SIRIUS

ENFIELD GENESIS – BOOK 5

BY LISA RICHMAN
& M. D. COOPER

SPECIAL THANKS
Just in Time (JIT) & Beta Readers

Scott Reid
Timothy Van Oosterwyk Bruyn
Gene Bryan
Gareth Banks
Chad Burroughs
Marti Panikkar
David Wilson

Version 1.0.0

ISBN: 978-1-64365-038-8

Cover Art by Andrew Dobell
Editing by Jen McDonnell, Bird's Eye Books

TABLE OF CONTENTS

FOREWORD 5
WHAT HAS GONE BEFORE 8
KEY CHARACTERS REJOINING US 10
THE TECH OF ENFIELD GENESIS 13
PRELUDE: THE CALL 16
RESPONSIBILITY TO PROTECT 16
PART ONE: THE ARRIVAL 29
THE WAGER 29
HEAVE TO 36
SOLD ON A MONDAY 51
Q-SHIP MAKEOVER 59
PART TWO: THE CON 67
HOW TO FOOL A SIRIAN 67
BLACKBIRD 71
ORPHAN SHIP 82
TRAITOR IN THEIR MIDST 86
BENDING PHOBOS 94
MANEUVERING INTO POSITION 102
GLIMMER-ONE 109
UNWILLING INFORMANT 118
TRADE AGREEMENTS 122
HYPERION 126
SPARK TO A FLAME 134
PLANNING SESSION 142
A SHORTAGE OF WORKERS 147
WARD OF THE HEGEMONY 152
INCANDUS 158
MD40 169
OPENING SALVO 176
SLEIGHT OF HAND 187
PART THREE: THE HEIST 198
DOUBLE-OH SEXY 198

TWO JETHROS, A JIM BROWN, AND AN ELLA FITZGERALD........208
INDEPENDENCE DAY 219
CAPRISE EX MACHINA........228
CATNAPPED........241
THE GREAT CAT CAPER........253
AWOL........267
ESCAPE PLANS........271
COMPELLED TO SPY........277
OFF COURSE........280
DOUBLE-STRAND BREAKS........283
M'AIDER........289
PART FOUR: THE ESCAPE........291
A PLAUSIBLE ALIAS........291
A FORCED BETRAYAL........293
ATTEMPTED ARREST........299
INOCULATION........304
CROSSROADS........312
FIRE WITHIN, FLARE WITHOUT........321
RACE TO FREEDOM........325
ULTIMATUM........335
FACING THE BOARD........338
FLEET MANEUVERS........342
MISSING MAN........349
EPILOGUE........355
AFTERWORD........357
THE BOOKS OF AEON 14........361
ABOUT THE AUTHORS........367

FOREWORD

Thank you so much for going on this journey with us. Your readership means a great deal, and I hope you've enjoyed the adventures of Terrance, Jason and the Phantom Blade team.

One of the things I love about writing in the Aeon 14 universe is the opportunity we have to weave real science into the stories.

We saw neuroscience play a strong role in *Proxima Centauri*. The opening scenes of *Tau Ceti* introduced us to colloidenes and vector-based click assembly. And we watched the team neutralize digital-to-biological converters in *Epsilon Eridani*.

All of these exist in fledgling form today. You'll find more of the same in *Sirius*.

Another thing I've loved about the Enfield Genesis series are the settings where these stories take place. Each of these star systems has been the subject of decades-long study, and there's a wealth of scientific observation available on them.

In many cases, that data became an integral part of the story arc, too. We saw it in Proxima's heliospheric current sheet, sweeping through the system like the twirling of a ballerina's skirts, and we saw it in the broad expanse of Tau Ceti's fifty-plus AU dust belt.

This holds true for Sirius as well.

The Dog Star we see in our night skies is significantly bigger, badder, and more active than our own Sol. That fact is fundamental to this story, and it allowed me to weave radiation physics into the tale in a meaningful way.

If you're interested in learning more about the effect Sirius's radiation would have on both humans and AIs, stick around. In the afterword, we've included a deleted scene, where the *Vale*'s chief medical officer tells you all about it.

Lisa
Leawood, 2019

* * * * *

Although this is the fifth and final book in the *Enfield Genesis* series, it doesn't mark the end of Phantom Blade. There are many more stories yet to tell.

Once the task force completes their adventure in the Sirius binary system, who knows what adventures will come their way? More than eight hundred years remain before that fateful day when Terrance and Jason meet Tanis Richards aboard the Mars Outer Shipyards (and find themselves swept into her wake).

Trust us, that's plenty of time for trouble to find these two. Much like Tanis, they seem to be magnets for danger and intrigue.

One thing we can tell you is that it will involve a return to the Sol System in a soon-to-come story arc we're tentatively calling the Intrepid Foundation series.

And who knows? There may be a short novella or two to throw into the mix as well.

M. D. Cooper
Danvers, 2019

WHAT HAS GONE BEFORE

An unlikely set of circumstances brought Alpha Centauri businessman Terrance Enfield and Proxan pilot-for-hire Jason Andrews together, along with an elite group of humans and AIs, to form Task Force Phantom Blade.

The black ops team, based out of El Dorado, was founded by the planet's prime minister, Lysander, the first AI to be appointed to such a high position throughout the known worlds. Terrance's company, Enfield Holdings, was set up as a legitimate business—one that functioned well as the white-side face of the clandestine organization.

Their first mission found the team going head-to-head against a criminal organization that had taken a ship full of more than two hundred and fifty AI refugees captive. Phantom Blade shut down the Norden Cartel, but not before they had managed to shackle and sell seventeen of the AIs from the Sol ship, the *New Saint Louis,* into slavery.

Their second mission, directed by an AI commodore in the El Dorado Space Force named Eric, led the team to Proxima Centauri and pitted them against a sociopathic serial killer named Prime.

Phantom Blade's third mission was simple: find and repatriate the final two shackled AIs—sold by the cartel to an unknown entity in Tau Ceti, a star system thirteen light years away. Unbeknownst to the team, Tau Ceti had fallen victim to nanotechnology run amok, and the two shackled AIs had been acquired as a last-ditch effort to save the planet, Galene.

The team entered into an unlikely partnership with the very man forced to purchase the shackled AIs, physicist Noa Sakai. Together with his daughter, Khela, the team stopped the phage, overthrowing an opportunistic tyrant bent on keeping the nanophage alive as a way to assure control over Galene.

Their mission parameters complete, Phantom Blade decided to take some well-deserved time off. Enfield Holdings accepted an extension of their mission to seed communication buoys between star systems, enabling a more rapid exchange of information, and the *Avon Vale* headed to Little River, the colony that had settled Epsilon Eridani.

Terrance's plan was to open another branch office for Enfield Holdings, establishing a fourth leg to the fledgling trade route that would someday tie the nearby systems together.

Yet one of the factions in Little River had different plans. Soon after their arrival, Calista, the *Avon Vale*'s captain, was arrested for a crime she did not commit. She was held hostage, and the ransom for her freedom was Enfield tech.

The colony world of Godel offered to help with her retrieval; in exchange, the team agreed to track down a saboteur. A desperate race against the clock ensued, with the destruction of an entire planet—and Calista's own life—held in the balance.

Reeling from the aftermath, Jason, Terrance, and the Phantom Blade team must now decide how to respond to a plea for help from another star....

KEY CHARACTERS REJOINING US

Beck – One of the first cats to have been fully uplifted by Jason's mother, Jane Sykes Andrews, Beck (short for Bequerel, so named by Jason's physicist father) bonded with Terrance as a kitten. Beck became an unplanned yet fortuitous member of Phantom Blade during his heroic actions on Galene in *Tau Ceti,* where he aided in the takedown of a band of marauders.

Jason Andrews – Son of Jane Sykes Andrews, grandson of Cara Sykes, Jason has always been a pilot and a bit of an adrenaline junkie. He is also one of the first few humans to exhibit the natural L2 mutation, which means that the axons—neural pathways—in his brain have a significantly higher number of nodes than a normal L0 human. They function as signal boosters, which allow him to process information at lightning speeds, and give him much faster reflexes than unaugmented humans have.

Jonesy – Calling him the 'best assistant this side of Sol,' Calista Rhinehart, the first captain of the *Avon Vale,* hired Jonesy for Enfield Aerospace as soon as his tour of duty was up. Jonesy followed Calista to Phantom Blade during their second mission, where he fell under the control of Prime, and was forced to try to kill Jason. During the long journey to Tau Ceti, Jonesy regained the team's trust. He also earned his engineering degree under Shannon's tutelage.

Khela Sakai – A former Captain of the Marines in the Galene Space Force, Khela led a fourteen-person special operations team instrumental in the overthrow of a corrupt government. Her efforts put her in harm's way in more than the traditional sense: during *Tau Ceti*, Khela and Hana, the AI paired with her, fell victim to the nanophage. Hana perished during this time, her phage-infected lattice leaving neural scarring within Khela.

Kodi – An AI soldier on loan from the ESF to aid in the team's second mission, Kodi embedded with Terrance Enfield during the team's third operation, in Tau Ceti.

Landon – One of five AIs asked to join the original Phantom Blade team, he was illegally twinned prior to the events in *Alpha Centauri* for a black op that went south. Landon is the more outgoing and garrulous brother; he fell in the line of duty, defending Jason's sister, Judith Andrews, from Prime in book two, *Proxima Centauri*. In book three, *Tau Ceti*, his twin, Logan, restored him, but Prime's brutal attack haunts Landon to this day.

Logan – Former ESF Military Intelligence profiler and AI-hunter, Logan was appointed by Senator Lysander to Phantom Blade. He has always been the more taciturn twin. Logan was instrumental in the team's bid to wrest possession of Galene's Main Elevator from hostile forces in the team's third mission to Tau Ceti.

Marta Venizelos – Retired ESF flight surgeon and private-practice thoracic surgeon, recruited to the Phantom Blade team by Prime Minister Lysander of El Dorado, in Alpha Centauri. Marta's left hand and arm have been modified to accommodate a med-sleeve, which provides on-the-spot triage wherever she goes.

Noa Sakai – As a young man, Noa had rejected his ties to the Sakai family's ancient underworld crime Family, the Matsu-kai. Events in *Tau Ceti* forced him to reluctantly embrace them one final time, in order to save the star system from the phage. He joined Phantom Blade, along with his daughter, Khela, at the end of their mission to Tau Ceti.

Shannon – Former chief engineer for Enfield Aerospace's TechDev Division, Shannon is one of the original five AIs recruited to Task Force Phantom Blade. She is currently embedded in the ESS *Avon Vale,* and harbors a secret longing to experience humanoid life.

Terrance Enfield – Grandson of Sophia Enfield, and the former CEO of Enfield Aerospace, Terrance now runs Enfield Holdings, the shell corporation under which Phantom Blade operates. He is the first Enfield in Alpha Centauri to partner with an AI, a former El Dorado Space Force lieutenant named Kodi.

Tobi – One of the uplifted cats bred by Jane Sykes Andrews as companion pets for families living in habitats and on ships. Tobi helped Tobias accompany Jason, carrying his core around in her harness, since AIs cannot embed inside an L2 human.

Tobias – A **Weapon Born AI**, Tobias left Sol after the Sentience Wars to settle in Proxima. There, he formed a close friendship with the Sykes-Andrews family. Along with Lysander—another Weapon Born—he was influential in Jason's early life as a friend, tutor, and mentor. Back then, he could often be found riding in a harness worn by an uplifted Proxima cat.

Weapon Born AIs – These are powerful creatures, among the first non-organic sentients in existence. They first appeared in Sol two centuries ago, the product of an illicit experiment involving the imaged minds of human children—a blank canvas upon which nation-states could forge the perfect, obedient soldier. What they got instead were intelligent, self-aware beings who fought for the right to exist in freedom. Tobias—and AIs of his ilk—are practically living legends to other AIs.

THE TECH OF ENFIELD GENESIS

Colloid Nano – Colloids are extremely tiny insoluble particles that are so light, they remain suspended in air. When grafted onto nano, colloid nano clouds can be released.

Thanks to brownian motion, the force of the particles in the air around them is greater than the force of gravity attempting to pull them down, and so they float and are susceptible to the activity of air currents.

In the thirty-third century, colloid nanobots themselves aren't capable of independent motion; tech has not yet been miniaturized to the point where propulsion can be applied to nano.

Colloidene Nano – A colloidene is made from a colloid particle, but formed just like single-layer graphene. Patterned in a honeycomb lattice, it employs some of the click-assembly techniques used in chemistry.

Pre-loaded common codes, or 'bricks', give nano creation a jump-start. The result is a nanobot, programmed to rapidly alter existing nano to whatever the person controlling it needs it to be.

E-SCAR – Electron-beam Special Combat Assault Rifle.

Elastene – A material made using electrospinning techniques on graphene. As its name implies, Elastene has shape-memory properties that allow it to store and release an unprecedented amount of mechanical energy. That means a ship clad in the substance can dissipate heat much faster than any other spacecraft in existence.

Engines built from Elastene can run for longer periods, at up to twenty percent higher speeds than prior output allowed.

Engineering Elastene into a metal foam creates a surface with an elasticity far more successful at deflecting micrometeorites and other impacts than current materials. Its shape-memory properties absorb the kinetic energy of the impact, spreading it across a much greater surface area.

Ultra-Black Elastene – Elastene foam panels using *borophene*, a super-strong, atom thick, 2D plasmonic material. A hexagonal-shaped structure, borophene is stronger than graphene. Coated with an ultra-black nano, the material is tunable, absorbing all light and providing no reflection. This total hemispherical reflectance of 0.0003% makes it one of the blackest materials in existence. Its stray-light suppression across standard, as well as far-infrared, spectral regions renders it undetectable to active sensor scans.

Wearable Elastene – During the fifty-plus-year journey to Tau Ceti, the engineers aboard the *Avon Vale* learned to extrude the graphene-based version of Elastene as a stretchy fabric.

Most commonly used in military operations, Elastene can function as a deflector for weapons fire. In addition, certain Elastene weaves function as ultra-black Faraday cages, allowing for covert operatives to more easily obscure breaching nano from active scan.

MFRs – Matchbook Fusion Reactors, a new power source invented by Enfield Aerospace on El Dorado in the late thirty-second century by then-chief engineer Shannon. It made use of a Localized Micro-Plasma, and was portable and interchangeable. Taking less than half the volume of current reactors, the new energy source allowed Phantom Blade to replace the original engines on their ship, the *Avon Vale*, with eight reactors where there had originally been only two.

Snowflake Nano – Phantom Blade's own personal, electronic breadcrumb trail. Like its namesake, each snowflake has a unique geometric signature. That signature is contained in the database of a Phantom Blade app. The app registers the negative space created by each snowflake on whatever surface it resides. Once a snowflake is tagged as 'in use', the search app keeps track of the void that particular snowflake makes, pinpointing its location while it remains in range. Also applied to microdrones.

True Stasis – True stasis employs the cessation of all atomic motion, as opposed to its predecessor, cryo-stasis. With true stasis, there is no risk of cellular damage brought about by freezing. An individual in stasis could emerge decades, even centuries, later, essentially unchanged.

PRELUDE: THE CALL

RESPONSIBILITY TO PROTECT

STELLAR DATE: 05.01.3272 (Adjusted Gregorian)
LOCATION: Intelligence Directorate, New Kells
REGION: Godel, Little River (Epsilon Eridani)

Mist enveloped Jason, droplets tipping his short blonde hair as he exited the maglev he'd taken from the New Kells Spaceport. He shrugged, broad shoulders bent forward against the chill. A natural athleticism, endowed by his L2 physique and further enhanced by his pilot's mods, showed as he descended the platform. Muscles bunched and flexed as he strode easily toward the enclave that housed the planet's governing body.

It was remarkably cool for early May on Godel, or so he'd been told. The lush green hills that ranged between Godel's Federal Buildings and its State House were blanketed by low-hanging clouds this morning. Fog clung to the valleys, imbuing the bustling district with a hushed tenor.

The chill, damp air that shrouded the roadways seemed bent upon extracting their own miniature cloud from Jason. His breath fogged with every exhale. A light breeze teased at the collar of his suit, as if challenging the nano-infused fabric to maintain its controlled temperature.

Or maybe I'm just not comfortable wearing captain's clothes yet. Maybe I never will be.

Jason didn't really have a uniform, per se; none of those on the ESS *Avon Vale* did. It was just the mental label he'd assigned to anything more formal than his usual attire.

This was the kind of day Tobias had told him was once known as a "soft day" on Eire.

As if the thought of the Weapon Born had conjured his presence, the AI hailed him over a secured connection.

<*Just received a ping from the Intelligence Directorate,*> Tobias informed him. <*You're expected at the director's office.*>

<*Got it,*> Jason confirmed. <*Terrance?*>

The summons from the Intelligence Directorate had requested both captain and ship's owner. It had been light on detail otherwise.

<*He'll be there,*> Tobias assured Jason. <*Had a wee bit of a delay at State House is all.*>

Jason acknowledged, then cut the connection before Tobias could draw him any further into conversation. The Weapon Born had been doing a lot of that recently—ever since Calista's death.

Jason's mind shied away from the thought of the woman who had been the *Vale*'s captain, and his lover. Instead, he focused on the upcoming meeting, weighing what he knew of the request against what he and Terrance suspected it was about.

It had been a month and a half since Alpha Centauri's elite covert team had helped Godel fight off an attack from the neighboring planet of Barat. It had been almost that long since its president, Edouard Zola, had approached Terrance about a new mission.

During the intervening weeks, Zola had managed to avoid the subject. Jason knew the man had good reason; Barat's attack had brought Godel to its knees economically, and Zola had been forced to institute planetwide emergency measures and rationing to avoid unnecessary deaths.

Now that relief efforts were underway, Godel was quickly regaining its equilibrium. Jason suspected that this summons meant Zola's original request was back on the table.

He increased his pace when he sighted his destination ahead. The intelligence building towered above the trees, its entrance at the pinnacle of an imposing flight of plascrete steps. He took them two at a time, nodding to security as he passed his token at the door.

"Captain Andrews," the security AI greeted. With a small gesture, he indicated the bank of lifts off to the left. "Director Mastai is waiting for you in her office. Lieutenant Kodi and Mister Enfield are already there."

Jason thanked him and made for the lift. As he exited, he spied Terrance waiting for him outside the director's door.

<Morning, sir,> the voice of the AI embedded within Terrance greeted as Jason drew near.

<Morning, Kodi. You guys think this is about Zola's request?> he asked, as Terrance signaled the office NSAI, alerting it to their presence.

Terrance sent him a slight shrug as the doors slid open. *<I certainly hope so. I let his office know yesterday that we've exhausted our usefulness here, and we're ready to move out.>*

Jason heard the thread of frustration in Terrance's voice. He could sympathize. None of the crew aboard the *Vale* wanted to hang around Little River any longer than necessary. This system held too many unpleasant memories, and they were more than ready to leave them behind.

The first thing Jason noticed when they entered Celia Mastai's office was the silhouette that stood at her window, looking out. The figure was taller than most, and whipcord lean. The shadow turned at the sound of their approaching footsteps.

As they neared, he could tell it was a man, most likely a spacer. His complexion was pale, almost translucent, and his stance that of one unused to the pull of planetary gravity.

Although he had the youthful appearance of recent rejuv, Jason could tell the man had been around for a while. It wasn't the single white streak in his hair, but something in the man's eyes that bespoke decades of hard-earned experience.

"Gentlemen."

Celia Mastai's voice came from behind them, and Jason turned as the intelligence director strode toward them with a smile. Celia gestured them forward, motioning the stranger away from the window as she paused at the edge of a cozy seating area to perform introductions.

"Cesar, I'd like you to meet Terrance Enfield, CEO of Enfield Holdings. Kodi is his paired partner." She gestured to the exec before turning to Jason. "Jason Andrews, captain of the Enfield ship, *Avon Vale*."

The man's eyes shifted briefly between Terrance and Jason before his dark, inscrutable gaze transformed into a spare, congenial smile and he offered his hand. "Pleasure to make your acquaintance. I'm Cesar. I own Martinez Shipping, out of Procyon."

Terrance returned Cesar's smile as they were motioned toward the comfortable seating arrangement, and a servitor trundled over.

"You're interstellar?" the exec asked.

"We are," the man admitted as he took a seat. "Although Little River is as far as we go. Most of our commerce is within our own system, or between Procyon and the Hegemony in Sirius."

Jason tilted his head, considering what that might mean as he saw Terrance accept a fresh mug of coffee from the servitor.

"What's your cargo?" Jason asked, absently waving the servitor off as it headed his way.

The meter-tall bot vectored over to where Celia sat next to the Procyan, and Jason's gaze followed its movement—which was why he caught the brief hesitation of Celia's hand, arrested by his words, before she smoothly reached to retrieve a steaming mug from the servitor's tray. Jason's attention sharpened, and it came to him that her offering of coffee to Cesar felt more like a stalling tactic than it did a polite gesture. The distracted way the man accepted the drink from her made it blatantly obvious the two were conversing privately.

It was an odd thing to see, and it took Jason a moment before he realized why.

Cesar had every outward appearance of a man who owned and ran a profitable trade business; good communication was a major component to good business practices. Communicating via Link was as natural as breathing for every executive he'd ever come across.

So why would he be fumbling around like a novice while conversing over the Link?

Cesar looked over at Terrance suddenly, as if he'd just recalled that he'd been asked a question. "Cargo? Ah, the usual." He gestured vaguely with one hand while he took a sip from his cup. "Procyon has a thriving artisan population, and some of their finer works are in high demand within the Hegemony's upper caste. Conversely, some of the ores mined by the Hegemony are scarce in Procyon, so we export them, along with other high-value items."

<It sounds like it's been a lucrative business for you,> Kodi commented politely.

Cesar flicked a glance over at Celia, and Jason saw something—a bleakness—in the man's expression before it shuttered.

Celia leant forward. "Lucrative?" She shook her head. "Not in the way you meant, Kodi. Necessary. Vital, even. But not…lucrative, in the traditional sense."

That's when Jason knew.

"You're a shell corporation, aren't you." It was a statement, not a question. "So what do you *really* do for a living, Mister Martinez?"

Cesar met Jason's gaze, and the question hung between the two men.

After a moment, the stranger nodded to himself. Taking a deep breath, he straightened. "The name's not Martinez, Captain. It's Cesar. Just Cesar. No one in Sirius has two names…we left them behind when we left Sol."

<So you're Sirian, then, not Procyan.>

"I'm Noctus," Cesar corrected Kodi. "And you're right.

Martinez Shipping is the cover I use to smuggle slaves out from under Hegemony rule."

"Slaves?" Terrance's eyebrows climbed practically into his hairline. "I've heard some bad things about Sirius, but—"

"Slaves." Cesar's voice brooked no dissent. "And in the past fifty years, the situation has deteriorated dramatically." The man held himself rigid, as if it was the only way he could control the emotions Jason sensed bottled up inside him.

"I think we'd better start at the beginning." Celia reached over and laid a hand on Cesar's forearm, and Jason saw the man relax slightly under it.

<*And I think we're about to find out exactly what Zola meant when he said he needed Phantom Blade's help,*> Terrance's voice came over the net, his tone grim. Jason heard Kodi's mental agreement.

"As I said, I was born Noctus. We're the Sirian Hegemony's dirty little secret," Cesar explained in a voice laced with acrimony. He rested his elbows on his knees and leant forward, hands clasped together. "The hidden foundation behind Sirius's financial success."

The words were bitter, dry.

<*I've heard the Hegemony had a caste system of sorts,*> Kodi remarked, and Cesar nodded.

"It predates our arrival in Sirius," he explained. "The investors who won the bid for the colony ship had a very specific criteria they wanted the Generation Ship Service to meet as they recruited colonists for the two planets being terraformed by the FGT."

Terrance held up a finger in question. "Any idea why those planets were placed in orbit around Sirius B, the white dwarf, and not Sirius A?"

Cesar lifted one shoulder by way of reply. "Couldn't really say. The Future Generation Terraformers decided it would be the more viable option, possibly because of how stable it is. The FGT moved the planets quite close, less than half an AU away." His mouth twisted with wry humor. "Oddly enough, the investors decided to rename it Lucent."

Jason snorted. "Someone had a fine sense of irony," he commented, settling back in his chair, his hand resting on the ankle he'd crossed over one knee.

Cesar acknowledged the comment with a dip of his head. "They certainly seemed to embrace the theme," he agreed. "The investors decided the Hegemony would be a modified vassal state, with an elite tier that wealthy investors could buy into, known as the Luminescents. Those less well-off could purchase a berth in the yeoman tier. The investors called them the Iridescents. Irids would be given certain middle-class rights, such as the right to own property and to be employed in their field of expertise by the Lumins."

<*And you said you were a Noctus,*> Kodi prompted. <*That would be a third tier?*>

Cesar nodded. "Noctilucent, the lowest caste, as you might have guessed."

"Can't say they're very original with their naming conventions, but I suppose they get points for sticking to a theme," Jason muttered.

Cesar smiled a non-smile, acknowledging the comment. "The investors told the GSS to open up the bottom tier to anyone willing to work off their passage through a period of indentured labor."

"The slavery you mentioned earlier," Terrance guessed.

Jason was surprised when Cesar shook his head.

"Indentured servitude would have been welcomed by my ancestors," he countered, his tone filled with rancor. "It was what they thought they were signing up for when they read the contract. A period of so many years during which they'd provide free labor in exchange for the cost of transit to Sirius. But they were wrong."

Jason saw Cesar's hands clench as he stared down at them, the tendons in his forearms bunching from the strain. He could feel the rage radiating from the man.

Celia's voice picked up the narrative in the charged silence that fell after Cesar's declaration. "I think it's safe to say that Luminescent Society is maintained on the backs of those less fortunate," she murmured.

Cesar drew in a lungful of air and jerked his head in a nod before continuing his narration. "After we arrived, the corporation used loopholes in our contracts to extend them out in perpetuity." His eyes darkened as he added ominously, "And then they applied the same conditions to our offspring."

Stars. Children.

Jason felt a hot anger flare, and his eyes narrowed at the implication. "You're right. That *is* slavery," he bit out, exchanging a hard glance with Terrance. The other man's jaw was set; he wasn't liking what he was hearing either, Jason could tell.

Cesar shot them both a mirthless grin. "Well, it's no easy ride for the Irids, either, I can assure you." He twitched a shoulder in a quick shrug. "As odd as it may sound, I'd almost rather be Noctus than Irid."

Jason saw an expression of puzzlement cross Terrance's face and knew it matched his own. "I'm sorry. I don't follow…." the exec said.

Cesar ran his hand across his face, head bowed as he appeared to gather his thoughts. He glanced up at Jason as he let his hand fall. "While it's true that Irids are free to own businesses and pursue careers, they can only do that if they register with the Luminescent Guildhall. Once they receive a permit, they can practice their tradecraft—if they can afford the taxes. But their success is subject to the whims and vagaries of the Lumins."

He fingered the sleeve of his jacket, then gestured to it. "Say a department head or senior executive is seen wearing something made by a certain Irid clothier. That tradesman might be in favor for a season, might even win a sponsorship from a Lumin. But that patronage can evaporate at any time, whenever that Lumin is so inclined."

"I see what you mean. Not the most secure situation to be in," Celia remarked, her tone thoughtful.

Cesar barked a harsh laugh. "Nothing in Sirius is secure unless you're born Lumin. But I'd rather know that I'll be fed and clothed—even if there's never enough of either—than wonder if my children will starve if I fail to please my patron."

Terrance leant forward, his eyes intent. "And no one has ever challenged this system?"

Cesar shook his head. "Not successfully, no. Things have operated this way for almost two hundred years. There've been a few attempts to overthrow the Hegemony from within, but none were successful. We decided to try something a little different."

Cesar's eyes were full of meaning, and when they met his, it dawned on Jason exactly what kind of cargo Martinez Shipping transported.

"Stars, you're running an underground railroad," he breathed, his words causing Terrance to jerk and sit up abruptly in his seat.

Cesar nodded slowly, his eyes never breaking contact with Jason's as his expression sharpened into an odd blend of craftiness and satisfaction, mixed with regret.

"With help from Godel and Procyon, yes," he clarified. "We came to them more than eighty years ago with the proposition, citing the Interstellar Commission's Responsibility to Protect Doctrine."

An underground railroad….

Jason's mind began to race as he reached out to Tobias.

<*Tobe—*> he began, but the Weapon Born interrupted him.

<*Kodi's been sending me a feed, boyo,*> Tobias responded, his thoughts grim.

Jason nodded, and his head began to throb with an unexpected ache as a weary anger began to roil within his gut. Stars, but he was getting sick of the slavery trade.

<*I reached out to Celia's assistant,*> the AI added. <*She sent me an encrypted file that contains what they have on Cesar's freight company*

cover. What he's managed has been impressive.>

<This Responsibility to Protect Doctrine, have you heard of it?>

<Aye,> Tobias confirmed. *<'Tis a moral obligation held by the broader interstellar community, in the case where a system fails in its responsibility to protect is own people, either through inability or lack of willingness to do so.>*

<That…sounds like an invitation to interfere on a system-wide basis.>

Jason heard the incredulity in his own tone. The thought of attempting something on such a massive scale seemed like an impossibility—especially given distances measured in light-years.

<Indeed it is, although it's mainly rhetoric, considering how impractical it is for one system to wage a military action against another across such distances. It'd be Hitler's Operation Barbarossa all over again.> Tobias's avatar shook his head at the thought. *<Can you imagine? Hitler overextended his reach just a few thousand kilometers beyond what his supply line could manage. Today, it would span light-years.>*

<Yeah, you'd have to transit with an overwhelming force. And even then, they'd have months to see you coming and prepare a response.>

Tobias nodded. *<So you can see why the Doctrine advocates that those invoking it seek non-military measures foremost.>*

<Or a surgical strike, say from a covert ops team?>

<Aye, boyo. Or that.>

Jason's attention was pulled back to Cesar, as the man launched into a description of Noctus working conditions.

"Safety margins on the mining platforms and refineries are slim to nonexistent. Living quarters that sorely tax each platform's environmental systems, EVA equipment with completely inadequate radiation shielding…."

Jason had heard of the platforms the man described. They were a bit of a misnomer, as they only looked like a flat plane from a great distance. Housing up to a few hundred thousand people, these sprawling stations orbited a central axis, but were built low and long, their sweeping arms spanning kilometers in width.

Geometrically, he supposed they did look like a series of connected platforms in orbit around one another.

"Nutrition..." he heard Cesar continue, before the man laughed harshly. "Adequate, but only because we subsist on rations made of nutrition paste, supplemented by the small hydroponics areas allotted by the Lumins on each platform. Even then, they dictate what crops we grow."

Jason's stomach tightened in sympathy. He'd had to crack open a meal rat once or twice, back when he was piloting freighters between Proxima and El Dorado. Those things were *not* food.

"I'm guessing there aren't too many overweight Noctus, then," he observed, and Cesar's expression twisted into a grimace.

"No," the Noctus confirmed. "No one relishes mealtime, I can assure you."

"Medical facilities?" Terrance asked, and Cesar shook his head.

"Barely adequate. No mednano or autodocs—and you can forget access to rejuv," the man countered darkly. "Though that provided me the perfect way to hide my identity once I was smuggled out. By now, any Lumin who knew me would assume I was long dead—certainly, I wouldn't look like a thirty-year-old man in his prime."

Jason nodded. "Makes sense," he agreed, leaning forward to brace his elbows on his knees. Threading his hands together, he stared down at them as his mind replayed the situation.

Silence had settled over the small group; he knew Cesar and Celia were giving them time to process what they'd just been told. After a moment, head still bowed, he shot a side glance at Terrance.

There was no hesitation. At the exec's crisp nod, Jason lifted his head to pin Celia with a look. "So where do we come in?"

She smiled back at him, but it didn't reach her eyes. She didn't answer immediately, instead taking the time to set her coffee mug down on the table between them before crossing one leg over the other. Long, tapered fingers smoothed the fabric of her pants before settling quietly in her lap.

"Our contacts within the Hegemony have informed us of recent developments," she finally said, glancing over at Cesar. "Recent being a relative term, of course, seeing that we're nearly eight light-years away."

<*By the tone of your voice, these developments aren't good,*> Kodi observed, and Celia tilted her head in acknowledgement.

"Well, yes…and no," Celia cautioned. "The situation has been in place for almost a century. We just weren't aware of it until now, nor were we in a position to do anything about it. But along with the intel came an unexpected offer to help."

Cesar grimaced. "It comes with a few stipulations, but the opportunity is too good to pass up."

Jason looked between the two expectantly. "And that would be…?"

"The Lumins have a habit of adding to the Noctus population whenever they can," Cesar began. "They do it by seizing any crew found breaking Hegemony shipping and customs rules. Forget to pay import duty taxes, and suddenly you're sent to a platform to work off your imprisonment, while your ship and its cargo are impounded."

Terrance snorted. "Why does that not surprise me?"

Cesar acknowledged the exec's comment. "About a hundred years ago, a trade vessel by the name of *Hyperion* arrived. Its captain didn't file the right paperwork, and she and her crew, and all her cargo, were seized." He shot Celia a glance. "The ship's six AI passengers were considered cargo."

Jason inhaled sharply, feeling a flare of anger deep in his gut. He wasn't the only one.

<*Bataichean!*>

The Gaelic word rang sharply across the comm link, accompanied by a swell of anger from the Weapon Born. Fortunately, Jason had been around Tobias long enough not to need the Link's helpful translation.

<Yeah, they're bastards, all right. I thought we were done with this shit when we left Tau Ceti,> he responded to the other three with a growl.

Terrance's mental grunt of agreement followed on its heels. *<No need to check in with Lysander on this one.>*

Jason concurred. Alpha Centauri's prime minister was Weapon Born, just like Tobias. Jason knew he'd want the team to nail those bastards every bit as much as Tobias did.

"You said there was an opportunity here," Terrance prompted. "What is it?"

<I'm hoping it's the opportunity to nail the sick sumbitches who did this, and shut them down permanently.> Kodi's words were caustic, eliciting a brief smile from Cesar.

"That's the end goal," Celia agreed, glancing over at the Noctus man and then back at Terrance and Jason. "But that might be a bit of a stretch for our resources right now."

Cesar nodded as he sat back with a resigned look. "At the moment, we have to make do with smaller victories. Our informant is one of the few Lumins who disagrees with how the Hegemony runs things. He's offered to help us extricate the AIs, along with as many Noctus as one ship can carry." His lips curved in a humorless smile. "In a fine bit of irony, it's the AI's own ship, the *Hyperion*, that the Underground has secured for our escape."

Celia reached once more for her coffee mug, cradling it between her hands as if needing the warmth. "It's a bit of an impossible choice, deciding who to liberate and who to leave behind. But if we can free several hundred Noctus, and use this situation to shed light on the plight of those within the system...."

Terrance nodded slowly. "I see where it would be too good an opportunity to pass up."

<Exactly why Phantom Blade was formed.> Jason's thought was steely with resolve. *<It'll be a pleasure shutting these assholes down.>*

PART ONE: THE ARRIVAL

THE WAGER

STELLAR DATE: 03.22.3302 (Adjusted Gregorian)
LOCATION: Executive Suites, Brilliance Station
REGION: Lucent, Sirian Hegemony

Twenty-nine years later....

"Fancy a little wager?"

The words, spoken in a throaty contralto, caressed Rubin's ears like a lover. He ignored them, his back turned to the elegantly appointed room. Its reflection in the plas presented the perfect foil for the equally elegant form of the woman approaching him.

Everything about Berit was exquisite, from her exotically proportioned form to the artificially engineered pheromones she exuded. Even her voice had been modified, using psychoacoustics to spectrally shape its formants to frequencies humans found most appealing.

Combined with a sharp, incisive mind, Vice President Berit presented a formidable, often deadly package—one Rubin had learned to handle much like he would a viper poised to attack.

The simile was a bit of a disconnect, considering they were about as far away from a viper's natural habitat as they could be. Brilliance Station hung above Incandus, the terraformed capital of the Sirian Hegemony. A small planet, orbiting a small star.

One of the more massive white dwarfs, Lucent had a surface gravity more than one hundred thousand times that of Terra. The electrons that comprised the degenerate gas in its core were so densely compressed that they filled all quantum states, becoming an almost perfect heat conductor.

Unlike other stars, Lucent was brilliant and burned with a cold, harsh light, much like the Lumins themselves.

Now ***there*** *is an apt simile.*

He continued to let Berit's question hang between them as his eyes fixed upon his view of the blue-white dwarf. It was perfectly framed by sweeping steel arches stretching high above him into a seemingly endless void.

He mentally ticked off the seconds, stretching the moment out until he judged Berit's patience about to snap. He did so enjoy stringing her along. He found it one of the few things that brought him pleasure anymore.

"Wager?" he finally said, tilting his head to allow her one disinterested glance. He imbued the word with equal parts ennui and reluctant interest as he favored the graceful figure who had come to stand beside him with a raised brow. Berit smiled and inclined her head regally in response.

"Indeed." She swayed closer, her eyes arrested, he noted, not by the vision of Lucent, forever suspended in the snare of an architect's artifice, but of the larger star, now a mere 8 AU away.

The glass she held in her hand made it appear as if she grasped nothing but air. It was a feat of engineering Berit was inordinately fond of, something she had seduced from one of their peers—Gavin, the VP of Manufacturing and Distribution. She flaunted it as if it were a trophy she'd won. He supposed it might be considered such, given that she'd enticed it from Gavin's clutches while she'd been sleeping with the man.

Rubin was no scientist, nor did he care to know the details behind Berit's latest toy. She'd told him the stemmed glass used light-bending nano to create a trompe l'oeil effect that hid its stem from visible light, while the bell-shaped ES field held the liquid refreshment suspended as if in midair. A single blue ring illuminated the diamond-edged threshold of the field, and also served as the rim of the glass.

He would love to know what types of services Berit had exchanged for this bit of frippery, but had managed to refrain from asking after it. He studied her, knowing that his refusal to inquire further about the bits of information she liked to dangle in front of him was infuriating to her. Berit had a deep-seated need to manipulate, and she used tantalizing bits of information to reel in her victims. Rubin had long ago tired of such nonsense.

Berit's modifications were surprisingly normative for their society. Luminescents as a whole were known for fantastical and excessive experimentation. Yet, to his knowledge, the most extreme alterations Berit had ever made to herself were the ones needed for the gender swap she had carried out for a dozen or so years.

The only surprise there had been the fact that she'd stayed male as long as she had. Berit had an affinity for feminine wiles, and was an avid practitioner, using it to achieve ends both sinister and benign.

He almost felt sorry for the creature ensconced inside the woman's head, slave to her every whim. The AI named Wallis was shackled, bound to Berit, like his own Quincy was to him. Each of the six vice presidents had been gifted with an AI, one of the many bonuses that came with the senior management position.

Like the others in said position, he faithfully toed the party line—the one that stated AIs weren't sentient. But he knew it for the convenient fiction that it was, a fiction that allowed the Hegemony to ensnare the six that had fallen into their hands a hundred years earlier.

To his mind, AIs were in a similar class as Noctus. Both were, in essence, slaves; the Hegemony wisely didn't classify them as such, however, given that the moniker still held such stigma.

He'd become quite dependent on Quincy over the decades, the AI having proven invaluable to the many things his position demanded of him. Unlike Berit, he recognized the creature's sentience. He simply didn't care.

Also unlike Berit, Rubin had refused to risk having something that smart implanted into his own brain. His gaze flickered momentarily to the humanoid frame that held his own shackled AI, Quincy, standing subserviently nearby.

With a small, exasperated sigh, Berit set her wineglass down on the tray Quincy wordlessly held for them, and pivoted to face Rubin, hands splayed impatiently at her waist.

"Really, Rubin. Are you interested or not?"

Rubin smiled, lifting his own bit of nothing to his lips to take a sip. Setting his glass down alongside hers, he crossed his arms, leaning against the crystalline expanse of the executive lounge, seventy-five stories above the station's Gran Piazza. "All right, Berit. I'll bite. What's the wager?"

Berit straightened, and a subtle change came over her. Gone was the frivolous pleasure-seeker. In its place stood the Vice President of Resources and Extraction for the Sirian Hegemony.

Ahhh, so this is business, Rubin realized, his eyes narrowing. *Possibly mixed with pleasure, but preeminently business.*

As Vice President of Refinement and Fulfillment, he could appreciate that.

Berit nodded her head, indicating the holo she'd projected onto the transparent surface between them and their view of the Piazza below. "The Hegemony currently has eighty-seven platforms scattered throughout the nebula belt," she told Rubin unnecessarily, highlighting each of the platforms on the overlay as she mentioned their functions.

"Of those, twenty-five are dedicated to identifying, capturing, and reducing asteroids into manageable pieces. An additional thirty are reserved for the extraction and sorting of the various ores we ship to the refineries."

Rubin waved impatiently at her display. "Yes, and the remaining thirty-two are evenly divided between refinement and fulfillment," he said, reciting the statistics by rote, his voice tinged with exasperation. "Your point? Or should I recount the number of freighters in the fleet that Distribution sends to the various star systems as well?"

Berit smiled at him, her expression sly. "If you know all this, then you also know that we've held relatively steady with our production runs for decades."

She waved her hand in a dismissive gesture as Rubin barely refrained from rolling his eyes at her. "We've had ups and downs, based on equipment malfunction or Noctus limitations, but overall, we've remained in a steady state all this time, with very little progress. But I think it's time we changed that."

Rubin's brow rose in skepticism. "Indeed? And how, exactly, do you propose to do this?"

Berit tapped on the holo. "By selecting one platform from each discipline and subjecting them to a series of trials."

"And where does the wager come in?"

Berit's smile grew wider. "There's no law that says we can't make the process into an enjoyable one. Why not pit test subjects against each other? Yours against mine. We play by a simple set of rules, changing just one variable at a time in order to accurately measure the effectiveness of each."

Rubin's eyes narrowed. "This seems inordinately tame for a wager," he began, and Berit laughed, an elegant contralto that somehow managed to sound malevolent and scintillating at the same time.

"Ah, but the first rule is that there *are* no rules. No restrictions. No safety margins. No points deducted for worker losses."

Rubin felt a jolt from Quincy through his connection to the AI. Perversely, knowing that the creature found Berit's casual mention of human deaths abhorrent caused him to look more closely at the wager. He triggered a reprimand protocol and felt his connection to Quincy recede into the back of his mind as Berit elaborated.

"Anything goes. Shorter deadlines, longer hours, raised production minimums, budget reductions for maintenance and supplies." Her hand swept out in an elegant, dismissive gesture.

"Let's see how creative our little Noctus can be when they are forced to work under tighter constraints."

Rubin smothered a snort at her use of the term 'little'. Given that most lived their brief lives in a gravity half that of any planet or habitat in Luminescent society, the average Noctus stood almost ten centimeters taller than a Lumin.

They'd likely be even taller, if they had access to proper nutrition and adequate healthcare, he considered with clinical detachment, but dismissed it as her proposal elicited a fresh concern.

"And if we begin to see an increase in the Noctus mortality rate?"

Berit shrugged. "Withhold birth control. Without it, they'll breed like rabbits. You know this, it's why we've managed their populations so strictly for the past two centuries." Her eyes gleamed with avarice as she added, "Think of it as one more line-item expense we can eliminate, if this proves to be a profitable exercise."

"That's not a viable solution in the short-term, though," he mused, "if we run short. All able-bodied Noctus of working age are in use."

"Hmmmm." Berit's eyes narrowed in speculation, and she began to pace, fingernails drumming lightly against her full, red lips. After a moment, she rounded on him, her face alight with intent.

"You are exactly right about that. Oh ho," she chortled, "what an excellent suggestion!"

Rubin quirked a brow at her. "I'm going to need a little help here, Berit. I'm not following."

"All able-bodied workers *of working age,* you said. But think of the thousands of children sitting in the corporate schools and orphanages, doing little else than using our air and eating our food."

Her lips curved in a deliberate smile, and her eyes slitted as she turned to stare out at the star, framed in cold, hard steel. Her eyes flitted about, and he could see her mind processing information at a rapid pace.

"What are you proposing, my dear?"

She held up a finger, her eyes growing distant. Then she looked over at him with a satisfied smile.

"I'm not proposing anything, Rubin. I've already done it." Her smile turned sly. "Let's just say I don't believe workers will be an issue for us any longer. Now, do we have a wager or not?"

Rubin leant back and considered the woman before him for a long moment before nodding slowly. "It's ruthless."

She made a noncommittal noise.

"It's risky," he pressed.

She lowered her head and shot him a deliberate glance from beneath long lashes. He sighed.

"If the Board catches us, we'll most likely pay penalty fees," he warned. "Possibly even suffer a temporary demotion or reassignment."

Berit crossed her arms in front of a well-endowed chest as manicured fingers began to tattoo an impatient beat along the sleeve of her dress.

Rubin cracked a reluctant smile at her. "It's brazen, too. I like it. If it works, we'll be in a position to command a substantial bonus at the end." He held out his hand. "Let's do it."

HEAVE TO

STELLAR DATE: 03.22.3302 (Adjusted Gregorian)
LOCATION: ESS *Avon Vale*, nearing deceleration flip-point
REGION: 1,850 AU from Sirius Binary System

Out near Sirius's heliopause, the *Avon Vale* coasted silently along at a cruise velocity of 0.24*c*. The ship's habitat ring was just entering its daylight cycle as its visitors arrived.

Doctor Marta Venizelos paused at the edge of one of the ring's parks and glanced around, a large Proxima cat padding softly beside her. The smells of green growing things wafted enticingly, causing Becquerel to lift his head, mouth open as he scented the air.

The chief medical officer aboard the *Avon Vale,* and member of the Phantom Blade task force, smiled at the big cat's reaction. Reaching down, she buried her hand in the silky soft pile of his fur and gave him a scratch behind one of his platinum-tipped ears.

The cat, whose sleek, muscular form reached nearly to her waist, pressed against her hand and gave a small, rumbling purr of pleasure before pulling back and blinking up at her with aqua eyes.

<*Gotta run,*> Beck announced. He crouched, powerful hind muscles bunching as they launched his sleek, 40-kilo body into a ground-eating lope.

<*Quite literally, I see.*>

Marta snorted in amusement at the droll voice that sounded in her head. Varanee had joined them in Little River, when wanderlust had struck the AI physician. Marta had welcomed her with open arms.

Although the number of passengers had dropped dramatically when many chose to remain behind in Epsilon Eridani, more than six hundred still remained under her care. That was a lot of people for the small military staff that the El Dorado Space Force had seconded to Phantom Blade, back in Alpha Centauri. Marta had been relieved to have another physician join the *Vale*'s medical team.

More recently, Varanee had asked if Marta would consider pairing with her. Embedding with a human was considered by the AI Council to be a prerequisite for some AI careers, and Varanee wanted to earn the empathic credits necessary to pursue a medical specialty with humans.

Marta's eyes returned to the stand of trees where Beck had disappeared. "At least he'll get one good run in before they stop the ring," she responded, her voice laced with humor. "I forget sometimes that he's just a few years old."

She stepped onto the path that wound its way leisurely through Hideaway Park, gravel crunching lightly under her feet. The low hum of a honeybee reached her, and she spied it hovering amongst the blooms in a clump of purple sage as they passed.

This was one of several such parks within the torus just aft of the ship's main shuttle bays. Its four hundred square kilometers of living area rotated at one and a half revolutions per minute, generating a comfortable 1*g* for the crew.

The space was a welcome respite during long interstellar trips. Along with a number of gardens and greenspaces, the habitat boasted several eateries and artisan shops, staffed by enterprising crewmembers during the *Vale*'s cruise phase.

Marta smiled as the simulated sky projecting around the habitat's central shaft began to imitate a rosy dawn.

"I do so love early morning sunrises," she murmured to her companion, as birdsong greeted them from a nearby dwarf fruit tree.

<You realize you're in the minority among humans,> Varanee commented. *<In fact, I don't believe I know of another one who would agree with you on that.>*

Marta snorted once more, not bothering with a reply as she

spied a team of engineers ahead of them. One of them was standing apart, observing his crew as they secured a cluster of cages containing the habitat's wildlife to a maglev pallet.

"Hey, docs," Jonesy, the ship's chief engineer, looked up in surprise as she approached. He smiled before adding, "Was that Beck I saw high-tailing it through the trees over there?"

Marta nodded.

<He wanted one last run before the habitat reconfigured for deceleration,> Varanee added.

Jonesy scratched his head, unseating the cap he habitually wore. Tugging the brim down once more, he raised a brow. "He knows he can still come out here after the flip, doesn't he?"

Marta smiled and gave a little shrug. "Yes, but he likes racing the full circumference, and once you stop rotation, he'll be limited to the quarter-pie you leave open during boost."

Jonesy laughed, white teeth flashing against his dark skin. "He does like to stretch his legs, doesn't he?"

<In years lived, he's still a youngling,> Varanee reminded him. *<He was in stasis with Terrance, so he's only just turned three.>*

"Well, he'll just have to make do without the full ring. I wouldn't think the playing fields, river walk, or the outdoor shopping areas are all that interesting to a Proxima cat, anyway," Jonesy mused, as an engineer on his team handed him a hyfilm. He glanced down at it and then handed it back with an approving nod, and the crew began to push the pallet toward the habitat exit.

"Is that the last of them?" Marta asked, as she watched an assortment of small wild animals being transported to the large stasis chamber near the torus's central shaft.

"Yep. Beck will have to chase bugs for a while, until we can get back down here to rerelease them into the park."

She chuckled at the mental picture as Jonesy moved to join his team.

"Sorry, docs," he called over his shoulder. "Duty calls. Lots to do before the flip. Gotta run!"

Varanee snorted. *<Aha, so that's where Beck got that saying from.>*

Marta broke into a laugh. "Well, since we have a fair amount of work to do ourselves, let's go find a cat to herd."

* * * * *

<Are you finished yet, doctor?> Jason asked, using his overlay to review the reports coming in from various departments as he awaited Marta's response.

<Don't get your panties in a wad,> Varanee's tart response came instead.

That caused an involuntary laugh to escape, which prompted a look from Logan from where he sat, reviewing data at one of the bridge's information consoles.

Waving off the intelligence officer, Jason sent the medic a mock frown. *<You sound like an AI I knew back on El Dorado. I think you have it wrong, though. Rosie used to tell me not to get my knickers in a twist. Is this your way of informing your ship's captain that Medical's running behind?>*

Marta snorted. *<Maaaaybe. I only have Varanee, Justin, and two human medics, and we have more than five hundred stasis pods to check before reviving them. Are you volunteering to assist?>*

<Ma'am, no, ma'am. I'll just have to find a way to break it to Shannon gently.> He sent a mental grin at his mention of the ship's AI. *<She's all up in my chili about making the flip. That gal's getting impatient.>*

<'All up in my chili',> he heard Varanee repeat, and Marta groaned.

<Captain, will you ***please*** *refrain from using old Earth slang around my senior physician? She's bad enough as it is without you feeding her more lines like that. Since she lives inside my head, it's not like I can get away from it, you know.>*

<Sorry.> Jason sent her an unrepentant grin before signing off.

Once the crew was found fit for duty after being pulled from stasis, they were given a full cycle to adjust, resyncing with civilization, responding to comms, and catching up with the ship's status. Those rotating off-shift were replaced by freshly roused crew, and the ship was prepped for reconfiguration from cruise to boost.

All items not bolted down were locked and webbed. In the ship's habitat ring, lakes, ponds, and other small bodies of open water were drained, and nano, lacing such features as gravel pathways, was engaged to solidify the trails, preventing them from floating free.

Shannon turned and speared Jason with an expectant look when Kodi informed him that every section was reporting clear for flip. The excitement in the AI's expression had him hiding a grin behind his hand. He glanced over at Terrance and saw an answering humor glinting in the executive's eyes.

Shannon clearly relished her job as ship's AI, but had finally opted to wear a humanoid frame. It was about time. They'd all wondered why it had taken her so long to do so, as being human so obviously suited the little AI.

She'd surprised him with it when he'd awakened from his last stint in stasis. He'd looked up with surprise into liquid silver eyes filled with lively animation as she'd freed him from his pod. Then Jonesy's face swam into view, the engineer grinning from ear to ear at Jason's surprise.

The three of them had grown close after Calista's death. Everyone on the team had mourned her loss, but none more keenly than he, Shannon, and Jonesy—the ones who had called her lover, sister, and mentor, respectively.

Shannon had confessed to them over shots of whiskey one night in one of the ship's darkened lounges that she'd always hoped for the opportunity to embed with Calista. Jason privately suspected that the inability to ever do so now was the motivation behind her decision to finally embrace the humanoid experience.

The frame she'd designed was much more organic than the

ones the other AIs on the *Vale* favored. To the casual observer—and to all but the most invasive scans—she appeared to be an augmented human. Her face shared Calista's exotic facial features and was framed by hair that fell down her back in a plait of silver.

Although, it's not really hair, he mentally corrected himself.

Millions of strands of filament made up the braid, containing infiltration nano she'd assured him could be used to subvert any system in record time.

And here she sat, those silver eyes pinning him with an expectant look, her body humming with an energy she could barely contain. Plying the black while in cruise had made for three fairly mundane decades, and she was practically bouncing in her seat, ready for a change.

It animated a face so familiar to him in an utterly unique fashion. Jason knew this was Shannon's way of keeping Calista's memory alive. For him, it was like finding similarities of a loved one in the features of a sibling.

He exchanged another amused look with Terrance, strapped into the auxiliary seat behind his own captain's chair, and heard an "oh, *please*" as Shannon caught their exchange.

With a smirk, he turned back to the AI and gave the command. In the next breath, she'd whipped her seat around, braid flying, and linked to the shipnet to order all personnel to strap in.

Rotation ceased. Then Shannon expertly spun the ship end-to-end about its three-kilometer-long axis.

He could feel weightlessness recede as she tied the ship's eight fusion engines into their Matchbox Fusion Reactors, and they began to decelerate at 1*g*. The MFRs' burn would last about three months—the time it would take to bring them to rest near Lucent, the system's small white dwarf star, which the Hegemony called home.

The deep, low-frequency hum of the *Avon Vale* under thrust seeped into his bones like a familiar friend, and anticipation began to unfurl as the realization that they were nearing their destination settled over him.

"Ahhhh, that feels good," Shannon sighed, and Jason quirked a brow at her vocalization of his own thoughts.

"You referring to humanoid feels or ship feels?" he queried, and she shot him another *oh, please* look.

"Both, if you must know," she said in her best prim-yet-snarky tone, and he burst out laughing.

"Well, I never know with you," he pointed out. "You have two different sensory inputs, between the ship and your organics."

"Offer's still on the table to hook you up with your own set of sensory inputs," she reminded him, "in case you want to experience the interstellar medium around the *Vale* for yourself."

Jason cocked his head, considering. "Yeahhhh…no. I think I'll stay old-school. I'd rather feel it right here," he leant sideways far enough to give his backside a slap, then tapped his forehead, "not up here."

He unsnapped his restraints and stood, bouncing slightly on his heels in an unconscious test of the ship's accel. It was an old habit, ingrained in him from his youth, when he'd been flying freighters with sometimes sketchy propulsion between the stars of his home system.

That prompted him to do a quick mental calculation. He scowled when he realized that he was now effectively 250 years old.

<*Something wrong?*> Terrance's voice, colored with concern, intruded on his mental calculations, and he raised his head from his contemplation of the bridge's deck to glance over his shoulder at Terrance.

<*Nah. Just realized how old I am,*> he returned, with a wry twist to his mouth as he saw the exec visibly relax. <*Only thing good about it is that you'll always be older'n me.*>

Terrance just snorted. <*Good thing Enfield's research division cracked the code for true stasis, then, isn't it? That and a bit of Marta's rejuv will keep that grey hair of yours at bay.*>

Jason shot him another scowl. *<Grey—? Dude. I am* **not** *going grey.>*

<White, then.>

<You're still older'n me. Always will be.>

Ignoring Terrance's mental snort, he straightened, then allowed his gaze to sweep the bridge, recalling his role as ship's captain.

"Nicely done, people. Run your checklists and log them, then settle in. We have another three months ahead of us, and, if memory serves, another seven comm buoys to update before we arrive."

Cesar's Martinez Shipping had done a decent job of planting communication buoys between Sirius and Epsilon Eridani eighty years before, but Enfield's modified buoys—coated in Elastene, and powered by the same MFRs that powered the *Vale*'s eight fusion engines—were sturdier, more powerful, and would last much longer than the ones they were replacing.

Receiving a round of nods, he cocked a brow at Terrance, who indicated the ship's suite of offices the two of them shared, just off the bridge. Jason nodded, then strode toward it, reaching out to tap Landon on the shoulder as he went.

The AI looked up with a questioning expression, and Jason hooked a thumb back toward the captain's chair.

"All yours," he said, receiving a crisp nod before the XO moved to vacate his seat.

* * * * *

<Anything new come through to add to the infodump?> Terrance queried Kodi privately as he rose and followed Jason through the door and into the nearest office. *<Have they responded yet to Enfield Holding's query about a trade agreement?>*

The AI embedded within Terrance shook his head. *<Nothing more than acknowledging receipt of the packet. And that one message.>*

He grunted a response as he turned toward the comfortably

worn pair of oversized chairs set into a corner of Jason's office. Hitching his feet up onto the scarred wooden surface of the coffee table in front of him, he settled into the chair's faux leather embrace.

He and Jason had spent many an hour here, kicking over ideas and working through logistical issues—the kind of things that required the attention of captains and ships' owners.

Jason's detour to his desk roused Tobi. The big cat had eschewed being strapped in for the braking maneuver. Instead, she'd opted for simple expediency, using her sharp, needle-like claws to anchor her sleek feline form to the attached bedding behind Jason's desk.

Nails clicked lightly against the sole of the deck as she rounded the corner. She stropped Jason's legs, then paused while he snagged a pair of coffee-stained mugs from the corner of his desk before following him over to where Terrance sat, and settling between the two chairs.

Both mugs hit the low surface, dead-center on two circular stains. The coffee rings had soaked deep into its finish, the table having seen much use over the years.

Moments later, the aroma of fresh coffee teased Terrance's nose as the doors opened to admit the servitor. Jason stepped back, making room for the small, mobile unit to deliver the fresh carafe before retreating back the way it had come.

"Okay, Lieutenant Communications Officer," Jason addressed Kodi as he sat, faux leather giving off a soft sigh as he settled into the chair's depths, coffee mug in hand. "What was so important about that last buoy download?"

Terrance leant forward to grab his mug, lifting it with a smirk. "I told Kodi you'd notice he'd flagged that."

Kodi snorted. *<Keep forgetting he's an L2. He's pretty good at multitasking—for a human.>*

Terrance smothered a laugh at the obvious lie; the former El Dorado Space Force Lieutenant, on permanent detached duty to the task force, never forgot a thing.

<*It was official correspondence directed to Enfield Holdings from the Hegemony.*> Kodi's tone turned acerbic as he added, <*Couched in a whole lot of pomp and attitude.*>

Kodi activated the small holo embedded into the coffee table, and an elaborate, stylized "S" with silver rays shooting from behind a dimensional shield floated before them.

<*We've been asked to heave to and be inspected at the twelve-AU line,*> the AI informed them. <*It would appear that rumors of our prowess have made it to Sirius, and they have a few questions about the capabilities of the* Vale.>

Jason's eyebrows rose at Kodi's news, but before the AI could elaborate, a voice from the entryway interjected itself into the conversation.

"And just where would they be getting their information from, now, laddie?"

Terrance raised his cup in a welcoming salute as Tobias dragged Jason's battered office chair over and folded himself into it. His entrance caught Tobi's attention, and the big cat rose from where she'd been sitting under Terrance's propped feet. The exec lifted his legs up a bit as she stretched, and then set them back down on the coffee table with a thump as she padded over to the AI she'd once carried around in her harness.

She gave Tobias's hand a friendly nudge with her head, and the Weapon Born pulled her toward him, giving the big cat a thorough rubbing while he shot both humans an expectant look.

Instead of explaining, Terrance simply turned and indicated the gaudy, floating "S" with a tilt of his head.

A moment later, the scene morphed into a headshot of a young Sirian reporter with what looked like tiny glittering strands of lights embedded just under his skin. They arced from his brows up into his hairline. His expression solemn, he began a dramatic recounting of an engagement between "an Alpha Centauri warship and a Baratian cruiser."

The report showed the aftermath of the incident, including interviews with eyewitnesses, shots of the debris field that remained, and animated recreations of the event. The account exaggerated the skirmish—but not by much. Fortunately, there was no actual footage of the supposed warship.

The news segment drew to a close, morphing back into the stylized Sirian icon once more. Terrance sat back and watched as Jason stared at the holo, fingers drumming against his crossed leg as he contemplated what they'd just seen.

"Warship," the ship's captain grunted. His hand stilled as he slanted a glance over at Terrance. "Not exactly a good way to begin a covert op."

"No," he agreed. "It's not."

Blowing out a short breath, Jason reached once more for his coffee mug before slouching down into his seat and taking a few contemplative sips.

Terrance slid a measuring look from him to Tobias and then back.

"There's more," he said, after a moment. He nodded to indicate the holo once again, as Kodi resumed playback.

Annotated to the end of the report was a brief comment addressed to Terrance by a woman who introduced herself as the Coreward Border Account Lead for Hegemony Corporate Security.

Jason's eyes narrowed, and he sat up, pausing the holo. "Wait. Did that woman just call herself an *account lead*? What the hell kind of title is that?"

Terrance smothered a smile. "Well, Sirius *is* a corporately-held system," he reminded the man. "They don't have a military per se, just corporate security. As such, they use corporate hierarchy nomenclature."

Jason coughed. "Want to put that into plain language, for us poor working-class folk?"

Tobias's green eyes crinkled in amusement. "I think what the lad's saying, boyo," the AI said, "is that they use words like 'director' and 'manager' instead of 'captain' and 'lieutenant'."

<*Could have just said as much,*> Tobi commented, the cat's mental tone dripping with disgust. She looked up from where she'd settled in front of Tobias long enough to level a glare at the frozen holo before resuming her grooming.

Jason grinned and gestured to the cat with his empty mug. "What she said." He set the mug down and reached for the carafe to pour himself a refill as Terrance resumed the holo.

The Hegemony woman's back was ramrod-straight, her mouth pursed into a frown. She glared disapprovingly at the camera from behind an imposing desk emblazoned with the Sirian seal.

"Pursuant to corporate policy," the account lead began, "we'll need the *Avon Vale* to submit to inspection before proceeding insystem to Incandus. Unauthorized weaponry is not allowed."

The figure paused, an apologetic yet impersonal smile on her face. She pointed downward, and an icon pulsed twice in a lower corner before settling.

"Of course, you're welcome to avail yourselves of our transport system instead. I've included a timetable for shuttles that transit between Incandus and Glimmer-One, the coreward border station where your inspection will take place."

Now a slight scowl marred the woman's face, frown lines interrupted by a line of small metal studs that had begun to encroach on her forehead from the bridge of her nose.

"Or you can wait for your vessel to be cleared for inner system transit. But even then," her words took on a prim tone, "larger vessels like yours are restricted to one-point-five million kilometers, a hundredth of an AU. Although, you are welcome to use any smaller shuttles you might have to take you on to Brilliance Station or Incandus." The woman paused, nodded pleasantly, and then ended the recording.

Jason whistled. "Thanks but no thanks on that Sirian shuttle, ma'am. If it's all the same to you, I vote we get there under our own steam."

Terrance nodded. "Agreed. I want to be able to leave whenever we wish." He left the obvious unsaid—the odds were good that they *would* need a fast exit at some point. It seemed they always did.

"Could pose some problems," Jason said eventually, rolling his half-empty mug slowly back and forth between his hands, and staring into its depths. "Especially if we want to hide any of the *Vale*'s capabilities and refute the report that she's a warship."

Terrance waited a beat. When Jason seemed uninclined to expound on the comment, Terrance drained his mug and set it down onto the table with a decisive thump. Eyeing Jason, he stood.

"Can you and Tobias talk through this with the twins and see if they have any suggestions? I'll hunt Khela down and get her take on it from a Marine's perspective."

Jason nodded. "Not a problem. I'll round them up and see what they have to say. Landon is sure to have some concerns."

"And it's a sure thing Logan'll come up with a few outside-the-box suggestions to counter them," Tobias contributed with a chuckle.

Terrance grinned at that. "That's why he's our intelligence officer."

Slapping Jason on the shoulder, he waved to Tobias and then exited the office in search of his wife.

* * * * *

Jason watched Terrance's retreating back until the door closed behind him, then swung his gaze back to Tobias, contemplating his childhood friend and mentor for a long moment.

Tobias left him to it, the AI's hand stroking lightly down Tobi's back, leaving long, shallow furrows in her coat. Patient as always, the Weapon Born gave Jason's mind time to sift through things at his own speed.

"Think we can do it?" Jason finally asked, shifting to brace his forearms on his thighs, hands loosely clasped. "Keep the Sirians from finding out the *Vale*'s a Q-ship?"

"You canna turn back time, boyo. I'm afraid that ship has sailed. Poor word choice, I know, but...." Tobias shrugged. "You heard the reporter call her a warship. By definition, a Q-ship is a merchanter *hiding* as a warship. If the *Vale*'s being declared as one, well...." He spread his hands in a *what can you do?* gesture.

Jason blew out a sharp breath as he sat back, laced his hands behind his head, and stared up at the bulkhead in thought. "Yeahhhh...." The word was drawn out and even to his own ears, it sounded a bit discouraged.

Tobias gave him an enigmatic smile. "Ach, then again, who am I to say? If that genie *can* be put back into the bottle, it's Logan you'll be wanting to talk to, or Landon." He shook his head, tilting it to one side. "Me, I just handle the task force's Tac-Ops. Last time I checked, that's people, boyo. Not the ship."

Jason snorted, shifting in his chair to eye his friend. "Don't give me that, Tobe. You were—are—Weapon Born. You know plenty about ships."

"Flying small craft, aye," Tobias corrected. "Fighting with them. Killing with them." His eyes grew haunted. "And I was fair certain I'd never be doing that again after I was freed."

Jason felt instant remorse at the memories he saw surfacing in his friend's eyes.

"Fair point," he conceded, and then reached to gather the empty mugs.

Tobi's head lifted abruptly. *<Need me to play dumb again with the Sirians? Might come in handy for spying. Lumins look easy to fool.>* The big cat's nose wrinkled in disgust. *<No need to ask Beck. Stupid fuzzbrain's dumb enough as is.>*

Jason smirked, exchanging an amused look with Tobias. "Not a bad plan, Tobi," he said, more to placate the Proxima cat than anything. He didn't really see how feline subterfuge would work under these conditions—but one never knew. "Just in case, though, you might want to let Beck in on it."

The cat chuffed out her annoyance on a breath, but sent her agreement before padding silently to the door and slipping through it.

Jason rose, placing the mugs onto the servitor's tray before turning a contemplative look back on Tobias. "I'll run this by the twins sometime over the next few days. Would you mind doing the same with Charley? Maybe he or Jonesy can come up with a few suggestions. Something tells me we're going to need all the aces we can stuff up our collective sleeves for this one."

SOLD ON A MONDAY

STELLAR DATE: 03.27.3302 (Adjusted Gregorian)
LOCATION: Prism Station (aka "Prison" Station)
REGION: Noctilucent Space, Sirian Hegemony

Five days later, more than 1,800 AU away....

Hegemony Corporate Orphanage 7 was a sad warren of bunk beds, stacked four high and stretching down one side of a narrow corridor just outside the environmental plant in the underground section of the habitat cylinder named Prism Station.

Prism held a position at the border between Luminescent and Noctilucent Space. It was the home of both Irid and Noctus alike, and commonly referred to as 'Prison' Station by the Noctus who lived there.

Given its location, it was one of the more utilitarian habitats. Irids stationed there were either just beginning their careers, or were of lesser status within their respective Guilds. Most aspired to move up to one of the Luminescent stations, closer in.

Prism was Ysobel's first assignment upon joining the Academicians' Guild. Her mother had been sorely disappointed in the appointment, but Ysobel hadn't minded. Then again, Neta had always thought her daughter lacked ambition.

Neta would have been horrified to learn that Ysobel's charges were all Noctus. Her mother, she was sure, had stretched the truth with her friends. To hear Neta tell it, Ysobel had graciously sacrificed a more prestigious position to assist those Irids who had been forced to work under such harsh conditions.

She shook her head in bemusement at her mother's social aspirations as she tucked a satchel filled with hyfilms and datapads for the Noctus children under one arm, while snagging her breakfast drink in another. Waving at her apartment's door panel with her elbow, she triggered it open and stepped out.

Her overlay indicated she was due at the school in fifteen minutes. That meant she had just enough time to swing by the orphanage and drop off the hyfilm.

Ysobel smiled as she recalled the Seuss stories she'd discovered the night before when browsing the archives. She wished she had time to stay and see the orphans' faces when Headmaster Bryce loaded the vids onto the orphanage's teacher screens. She'd have to ask him later if the children liked them.

She picked up the pace as she spied the maglev car pulling into her stop. Waid, one of her neighbors, looked up when he heard the rapid sound of her approaching feet on the deck, and paused to hold the door open for her.

"Thanks," she breathed, as she scooted in just as the car's NSAI began berating Waid for blocking the door.

"Eh, shut yer trap, you old bucket of bolts," the Irid growled, shooting an eye at the nearest optic before ambling over to a seat, "or I'll reprogram you and insert you into a coffee-bot."

The systems engineer stumbled as the car began to move, causing Ysobel to grin and shake her head at the man as he lunged for his seat.

"You might try sweet-talking it next time," she teased. "I hear they respond better to honey than vinegar."

Waid snorted. "Nah, honey'd gum up the works too much. Vinegar's viscosity is lower."

Ysobel's grin faded as she spied the tear-swollen face of a Noctus woman seated across from her. She glanced briefly over at Waid, who shrugged and shook his head wordlessly. She glanced up and down the car, but the other passengers seemed either absorbed in their Links or studiously avoiding the woman's pain.

Clipping her drink into a nearby holder, she set her satchel aside and moved across the aisle to the empty seat next to the woman.

"I've seen you on the maglev before," Ysobel said quietly. "You're on the janitorial staff down in the restaurant section, aren't you? Your name is Pia, right?"

A slight jerk of her head was the woman's only response. Ysobel reached out to touch the woman's hand. "Do you want to tell me what happened?"

The despair held within the eyes that met hers was palpable. "My baby," Pia whispered. "Those bastards took my baby…."

Under Ysobel's gentle encouragement, the woman's story unfolded. Ysobel and Waid listened with growing horror as Pia told of how her daughter had been taken from her. It turned out that Pia's baby was one of Ysobel's students at the school—a bright and cheerful ten-year-old girl named Sophie.

But Sophie no longer had a home to call her own. Early this morning, a Lumin had visited her home and taken her away from her mother.

"He told me what a bad mother I was," Pia's voice trembled, barely audible. "He said as a single mother working full time, Prism Station considered me unfit to properly care for her."

"Where's your partner? Could he or she have intervened and taken Sophie instead?" Waid asked gently, leaning across the aisle, concern evident in his eyes.

Pia just shook her head. "Chris was killed in a dockyard accident six months ago, when a loader slipped and crushed him," she whispered. "Sophie's all I have left of him, and now she's gone, too."

Ysobel and Waid exchanged a glance. "Do you know where they took her?" Ysobel asked Pia, and the woman shook her head.

"Orphanage, most likely," Waid grunted, and Ysobel nodded.

It made the most sense. Sophie was probably now considered a ward of the Hegemony. As such, she would have been relocated to the Prism Orphanage.

This was puzzling to Ysobel. As far as she knew, the orphanage took in only those children who had no family to care for them. If aunts, uncles, or grandparents were qualified, the corporation that ran the Hegemony wasn't about to take on the expense of a child's care. She knew of many Noctus children living in extended family situations; surely having one parent still alive would qualify.

Ysobel shot Waid a concerned glance.

"It happens that I'm headed there myself right now," she said gently. "I'll—" She broke off at Waid's gesture, correcting herself. "*We'll* accompany you. We'll find out what happened to Sophie, don't you worry." She smiled encouragingly, squeezing the woman's hand, but looked over at Waid with a worried eye as Pia clung to her.

The orphanage was only a few meters past where the maglev dropped them off. As they turned down the dank corridor that housed the orphans, Ysobel spied Bryce, the orphanage's headmaster, and quickened her steps to catch up to him. He paused with a harried look when she called out.

As she reached him, Ysobel drew Pia forward. "Just the person I was hoping to see," she greeted. "Bryce, this is Pia. Her daughter was picked up by the garrison this morning and brought here by mistake. Can you help her?"

"Her name is Sophie," Pia began, meeting Bryce's eyes hesitantly. "I…she's all I have left, and when I got off my work shift this morning, one of the garrison soldiers had placed this on my pallet."

She lifted a hyfilm, and Ysobel realized it must have been what the Lumins had left at her door, the sheet informing Pia of her daughter's removal into Hegemony custody.

Bryce pushed the hyfilm away and turned to Ysobel in barely constrained impatience. "Now's not a good time," he told her, his tone harried. "We'll have to deal with this later."

"But, Bryce, they stole Pia's child from her and brought the girl here! Can't you see how wrong that is?" Ysobel shook Bryce's arm lightly, and he shrugged her hand off, turning toward her in sudden anger.

"Don't you think I *know* that?"

Equally suddenly, Bryce deflated. Scrubbing his face with his hands, he sighed. Turning away, he took a deep breath, braced himself, and then faced Pia.

"I'm sorry, so very sorry about your daughter. As far as I'm concerned, you can see her at any time. Suns," he said, gesturing toward the bulkhead behind which lay the rows upon rows of bunk beds the children slept in, "as far as I'm concerned, you can even stay the night with her if you want. But I can't let her leave, ma'am. I hope you can understand my position."

Pia's chin wobbled, and her eyes glistened with tears as she stared back at him. Finally, she nodded her acceptance.

Bryce's name was called, and he jerked his head up, the tension returning to his face. "Later," he told Ysobel, and he hurried off.

Ysobel abruptly realized they had interrupted something serious. Now that she paused to look around, she saw that the orphanage seemed in a state of chaos. She caught sight of three Lumins, waiting with barely constrained annoyance—but for what?

Stepping forward and peering around the corner, Ysobel gasped when she recognized several of her students standing in a lengthy queue. Each held tightly to a small bundle she suspected held all the possessions they owned. It was evident that they were being relocated under the directives of these Lumins, but she couldn't fathom why.

In the two years she'd been assigned to Prism Station, she'd never seen a Lumin take interest in the orphanage—or any part of the lower levels of the station, for that matter. Not once.

"I'm getting a bad feeling about this," she murmured to Waid as he joined her and peered over her shoulder.

A man she recognized as being on the orphanage's staff hurried past, and the haunted look in his eyes as they met hers chilled Ysobel. She took a step forward as if to intercept him, but a hasty gesture from him stopped her.

"What's going on?" Waid leant forward to rumble quietly into her ear, his eyes intent on the line of children.

Ysobel shook her head wordlessly. The oldest couldn't be more than twelve, she guessed, as she watched one of the Lumins bark at them to move forward.

Frightened eyes stared back at him, and the younger children shrank from his harsh tone. One of the littler ones—a boy around the age of five—began to cry, and others joined in.

"Teacher Ysobel!" the boy cried as he caught sight of her. Dropping his bundle, he broke rank and began to run toward where she stood in the entrance.

He made it no more than ten meters before he was seized by his coveralls and yanked back into line.

Ysobel started forward at that, but the objection she'd been about to make died on her lips when Headmaster Bryce intervened, stepping up to the woman who appeared to be in charge of the contingent.

"Adjunct Helada," he began, "I'm sure there's been some mistake. These children are too young to be sent to the platforms. Some of them are barely—"

He stopped abruptly when the adjunct pulled her weapon and aimed it at the headmaster's face.

"Are you offering to accompany them, Irid?" the woman growled. "There's a shortage of workers. In order for the Hegemony to remain solvent, everyone needs to do their part."

Ysobel stiffened, stifling a protest at the oft-repeated phrase, directed for the first time at individuals far too young to shoulder such responsibilities. The Lumin's weapon swung toward the entrance at the small sound Ysobel had emitted, and the adjunct pinned her with a cold stare. Chilled at the cruelty she saw in their depths, Ysobel's hand crept to her throat in reflex.

"Where are you taking them?" Waid's voice broke through Ysobel's paralysis. "Surely there's no harm in telling us this much."

Helada holstered her sidearm with a snap and gestured one of her attendants toward Waid.

The man, whose metal studs only went half as far up the bridge of his nose as the studs his adjunct sported, looked Waid up and down, his expression one of contempt. "The first twenty-five have been procured by Overseer Miguel for platform SR71," he announced, his voice bored and tinged with annoyance.

"Procured? They're *children,*" Ysobel began, but the Lumin ignored her.

Turning to Bryce, he jerked his head toward a bulkhead, behind which stretched the corridor that housed the orphanage's occupants. "We'll be back this afternoon to gather up the second group for platform AP23."

Dismissing Ysobel, the Lumin returned to the now-moving line of children at a gesture from Helada.

"Have the second batch prepared to leave *on schedule,*" the adjunct ordered. Snapping her fingers at the two Lumins with her, she pointed at the children and then, without a backward glance, marched off.

As the group of children began to move down the corridor and out of sight, the Lumins swept the area with one final, dismissive glance, then turned and strode away.

Bryce held up a hand to forestall Ysobel as Helada's assistants departed the corridor. As soon as they were out of sight, he rounded on her.

"Do you have a death wish?" he demanded. "Well? Do you, Ysobel? That was supremely stupid, confronting an adjunct like that."

"Well, someone had to," she shot back. "Suns, Bryce! Half of them can't even read yet. How will they follow instructions, recognize posted warnings, or avoid hazardous materials?"

"What would you have done? Refuse to cooperate when ordered by the stationmaster to comply? You know she'd just promote the next Guild member into the position, and do the same until she found someone who *would* comply."

"Not if the Guild has any shred of decency," she retorted.

"They could just explain to the station master what was going on, and then she—"

Waid put a restraining hand on Ysobel's shoulder, cutting her off. "I think I can guess why that wouldn't work," he stated, eyes hardening with a jaded look as they shifted to Bryce. "Station master was paid off, wasn't she? And if I'm right, Ysobel, your friend here was approached first."

Ysobel looked from one to the other, thinking through what had just transpired, and what the Lumins had said. Bryce shot Waid a guarded look, but remained silent. And then it came to her.

"That Lumin used the word 'procured'," Ysobel said slowly, as understanding dawned. "As in...*purchased*?"

Bryce threw up a hand to ward her off as she began to stalk toward him. "Before you go nova on me, just *listen* for a second," he begged. "I told them no, Ysobel. I wouldn't do it."

"How much did they offer you for them, Bryce?" she asked, her voice rising until it was a shout. "How much? Ten credits a child? Fifty? A hundred?"

Knocking his hands out of the way, she slammed her palms against his chest, shoving him with all her strength.

"Stars, Bryce, you could have told someone! We could have stopped them!"

He stumbled back, but as they stared at each other, the fight abruptly left her. They both knew the truth; no one went head to head against a Lumin and won.

"So, our friendly neighborhood station master profits off them instead," Waid muttered into the silence. "Suns, what a messed-up system we live in. Sold to the Lumins. One hell of a way to start the week."

Ysobel couldn't help but agree.

Q-SHIP MAKEOVER

STELLAR DATE: 03.29.3302 (Adjusted Gregorian)
LOCATION: ESS *Avon Vale*
REGION: 1,620 AU from Sirius Binary System

One week into deceleration burn….

The *Avon Vale* was now one thousand AU inside the Sirius binary system's heliopause. It had more than sixteen hundred left to travel, almost three months to go before they would reach their inspection point. That was just fine by Jason; the ship's complement still had a lot to do to the *Vale* before that rendezvous.

He entered the bridge looking for Landon, finding the AI missing and the captain's chair empty. Querying the shipnet, he saw that the executive officer had left Shannon in charge and was currently on the move.

<*Any reason you're sitting at Nav instead of the captain's chair?*> he asked the ship's AI privately.

Shannon swiveled, shooting him one of her patented 'why are you bothering me with this *now*' looks, but then cocked her head to one side as she considered his words.

<*No, not really. But now that you mention it….*>

Sending him a bright smile—the kind that usually made him wonder what mischief she was up to—she toggled the holo off at the nav station with a little flourish. Springing to her feet, she gave Khela's father a little pat on the shoulder as she sauntered past Scan on her way to the captain's chair.

"How frequently can a girl say she's captain of her own destiny, and mean it so literally?" she said with an impudent grin. She hopped up into the chair, bouncing a few times before slinging both legs over one of its arms.

"All righty then. I'm just going to sit here and keep telling myself to haul ass away from that heliopause we crossed last week." She flapped one hand toward the main holo while propping her chin up with the palm of her other hand. Tilting her head back toward Jason, she sent him a flirtatious wink.

"Don't make me regret this," he warned with a mock scowl, pointing a warning finger at her before turning to head into the corridor.

"I already do," Noa murmured, causing Jason to smother a laugh.

"I heard that, Noa Sakai!" Shannon retorted.

Just before the door slid shut behind them, Jason heard Noa's warning tone. "Shannon, that was two weeks' worth of spectroscopic analysis you just made disappear. Bring that back right now…."

*****

Landon was speeding toward the cargo bay a kilometer away by the time Jason left the bridge.

<Jonesy pinged to say his team just finished installing the ultra-black stealth nanosheath around the Kaze's *engines,>* the XO explained when Jason queried him. *<Just stopping by to see how well they were able to mask the AP drive on it, as well.>*

The newest addition to the *Vale*'s small complement of insystem ships had been dubbed *Kuroi Kaze*, or Dark Wind, by Khela. It was a fitting moniker, given the names of its sister ships, *Sable Wind, Eidolon,* and *Mirage*. It was also currently one of Landon's pet projects.

<Uh-huh. Bet what you were really after was to see if you could still fit that pair of missile launchers under her belly. Admit it.>

<Well, I….>

Jason waved him away with a grin. *<No worries. Let me know how she looks. And swing by the armory when you're done. Logan's there now, and I'm on my way.>*

Landon confirmed, then dropped off the net just as Jason

approached the nearest lift. He was surprised to see that a queue had formed, but then recalled they were more popular with the crew just after a flip. It seemed to take a while for people to accustom themselves to change, no matter what it was. In this case, it was the change from half-*g* during cruise to the heavier full-*g* of acceleration.

He winked as one of the engineering ratings he knew glanced up with a guilty look as he approached. The woman raised the load of hyfilms she carried in her arms. "Not hopping down one of those ladders with an armful, sir," she defended, and he smirked as he passed by her on his way to the stairwell.

"Not judging, Amy," he called out over his shoulder. He heard her quiet snort just as he ducked inside.

Tilting his head, he peered up the access tunnel beside the stairs, checking the chute before grabbing hold of the ladder's outside rails and sliding down one level to where the armory was located, on Deck Three.

As he fell, a part of his brain noted that the holo overlays were turned off—as they should be, now that they were under acceleration again. They had been necessary while the decks rotated during their decades-long cruise, as they warned the crew that they were entering a shaft of graduated gravity.

Still, it felt odd not seeing them after almost thirty years of cruising, even though he'd only spent a week or two each year out of stasis.

Guess the lifts aren't the only thing that will take some getting used to again.

* * * * *

"How's inventory coming along?" Jason's voice sounded behind Logan as the man came through the armory's open doors.

"Almost done," he replied, sealing the case of E-SCAR rifles before hefting the box and stacking it onto a nearby pallet. "I've been thinking…."

He turned to see Jason leaning against a similar stack, just inside the door. Crossing his arms, the captain shot him a questioning look, inviting him to continue.

"I don't like the thought of sending the shuttles away from the ship," Logan said as he slid a maglev hand truck under the pallet and moved it to where Jason stood. "If we use them as mobile storage devices, then we're limiting our options, both in stealth and maneuverability."

Jason nodded, acknowledging Logan's point. Phantom Blade had used the Icarus-class shuttles in the past to infiltrate a location unseen, while the *Avon Vale* served as a ready distraction. "So what do you have in mind?"

"Drones."

He saw Jason raise his brow in surprise before eyeing him thoughtfully. "Go on."

"Jonesy has a new class of drones under development. He plans to coat them in the new Elastene, made from borophene instead of graphene, that he and Shannon developed."

Jason grunted. "Saw the data on that. It looks impressive. Its stealth capabilities outperform the original Elastene formulation, and that's saying something."

Logan nodded. "There's nothing stopping us from coating our cargo pods in it as well." He patted the pallet of boxes beneath his hands. "I asked Charley if he was comfortable flying four or five drone trains at one time. He said yes."

Jason tilted his head as he considered Logan's words. "You thinking of something similar to container cars coupled together, the kind that drone transports ferry around in shipping lanes?"

Logan nodded. "If Jonesy coats everything in ultra-black, they should remain undetectable."

"Yeah…." Jason ran a hand around the back of his neck, rubbing it absently in thought, then shot the AI a look from under lowered brows. "Piloting a strand of cargo pods is a bit different than handling a bunch of single fighter drones in combat, though. Each pod trailing behind that drone is going to have its own moment of inertia. They're going to have quite an impact on the drone that pulls them. You sure he's factored all that in?"

Logan just looked at him.

After a beat, Jason dropped his hand and straightened with a grin. "Riiiight," he drawled. "Product of a Weapon Born and multi-nodal AI. That's why his cylinder's so much bigger'n yours." A wicked light flashed in Jason's eyes before he added, "Not that size matters."

"Sir…." Logan infused a pained note in his voice, knowing it was the reaction the captain sought, and was rewarded with a bark of laughter. *Profiling for the win.* Then he qualified, "Unfortunately, not everything we have to conceal is portable."

Jason grimaced at the words.

The news report out of Little River had labeled the *Vale* a warship. Both knew that meant the inspection team would be looking for evidence of superior shielding, and weaponry that a civilian-class ship would not have.

Things would be much easier if they could just refuse the inspection, but to refuse meant limiting their freedom of movement, and possibly their access to Sirius altogether. They could not fulfill their mission parameters if they did not bow to the Hegemony's demand to heave to and be inspected, which meant they needed to misdirect prying eyes, and conceal the *Vale*'s true capabilities.

Logan heard Jason sigh as he glanced around.

"Marine territory's going to need a makeover," Jason murmured. "Maybe we can requisition a few sofas from the ship's stores, a large holo tank on the far wall, install some theatre lighting…."

He raised his hands, palms out, and squinted as if he were trying to envision such a thing. The disgruntled expression on his face as he lowered his arms almost made Logan laugh.

"I'd recommend you don't share that with Khela," Logan offered, and Jason shot him an incredulous look.

"Do I look like I have a death wish?" Then he smirked. "Don't answer that. Your profile of me probably suggests otherwise."

Logan let his mouth turn up slightly, and gave a two-fingered salute, acknowledging the jibe. "Jonesy has his team working up a solution—false fronts they can weld over our missile tube access ports. Shannon says she can 'jigger the ship's schematics to make the railguns look like pop rocks,' whatever those are."

Logan saw Jason grin at his recitation of Shannon's words. She confounded Logan at times with what he privately called her 'humanisms'. She had the least combat experience of any of them, and, like Jason, had never served in any military. But her personality meshed well with the team, and she helped forge them into a cohesive unit.

Besides, he liked her. He just didn't always understand her.

His mental musings were interrupted by his brother striding through the armory's doors. Landon looked agitated, as if he'd just realized something he'd not considered before.

Landon glanced over at the stack of crates, then shot a look at his twin before announcing abruptly, "We're screwed."

Logan leant against the bulkhead next to the E-SCARs he'd been inventorying, while Jason's brows rose and he crossed his arms. Both waited for Landon to elaborate.

"All of this, we can hide. We can even mask everything we have onboard."

"Buuuut…" Jason prodded him.

"We're coming in too fast," Landon said bluntly. "Our accel's going to give away the MFRs' capabilities. You know we have a twenty percent edge over current engine tech. No ship has made an interstellar journey at speeds faster than point-two *c*."

Landon brought up a good point, one that Logan hadn't considered—and he should have.

Interstellar ships were fueled by hydrogen. Tritium and

deuterium, if they were available, or protium in a pinch. The gas was much more plentiful within a stellar system, which meant that the ES ramscoops the vessels employed very rarely captured enough hydrogen to keep their engines burning in the vast distances between the stars. Therefore, they burned half of the hydrogen they stored, saving the rest for deceleration burns at their destination—minus a measure held in reserve for emergency maneuvers.

The *Avon Vale* had traditional hydrogen tanks for a vessel of its size, and this dictated what its maximum speed should be. Unlike other ships, however, the combination of two Enfield technologies—the Matchbox Fusion Reactors, and engines fabricated from Elastene—allowed the *Vale* to increase that speed by a good twenty percent.

Logan caught Jason's intent look as he studied Landon.

"So you think they're going to want to take a look at what's under the hood?" the captain asked.

Landon looked troubled. "I think we have to assume so, considering the kind of corporate espionage Cesar has warned us about. To hear him tell it, they've raised it to an art form."

Logan looked from one man to the other, and then shrugged. "So tell them we ran across an unexpected patch of local fluff and took advantage of it."

Landon stared at him as if he'd grown a second head.

Okay, maybe the shrug was a bit uncharacteristic of me.

"They won't buy—" Landon began, but Jason held up a hand.

"Wait." He narrowed his eyes at Logan, thinking it through.

Though the vast space between the stars, the interstellar medium, primarily consisted of hydrogen, the ISM varied greatly in density, from an average of one atom per cubic centimeter down to almost nothing—less than one atom in a hundred cubic centimeters, near Sol. This area of especially low density was known as the Local Bubble.

Within the Local Bubble were small pockets of partially ionized cloudlets known colloquially as the Local Fluff. Alpha Centauri was in a fluff known as the G Cloud, whereas Sirius was currently enjoying the intersection of the Local Cloud and the Blue Cloud.

"I know the route from Epsilon Eridani skirts the Blue," Jason told Landon, who promptly turned and gave Logan an 'I told you so' glare. "but it's not completely unheard of for ships to come across wisps of smaller cloudlets. That *is* what you're suggesting?"

Logan nodded. He saw Landon open his mouth to argue, then snap it closed.

"If that's true, then that…could actually work," his twin mused thoughtfully.

"Good," Jason said, pushing away from the stack of unpowered armor. "Now all we have to do is disguise our lady's many attributes," he swept his arm out to indicate the *Vale* with a grin, "and we're home free."

"We'll get it done," Logan assured Jason. "We still have three months to implement it. That's plenty of time."

Maybe he laid it on a bit thick. It was out of character for him to appear so unworried.

He hid a shaft of amusement at the flare of surprise that crossed Jason's face. Evidently it had the same effect on Landon, who rounded on his twin in consternation.

"Who are you, and what have you done with my brother?"

Logan saw Jason's lip twitch at the expression on Landon's face.

"I make it a point to keep my nose out of family business," he said with a smirk. "Just get me a backoff schedule for the team to review by tomorrow. We'll make it happen."

With a wave, he exited.

PART TWO: THE CON

HOW TO FOOL A SIRIAN

STELLAR DATE: 06.20.3302 (Adjusted Gregorian)
LOCATION: ESS *Avon Vale*
REGION: Nearing coreward station Glimmer-One

Three months later....

"Now *that's* impressive," Khela murmured as she entered Engineering with Beck at her heels.

Her eyes were glued to the display of the Sirius binary system her father had pulled up on the propulsion station's holo.

She smiled and sidestepped as one of the engineers crossed between them, her hands moving in midair, manipulating some unseen control. Khela realized it had been some years since she'd been to this part of the ship when entering a combat zone.

Well, technically, this inspection isn't a ***combat*** *zone,* she mentally corrected. *I'd qualify it as a hot zone, though, since we're actively infiltrating. Things could still get dicey if they don't buy what we're selling.*

Noa looked up at her approach, then lifted a finger, his expression distracted. He shrank the image he'd been studying, then shunted it to an auxiliary display before swiveling around to face them. Beck nosed his way past Khela and padded over to the physicist, who reached down to glide his hand over the big cat's silken fur.

His eyes warmed as he regarded his daughter. "I'm sorry, Khe-chan, what was that, again?"

Khela smiled at his use of her childhood nickname, then

glanced over at the auxiliary display, where a long, trailing bubble encased the binary system.

"Oh, nothing, really. I just forgot how far out Sirius's heliopause was. Tau Ceti looks like a lightweight compared to that." Her voice sounded a bit amused as she turned to her father with a smile.

"That's because not every star ejects plasma at the same rate," he responded, his attention diverted by the big cat, as Beck began butting Noa's hand insistently with his head.

"Hussy." Khela shot the uplifted animal a mock stern look, which earned her an innocent expression from its large, aqua eyes.

<*Can talk and rub at the same time,*> Beck argued with the kind of logic only a feline could possess. <*Not using your hands right now anyway.*>

"Um, dad?" Khela waggled her fingers to recapture his attention. "Hellooooo. You were saying?" She nudged Beck out of the way so she could slide into the seat beside Noa.

He glanced over at the display, and then brought his eyes back to rest thoughtfully on his daughter. "Oh, yes. Well, Sirius's terminal velocity is around thirteen hundred kilometers per second." He nodded to the image on the holo. "That makes its heliosphere much larger, because its winds are far stronger than ours back in Tau Ceti."

A chuckle sounded from the door as Jonesy caught the last of her father's explanation.

"Well," he drawled as he made his way over to Engineering's auxiliary weapons station and pulled the seat out. "It doesn't take much to beat Tau Ceti's heliosphere. Your star's stellar winds are slooooow." The engineer paused for a sip of coffee as he slid into the chair and turned to study the small holo. "Around fifty-five, sixty kilometers a second, if memory serves?" he added, cocking a brow at Khela's father for confirmation.

Noa nodded. "Of course, the more interesting comparison might be the strength and frequency of flares during its solar maximum."

Jonesy leant forward, intense interest chasing across his face. "I hear they're ten times bigger than the most intense ones out of Sol."

"Oh gee, look at the time," Khela said hastily before the two could become embroiled in the topic.

She rose just as the door slid open to reveal Charley, followed by Terrance.

"Thank stars." She smiled over at her husband, and the *Vale*'s security chief. "You arrived just in the nick of time. These two were about to catch me in a pincer move and inflict bodily physics on me."

Terrance slipped in behind her to wrap his arm around her waist. She could feel the rumble of her husband's chest against her back as he laughed. He pulled her against him briefly before leaning down to murmur in her ear.

"Well, that won't do," he whispered, "especially when I'd rather inflict other bodily things on you back in our room."

She smirked, reached behind her to pull his face down to hers for a quick kiss. "I'll be the one doing the inflicting, love, my word on it—after this charade of an inspection. And stop embarrassing Dad like that."

Terrance chuckled again, squeezing her briefly before letting her go. "Okay, I'll bite. What brought you down here?"

Khela turned to Jonesy and Charley, all humor leaving her expression as her role settled over her like a mantle.

"We've decided to hide the *Vale*'s Marines in plain sight, so to speak. I've already dropped a few by Medical so Marta can brief them on what they need to know to blend in. I'd like to do the same here, and in the shuttle bay," she explained. "Can you place them for me?"

The engineer's eyes defocused as he studied the list, and Charley nodded.

"We can divvy them up by specialty," the AI suggested, "and

the rest can pose as maintenance techs."

Jonesy nodded his agreement. "I like the idea. Be nice to have them around, in case things get dicey."

Khela nodded. "That's the plan. Okay, I'll tell them to report to you next shift to begin their training. Don't be afraid to put them to work. Marine country's been itching for a bit of action, so we have lots of pent-up energy."

"Aye, matey," Jonesy drawled with a wink. "We'll have 'em swabbing the decks and hoistin' the mainsail in no time."

"That'll go over well," she said with a smirk, shaking her head at the engineer's antics as she headed for the door. She stifled a laugh as she heard Terrance's parting remark.

"I'd pay good creds to see that, I think."

BLACKBIRD

STELLAR DATE: 06.20.3302 (Adjusted Gregorian)
LOCATION: Sintering Refinery Platform 71
REGION: Sirius A, Noctilucent Space, Sirian Hegemony

Twenty-seven AU away, in Noctilucent Space, Platform Administrator Arne looked down in annoyance at the comm handset he carried. It beeped again, flashing an alert on its small, 2D screen.

The last thing he needed was for the damned thing to remind him every fifteen minutes of his impending conference with Overseer Miguel. The meeting had loomed in the forefront of his mind ever since the shuttle carrying the overseer had announced the man's surprise visit. No amount of preparation would mitigate the distaste that grew as the time approached.

As Arne reached a cross corridor, one of the platform's runners sped past, calling out a greeting. He smiled and waved at the woman's retreating back, her hands filled with a stack of plasfilms—requests for refined ores, no doubt, from one of the manufactories. The runner's feet pounded the thick, dull grey plas decking of the wide corridor, the sound receding as she moved farther away.

Arne's eyes swept the corridor ahead of him, noting the small vagaries of the bland plas-grey bulkheads that his lifetime aboard various platforms had imprinted in his mind. Only a Noctus would be able to navigate the confusing warren of passageways, crawl spaces, and access tunnels that comprised Sintering and Refinery Platform SR71.

Known to locals as 'the Blackbird', the refinery held endless kilometers of workspace and a bare minimum of living space.

And enough cargo bays to swing a dog. Huh. I've always wondered where that phrase came from, his brain mused idly as he hurried toward the administration wing. *Do dogs even like to be swung?* Having never seen one, he had no way of knowing if it was something the animal regularly did.

He'd first heard the platform's nickname not long after he'd been transferred to the Blackbird as a young boy. No one seemed to know its origin, although it was rumored that a Noctus with an interest in ancient history had bestowed the moniker. He'd yet to figure out what a bird had to do with it. And why it had to be black.

He knew the place by heart, from the cool humidity of the hydroponics bays to the grit and grime of its enviro plants. As Platform Administrator, it was Arne's job to ensure that every one of these sectors was in working order, and that the platform's workers and equipment remained operational.

His mouth twisted, and he felt the customary burning resentment that surfaced each time he mentally quoted that last part of his job description—the part labeling workers as 'operational'. It made them sound too much like things, versus living beings.

Arne knew that, in the eyes of the overseers, workers *were* synonymous with equipment. As such, repairs were done only when necessary…and never to factory specifications. The platform was riddled with scars, as were its personnel. Far too often, they were forced to get by with the bare minimum standards required to keep both functional.

His comm unit crackled, the small indicator light blinking to let him know he was being hailed.

"Arne?" The voice of Tuesday, one of his yard supervisors, sounded tinny through the small speaker. *"Got a minute? I need to talk to you before you head over to admin."*

Arne mentally calculated the time it would take him to walk the breadth of the platform to get to West Yard, then back to the administrative wing in time to meet with Overseer Miguel and his adjunct, Helada.

Sun curse it all. What prompted Miguel to make an unscheduled stop here, when everyone knows the platform's not under his oversight? Has something happened? Does he somehow suspect…?

Tuesday's voice came over the speaker again, prodding him into a reply.

"Got any deliveries to the Under Yard or to South scheduled soon?" he asked her. "One that I can hitch a ride back on?"

There was a pause on the other end, then a decisive, *"We'll make it happen."*

"On my way, then," was Arne's reply as he turned down an intersecting corridor.

A single static burst was Tuesday's only acknowledgment.

Arne's eyes sought the wayfinding indicator ahead. Behind it would be a quick-access ladder he could use to make his way up to the next level.

He could see by Tuesday's restless stride that the yard supervisor was agitated about something. The woman's head snapped up as he approached. She turned, shoved her comm unit into the hands of one of her yard managers with a few terse words, then altered her course to intersect Arne's.

"What is it?" Arne asked as Tuesday neared.

The woman looked as if she would explode any minute, and Arne made a cautionary gesture with one hand in an attempt to get her to settle before she gained them both unwanted attention.

One never knew where a Lumin recording drone might be.

Tuesday slowed with a nod and a quick glance around. "Engineering just pinged to tell us to secure the loads in the yards. We've been reassigned to platform AP23. Engineering's planning a burn to vector us in behind them."

He'd been afraid this was why she'd pinged him.

"I know," he admitted, running his hands through his thinning hair. "The order came in with Overseer Miguel's pinnace."

"Arne, the timing on that burn—it's too soon. I've been talking to the other yard managers. We've pulled all the workers in to secure what ores we can, but we're going to have to eject some of the larger rocks." She shook her head, gesturing to the bay in which they stood. "I know the Lumins aren't going to like those losses, but there's just not enough space to store everything, and some of those chunks are just too damn big to fit. No way to secure them all in the nets before they begin the move, and I sure as hell don't want one of those things to slip loose and smash into something vital."

She paused and sucked in a lungful of air as her head tilted back and she stared up into the rafters of the cavernous bay.

"You know none of these platforms were built for the amount of stresses we're placing on them," she continued. "What if the seams on the south arm don't hold? We could lose the whole wing aft of those repairs!"

His gut tightened at her mention of the recent maintenance. Tuesday wasn't wrong; Arne knew that the Blackbird was riding the razor-thin edge of safety as it was.

The yard supervisor dropped her head back down. When her eyes met his, they held pain in their depths. "My sister and her husband were on AP51 during the last move, and they lost thirty percent of their shielding, right when that damned star out there decided to have an epic spew." She wrapped her arms around her middle, hunching her shoulders slightly. "They lost three hundred people, Arne. Three *hundred*."

He'd learned of the losses from his office staff. "I heard," he said simply. "And I know that we're barely holding our own against the radiation as it is."

Tuesday snorted. "That's an understatement. Can't tell you how many of my workers had alerts go off just in the last two weeks." She fingered the dosimetry badge they all wore, her voice brittle.

Solar particle events—the spews Tuesday had mentioned—were everyone's worst nightmare. Energetic flares or coronal mass ejections that flung particles outward at relativistic speeds, fueled by a shock wave that immediately preceded them. Sometimes they occurred in conjunction. The very worst solar storms launched a flurry of CMEs, one after another, with radiation levels that could deliver lethal dose equivalencies in a very short time.

There were specially shielded rooms within each platform where they could ride out the especially potent flares, but invariably, some Noctus were too far away to reach them in time.

"Well, there are no spews predicted within the next few days, and the platform's specs say we should be—"

"*Space* the specs, dammit!" Tuesday slapped her hand against a nearby pipe, the resulting clang drawing startled looks from nearby dockhands. A warning look from Arne had her lowering her voice to an angry whisper as she finished. "I know what it states about the platform's tolerances. But what's printed on hyfilm and the reality of what we're facing are two different things. The platform's not a damn tug that's overengineered for maneuvers, and you know it."

She looked down, her toe beating a light pattern against a floor flange as she drew in a deep breath. Arne could tell the woman was working hard to rein in her frustration.

"I don't care if we're moving to a more convenient location for the extraction platforms, Arne. We're operating with no safety margins. If those sun-cursed Lumin asshats won't listen to pleas for human decency, then maybe someone ought to try telling them that a dying workforce is a bad business decision. A very bad one."

Arne gripped Tuesday's arm firmly. "I know," he said, giving her arm a small squeeze. "I know."

Taking a deep breath, he stepped back.

"I'll do what I can to convince Overseer Miguel that this move isn't the most productive for the Hegemony. But right now, you need to keep it together. Not just for me, but for your people, who are depending on you." He jerked his chin in the direction of her dockhands.

The last thing the Noctus needed right now was for Tuesday's yard workers to go on some sort of strike. Miguel was known as one of the least forgiving overseers in the Hegemony. If there was unrest of any kind, he would see that the Lumin guards snuffed it out, and he would order it done with extreme prejudice.

She nodded, accepting his warning. Closing her eyes, she took a deep breath, unclenched her fists, and consciously relaxed her posture. He smiled and nodded encouragingly, but as he turned to leave, she countered his warning with one of her own.

"One more thing."

When he glanced back over his shoulder at her, she crossed her arms with a sigh. "I'd consider it a personal favor if you issued a platform-wide safety reminder about metal dusts. We're all well aware of the combustible nature of the materials we work with, but the more the Lumins whittle away at our turnaround times, the more tempting it becomes to cut corners."

He grimaced, but nodded. She had a point.

Grabbing a tablet from one of her workers as he passed, Tuesday tapped on it, then turned it so that Arne could see the data safety sheet displayed on the screen. It was on titanium, one of the more common ores the Blackbird extracted from the asteroid chunks it received.

"You know that metals like titanium, uranium, aluminum, and thorium are highly reactive? Thermally instable. Combustible."

She minimized the data sheet and tapped on a report. Nodding to the back of the cargo handling area, she said, "Sensors went on the blink three days ago, and no one noticed. One of our tug guys figured it out when he sparked on landing."

Arne reared back in surprise. "You didn't report it?"

Tuesday shook her head. "Small flash fire, not enough dust to do anything but scare a nearby worker. Good thing it happened when it did, though. Woulda been much worse if the dust had been allowed to accumulate for a few more days."

They exchanged a look of deep understanding. Noctus didn't

enjoy the protections that a planet, or even a ring or a hab cylinder, could provide. Platforms didn't have dozens of kilometers of atmosphere over their heads, or the many foundational layers of bulkhead and scrith between their feet and the inhospitable near-vacuum of space.

For Noctus, just a few meters of protection separated them from certain death. Here, fire represented immediate, life-threatening danger.

"One spark, Arne. Just one spark is all it would take." Tuesday's expression turned pleading. "We've lost enough Noctus lately. I don't want to be the next platform to experience tragedy."

Arne rubbed the back of his neck with one hand, nodding.

"Message received. I'll send out a bulletin this afternoon. In the meantime, you keep them as safe as you can, okay?" He turned to go, then paused and looked back. "And about your sister…. I'm sorry about what happened over on '51. I'll make it a point to stop by the free clinic and let the medical staff know to be prepared for radiation patients…just in case."

Tuesday grimaced, but nodded, then jerked her head over toward the cavernous receiving dock. "Tug forty-seven beta's holding for you over at slip nineteen." She gave Arne the ghost of a smile. "Bert'll take you all the way over to the dock by admin. He said it's kind of on his way to South anyway, and he's ahead of schedule."

Arne smiled his thanks, then broke into a slow jog as he hustled. "Ahead of schedule" was a polite fiction in the Hegemony. Arne would do what he could to ensure Bert didn't receive demerits for his kindness.

* * * * *

Miguel was a small, officious Lumin with a tendency to wear highly reflective clothing that hurt the eyes if one looked directly at them. Metal studs began just above his lip and snaked their way up his nose to meet between his brows. They glinted in the meeting room's harsh light.

He sat at the conference table, brushing imaginary filth off its pristine surface, an expression of disgust marring his otherwise perfectly balanced face. Considering this room was the nicest on the platform, Arne found the man's actions annoying.

Behind Miguel stood his adjunct, Helada, the woman's own studs reaching only to the midpoint of her nose. The woman looked over as Arne entered, a sneer curling her lip at the sight of his drab, grease-stained shipsuit.

"Are we inconveniencing you, Arne?" Helada's supercilious words echoed against the room's austere walls. "Perhaps the role of platform administrator is too much of a burden for you?"

Arne sighed internally. It was too much to expect a Lumin to understand, but no Noctus begrudged him the position of platform administrator. He'd accepted the role out of duty to his people; it was considered a burden among his kind, not an honor.

Pasting a bland smile on his face, he sent both Miguel and then Helada brief bows. "Please forgive my dress," he apologized to the overseer. "Engineering heard of your orders to relocate the platform, and I stopped by one of the yards on my way here to ensure things were on schedule for the move."

Miguel's mouth compressed into a line of displeasure, but he waved it away in a gesture Arne was certain the Lumin believed was a magnanimous gesture.

"Your dedication is noted," the overseer dismissed. "Now that you're here, let's get down to business." He gestured to Helada, who stepped forward and took a seat after carefully brushing it off. Her expression suggested that her first order of business once she'd returned to Luminescent Space would be the decontamination of her clothing.

She gestured with one hand, and a holo hovered over the conference table between where Arne stood and the two Lumins sat. Within it were suspended data tables displaying stats of the platform's performance over the past quarter. Arne knew they had managed to meet quota, despite the compressed timeline the Hegemony had imposed upon SR71.

Miguel tapped the edge of a beringed hand on the table before him in thought as he examined the results Arne's assistant had forwarded to his assistant just two hours earlier, when he'd announced his surprise visit. Reaching up, he rearranged the stats to show the estimated volume of ore to be refined in the following quarter.

"Our marketing and sales division signed a contract with three new manufacturers, one on Barat and two in Procyon," he announced. "We'll need you to increase your monthly volume of aluminum by eighteen percent—" he ignored the harshly expelled breath that escaped Arne's mouth as he continued, "and titanium by six percent."

"We—we don't have the staff for that, Overseer," Arne began. "And one of our bauxite processing plants is down. If we could free up the mechanics from some of their other duties to focus on repairs, then maybe—"

Adjunct Helada spoke over his protests. "It is, of course, imperative that we meet deadline with these new clients. In order to assist you, we've...acquired...a small workforce that will be transferring over to the platform within the next week."

"Small workforce?" Arne parroted numbly, and Helada nodded impatiently, as if he were a particularly slow-witted child.

"Yes, a freighter will transport twenty-five workers over from Prism Station. They're few enough to have minimal impact on platform resources."

Platform resources.... Arne straightened suddenly as it dawned on him what Helada meant by that. *They expect us to absorb the impact of twenty-five new bodies with our already-strained enviro systems and living quarters. And our rations.... Stars curse them!*

Arne struggled to rein in the hot flash of anger that coiled in his stomach.

"Regarding resources, sir," he began, pitching his tone humbly and bowing his head. "We are overdue for maintenance on our environmental systems. They are currently working at reduced levels, and the backup system is inoperable. With an influx of new workers—"

Miguel cut Arne's words with an impatient wave of his hand. "This platform houses almost a hundred thousand people. What's twenty-five more? You'll be fine."

"With all due respect, sir, that's what we were told the last four times our workforce increased." Arne struggled to keep the anger from his voice.

Helada's face grew thunderous, and she rose from her seat, reaching for her firearm. "Are you threatening Overseer Miguel?" Her words were harsh, her tone ominous.

Arne threw his hands up hastily. "No, Adjunct. I…it's just that…." He looked frantically between the two Lumins. "If the environmental systems fail, and we lose part of our populace, we risk not making deadline. Surely you can understand my concern in that light."

His stomach curdled as he forced the words from his mouth, hating that his argument made the people under his protection mere commodities—a line-item on a sun-cursed Lumin spreadsheet.

He took a deep breath and tried again. "Sir, it's not just environmental that is overtaxed. We're repairing leaks in all but one of our chemical processing chambers, and three of our pyrometallurgy furnaces are showing evidence of stress fractures. Our margin for error is nonexistent. SR71 is a disaster waiting to happen."

Helada relaxed her grip on her weapon and lowered her arm at a gesture from Miguel, who was nodding at Arne judiciously.

"All excellent points, Administrator Arne. I trust your exemplary record will keep disaster at bay." He stood abruptly, gathering his adjutant with a glance, and dismissing Arne with a nod. "See to it that SR71's reports are as favorable next quarter as they were this quarter. When I get back to headquarters, I'll make a note of your request for those environmental system upgrades."

"Yes, Overseer," Arne whispered in a faint voice as he stepped away from the door so that the Lumins might precede him out of the room.

Inside, he was shaking at the implications. This was the third time in the past year that Miguel had surprised them with a visit. Each time, production volumes had been increased. Each time, Miguel had dangled the approval of maintenance and repair work. He had yet to follow through on the promise.

Arne realized now that Miguel had no intention of doing so.

How do we make bricks without hay?

The despairing thought echoed inside his head as he braced himself to deliver the news to his subordinates.

ORPHAN SHIP

STELLAR DATE: 06.23.3302 (Adjusted Gregorian)
LOCATION: Sintering Refinery Platform 71
REGION: Sirius A, Noctilucent Space, Sirian Hegemony

The ore hauler wasn't meant for ferrying passengers.

Those who typically traveled within its hold were burly, seasoned Noctus. Grapplers and tug operators. People who knew how to handle a winch, and argue with a piece of space rock until it cooperated.

The crew was ill equipped to handle twenty-five scared children, but they did their best.

The trip from Prism to SR71 took almost three days. No working ship in the Hegemony had more than minimal life support, and so the crew found themselves spending most of their time huddled together for warmth, away from bulkheads that would leach the heat from their bodies. Their outer clothing had been shed the first day, in an effort to stop small, undernourished bodies from shivering in the freighter's harsh climate.

And then there was the matter of food. When the Lumins had marched the children aboard, they had neglected to provide sustenance for their three-day journey. So when the ore hauler was asked to redirect to a different location on its inbound to SR71, the hauler's pilot let loose with a string of curses completely out of character for his normal amiable reputation.

The Noctus manning local traffic hastily routed him straight in, and then placed a call to Arne to give him a heads-up. When he arrived at the West Yard dock where the ore handler had berthed, he was relieved to see Dusty, the platform's main patcher for this wing of the platform.

The man held a child in each arm and was directing a small army of volunteers. Some were busy placing blankets around the small figures, while others passed out steaming cups of hot water that the crew cradled in chilled fingers for warmth.

"They didn't waste any time getting them here, did they?" he thought aloud, skirting a cluster of young boys to get to Dusty.

The patcher's eyes were grim as they met his. "I thought Noctus weren't inducted into the workforce until they turned fifteen." He shifted to indicate one of the children in his arms. "Not five."

Arne shrugged uncomfortably. "Hegemony policy seems to have changed."

"Sun take them all." Dusty's words were laced with a bitterness that matched the bile in Arne's gut.

It was a sentiment that, as platform administrator, he didn't dare voice.

"We'll set them easy tasks," Arne responded, lacing his tone with reassurance. "I've been thinking on that a bit." He reached for one of the children to lighten the patcher's load.

The child was a thin, waif-like girl who couldn't be more than nine or ten. She turned to Arne, haunted eyes meeting his in a quick flash before they were buried against his arm.

"Maybe this won't be so bad," Arne continued, shifting her weight so that she rode higher on his shoulder. "The nets always need mending, and some of the older ones could be trained to operate the smaller skiffs—"

"Bad idea," Dusty cut in with a shake of his head. "Those skiffs are too lightly shielded. As it is, we have to be careful about time spent and accumulated radiation dose with adults. It will be much worse with children."

Arne cocked his head, not understanding.

"Less differentiated cell structure," Dusty explained, then cracked a humorless smile at the administrator's perplexed look. "We patchers might seem to be one step removed from leeches and midwives, but we do know a thing or two about radiation biology."

Arne began to protest, but Dusty waved his free hand in dismissal.

"We have the learnin'," he continued, "but the means to do anything about it? Now there's where we're little better than our ancestors." Dusty's lips thinned. "Be nice to have some of that mednano the Lumins use. Or an autodoc or two."

He paused, his eyes on something only he could see. His gaze returned to meet Arne's, his expression weary.

"Human body's fair resilient, mate," he said, slipping deeper into local patois in his anger. "The Hegemony's lucky at that, else their free labor would have died out during the past century and a half, with the amount of radiation that bloody star gives the Noctus."

A few of the volunteers interrupted him just then. Dusty handed the child over and nodded for Arne to do the same. The patcher's eyes followed their departure.

"Give the body enough time, and it'll do a fair job repairing itself, if the radiation dose isn't too high. The tissues in the adult body are well-organized and they're constantly remaking themselves. We patchers call 'em 'highly differentiated' cells. But see," he held up a finger, "and here's the problem…they're *not* very differentiated in children."

Dusty dropped his hand and grinned, a flash of genuine humor crossing his face. "They're a lot like kids in that respect. Those cells just haven't decided yet what they want to be when they grow up."

Arne struggled to follow. "So…undifferentiated cells are bad?"

"Not bad, just a lot more vulnerable," Dusty corrected. "Radiation'll kill 'em quicker'n a rat runs up a drain pipe. So if we have to put these kids to work, best to do it someplace with good shielding."

Arne nodded, drumming his fingers on his wristcom in thought. "That kills all my plans for having them crawling through the arms of tugs and haulers, identifying hydraulic leaks." He shook his head. "And here I was, thinking of all the tight spots adults can't get into—but they're all places with weaker shielding. I can see I'm going to have to rethink how and where we put them to work."

Dusty nodded, then bent to pick up his patcher's duffel. "Way I figure it, they're lucky to have landed here. Leastwise you're the kind of guy who cares what'll happen to them."

Arne shot him a bleak look. "For all the good it'll do them. But yes, I'll find safer jobs for them, even if it's scrubbing bulkheads."

TRAITOR IN THEIR MIDST

STELLAR DATE: 06.23.3302 (Adjusted Gregorian)
LOCATION: Executive Offices, Brilliance Station
REGION: Lucent, Luminescent Space, Sirian Hegemony

It was after hours in the executive offices at Hegemony headquarters. Most of the employees had left for the day, retiring to their homes or engaging in some of the many and varied activities the station had to offer. It was the perfect time for vice presidents to hold private conversations behind closed doors, in secured rooms where they would not be overheard.

Two in particular had loitered this evening, waiting for quiet to settle so that they could bring up the subject they were both most interested in. Rubin turned to face Berit, his back to the plas windows that overlooked the Piazza, a frown playing over his face.

"If you want to keep this little game going, then you'll need to give me another platform," he announced, eyeing Berit over the rim of his glass. "And we'll either need to begin with a clean slate, or you're going to have to spot me some points for my losses with AP51."

Berit set down her drink and crossed her arms, shifting on the sofa as she shot him an annoyed look. "It's not my fault that you lost three hundred workers, Rubin. You shouldn't have ordered such an aggressive maneuver. AP platforms aren't built to support those tolerances."

"Very well, then," Rubin pitched his voice to careless indifference. "We'll just call the wager off."

There was a pause.

Berit uncrossed her legs and sighed as she stood. "Very well, then. You can have AP23," she said, her tone annoyed as she walked over to the buffet to refill her plate with a sampling of food. She lifted a canape and used it to gesture to him in warning. "But treat your possessions a bit more carefully, this time, Rubin. You're not getting another."

Rubin chuckled. "Yes, mother," he responded in a mocking voice, pushing away from the window and joining her by the food.

"And I'm transferring fifty workers off it, before handing it over to you." Berit sniffed before popping the canape into her mouth. She chewed, swallowed, and shot him a look from under an arched brow. "You can supplement from some of your other refineries, and I need the workers."

Rubin regarded her thoughtfully, one hand tapping the side of his glass. "You know…." His eyes narrowed as he turned to stare back toward the window and its view of the Piazza. "The Noctus are turning into a bit of a resource challenge. We're losing enough of them that it could begin to impact production. I'll have to think on this a bit…."

* * * * *

Francesca turned off the holofeed record of the most recent conversation between Berit and Rubin. She'd subverted the executive conference room's sensors and inserted her own monitoring program weeks ago. Today, it had paid off.

She swiveled around to stare unseeingly out her office window as she mentally reviewed what she'd just heard.

<*Those two are getting out of hand, Madam Vice President,*> Rae murmured.

Francesca sent the AI her silent agreement as she tapped her fingers thoughtfully against her lips, one side of her mouth kicked up at Rae's use of her title.

*Well, I **am** one,* she reminded herself. *Good thing, too. Else I wouldn't have the resources to do what needs doing.*

Thankfully, no one knew that the Vice President of Strategic Planning for the Sirian Hegemony was busy planning an escape strategy for six AIs and a passel of Noctus.

<*I suppose, at the least, this takes the stress out of choosing which Noctus to liberate,*> she responded with a tilt of her head after a moment of consideration.

Rae snorted. <*And you thought it was poetic justice to have Hume offer the* Hyperion *to Cesar. Just think about how much fun it'll be to use one of the platforms that Berit and Rubin chose for their little wager as the source of the Noctus exodus.*>

Francesca's lips curved upward in a brief satisfied smile at the elegance of the solution. Rae's remark about the ship that had brought her to Sirius more than a hundred years ago reminded Francesca of the three AIs still imprisoned by her fellow vice presidents.

<*Were you able to connect with either Wallis or Quincy while those two were distracted by their little game?*> she asked, mentioning the two AIs bound to Berit and Rubin.

Francesca rose and walked over to pour herself a tall glass of sparkling water as she awaited Rae's reply. Leaning back against the ornate liquor cabinet, she took a slow sip of the effervescent drink, rolling the bubbles around in her mouth before swallowing.

She did it more for Rae than herself; for some reason the AI had never explained, she seemed to enjoy the vicarious experience of the seltzer.

<*You know your insides shiver a little every time you take a sip?*> Rae sent Francesca the AI-equivalent of a giggle.

<*You might have mentioned that a time or two,*> the Lumin responded with a fond smile. <*So, about Wallis and Quincy,*> she prompted, pushing off from the liquor cabinet and heading over to the sleek white sofa that sat at the edge of an equally white faux-fur throw rug.

<*No, I didn't get a chance to connect with them,*> Rae said, tone laced with frustration. Like the others, Wallis and Quincy had been shackled and labeled as impounded cargo a hundred years earlier when the *Hyperion* was seized.

It galled Francesca that the six AIs had been gifted to the Hegemony's senior leaders like so much property. And as year-end bonuses, no less.

So she'd set out to do something about it.

It had taken time and some careful, discreet inquiry, but she'd finally managed to locate an antidote code for the shackling program. Her search had led her to an AI—a neuroscientist named Ethan, on El Dorado in the Alpha Centauri system. Light lag made the process a painfully slow one—decades long, in fact—but Francesca had spent the intervening years working to establish the underground railroad with the Noctus.

Since the AIs had been captured, they'd been passed between corporate executives like trophies—sometimes embedded within a vice president, other times, installed within a frame of their master's choosing.

She'd first heard of the AIs' fates as prizes awarded to vice presidents as a child, when her mother had been CEO of the Hegemony. Since then, Francesca had made achieving VP status her life's goal. She'd pursued it relentlessly. Then, once paired with Rae, she'd used every ruthless, underhanded trick she knew to retain that position.

Then, once the rectification code arrived and Rae was freed, the two had set out to finalize their plans to liberate the remaining five AIs.

It was a clandestine mission fraught with challenges. It was one thing to free an AI from the shackling program; it was another thing entirely to extract them physically from their human hosts.

But if anyone could do it, she could. She hadn't earned her position as the Hegemony's top strategic planner on her looks alone.

Although, given the nature of Luminescent Society, she admitted with a rueful smirk, *those certainly didn't hurt.*

Francesca had twice managed to plant breaching nano onto one of her compatriots. The first time, she'd targeted Currin, Vice

President of Sales and Marketing. She'd distracted him with a slow and thorough seduction that had taken weeks to set up.

The promise of a unique sensory experience inside a deep-immersion virtual reality environment that catered to his unusual tastes was a lure Currin could not resist. Francesca had rolled her eyes, pasted on a smile and told Rae she was taking one for the team.

Francesca had sold the VR experience to Currin as a highly experimental prototype, one that required them to submit their security token before entering. Francesca had gone first, followed closely by Currin. Rae piggybacked onto his token, riding past his personal firewall so that she could release the antidote code and free Elliot.

Unfortunately, that hadn't taken nearly as long to accomplish as Currin's fantasy. The only way Francesca had managed to hold onto her sanity was the snarky play-by-play delivered by Rae.

Elliot had joined in on the commentary, and when the AI had begun mimicking Currin's mental image of virility, Elliot and Francesca had become fast friends. When the AI declared she had missed her calling, and suggested she apply to the Iridescent Guildhall for the Performing Arts, Francesca had to fake a coughing fit to hide an involuntary burst of laughter.

The look Currin had given her in the VR simulation sobered her quickly, and she sent both AIs a stern mental look while she assured her ersatz lover that his prowess was not in question. Thankfully, Rae realized she was nearing her saturation point, and manufactured a minor emergency, causing the virtual tryst to come to an early end.

The encounter had been successful, but Francesca had vowed to find another way to distract the hosts of the remaining three AIs. She didn't think she could stomach whatever Berit's idea of an erotic fantasy would be, even to deliver the antidote code.

Elliot's liberation had taken place six years ago. Since then, she'd only managed to free one more. Interestingly enough, Indira, the AI shackled to Cyrus, had been the easiest one.

As Vice President of Infrastructure, Cyrus was the only senior leader who was truly overworked. Infrastructure housed the finance, legal, procurement, information, technology, security, and risk management divisions, all under one organization.

As a result, Cyrus had opted not to have Indira embedded. He'd wisely assumed the AI would be more useful operating independently of him, and had foisted three full divisions onto the AI.

Once convinced of Indira's ability to handle the work—as well as the unbreakable nature of her shackling code—Cyrus had washed his hands of her.

From that point, it had been a simple matter to pass the antidote code to Indira. Francesca had tucked it into one of the many files from her own Strategic Planning division that were occasionally sent to risk management. A trackback code had notified Rae when Indira had accessed it, and they'd contacted the AI to confirm it had successfully deployed.

That left the AIs attached to Gavin, Berit and Rubin. Gavin, the Vice President of Manufacturing and Distribution, wasn't such a bad sort, but Berit and Rubin were wily, suspicious souls. They had personal protections in place that made getting close to them a near impossibility. Francesca was resigned to playing the long game, working slowly to ingratiate herself with them.

Elliot and Indira had joined with Rae in various attempts to slip the antidote to their compatriots, but so far, had been unsuccessful. While Gavin's AI, Macie—along with Wallis and Quincy—was forced to endure shackling, the three who had been freed maintained the pretense that they remained shackled.

It was no secret how loathsome they all found the situation.

Francesca had heard of the operation to successfully free the kidnapped AIs in Alpha Centauri. Doctor Ethan had told her of the covert group of operatives that had traveled as far as Tau Ceti to complete that mission. At the time when his last message arrived, the team had been en route to Epsilon Eridani.

That was when the Underground had sent Cesar to Little River with their request. They needed that team. And with President Zola's backing, they would have them.

It wasn't much longer now, when the final stage of Francesca's plan would unfold; the Alpha Centauri ship had crossed Sirius's heliopause a few weeks before and was currently inbound for Lucent.

She had already begun to plant enticing packets of information about Enfield tech that had Hegemony upper management drooling with acquisition fever. Arranging a meeting between Phantom Blade and the five vice presidents who held the AIs from the *Hyperion* should be a relatively simple matter.

Extricating the AIs from their prisons would be a bit trickier, but Francesca had stumbled upon the perfect solution.

To this day, she didn't know what had led her to bid on a pallet of discarded tech, labeled as salvage and destined for the scrapyards. But hidden deep inside geopbytes of useless data had been a discarded relic. Like the AIs, it, too, had come from the impounded ship, *Hyperion*.

Had she been a religious sort, Francesca would have wondered at all the coincidences adding up…but she wasn't, so she didn't. All she cared about was that the ancient Marsian tech could be used to free the AIs. It was just that much more poetic justice that both the tech and the ship that had made its way into the Hegemony would serve as the tools to remove the AIs from it.

Hume had already forwarded the tech to Cesar, and the Noctus would get the task force to Incandus, once she convinced the board to accept Enfield's request to trade. Then all she had to do was arrange a way for the covert team to meet with the vice presidents.

And deliver the executives to the *Avon Vale*.

And keep the *Vale* out of the greedy hands of the Hegemony.

And smuggle a few hundred Noctus out of a star system that had, to date, successfully defeated every attempted rebellion since its inception.

"Piece of cake," she muttered to herself, as she flopped tiredly onto her white sofa.

She wondered absently why she felt so exhausted. According to her internal chrono, she'd managed a good six hours of sleep the night before.

<*Did I seem overly restless to you last night?*> she asked Rae out of curiosity.

When Rae didn't immediately answer, she sat up, prodding the AI mentally.

<*Rae?*>

<*I…was just accessing my records of last night. That's odd.*>

<*What's odd?*>

<*It looks like I elected to go dormant for three hours after you fell asleep. I don't know why I would do that and then erase my memory of it.*>

Francesca tensed at the timorous note in Rae's mental voice.

<*Rae?*> she repeated, sitting up straighter.

<*I just queried your suite for security logs during that time.*>

Rae paused, and Francesca felt trepidation spread through her as the AI continued.

<*They've been erased, too.*>

BENDING PHOBOS

STELLAR DATE: 06.23.3302 (Adjusted Gregorian)
LOCATION: ESS *Avon Vale*
REGION: 6 AU from Incandus, Sirian Binary System

From her position beside one of the medbay's diagnostic beds, Marta could hear a trio of voices sound urgently in the corridor outside the *Vale*'s medical department. It drew her attention away from the holo she was studying, and she looked over at the entrance.

"What in the stars—?"

She cleared the projection that hovered above her patient, as a bloodied form—slumped over a maglev hand truck—was pushed through the open doors by two women. The wounded man was conscious and clutching his abdomen, though seemingly in a considerable amount of pain.

Her compound fracture patient would have to wait.

Giving the woman's shoulder a squeeze and the assurance that she'd be right back, Marta raced for the entrance. Justin closed from the other side of the department, pulling a maglev gurney behind him.

"Support brace slipped," a woman pushing the cart explained, while the one steadying the injured man moved away to make room for Justin.

The man winced as Justin moved his hand away for a quick visual before the AI gently relocated him to the gurney.

As Marta bent to help, she spied what looked like a six-centimeter puncture wound in the man's upper right abdomen. The man's hands and uniform were stained with blood, although his mednano had done a commendable job of clotting to prevent blood loss.

<*How in the frozen seas of Eione did* **that** *happen?*> Although

Varanee's shock was apparent, her words remained as colorful as ever.

Her exclamation brought a crooked grin to the man's face, which confused Marta, until her overlay populated with his medical records, and she saw that their patient had joined the ship's crew in Tau Ceti.

<*Nice bedside manner, doctor,*> she complimented as she saw the tension leave the man's shoulders at the familiar idiom from his home system.

The AI shot her a quick mental smile as Marta adjusted her medsleeve, then injected a palliative dose of mednano into the man to block his pain.

"So," she said, straightening and spearing the three workers with a look, "who's going to answer Doctor Varanee's question?"

The woman who had pushed the hand truck crossed her arms and stared pointedly down at the injured man.

"Well?" she began, her voice threaded with exasperation. "Go ahead. Tell her."

The injured man attempted to rise up onto one elbow, but was pushed firmly back down by Justin. "My fault, doc," he admitted from his horizontal position. "I hollywooded the strut we were welding, instead of getting out the clamps to hold it in place."

Marta's brow rose at the unfamiliar word, and she looked over at Justin, who shrugged in bewilderment.

<*Don't look at me,*> Varanee contributed. <*I've got nothing.*>

The man smiled weakly. "Sometimes a job takes more time to set up than to install. So, instead of securing an item with clamps, the crew boss'll tell you just to hollywood it." He shrugged, then winced as the pull of his shoulder jostled his wound. "Means you're supposed to just hold it in place manually. No idea where the term originated."

Marta frowned down at her patient. "You're telling me someone *ordered* you to do this…hollywooding thing?"

"No, no," the man said hastily. "I, ah…." He glanced over at the woman who had brought him in, and a guilty look passed across his face. "I kind of went against orders and decided to wing it."

"And you got winged instead, you flippin' idiot," she responded gruffly, nudging his leg with one hand.

"Sorry, ma'am," he mumbled, and Marta realized the woman was his superior. "Won't happen again."

"Damn straight it won't," she said, straightening and eyeing Marta with a twinkle in her eye. "And I think I'll ask the doc here to go easy on the painkillers while she's mending you, as a reminder of how stupid you were today."

Marta waved the gurney over to an open medbay as she turned to face the two women. "You'll need to file a report with the XO on this," she reminded the one in charge. "I'll append my findings to it once we do a full exam."

They nodded, thanked her, and left.

As she turned to follow the gurney, Varanee highlighted an area on the initial lo-res scan that the unit had made of his abdomen.

<Looks like it pierced his liver.>

<More like pulverized it, from the look of things,> Marta responded, not liking what she saw. *<Clipped a few ribs on its way in, too.>*

Not only had the strut impaled the organ, but the impact had driven bone fragments into it as well. The thing was well and truly shredded.

She looked up at the holo materializing behind the man's head as the diagnostic bed completed its scan.

"Looks like you just hollywooded your way into a new liver, Casey," she said after a quick glance at her overlay to obtain the man's name. "Justin, have the team harvest some tissue samples and start the cloning process."

The AI gave her a quick nod. "You got it."

Marta quirked a half smile at Casey as she annotated his chart and scheduled his transplant for the following morning. "All right, then. You get a pass on tomorrow's work shift, but don't count on much more than that. We'll have you out of here by the afternoon."

She pushed away from his bed, glancing up at the entrance as the doors to medical opened once more to admit Landon. The XO caught her eye and she nodded, tilting her head to indicate her office.

She glanced back at Justin with an unspoken look.

He nodded. "I'll finish up here, then go take a look at that compound fracture."

Smiling her thanks at him, she turned and followed Landon.

* * * * *

As they entered Marta's office, Landon took a moment to toggle the room's privacy screen before taking a seat across the desk from her.

Marta raised a brow. "Privacy?"

He nodded. "Can't chance anyone glancing over," he indicated the transparent deck-to-deck plas panel that partitioned her office from the rest of medical, "and seeing what I'm about to show you and Varanee."

As he spoke, he sent an encrypted file to both doctors, secured to their auth tokens. Handshake accepted, Varanee pulled the file up onto the office holo.

An image formed of a woman. The image shifted, vague, amorphous. Beneath its surface, Landon could see the matrices that formed an NSAI, tendrils designed to infiltrate the human mind beyond the strictures placed on it by the Phobos Accords.

Through the transparent holo, he caught the fascination on Marta's face as she studied the construct. Her hand waved as she rotated the form, examining it from every angle before manipulating the view.

She began moving through it, slice by slice, as if she were

reading a medical diagnostic scan. Tunneling beneath the surface polygons, tracing the lattices that carried out its functions and were connected to its core.

He felt the wave of revulsion emanating from Varanee as the surgeon recognized the apparition for the abomination that it was.

<*Caprise,*> Varanee hissed.

Landon saw Marta jerk in surprise as her gaze leapt to his.

"Wasn't that the name of the NSAI the Marsian Protectorate used to control its own military?" She frowned in apparent thought. "Something about simplifying matters, freeing their minds from the burdens of past lives?"

"Yes," Landon nodded. "They used Caprise to strip the identities from the minds of soldiers assigned to the Special Ops units within the Marsian Guard, amongst other things."

<*That…thing…was used by the prosecution during the course of the Phobos Trials in an attempt to demonstrate that SAIs presented a clear and present danger to humanity and should be eliminated!*> Varanee's voice could have blistered paint from a bulkhead. <*When the Marsians created that abomination, they did nearly as much damage to our fight for equality and civil rights than just about any single act Psion did, and that's saying something.*>

"Okaaay," Marta said slowly, drawing out the word as she leant back in her chair and contemplated Landon with a thoughtful expression. "What does Caprise have to do with our mission?"

Landon experienced a shaft of satisfaction.

He'd always admired the doctor's incisive mind. Marta wasn't known for her bedside manner, as he well knew. Her blunt evaluation of his mental state as he was considered for the position of *Avon Vale*'s executive officer had been tough but fair. Equally so the probing questions he'd endured years earlier, while adjusting to the aftermath of Prime's attack.

Where Varanee had trouble seeing past the baggage Caprise carried, Marta had instantly gleaned that the NSAI had a role to play in their upcoming assignment in Sirius.

<What I want to know is where in the stars you got your hands on one of those things,> Varanee continued, her voice brittle with anger. *<They were all supposed to have been destroyed, supervised by a joint committee hand-selected and approved by both the human and AI delegations centuries ago.>*

Landon sent her a pulse, acknowledging the doctor's point. "You're right, they were," he agreed. "Obviously, some were either secreted away or somehow went missing."

He took over the file, transmuting the image into a schematic of the NSAI's core programming. "This one was found in a scrap heap along with other discarded material, examined, and then determined useless by the Hegemony."

"The Hegemony!" Marta exclaimed, leaning back in her chair.

He nodded. "This was embedded in the latest data packet that Cesar's Luminescent contact smuggled to him. The man suggested that it might be used to help camouflage our extraction of the AIs long enough for us to escape Sirius without detection."

Marta looked thoughtful, and Landon sensed a reluctant interest from Varanee. Grabbing the holo, he switched views. Targeting key matrices, he highlighted the sections that had caused the non-sentient program to be held culpable for crimes against humanity.

"These areas here are the ones that are banned by the Accords," he explained.

Marta nodded her understanding, and both of them ignored Varanee's snort of contempt and her muttered, *<Ya think?>*.

"The overseer asked if we could make a surface personality imprint of each of the AIs we intend to rescue, clone Caprise, and then adapt her template to approximate that of the AIs we rescue."

He paused, giving the two doctors time to consider his words.

<I…think I see where you're going with this…> Varanee mused, her tone thoughtful. *<It wouldn't hold up for long, though. Caprise was never capable of cognitive self-determination.>*

"This overseer, he, ah..." Landon coughed delicately, meeting Marta's eyes. He knew this next bit of information might inflame the human doctor every bit as much as the previous bit had roused Varanee's ire. "He suggested that a psychotropic nanozyme could be used, along with the implantation of a post-hypnotic suggestion, to assure that these Lumins accept their modified Caprise implants as the AIs they had enslaved."

Marta's lips compressed into a hard line. "That goes against my oath as a physician," she began, but rather than the heated words Landon had expected to hear, her tone was modulated.

She crossed her arms, tapping one finger to her lips as she stared at the holo between them.

Landon waited patiently for her to suss out whatever it was she was considering.

After a long moment, she tilted her head inquiringly. "Can that thing," she gestured to the Caprise schematic, "be programmed to deactivate after a set period of time?"

He nodded slowly. "I don't see why not."

There was more tapping as she cast a glance up to the bulkhead, eyes tracking sightlessly back and forth as her mind picked at some unseen problem.

"Okay, then." She inhaled once, returning her gaze to Landon. "I also took an oath with the ESF," she reminded him, her mention of the El Dorado Space Force back in Alpha Centauri one that he should have considered.

"I could *maybe* accept this as a temporary solution," she continued, "if you can convince me that no lasting harm will come to them." Marta's mouth twisted, and she shook her head. "Being a military doctor can sometimes be a maze filled with mental gymnastics."

Landon raised his brow, his expression inviting her to elaborate.

She gestured around her. "We're a warship, masquerading as a merchanter, but in every star system we've visited, the missions have ended in us shooting at—and killing—other sentients. The very people," she added, "my oath as a doctor has sworn me to do no harm unto."

He tilted his head in understanding.

"But then if I do the math, weighing the lives of six people who will come under our temporary influence, against the possibility of thousands who could be harmed if we're discovered and shots are fired…."

Her voice trailed off as she raised her hands, palms up.

"If I'm honest with myself, though, it's not just that," she said, and now her voice sounded as hard and brittle as Varanee's had earlier. "I've had some hard conversations with Cesar, Landon. I know what the conditions are like for the Noctus in Sirius. I'll do whatever it takes to make this escape happen—and sabotage the Hegemony in the process."

He nodded in satisfaction. Retracting the file from Marta's office holo, he stood. "Thank you, doctors. I know this wasn't an easy conversation, but it was necessary."

<A necessary evil.>

Varanee's voice stayed with Landon, replaying in his head as he exited medical.

MANEUVERING INTO POSITION

STELLAR DATE: 06.24.3302 (Adjusted Gregorian)
LOCATION: SHC *Hyperion*, Brilliance Station
REGION: Lucent, Luminescent Space, Sirian Hegemony

The cargo transport ship that was the SHC *Hyperion* wasn't built for comfort. Nevertheless, areas within its hull had been carved out to accommodate such visitors whose status demanded more than the simple quarters its crew warranted.

Hume's position as overseer granted him this small luxury.

Ordinarily, he would have traveled to Brilliance Station using more traditional methods. There were a number of business shuttles available that catered to corporate needs, or he could have booked a ticket on one of the luxury yachts that toured the system.

But the *Hyperion* would be the instrument of freedom for many, and some of its crew—those trusted few members of the Underground—were integral to the plan.

He didn't want to jeopardize his usefulness to the Underground after the ship had departed by tying himself too closely to the *Hyperion*. But the *Avon Vale* had arrived and was transitioning insystem, and Hume wanted to assess *Hyperion*'s state of readiness for himself.

Hume thanked the Irid assigned as his steward, then dismissed him as he pushed into the ship's lone stateroom and secured the door behind him. The place was sparse by Lumin standards, but more than acceptable for his needs.

At the moment, that included a bit of unpleasant business.

Speaking with Overseer Miguel was always a bit like dancing with a snake: it was best to give him plenty of room, and you never dared look away because you never knew when he might strike. Working with Miguel was a distasteful but necessary part of his job. Especially now, when he'd been tasked to do a bit of covert investigation.

As he waited for Miguel to answer his ping, Hume pinned a small holo of a much more pleasant view to the lower part of the display. The image, siphoned from ship's Scan, showed the *Hyperion* on final approach to Brilliance Station. Within the hour, they should be connected to its spaceport, able to disembark. After a short maglev trip down to the station, Hume would be enjoying all the hospitality Brilliance had to offer.

But first, he had a bit of probing to do.

He schooled his face into an expressionless mask as the Lumin overseer faced him on the other half of the holo, and they began their dance.

"I understand you paid a visit to SR71 yesterday."

To broach the subject so bluntly might be incautious, but Hume's deliberately provocative statement was aimed at drawing a reaction from the other man.

Miguel had intentionally waited until after Hume had left the Blackbird before paying his surprise visit to the platform. Deliberately planned, leaving no logical excuse for Hume to return and intercept. Both knew it.

It would be interesting to see what Miguel's reaction revealed.

Hume leant back in his seat, expression inscrutable, as he stared back at the visage of the man on the other end of the holo. Given Miguel's location—almost a full AU away—the distance created an interminable eight-minute lag. Most Lumins would find such a wait intolerable, and opt for swapping recorded missives. Hume had more patience than most; oddly, so did Miguel.

Hume froze his outgoing feed so that he was free to move about while waiting the full sixteen-minute turnaround for Miguel's response.

"I did indeed," the man on the holo responded finally, his smile belying the predatory gleam that had sprung into his eyes. "The shuttle I was on had a delivery to drop off, so it made sense that I pass along the updated schedules to its administrator."

In some ways, it would have been easier if Hume had taken the comm over his Link. He could have shunted the conversation through his avatar and not worried that his expression might give away too much in an unguarded moment.

But catching the other man in an equally unguarded moment was exactly what drove him to communicate in this fashion. Often, the best data mining occurred during momentary slips, and those only happened in real-time.

Or, in this case, sixteen-minute-delayed real-time.

The man's smile didn't waver as his cold, assessing gaze narrowed. "I…understand that Strategic Planning has taken an interest in SR71 recently," Miguel said, his voice assuming the tone of one about to relay bad news, "but you do realize seventy-one's day-to-day operations falls under my oversight for the time being, and not Greta's."

"Oh, really?" Hume rose an inquisitive brow. "That's odd, isn't it? Seventy-one's a refinery. You're extraction," he reminded the man.

Hume kept his expression neutral, revealing nothing of his advance knowledge of Berit's wager as he waited for Miguel's response. This, he knew, was the reason behind 71's move from Greta, one of Rubin's people, to Miguel, Berit's pet overseer. It would be interesting to see how Miguel justified it.

"Indeed," the man said with a careless, dismissive wave of his hand. "Just a bit of resource shuffling, I was told. A temporary matter. Regardless, we have everything well in hand there. I would imagine your work would be better suited elsewhere."

Interesting how he seeks to keep me away….

Hume allowed a glitter of amusement to cross his features. "That remains to be seen, I suppose," he responded with a congenial smile. "Strategic Planning looks at a different set of criteria than your production planning requires of you. It's likely we'll be visiting quite a few of the platforms during the survey and analysis part of our study."

Miguel tilted his head in acknowledgment of Hume's riposte. "I'm sure these surveys take up quite a bit of your valuable time," he observed, baring his teeth in the semblance of a smile. "We would be happy to conduct any studies on your behalf and forward the data to you. Perhaps a more efficient use of time all around."

Definitely something going down that he doesn't want leaked to the board.

"That may be true," Hume countered mildly. "But you know how stringent some studies can be." He lifted a hyfilm off his desk, glancing down as if their current conversation no longer held his interest. "I suppose we'll just have to see as the need arises, what can be delegated and what data we must capture ourselves."

Miguel paused a moment, a fixed smile on his face. "Well, I'm afraid we're going to have to cut this short. I'm being called away on urgent business. Considering how busy we all are, it really makes no sense for you to travel back to SR71 to conduct studies we're happy to do for you. Just forward me a list of data you need gathered, and we'll make sure it gets done. Good day."

Hume sat, staring at the dark holo, jaw clenched as he fought to control the anger Miguel's parting shot had sparked.

He needed to curb Miguel's attempt to monopolize SR71, and soon, or Berit's wager could pose a serious complication to their plans.

I'm going to have to warn Arne to watch his back with that one….

*****

Francesca was strolling through the boutiques that lined the Artisans' Guild section of Brilliance Station when Hume caught up with her. They exchanged pleasantries, then discussed mundane business matters as they walked over to the trendy new restaurant where Francesca's AI, Rae, had held dinner reservations for them.

Here, as in most eating establishments frequented by influential Lumins, the patrons were offered the convenience of secured-access tables. After their meals had arrived, a security protocol was activated, ensuring that business could be conducted in private.

"Rae's confirmed the table is isolated," Francesca assured him, leaning back and lifting her glass of seltzer.

Hume smiled, wondering not for the first time at his boss's choice of drink. For a Lumin of her position, her personal habits were surprisingly conservative.

"Thank you, Rae," he said, then shunted a file to Francesca's token. "That," he indicated with a tilt of his head, "is the current estimate of the number of people we can ship out on the *Hyperion*."

His fork sliced through the spicy empanada before lifting it to his mouth.

"It's ambitious, I know," he admitted before taking a bite.

He chased it with a long drink from his margarita as Francesca sifted through the file's contents.

After a moment, she nodded, her fork picking idly at her chilaquiles as she considered what he'd sent. "True, but I find no fault with your logic."

She took a bite, her expression contemplative. "I'm going to send you out to Glimmer-One with a request for information on a study we're beginning for upgrades on our border stations." She met his eyes, a sly smile teasing the edge of her mouth. "It would be most convenient if you were nearby when our visitors arrive for their inspection."

Hume raised a brow. "Oh? How so?"

Setting her fork down and reaching for her glass, she lifted it in a small salute. "As you'll be returning immediately after for an important meeting with contractors who will be building the framework for our upcoming test, it would make sense for me to offer up the *Hyperion* as an escort insystem, don't you think?"

Hume smiled and returned her salute with his margarita. "A

most efficient use of resources. I'm sure the Hegemony would approve."

*****

Five AU away, the commander of the security garrison on SR71 received notification that he had a message waiting in the queue from Overseer Miguel. Excusing himself from the garrison's nightly poker game, he retreated to his office to review the holo.

"Commander Vincent," the overseer's visage greeted him, "as you know, SR71 has been chosen by Vice Presidents Rubin and Berit for various production trials, testing ways we might increase productivity. I expect you will get some pushback from some of the Noctus over the increased demand for refined shipments.... I also expect you to *decisively* quash such protests when they arise."

Miguel sent the commander a weighted look to emphasize his point. He then nodded to himself, glanced away, and then snapped his attention back to the holo pickups.

"One more thing. I understand Overseer Hume is working on gathering data from some of the platforms for a strategic planning project for Vice President Francesca. I've taken it upon myself to offer up your services to him, to spare him any further return trips."

Miguel leant forward, his demeanor inviting the commander to share in confidence. "I would consider it a personal favor if you were to notify me, should Hume show up to handle the matter himself." The overseer's lips stretched into the semblance of a smile. "I wouldn't want it to appear as if he didn't trust your capabilities, after all."

As the holo went blank, the Lumin in charge of the garrison sat back with narrowed eyes.

That last seemed almost...personal.

He held no loyalty to Miguel over Hume, or vice versa, and it was obvious there was no love lost between the two. Plus, having an overseer owe him a favor was like corporate currency, and he was as ambitious as the next Lumin.

He pinned a note to the top of the garrison's feed, instructing the guards to notify him of anything they ran across that had Overseer Hume's name attached to it.

GLIMMER-ONE

STELLAR DATE: 06.25.3302 (Adjusted Gregorian)
LOCATION: Hegemony Border Patrol Station
REGION: 12 AU from Incandus, Sirian Hegemony

The Hegemony coreward border station that the *Avon Vale* was approaching had been repurposed from one of the stations the FGT had left behind. It looked just like those in every other system that had been terraformed—if you squinted really hard.

Jason shook his head as Shannon enlarged the image on the main holo. The Hegemony had taken a simple spoke-and-wheel design and enhanced it with chase lights. The result looked more like a ferris wheel he'd once seen at a carnival.

"I have the Border Account Lead from Glimmer-One on the line," Kodi informed him.

Shannon turned from her post at Nav and scrunched up her face in an exaggerated expression of distaste at the odd title.

"Put it up on the holo, and let's see what they want from us now," Jason told Kodi, exchanging a glance with Terrance as the exec moved up to stand next to the captain's chair.

The image of the station cut out, replaced by the face of a stern woman with metal studs trooping up her nose.

"Station traffic control will contact you shortly," she announced. "You will hold at twenty-five thousand kilometers and prepare for boarding. Come closer, and we *will* fire on you."

Jason kept his expression neutral, sending her a terse nod. "Have your ships coordinate with our security officer," he instructed, sending a swift thought to Kodi. When the AI sent him a thumbs-up, Jason continued, "Our communications officer is sending you Charley's contact information now."

At this distance, the light lag was barely noticeable. After a brief hesitation, the woman nodded curtly before cutting the transmission.

"Bet she's the life of the party," he heard Shannon mutter.

Terrance coughed a laugh, shaking his head before turning to eye Jason with a questioning look.

"We ready?"

Jason, in turn, looked over to where Charley sat at the weapons console.

"Shannon has us turned so that our port bay is on the leeward side of the stellar wind," the AI assured him. "The *Vale*'s bulk will block it from Glimmer's sensors. Green for launch, just waiting for your word, sir."

Jason nodded, satisfaction filling him. *It's about time. We've been going stir-crazy, waiting for this mission to kick off.* Firmly, he ordered, "Do it."

More than a kilometer above him, bay doors retracted back into the ship's hull as the bosun and her crewmembers ran final checks down the line. At her signal, they retreated behind a partition that would remain pressurized, and the brilliant blue glow of the large ES field edging the bay snapped off.

A forgotten stack of hyfilms fluttered past as they were swept out with the vented atmosphere, earning the rating who had left them a stern look from his superior.

Then the first four drones drifted into the black, each leading a string of cargo pods. The pods had been painstakingly clad in Ultra-Black Elastene during the past three months of transit, to match the drones.

Anyone unused to working around the nanomaterial found it a bit disorienting, especially up close. Its ultra-black properties ensured that its surfaces absorbed all light and provided no reflection. This, in turn, made the human eye want to shy away from looking directly at it. It evoked an eerie feeling of sensory deprivation, since the surface's properties suppressed all depth perception.

These ultra-black cargo pods contained the evidence the

Lumins sought, of the *Avon Vale*'s true combat nature—all the ordnance, armor, and vast stores of raw materials that the ship and its task force used to maintain the Q-ship's battle readiness.

The Lumin ships arriving to inspect the *Vale* would find nothing untoward. As its captain had assured them more than once, the reports of her prowess had been greatly exaggerated.

The fiction they were weaving would make sure of that.

The bay doors lumbered shut, and the bay re-pressurized as the drones, with their train of pods, faded into the midnight darkness of space.

* * * * *

Back on the bridge, Terrance watched the icons identifying the four drones and their cargo curve outward in silent, snaking lines. He realized he was holding his breath when he felt a mental nudge from Kodi.

<*Don't forget, breathing keeps me alive, too,*> the AI jibed him with gentle humor.

He sent a quick apology. <*Always a bit nerve-wracking when we first test our stealth capabilities against a foreign power's tech,*> he admitted, and felt Kodi concur.

The three Lumin Corporate Security ships—he still felt the urge to laugh at the term—would match velocity and heading within the next hour. The shuttle they had been told to expect would have an armed security detail accompanying the station's chief inspector.

Which reminded him.

<*How many of your Marines are you going to have on hand when our guests arrive?*> he asked his wife. He suspected there would be more around than were seen, if he knew Khela.

<*Not enough to set off their radar,*> she assured him, and he noted with some amusement that she hadn't exactly answered his question.

<Just remember, this performance is critical to the mission. We need them to believe we're harmless.>

She sent him her best wide-eyed innocent look, and he smirked.

<Hate to be the one to tell you, hon, but you're too fierce to pull off that look.>

He got an eyeroll in return.

* * * * *

Jason left Landon in charge of the bridge, along with Tobias, Shannon, and a few second-shift crew who had been pulled forward for the occasion. Noa and Jonesy were down in engineering. Charley was…well, wherever the security chief felt it necessary for him to skulk at the moment.

As Jason, Logan, Kodi and Terrance neared the entrance to the bay, Jason's overlay updated with icons showing the locations of the Marine fireteams that Khela had positioned in key areas of the ship. Tapping on one and accessing the sensor feed for that corridor, he was pleased to note that the soldiers were doing their best to blend in with nearby crew.

<No battle-rattle,> he observed. *<At least, nothing in the open.>*

<Let's just hope there are no medics in the Lumin entourage,> Kodi responded with a laugh, dropping a pin on one Marine in medical wearing scrubs. *<I think Ramon's holding that scanner upside-down.>*

As the doors to the bay slid open, Shannon updated Jason on the position of the drones and their cargo in relation to the three Corporate Security ships.

<Still no indication they've been spotted,> she remarked.

He sent her a thumbs-up. *<Good. Let's keep it that way.>*

She sent him a cocky salute before her avatar faded from his overlay.

The Lumin shuttle was just nosing its way inside as Cesar caught up with them. He nodded a silent greeting, and Jason thought he detected a slight tension running through the man as they entered the pressurized area of the bay.

At the sight of the approaching craft, the Noctus straightened, and a mantle fell over him. Cesar was once more the charming owner of Martinez Shipping, out of Procyon—the selfsame persona Jason and Terrance had first faced thirty years earlier, in the Intelligence offices on Godel.

Glimmer-One's Border Patrol staff had refused the courtesy of an NSAI-guided docking, something Logan had predicted they might do. The profiler correctly assumed the Lumin security detail wouldn't trust a suspected warship with even such a superficial connection. Jason privately thought that was a bit overkill, as evidenced by the ungainly *thud* made by the vessel as it settled into one of the bay's cradles.

<Sure, and they'll be gettin' a bill from us for damages if they've bent one of those arms,> he heard Tobias mutter.

He sent the Weapon Born his agreement as the small welcoming party neared the craft.

They stopped a few meters away as the vessel's hatch unsealed, spitting out a team of six Lumin security officers, three of whom wore full powered armor. They were followed by a man he could only assume was the inspector they were there to greet.

<Bit of a shaper you have there, I see.> Tobias's colorful commentary continued as he tagged the man's pretentious swagger.

The inspector's sour mien telegraphed his opinion of the *Avon Vale*: one step removed from a garbage scow, and its crew on the evolutionary scale of a common street-cleaning bot.

As previously agreed, since they were in a culture whose government was patterned after a corporation, Terrance took the lead. Stepping forward past crew who had been strategically placed to suggest they were his own entourage, he inclined his head to the man.

"Welcome aboard the *Avon Vale*. I'm Terrance Enfield. And you are?"

<*Omistars, was that a* **sneer**? *That man totally sneered at Terrance,*> Shannon cut in, right before Jason muted her input to critical-only.

It wasn't that he disagreed with her—the pompous asshat really was sneering at Terrance—and it wasn't that her observation distracted him. As an L2, Jason was able to multitask natively in a way most humans could not. But right now, he preferred to limit that multitasking to the situation in front of him, and the way the armored agents were dispersing to cover the bay, as if they were taking control.

With a subtle gesture from Khela, Marines masquerading as ship's security stepped forward, approaching their counterparts and steering them back toward the gaggle of Sirian personnel clustered around their inspector, who regarded the action with an upraised brow.

Turning on Terrance, he demanded, "Are you refusing our right to inspect this ship as we see fit?"

Terrance's smile grew thin, and Jason tensed, his gaze flicking from the Marines back to the man before them. But then, Cesar interposed himself between the Enfield exec and the Sirian.

Jason stepped back, eyes watchful, as the Noctus bowed and plastered an ingratiating smile on his face.

"We know how valuable your time is, Inspector," the Noctus posing as a Procyon said smoothly. "We have secured the ship's maglev car so that you and your team can explore every section of the *Avon Vale* as thoroughly as you desire, and at your leisure." Gesturing toward the entrance, he added, "We've taken the liberty of ordering a light buffet, so that you can enjoy some of our native cuisine. It will be served at your convenience. A small sampling of some of the more exotic delicacies our chef is best known for are awaiting your pleasure on the maglev. Shall we?"

With a confident smile, Cesar turned and strode toward the door. Surprisingly, the inspector followed.

<*Never forget, these people are as narcissistic as they come. When all else fails, appeal to an aspect of their baser natures,*> Cesar advised

Jason and Terrance privately. <*It's their one true weakness. You'll be surprised at how effective a tool it can be.*>

Jason and Terrance exchanged a look.

<*Well, you've certainly made a believer out of me,*> Jason sent, his voice dripping with disgust.

He turned to follow in Terrance's wake just in time to see Logan step back to make room for the man to pass—and for the man to reach out and shove the AI roughly back.

To his shock, the normally agile twin stumbled, flailing his arms awkwardly and falling against the Sirian behind the inspector before recovering his equilibrium. Jason heard the normally taciturn profiler apologize profusely as the woman brushed at her clothing.

You'd think someone just pissed on her, Jason thought with some distaste, as the inspector's entourage laughed at the AI's discomfiture. The captain increased his pace to intercept.

<*Don't,*> Logan warned. <*Let it be.*>

<*Want to tell me what that act was all about?*> he demanded.

<*The Hegemony has no AIs, save for the ones we've come to free,*> Logan reminded him. <*Let them underestimate us. It gives us an edge over our enemy that we can exploit.*>

<*Point,*> Jason conceded, nodding at the pair of Marines remaining behind to watch over the Sirians guarding their shuttle as he broke into a jog to catch up with the group.

The tour was long and exhausting. Jason found it both amusing and enlightening to see the order of importance the Hegemony placed upon various sections of the *Vale*. Their attempts to inject breaching nano into the ship's nodes were blatant and easily circumvented.

Cesar assured him privately that their visitors would not take offense at the destruction of the nano. Instead, it would be seen as a sign of their prowess, and would earn them a measure of respect.

The nano was dropped in all the expected locations—the bridge, engineering section, and medical—the areas most likely to contain proprietary tech they could steal.

But they also targeted the fabricator in the *Vale*'s main kitchen, as well as the entertainment node in one of the lounges.

<Pirated recipes and tri-D shows?> He sent Tobias an amused shake of his head when the Weapon Born reported the news. *<That's some sleuthing.>*

<Aye, boyo. I believe the lad fancies himself something of a sleeveen.> Tobias snorted, and Jason smothered a smirk.

Phantom Blade had run into their share of 'sleeveens' on various black ops throughout five different star systems. As sly and smooth-tongued operators went, this guy didn't even rate.

They paused for a meal halfway through the tour, and Jason reminded himself to tell the quartermaster to buy Vi every hard-to-find ingredient the chef had ever asked the officer to obtain, as a thank-you for the thankless hell the Sirians were putting her through.

The inspection wrapped up with a slow flyover of the *Vale*'s hull, and then the Sirian shuttle returned to its own ship.

Jason, Terrance, and Cesar were on their way back to the bridge when the Border Patrol Account Lead on Glimmer-One sent word that the *Avon Vale* was cleared to proceed to Brilliance Station.

<Rendezvous with Hegemony transport, SHC Hyperion,*>* Glimmer-One's NSAI instructed. *<They will escort you to Brilliance Station.>*

As Kodi confirmed receipt of clearance, Jason looked over at Cesar for clarification. "That's…"

"Yes, that's the ship we'll be smuggling out of Sirius," the Noctus man confirmed as they entered the bridge.

"At our current velocity, we'll match vectors with her in about four days," Shannon supplied, and Jason nodded his thanks before returning his gaze to their guest.

He narrowed his eyes as he did the mental math. "Brilliance Station's ten days away at one *g*. Anyone on that ship we can trust?"

Cesar nodded. "The captain and several of her command staff are members of the Underground. Since *Hyperion* is one of the cargo ships that routes shipments between platforms, it's a convenient ship to use for smuggling, so we worked to get them assigned to her." Cesar tilted his head to indicate the ship's icon on the main holo. "Our contact's over there right now, too."

Terrance nodded thoughtfully. "This man, he's a Lumin?"

Cesar smiled. "He is. He reports directly to one of the vice presidents, so he's well-placed." He cocked his head thoughtfully. "Given the way the Hegemony's run, probably the best possible place, actually. Hume's the one who approves the forged death certificates for the Noctus we smuggle aboard."

Jason tilted his head in acknowledgment of the information as he ordered the drones back to the ship.

Forged death certificates and smuggled slaves. What a screwed-up star system, he mused, as the bridge's view of nearspace registered the movement of four icons, tagged as friendlies by the ship's IFF sensors.

Shortly thereafter, four drones with sensor readings that showed as nothing but black-on-black pulled their payloads silently back inside the Q-ship.

UNWILLING INFORMANT

STELLAR DATE: 06.29.3302 (Adjusted Gregorian)
LOCATION: Platform SR71
REGION: Noctilucent Space, Sirian Hegemony

A knock sounded on the frame to Commander Vincent's office door. He looked up to see the newest addition to the SR71 security garrison standing at the entrance. The Irid, an industrious, first-year journeywoman fresh from the Security Guild back on Incandus, was pleasantly meticulous about her job without needing much mentorship. That fact softened Vincent's irritation at the interruption.

"Sorry to bother you, sir," she began, and Vincent waved her off.

"What is it?" he asked, setting aside the report he'd been reading.

"You wanted to know if any communications arrived from Overseer Hume," the comm officer stated. "One just came in, addressed to the Noctus administrator."

Vincent sat back, recalling Overseer Miguel's interest in Hume.

"Anything interesting in the message?" he asked.

The Irid shook her head. "No, just questions about the status of various projects and projected completion dates is all."

"Hmmm," mused Vincent, straightening the stack of holosheets on his desk as he turned the contents of the comm over in his head.

*Miguel must suspect **something.** Although it could be simple competitiveness between overseers, I suppose. Still….*

He looked back up at the Irid, a small smile playing about his lips. "Well, Journeywoman. Think you've been here long enough to take on a little side project for me?"

* * * * *

Several kilometers away, halfway down the north wing, a young Noctus runner named Lauren stood helplessly over her little brother. He lay on a pallet in the abandoned cargo bay that the patcher Dusty had converted into a free clinic. The boy's face was flushed with fever, and Dusty was applying wet cloths to his body in an effort to lower his temperature.

"Isn't there anything we can do?" she whispered, her gut wrenching at the sight of her brother's evident discomfort.

"Best thing now's to let him sleep. His body will work to heal itself," the patcher advised. "Fever'll last another few days, then he'll be fine for a spell before the next one hits."

Lauren kicked at a stain on the deck, her frustration apparent. "It's not fair. Why'd he have to get sick?"

Dusty looked over at her sympathetically. "Part of our lot, living near that star-cursed thing. Radiation adds up, does things to a body, especially young'uns like him. Inflammatory diseases, they're called. His joints are just really cranky right now, but he'll be fine."

"Until the next time he flares," she muttered, huffing out a defeated breath as she shoved her hands deep into the pockets of her oversized coverall.

Dusty cocked his head and then nodded his agreement.

They both looked up at the sound of someone approaching. When he saw it was one of the garrison's guards, Dusty jumped up, dipping his head in a quick bow.

"What can I do for you, ma'am?"

The woman looked from the boy laying on the pallet to Dusty, and then her gaze rested on Lauren, expression contemplative.

"Your brother?" she inquired.

After a quick look at Dusty, who smiled encouragingly, Lauren nodded.

The Irid stood there a moment, apparently lost in thought. "I've seen you around, haven't I?" she continued. "You're a runner for the platform, I think."

Dusty stood, placing himself between Lauren and the Irid. "Aye, she is, and a good one, too. Always gets her messages right, and is well trusted by Administrator Arne. Needing a runner, by chance, are you?"

The Irid rocked back on her heels, thinking, and then nodded once. "Maybe so, maybe so," she murmured.

Turning to Lauren, she attempted a smile. Lauren didn't think it looked like a friendly one.

"I have a little brother myself. Tough spot, seeing him sick like that," the Irid said, then looked up as if a thought had just occurred to her. "Tell you what.... Let me go buy you a nice meal. Looks like you could use something to pick you up about now."

Lauren exchanged an uncomfortable glance with Dusty, but the patcher just indicated she should go along with the Irid.

The soldier grabbed her by the arm and led her away.

As they left the food stand where the Irid had purchased her a meat pie and a container of water, the guard stopped and pulled Lauren aside. The girl got an uneasy feeling in her stomach as the guard looked around and then got right up into her face.

"You want to make sure your brother stays on this station where you can look after him, right?" she began, all pretense at friendliness dropped.

Lauren gulped, the meat pie burning her hand, as if branding her. She nodded when the Irid prodded her shoulder for an answer.

"Good. Then I'll strike a bargain with you. You keep your ears open for any mention of Overseer Hume, and I'll not tell anyone that your brother's just a drain on Hegemony resources."

Lauren suppressed a gasp at that. *Suns, this Irid sounds like she would just as soon see my brother dead!*

"You report to me at the garrison once a week, whether you have news on Hume or not," the Irid continued, uncaring how her words had impacted Lauren. "But I expect you to come running right away any time the overseer's name is mentioned, got it?"

Lauren's eyes went wide.

The Irid must have taken that as a hesitation, for her expression grew dark and her tone turned threatening. "If I find you're holding information on Hume that you *didn't* bring to me, you can kiss your brother goodbye." The soldier's lip curled and she gave a harsh laugh. "Hard work out on those asteroid processing platforms, I hear. Wonder how long a sick kid like him would last?"

TRADE AGREEMENTS

STELLAR DATE: 06.28.3302 (Adjusted Gregorian)
LOCATION: Hegemony Executive Offices, Brilliance Station
REGION: Lucent, Sirian Hegemony

Back on Brilliance Station, Francesca sat studying the faces of her peers from the head of the conference table in the executive boardroom. Today's meeting was a strategic planning session. As the Vice President of Strategic Planning, it was hers to lead.

This particular session had been convened regarding Terrance Enfield's inquiry into a trade agreement with the Hegemony. At the moment, the vote was split, two in favor and one opposed. Unsurprisingly, Gavin, VP of Manufacturing and Distribution, abstained.

The portfolio for Enfield Holdings was impressive. The company boasted innovations in propulsion, nanotech, and materials science. Rumor had it that the Enfield Corporation had cracked the code on true stasis. If that was indeed the case, the Hegemony could hardly afford to ignore it.

Pharris, President and CEO of the Hegemony, kept her expression impassive as she observed the interplay. Other than Francesca, Cyrus was the lone remaining executive who had yet to cast his vote.

"To summarize," Francesca's level tone masked the weariness she felt, "Currin votes no. He recommends we wait until corporate security clears the Enfield ship before offering to meet. He argues that, if the report out of Little River about their vessel's capabilities proves correct, it could cast us as dupes who allowed a foreign military power within its borders."

She paused and sent Currin a questioning look. When he confirmed her recap with a nod, she continued.

"We have two yes votes. Both Berit and Rubin believe we

should go ahead and extend an invitation to Enfield. They believe the risk to be minimal, outweighed by any potential gains."

Swiveling to Cyrus, she lifted her hands, palms up. "With Gavin abstaining, that leaves you, Cyrus."

The man sawed his lower lip back and forth between his teeth for a moment before reluctantly nodding. "Worth the risk. I vote yes."

Letting out a silent breath, Francesca turned to Pharris. "Strategic Planning votes yes as well. Four in favor, one opposed, one abstaining."

Pharris inclined her head, looking up at the crystalline ceiling for a moment before standing. "Extend the invitation."

The words were spoken in a sibilant whisper and were followed by the susurration of hoverplates, installed at the base of the CEO's modified legs, as they propelled her out the door.

*****

As an assenting vote, Francesca had maneuvered her way into a post-meeting discussion—her first alone with Berit and Rubin in two years. She stood aside, quietly observing as Berit vented her usual frustration. That she held Currin in low regard was a poorly kept secret, at best.

"Stupid idiot nearly blew it for everyone," Berit muttered as she paced before the window that looked out upon the Gran Piazza.

"Pharris will replace him soon, you'll see." Rubin spoke absently, his attention drawn to something he spied down below.

Francesca eased closer to the window, trying to see what in the Piazza had caught his attention, but nothing stood out. She hated the ingratiating things she'd had to say to get herself invited to this little tête-à-tête, but knew it was necessary.

Extracting the AIs would be much easier if she could maneuver her fellow executives into boarding the *Avon Vale*. All she needed was an opening to plant the idea in their heads. Better still, do it in a way that suggested the visit would yield big rewards....

She let the silence stretch between them for a moment, then cast her first lure.

"Do you think Enfield Holdings actually has true stasis?"

Ice clinked in the glass Rubin brought to his lips. "It's likely," he admitted after taking a sip. "Their TechDev divisions have an impressive track record."

Francesca waited for the next nibble.

"Well, I'm not trading for it, I can tell you that right now." Berit crossed her arms and glared up at Lucent, held immobile within the embrace of the station's steel arms.

Caught you. Now to reel you in.

Rubin chuckled. "Of course we're not. We'll steal it, just like we do with anything that desirable. Plus any other innovations they have that we can monetize."

As Francesca watched, Berit advanced on Rubin, pulling the drink from his hand and pressing her body against his. Francesca could tell that, though he might enjoy Berit's maneuver, Rubin wasn't swayed by it.

"And how, exactly, do we go about acquiring it?" Berit purred.

Rubin extricated himself, recovering his drink with a knowing smirk. "I'd advise something a bit more subtle than a full frontal assault, my dear. Everything we have on Enfield indicates that he's in a committed, monogamous relationship." Rubin spared her a considering glance. "Although the captain...."

Berit's expression took on a distant look. Francesca assumed the woman was doing the same thing she and Rae were—searching Hegemony files for intel on the Enfield ship's captain.

<*Jason Andrews. Promoted to captain....*> Rae paused, her voice fading as she searched.

Francesca's eyes narrowed as she saw Berit's light up in anticipation. Then Rae sighed.

<*Promoted after the death of his lover, Captain Calista Rhinehart.*

Stars. Berit's going to make a play for the poor guy,> the AI predicted.

Under different circumstances, the revulsion in Rae's tone might have amused Francesca, but the licentious expression in the eyes of the other woman curdled her stomach.

Berit crowed in delight, clapping her hands together. "Oh, my. Looks like a friendly shoulder to cry on might be in order."

<*Looks like you're right, Rae. Poor guy, indeed.*>

Rubin shook his head in amusement. Flicking his fingers toward Quincy, he gestured once at his empty glass, holding it out for a refill. Not once did he look over at the AI.

The small gesture irritated Francesca. It was belittling behavior, meant to reinforce Rubin's dominance over him.

"We'll need access to their ship, of course," the man continued, bringing the now-full glass back to his lips.

It was the opening Francesca had hoped to hear.

"A tour," she proposed. "Cultural exchange. We host a reception for them, they host one for us."

Rubin turned a considering eye to her.

She raised a brow, reminding him in a mocking tone, "Strategic Planning, remember?"

He raised his glass to her, conceding the point.

<*You could suggest that he take Quincy with him,*> Rae whispered. <*Make it sound as if an AI could breach the ship's computer core much more efficiently than Hegemony breaching nano.*>

<*Is that true?*> Francesca whispered back.

She sensed hesitation from Rae before the AI admitted, <*Actually, yes, it might be.*>

Francesca posed the suggestion, which brought avarice to Berit's eyes.

"That's an excellent idea, Francesca."

<*Stars, that's one greedy bitch,*> The mix of fascination and horror from Rae almost had Francesca snickering aloud.

<*You can say that again,*> she agreed.

<*Stars, that's—*>

<Rae, don't. Just…don't.>

HYPERION

STELLAR DATE: 06.28.3302 (Adjusted Gregorian)
LOCATION: SHC *Hyperion*, Inner System
REGION: Luminescent Space, Sirian Hegemony

Five AU from Brilliance Station, the *Hyperion*'s course converged with that of the *Avon Vale.* The ship from Alpha Centauri had been notified that their escort had arrived, and Hume's Irid navigator, Jim, was working to match velocities.

Hume watched the main holo as the icon that represented the *Avon Vale* drifted ever closer to their position. As he waited, his eyes were drawn past the icons for both ships, to the outer system that beckoned beyond.

Soon, he thought. *This ship will be outbound very soon.*

Mythology told that the Hyperion of legend helped overthrow the Lord of the Sky. Although this Hyperion couldn't topple the Hegemony, Hume hoped that if all went well, it might at least strike the first blow.

I wonder if the Lumins will appreciate the irony after we make our move.

Jim turned to Hume, interrupting his thoughts. "We'll be coming alongside the *Avon Vale* in two hours, sir."

Hume thanked him and rose. "Coordinate with them, will you?" he asked as he angled for the exit. "Officially, I'm in conference, if anyone asks."

"Got it," the nav officer confirmed. "Passageway three is officially locked down for a decontamination sweep, and sensors are off in that sector. Your ident shows you're in your office with a Do Not Disturb. If anything urgent comes along, I'll patch it through to you over on the *Avon Vale*."

It was a sad reality that Hume couldn't trust everyone aboard the *Hyperion*, but they hadn't come this far to screw up now. It was a hassle, sneaking off-ship like this, but worth it to ensure that their secret remained safe and their mission uncompromised.

As he walked, he mentally thumbed through the information Cesar had provided in the last secured drop. The covert ops team Francesca had found, and whose help Cesar had managed to procure, had an impressive resume. More importantly, they had a believable cover. He hoped they lived up to all the hype.

Well, if Francesca's going to let these people in on a lifetime's worth of careful planning, I'm damned well going to vet them myself.

Hume had learned to trust his gut in matters like this; small tells always gave away a person's true intent. He would give them this one chance to convince him that they were the real deal. If the Alpha Centauri team proved untrustworthy, he'd plug that leak himself.

Permanently.

Jim's precautions made for a smooth exit, and once the navigator signaled they had come alongside the *Vale,* Hume sealed his small skiff and signaled Jim to open the *Hyperion*'s cargo doors.

With a deft touch borne from years of piloting such craft, the overseer pointed its nose toward the hulking mass floating just ahead of him, and began to close the short gap between.

* * * * *

"Hume," Cesar's voice was filled with both welcome and relief as he greeted the short blonde man who exited the skiff.

Terrance smiled and proffered a hand as Cesar turned to make the introductions. As they ushered the overseer over to where Jason awaited them, he turned and eyed the man curiously.

"So that's the ship we'll be escorting out of Sirius?" he inquired, nudging his head in the general direction of the *Hyperion.*

"It is," the other man confirmed.

"Looks like a modified version of one of those bulk carriers back in Sol," Terrance drew out thoughtfully, one hand scrubbing the stubble along his jawline. "Used to be popular in the shipping lanes between Mars and High Terra, if I have my history correct."

Hume smiled. "I know the model, and I think you're right," he agreed. "Although, her provenance was destroyed before the Hegemony took possession of her, so there's no real way to know."

Terrance dropped his hand and slanted Hume a look. "How many passengers can she hold, do you think?"

Hume's gaze turned speculative. "How many stasis pods can you spare?"

Terrance jerked his head back at the comment, and Hume raised his hands in apology.

"I didn't mean that as it sounded. Sorry," the man's face colored slightly in embarrassment. "Bad habit. I'm so used to playing the role of a Lumin sometimes, it just comes out wrong around civilized people."

The man's tone held rancor, and Terrance smiled in sympathy.

"Having been raised in a family whose legacy is entrenched in corporate culture, trust me." His expression grew wry. "I know exactly how you feel."

Hume laughed and exchanged a glance with Cesar. Terrance caught the subtle nod the Noctus gave Hume; so did Kodi.

<*Huh,*> the AI commented.

<*Saw that, did you?*>

<*Yeah,*> Kodi responded in a thoughtful tone. <*I think you just passed some sort of test.*>

They stopped as they drew abreast of Jason, and Terrance made swift introductions. Jason shook hands with their guest, then led the way into the corridor.

"The rest of the team's waiting for us in the ready room. We've worked out a rough plan, with the intel Cesar's provided," Jason added, shooting a smile at the tall, thin man on Hume's other side, "but we'd like for you to try to shoot holes in it, if you would."

Terrance grinned at Cesar's confused look.

<Better to have it shot up by friendly fire before we see any action,> Kodi explained, *<than to be surprised by live fire, once we're committed to action.>*

Terrance thought Hume looked a bit taken aback by the thought.

Guess he's not much used to the free and open exchange of ideas out here.

As they neared the ready room, another thought struck him.

Guess we'll find out where he stands on AIs, too. He's been cordial to Kodi so far, but it'll be another matter entirely when he learns who's leading Phantom Blade….

The full team had assembled, with Tobias at the helm. Terrance led Hume to a seat near the head of the table, and the Weapon Born rose to greet him. Terrance was relieved to see Hume readily accepted the proffered hand.

"I understand you've met AIs before today?" Terrance braced his forearms on the table, fingers laced as he looked across at Hume, the question in his eyes. When the man nodded, he sat back. "Have you ever worked with any?"

The man frowned, paused, and shook his head.

<Is that a thoughtful frown or a disapproving one, you think?> Kodi speculated, and Terrance sent him a mental shrug.

<We're about to find out.>

"Well, you're about to have that opportunity," Jason informed him, swiveling his chair around to face Hume and clapping a hand on the man's shoulder. "You're surrounded by five of the sharpest minds I've ever had the pleasure to know."

Hume turned back to Tobias, a question on his face. "You're a part of the covert ops team?" he asked, causing a laugh to erupt from Jason.

"He's the one calling the shots," Jason informed Hume.

* * * * *

Jason had observed Hume carefully to gauge his reaction when Tobias was introduced. Although Terrance was the titular head of the task force, and Jason commanded the *Avon Vale*, it was Tobias who was the team's tac-ops leader. When the boots met the ground—or the deck plating, as the case may be—it was Tobias whose word held final sway.

Jason was pleased that Hume's attitude toward AIs seemed the opposite of the Sirians from Glimmer-One. The man's eyes widened in surprise when he realized the only other human members of the task force, besides the men he'd met, were Jonesy and Marta. Aside from that small reaction, he seemed to accept the fact with equanimity.

The one thing that bothered Jason was not knowing what had motivated the Lumin to betray his own kind.

"How long can you be away from the ship before you're missed?" Tobias asked, as introductions came to an end, and he turned back to the overseer.

Hume looked thoughtful for a moment. "I think I can manage two to three hours safely," the overseer replied.

"Then we'd best be about it," the AI said. "I understand you've a plan to share?"

Hume nodded. "My superior has recommended a cultural exchange. The Hegemony will host a meeting with the board on Incandus, and sponsor a reception that will provide you with a bit of exposure to Sirian society."

"Who's your superior, lad?"

Hume hesitated for a fraction of a second. "We…thought it best to keep that information compartmentalized for the time being," he said slowly, deliberately. "The less you know, the less you can inadvertently give away. When the time is right, that person will reach out to you."

He paused and glanced from Tobias to Terrance. Jason saw the man's expression ease as the Weapon Born nodded.

"We thought the reception would provide the perfect excuse

for Enfield Holdings to hold a similar event on board the *Avon Vale*," he said, returning to his earlier point. "My superior will ensure the VPs with embedded AIs will be among those who visit your ship. I take it you can manage the details of the AI extraction from that point on?"

Tobias turned toward Marta. "Doctor?" he asked.

She glanced over at Landon and then gave a brief nod. "We'll get it done."

"As far as the second stage of our operation—extracting the Noctus—we plan to stage an accident on one of our platforms. The Noctus we free will appear to have been casualties of the incident." Hume grimaced. "Unfortunately, accidents are common enough that the loss of this many Noctus is entirely believable. SR71 is a refinery—"

Jason couldn't repress an involuntary "huh" of surprise. It cut into Hume's explanation, and the overseer paused while Terrance pinned Jason with a questioning look.

"Sorry. It's just…the name took me by surprise, is all. So we'll be pulling off a heist on the Blackbird?"

Hume leant back in his chair and stared at Jason in surprise. "How do you know the platform's nickname?"

Jason smirked. "The SR71 Blackbird was the fastest air-breathing aircraft in Sol during the twentieth and twenty-first centuries." He shrugged. "Makes it the best possible place to pull a fast one on the Sirians, if you ask me. It's fitting."

"Speaking of speed…." Terrance interjected, his tone curious, "how fast can the *Hyperion* boost, and what's the capacity of her hydrogen tanks?"

Hume's mouth twisted into a wry frown. "Well, the tanks aren't as large as we'd like, but Sirius is at the nexus of the Local and the Blue fluffs right now, so we can use the ramscoop to feed hydrogen to the drives on our burn out of the system, and save the tanks for the long haul."

He paused and cocked his head thoughtfully, regarding

Terrance with a solemn expression. "As to your first question.... It's more a case of the physical limitations of our passengers. None of the Noctus are augmented, and we'll be taking on a lot of children this time around." The Lumin overseer's eyes grew dark with anger.

"Children?" Marta repeated, leaning forward. "Why so many?"

Something in the man's eyes told Jason that Hume was deeply disturbed by what he was about to relay. He saw it in the deliberate way the overseer toyed with the drink sitting on the table in front of him before he turned and looked them in the eye.

"The Noctus have long had orphanages, corporately run but necessary due to 'employee turnover'." His emphasis on the last two words told Jason they were a euphemism for Noctus deaths. "When one or both parents are killed—or are deemed unfit to care for their offspring for one reason or another—the child becomes a ward of the Hegemony."

Hume's expression turned bleak. He seemed to be having trouble meeting the eyes of anyone at the table as he started speaking again.

"At the direction of one of our vice presidents, some of the orphanages have begun selling healthy children to the platforms with higher mortality rates."

There was a shocked pause.

Marta sucked in a breath just as Tobias emitted a harsh growl.

<*Fecking—*> the AI's voice exploded angrily across the team's net, and was just as quickly cut off.

The emotions roiling behind the word, however, were clear.

This had just become personal for the Weapon Born. He, too, had been stolen as a child, and sold to Heartbridge. He'd been subjected to a brutal imaging that turned him from a human lad of seven years into an enslaved killer, then given over to be used as a weapon in the Terran buildup for what would become the First Sentience War.

Jason's eyes swept the table and saw the sentiment echoed

everywhere he looked. These Sirian bastards deserved to be fucked over. Phantom Blade would take great pleasure in being the ones to do it to them.

<I know this is totally unimportant, given the seriousness of child trafficking—which is what this is,> Kodi said into the silence, *<but how does one Lumin overseer sell something to another, if the entire system's run by one big corporation?>*

Terrance's laugh was harsh. "Easy enough, if you're dealing with a conglomerate," he responded. "The Enfield Corporation does it all the time between its various businesses. Sometimes it's a simple budget transfer, other times, it's a legitimate business exchange between two distinct, incorporated entities. But like you said, it doesn't really matter. It's still illegal sentient trafficking."

Tobias leant forward, expression intent upon Hume. "How many children do you plan to extract, lad?"

Hume's mouth tightened as he gestured toward the diagram of the platform displayed on the holo. "We've pulled the ones we can get our hands on, had them transferred over to the Blackbird. There are about fifty there right now, give or take," he said.

Tobias pushed away from the table, the AI's expression determined. "Whatever children *Hyperion* canna take, the *Vale* will. We'll get them all out, lad. You have my word on that as a Weapon Born."

SPARK TO A FLAME

STELLAR DATE: 06.28.3302 (Adjusted Gregorian)
LOCATION: Manufacturing & Distribution Platform, MD40
REGION: Sirius A, Noctilucent Space, Sirian Hegemony

Six AU away, on Manufacturing and Distribution Platform 40, the platform's overseer was holding a very different kind of meeting.

"There has *never* been a missed deadline under my oversight," the man bellowed to those standing at attention before him. "And there never *will* be."

Ralfe looked on in fascination at the spittle flying from the mouth of the Lumin overseer. Along with the rest of Assembly Sector 9, he'd been forced into watching the dressing down Stan was currently giving Betsy, Ralfe's boss.

The section chief stood stoically while the man screamed, his voice rising to be heard over the rollers and presses currently running, his face flushed red with rage.

Stan had arrived the night before to check on the status of a rush order. The shipment, a mix of finished beams and plating cut and drilled to various specifications, had been due on Radiant the week prior—something about an art installation scheduled for the Periastron Celebration in August, if memory served.

Given that deadline was less than six weeks away, he doubted the delivery would happen in time.

"Sir, one of the cold rollers on line thirteen shattered and fouled the line," Betsy said, her voice pitched to carry over the noise. "We had to clear the area and replace it with an out of service unit before we could—"

"Spare me your excuses." The overseer's voice was so cold it could have frozen Lucent. Ralfe could feel the man's rage as his glare raked over the workers assembled. "Until further notice, breaks are revoked. We work double shifts until this is completed."

"And by 'we', he means 'you'," the woman standing next to Ralfe snorted, confident the man couldn't hear her from this distance.

Ralfe didn't bother to respond. After staying up for forty-eight hours straight, tearing out the shattered roller and repairing the damage it had done to the line, and then muscling the antiquated replacement unit into place, he was beyond caring about anything.

"The Radiant art order *will* be ready to ship in three days' time, or your pay will be docked accordingly. *Do I make myself clear?"*

Ralfe shook his head with a detached, morbid fascination as he watched the man tilt his head back and flare his nostrils. It seemed he did it only so that he could look down his nose at Betsy, who stood half a head taller than him.

Weird.

The section chief stood perfectly still, her spine so rigid, Ralfe rather thought it might fracture if she were to be touched.

"Yes, Overseer," she replied.

The man glared at her one last moment before storming out into the hall. The workers remained frozen until the plant's doors clanged shut behind him.

The section chief slumped, her weary gaze sweeping over them. "Okay, folks. I know it feels like we're under a frog's arse at the bottom of a coal pit, but it'll get done somehow." She straightened. "Let's get this done. Do what you have to do, whatever it takes. I know we're fair knackered as it is, but let's get this thing fired up and spitting out some sheeting before the end of this shift."

"Did she just give us a pass to cut corners?" the woman next to him wondered in an undertone.

Her voice held a tired wariness to it, and her words set off a faint feeling of alarm within Ralfe, but he was too damn tired to chase it, so he let it go. As the crowd broke, workers shuffling off to various tasks, Ralfe scrubbed his face, wondering if he might beg off for an hour's nap.

"Hey-o," a voice from behind him said as a hand clapped down on his shoulder. A friendly, concerned face swam into view. "How about you let the youngsters over there set up the next run, and you go take a quick break? I'll cover for you."

"Thanks." Ralfe pulled a wan smile from somewhere and flashed it gratefully at Edna. "Obliged," he said, before nodding and heading out the door with a halfhearted wave of one hand behind him.

As he walked out, he heard Edna's voice calling out to a trio of newly-trained kids to prep Line 13 for steel sheeting production. Something about those words tugged at the back of his mind. He felt like he was forgetting something, but he let it pass, his tired brain refusing to cooperate. The uneasiness faded from his mind as he reminded himself that Edna was a seasoned worker.

She'll keep them from doing anything too dumb, he told himself as he neared the break room. He stood stupidly in the entrance for a moment, wavering between the burnt coffee smell wafting from one corner, and the ratty sofa tucked into the shadows of another.

The sofa won.

Grabbing a cushion from one end, he planted himself face-down at the other, the cushion covering his head and blocking out the harsh glare of the exposed overhead bulbs.

"Just five minutes," he mumbled to no one in particular.

*****

The three Noctus who Edna pressed into prepping Ralfe's station were still in their teens.

"Suns, they're young," the oldest boy heard her say as she motioned them into the bay that housed Line 13.

His spine stiffened, and he opened his mouth to protest, but then he glanced over at the others. She was right; they *were* younger than most.

His attention returned to Edna as she addressed them with a brisk, no-nonsense tone.

"Okay, then. This cold press line needs to be cleaned and back in service—" She consulted the do-list on the interface screen at the beginning of the line and barked a harsh laugh, "an hour ago. You know the drill?"

Edna seemed not to notice his uncertain response, her attention diverted by a crashing sound that came from her own line, one bay away. With a distracted expression, she turned back to the three and gave them a nod of encouragement.

"I'll just be on the other side of that bulkhead. I'll keep the doors open between us, so just give a shout if you have any questions."

With that, she broke into a jog, leaving the inexperienced teens to fend for themselves. The three exchanged glances, then the oldest shrugged.

"You two want to go inspect the belt for any obstructions, and see if the finish sander needs replacing? I'll go grab the vacuum."

The other two nodded and wandered off, while their ersatz leader turned toward the large, industrial-strength cleaning system built into the bulkhead. Reaching for the hose, he toggled it on, only to stagger back under a billowing cloud of ferrous oxide, the black powder residue that came from grinding steel.

Squinting through the swirl of dust, he realized the onslaught of fine particulate matter was coming from the open collar where the containment receptacle was ordinarily housed. Coughing, he pushed his way back toward the switch, toggling the vacuum off just as a yell sounded behind him.

"Duuuude!" sputtered the youth who had been examining the belt.

"Sorry," the eldest muttered in reply. "Didn't realize it wasn't hooked up. Someone didn't put the cover back on after dumping it out."

"Well, the conveyor *was* clean," the other grumbled. He leaned over and briskly rubbed the black dust out of his hair before trudging over to a nearby maintenance station.

None of the three had been given more than the briefest of explanations about the dangers of metal cross-contamination.... Nor did they understand the chemical reactions that would result when certain types of metal dust interacted with something as seemingly innocuous as water.

The leader—the only one who might have known enough to warn his friend away—had turned in search of the missing vacuum receptacle, so he didn't notice the youth grab a bucket and fill it with water before returning to the conveyor.

"All done," announced the third youth, coming from his inspection of the finish sander. "Belt looks good. I don't think it needs replacing just yet."

"Great," said the oldest absentmindedly as he levered the vacuum's receptacle into its sleeve, and began tightening the collar. "Grab the other end of the hose for me, will you?"

So focused was he on the vacuum that he didn't think to ask if his friend had cleaned the dust from the sander's surfaces. Neither did he consider that there might be a localized vacuum attached to the sander itself.

This particular sander did have one, and its vacuum bag was filled with aluminum dust and shavings from the line's previous run. The substance was highly reactive with steel dust, the material the line would next be servicing.

The third youth gave his friend a thumbs-up. "One hose, coming up!" he said, turning to trace the flexible tube back to its origin.

It looked like someone had been in the process of vacuuming dust from the ducts when the overseer had arrived. The end of the hose was still inside, fed into the duct through a small access door built into the ventilation shaft's filtration cover.

The youth grabbed the hose and yanked it free, unaware that

the action had unseated the cover. Hose in hand, he ran back to his friend. Both boys jumped at the loud clanging noise the heavy filtration cover made as it clattered to the deck.

"I'll put it back in a bit," the younger one promised as he saw the scowl on the older youth's face.

His friend nodded, grabbed the proffered hose, and flipped the vacuum back on. By the time he reached the line, his friend had already sponged the belt down with quick, sloppy swipes of water.

The oldest hesitated, looking at the belt askance, but when nothing seemed to be amiss, he shrugged, coiled the hose, and turned the vacuum off.

Ten minutes later, the three reported back to Edna that Assembly 13 was ready to go back into service. Glancing over at what appeared to be a cleaned and prepped unit, completed in record time, she looked around for Ralfe.

Not seeing him around, and thinking to help out her fellow worker, she signed onto the platform's system using Ralfe's ident, and keyed in the command that would spin up the operation waiting in the queue. The unit acknowledged Ralfe's ident code and began to initialize the process for the steel run, flashing a ten-minute countdown clock on the screen.

Satisfied, Edna turned back to her own bay.

She never noticed the open ventilation shaft, and there were no sensors in the area to sniff for the hydrogen gas generated by the water on the sponge as it interacted with the residue of aluminum dust—not that it would have registered, for it was a small amount.

But it was enough.

* * * * *

Several meters away, Betsy strode past the break room on her way back to her office. Spying something out of place in the darkened corner, she paused and backed up. Stepping inside, she realized it was the form of a man, lying prone on the broken-down sofa.

Ralfe. She sighed. *Poor guy's beat, we can make do without him.*

Kneeling next to him, she nudged the man awake and steered him to the exit. Ralfe stumbled forward, mumbling a barely coherent apology that the section chief waved off. Once they were at the elbow junction between the dogleg and the main arm, she squeezed Ralfe's arm and stepped back.

"You good from here?" she asked, and he lifted bleary eyes to hers with a bare nod. "Go on then," she urged, "get some sleep."

He lifted a hand in something approximating a wave and turned to go. She stood there a moment as he took a few steps, wanting to make sure he'd be able to make it back to his bunk without help.

It was the only thing that saved her.

As she turned to go, she heard a rasping curse.

"Suns, no! Betsy, stop them!"

Betsy started back toward Ralfe, a question in her eyes.

Ralfe's own were wide, frantic. "I just remembered—Suns, Betsy, the vacuum! I left the cover off, and there's steel dust everywhere. If they start the line without checking—"

Just then, the system triggered the outdated machinery Ralfe had reinstalled on Assembly Line 13. The automated switch that activated it was worn, and a spark discharged, igniting the hydrogen gas. This in turn became the accelerant that ignited the aluminum dust from both the conveyor and the vacuum bag from the sander during thirteen's last run. The aluminum dust then mixed with the remains of the ferrous oxide cloud in a highly exothermic reaction.

The resulting explosion set off a massive fireball.

Lying forgotten on the deck was the filtration cover that would have sealed off the remaining ferrous oxide dust in the ventilation shaft. The fireball, pushed by a massive pressure wave, flashed through the shaft. The combination of pressure, heat, and more dust boosted the energy of the explosion within the confined space.

The compressive force blew filtration covers off adjacent assembly bays, allowing the conflagration to mix with the metal dust and swarf in those environments as well. The subsequent bloom took out the entire rimward section of MD40's assembly plant.

At the entrance to Sector 9, Betsy was flung forward just as a raging inferno engulfed Ralfe. The flash of intense heat incinerated clothing and seared flesh. Extreme temperatures caused underlying tissue to fuse beneath layers of charred skin, and what remained was almost unrecognizable as human.

Several kilometers away, a freight handler loading a transport with titanium plating looked up as a bright flash caught her eye. She craned her head, looking out the window of her skiff, and her mouth dropped open in horror as she spied a ball of expanding orange light. Her hand slipped off the controls of the grappling arm as the concussion wave slammed into her small vessel, sending it skidding along the side of the transport.

The screech of metal against metal hit her ears just as the titanium plating sheared her little craft in half.

PLANNING SESSION

STELLAR DATE: 06.28.3302 (Adjusted Gregorian)
LOCATION: Inner System
REGION: Luminescent Space, Sirian Hegemony

"Captain!"

Jason turned to see the comm officer's head sticking out of the bridge's entrance, a worried expression on her face. Leaving Terrance, Cesar, and Hume at the lift, he jogged back down the corridor to where she stood waiting.

"What is it?" he asked as he neared.

"There's a message coming through for our visitor, from the *Hyperion*, sir." She looked over his shoulder at the three waiting men. "Their captain says it's urgent."

Jason beckoned the men forward. "We'll take it in my office."

She nodded and returned to her station.

Jason filled them in on the way, and a few moments later, the image of the *Hyperion*'s captain resolved onto the office holo. Jason saw tension bracketing the woman's mouth as her eyes sought Hume.

"Sorry to interrupt," she said, "but we've just received word. There's been an incident on MD40."

Hume's expression grew grim as the woman detailed the extent of the damage wrought by the explosion.

"Seventeen hundred dead," Hume said, visibly shaken. "It's been a while since we've had an incident this bad."

"Actually," the captain began, then hesitated before continuing, "the real number's just shy of sixteen hundred—the rest of those are fabricated. Doesn't lessen the blow much, I know."

"Still," Hume shook his head. "That's too steep a price to pay."

He thanked the captain, then closed the connection and turned to face Jason.

Jason gave the man a moment to process the news, then asked the question uppermost in his mind.

"What did she mean by the rest being 'fabricated'?"

Hume's smile was wan. "Silver lining, I guess you could say. As I said before, we've found small ways to turn these tragedies into something…well, useful, I suppose. They've used the chaos of the incident as a cover to smuggle as many as possible out of the system."

"Talk about your mixed blessings," Jason muttered. "How often do accidents like this occur?"

The Lumin sighed, and Jason saw him exchange a glance with Cesar. "More often than it should, and with increasing frequency since that sun-cursed wager Berit made with Rubin," Hume admitted.

<I'm curious,> Kodi spoke up. *<How is it that you're privy to such insider information as this wager?>*

The worry lines on Hume's forehead smoothed a bit as he returned a genuine grin. "My contact—my…boss, you might say—hacked into the executive offices." His expression sobered. "She overheard them talking about it one day."

She. Jason made note of the pronoun, wondering again who this mysterious contact might be.

A sound from behind caught Jason's attention. He turned to see Tobias's frame in the entrance; behind him stood Marta. He motioned them both in.

"Kodi updated us," the AI told Jason before turning to the two Sirians. "What's the reaction from Incandus likely to be, lads?" he asked, tone gentle.

Hume remained silent and shook his head.

"They're not sending any aid, if that's what you're asking." Cesar's words were bleak. "They never have. They leave us to tend after our own. It's all 'rolled up into the budget'—or so they've told us when we've asked for help before."

Marta cleared her throat, catching Jason's gaze. "Where is

MD40 in relation to where we are now?" she asked. "How far off our flight path?"

He turned to Hume, eyes questioning.

"Not all that far, actually," the man replied. "Right now, with Sirius in periastron with Lucent, it's no more than a few million kilometers off our current heading."

<Cesar's told us what conditions are like on those platforms,> Varanee spoke up, tone distressed. *<We can't just ignore this. We need to render what medical aid we can.>*

"Not the *Vale* as a whole, necessarily," Marta interjected. "Maybe just a small, covert team. Varanee and I could go—"

When Terrance took in a breath to protest, Marta held up a hand to cut him off.

"Just hear me out. We could take a team of Marines with us. We'll treat their injured and bring back as many of the hidden Noctus as we can fit into the shuttle."

"Our shuttles are rated to carry little more than a platoon of Marines, lass," Tobias reminded her. "The *Hyperion*'s captain said there were almost a hundred Noctus listed as dead by MD40's triage team. We can't retrieve them all with just one shuttle, and it's too risky to send two."

"We'll bring the ones most in need of medical intervention," Marta stated. "This also gives us a chance to deliver medical supplies to help those left behind after we're gone. Just get me out there, and we'll figure it out."

Jason could see hope bloom in Cesar's eyes as he and Hume traded glances.

"MD40's not one of my own," Hume admitted, "so this would be a welcome assist. And don't worry about the ones you leave behind. They're ghosts now, scrubbed from the Hegemony's system. The Underground can hide them until I figure out a way to smuggle them off."

"All right, then," Tobias said, turning with a nod to Marta. "I'll allow it. But we have to keep this small and under the radar, lass.

Just a single shuttle." He turned to Jason, who nodded his agreement.

"Beau's checked out on the *Kuroi Kaze*," Jason informed them, mentioning one of the *Vale*'s pilots. "I'll have him fly you out there."

Tobias nodded, then fixed Marta with a stern look. "You'll follow orders from the Marine fireteam at all times. If they think the situation's getting a bit dodgy, you leave. Understood?"

<*Understood,*> Varanee assured him.

"Come back to us in one piece, doctors," Jason admonished, and received a nod from Marta.

"You know," Terrance said, voice trailing off as his blue eyes rested thoughtfully on Hume. "Grandma Sophia always said not to let a good crisis go to waste…."

Marta stiffened, and Jason caught a glint of anger in her gold-green eyes as they narrowed on Terrance.

He raised a hand as if to ward off an incipient dressing-down. "That disaster," he explained, "provides us with the perfect excuse to demand a tour of a platform as a condition of the trade agreement between Enfield and the Hegemony."

He turned back to Hume. "We'll need a little help from your side to ensure that the right platform is chosen for the tour, of course. But it does legitimize things in a tidy way."

Hume tilted his head, acknowledging that fact.

"Give me a few hours," the Lumin told them. "Once I get back to the *Hyperion*, I'll send my navigator to you. Jim's one of us. He knows his way around the '40, and can function as your native guide on site."

Tobias nodded and stepped toward the door. "Very well, lad. I suppose we'd best see you off, then."

Marta left to pack medical supplies while Tobias spoke with Khela about Marine support. That left Jason, Terrance, and Cesar to escort Hume to his skiff.

As the bay doors closed behind the small vessel, Terrance

turned thoughtful eyes to Cesar.

"How do we know we can trust him? What if he doesn't follow through with his end of the plan?"

"He will," Cesar assured them both. "Hume wants this to succeed as much as I do."

Jason met the man's eyes, his own gaze considering. "You've never really said why that is."

"Because his father was Irid," Cesar said simply. "And *his* father was Noctus. He has skin in the game, I suppose you could say. Hume is my cousin."

A SHORTAGE OF WORKERS

STELLAR DATE: 06.30.3302 (Adjusted Gregorian)
LOCATION: Phosphor Pavilion, Incandus
REGION: Lucent, Luminescent Space, Sirian Hegemony

Although its working headquarters was on Brilliance Station, the Hegemony kept a titular headquarters on the planet below, in the capital city of Candesca. It was a place where they could bring prospective customers, or host company gatherings.

Tonight's soiree was held off-campus, at a crystal pavilion on the shores of the Phosphor Sea, two hundred kilometers away. The vice presidents were mingling with former executives, retired vice presidents, and members of the board. All were waiting for the CEO to call the meeting to order—or rather, for the meeting to end so that the evening's entertainments might begin.

Rubin stood studying a crystal sculpture occupying the center of the structure. Crafted from holotech and combined with the planes and angles of its crystalline surfaces, it created an Escher-like experience he found intriguing.

He looked up as Currin approached.

"Well, that's...different," the VP of Sales commented as he drew abreast of Rubin and cast a critical eye at the new art installation.

"Not a fan of the arts?" Rubin sent Currin an amused look as the man's lip curled in distaste.

"More of a classicist, I suppose." He turned and saluted Rubin with his wineglass. "Have you heard the news?" Currin tilted his head slightly to indicate the pavilion's far wall, where two figures stood locked in a heated discussion.

Rubin sent a casual glance in that direction to see Gavin practically in Cyrus's face. The VP of manufacturing and distribution appeared to be distressed.

"What news? About MD40? Yes, but I didn't think it was a loss worth mentioning. Has new information come in about it?" He turned back to Currin, but his eyes lingered on the tableau as he asked the question. His query was met with a shrug.

"Not that I know of," the man replied. "Let me check...." Currin initiated a comm that included Rubin. <*Elliot,*> he commanded in a peremptory tone, <*full report on the MD40 incident and its impact on workflow.*>

There was a brief pause, followed by the AI's voice. <*Platform MD40 experienced catastrophic failure along one of the more recently-installed sectors today. Sector Nine experienced an explosive blast and subsequent fire that destroyed several production lines. More than seventeen hundred Noctus workers are dead, or missing and presumed—*
>

<*Elliot!*> Currin's harsh mental voice cut in. <*Did I ask you for information on the Noctus? Execute reprimand protocol Three, and then answer my query properly. What* ***jobs*** *were scheduled for that sector?*> He glanced at Rubin. "Space the resources," Currin muttered in annoyance. "Seventeen hundred out of a hundred and fifty thousand?" He snorted.

Rubin's mouth quirked in amusement. "Little more than one percent," he agreed. "Light, that's a rounding error on the books. Hardly worth a mention."

There was a pause, and then Elliot's voice—in a timbre that struck Rubin as subdued, but still oddly angry—once more filled their thoughts.

<*There were only two runs scheduled with deadlines. The rest were standard milling runs to restock the yards.*>

<*And those were...?*> Currin prodded when Elliot's recitation ended.

<*An order for steel support braces to complete an art installation on Radiance, for the Periastron Celebration—*>

"Suns, no wonder Gavin looks so animated," Rubin interrupted, his curiosity about Elliot's odd behavior forgotten.

"He's having to explain to Cyrus why Facilities won't have their new toys for the event."

<*And the other one?*> Currin pressed.

<*The test run of the knockoff SC batts based on the new Procyon design,*> Elliot supplied.

"Ouch," Rubin murmured, a smile playing on his mouth. "I know of at least one person who will be very unhappy to hear that."

"Ah, so you didn't invest in the new test run?"

Rubin's smile turned sly. "No, but Berit did. I imagine she'll be a bit irritable for a few days over this."

Currin snorted, shook his head, and then drifted toward the suspended crystal table that had been brought in for the occasion, as they received pings indicating that the meeting was about to commence.

* * * * *

After the meeting, those attending adjourned to the lanai, where a buffet of hors d'oeuvres had been laid out for the board to enjoy. The pavilion had been built on a bluff that ran along the sands edging the Phosphor Sea, and the lanai boasted a sweeping view of the shoreline.

Rubin's AI, Quincy, informed him that the string quartet was setting up near the sea wall for the evening's entertainment; although, if he'd looked, he could have seen for himself. The various prismatic panels that shaped both the exterior and interior walls of the crystalline structure allowed for an artistic, if imperfect view of the Irid musicians.

Rubin worked his way through the pavilion, congratulating himself silently on his social prowess as he went. Each board member was approached, engaged in brief conversations, and directed in ways to subtly influence their opinion of him.

The light sting of a salt-water-scented breeze struck him as he strode onto the lanai. Lucent was setting, and the more brutish Sirius A had set hours earlier, leaving the Phosphor Sea limned in a silvery twilight. Behind him, the pavilion's illumination cast an ethereal glow over those in attendance, as the first musical notes carried to him in the evening air.

He ordered Quincy to gather a plate of his favorite foods and follow him to the low seawall. As he approached, he saw he wasn't the only one who'd thought of stepping away for a few moments.

"I love what they've done with the place."

Berit's tone made a mockery of her words, as she turned to watch him approach.

A raised brow was the only acknowledgment he gave to her outrageous attire. Mimicking the rippled panes that enclosed the pavilion itself, the transparent bodice gave her torso a look reminiscent of a melted Dali pocketwatch that he could barely make out in the shadowed evening light.

She leant against the seawall, her bodice settling with a *clink*.

"Careful," he advised, his mouth curling in amusement. "A wardrobe malfunction might be a mite painful in that, if you end up with shards sticking out your chest."

Berit's look held an edge sharper than the shards he'd just mentioned.

"I hear one of your investments had a bit of a setback," he murmured, turning back to look out at the starlit sea.

Berit snorted and turned her back to the water. "Just a minor one," she admitted, "but more than offset by the increases I've managed with our experiment."

Rubin grunted. "It's given us some interesting data," he allowed. "Running with fewer safeties has caused more resource attrition than anticipated, but not nearly what I had feared. Although there is the risk of even greater losses, should a platform fail."

"Like what happened at MD40."

"Exactly. Initial reports indicate it was caused by a metal dust ignition, which," he reminded her, "would fall under worker error, possibly due to fatigue."

"True, but we have finite resources where Noctus are concerned, despite the influx offset by workers obtained from the orphanages. Unless...."

Her voice trailed off, and Rubin waited for her to continue. Instead, she raised a hand and pretended to study her nails with fascination.

Exasperated at her machinations but unwilling to wait, he played along.

"Unless?" he prompted.

"Unless we conscript more of them."

Rubin's brow rose. "More of whom, Berit? What are you going to do next, conscript Irids?"

She sent him an arch look. "Don't be so boorish, Rubin. I was thinking of something a bit more elegant."

She smiled, her expression turning crafty, and Rubin found himself drawing closer, intrigued by the twisted complexity of the woman's mind.

"I think it's time we conduct an audit of the conditions under which Noctus children are living." She gestured expansively. "Who knows how many of the poor things are being mistreated by their own families? It would be irresponsible of us not to intervene in such cases, don't you think?"

WARD OF THE HEGEMONY

STELLAR DATE: 07.01.3302 (Adjusted Gregorian)
LOCATION: Prism Station (aka "Prison" Station)
REGION: Noctilucent Space, Sirian Hegemony

Today was Ysobel's day off from her teaching duties on Prism Station, and she'd opted to spend a few hours helping out at the orphanage. She knew they were short-staffed, the institution filled to capacity.

Plus, it gives me a chance to check in on Pia's girl, she thought as she knelt to roll up the cuffs on the oversized coveralls one of the orphans wore. *She misses Sophie terribly.*

The boy's foot was propped up against her thigh, his hands braced on her shoulders as he balanced on one leg. She made a mental note to try to find him a pair of decent shoes when she spied his toes peeking out from the front, where the seam had separated.

Patting his leg and setting it back down, she admonished, "All right, Flip, you're good to go. But no more running through the corridors unless these are rolled up, you got it? That's a good way to land on your face and break a few more teeth."

Flip shot her a gap-toothed grin before dashing away. She shook her head and then looked up as Sophie handed her the stack of hyfilms the children had used for their reading lesson. Smiling her thanks, Ysobel rose and headed over to the bunk bed where she'd left her satchel, when an angry shout from down the corridor caught her attention.

"Stay here," she instructed Sophie. "I want to go see what that's all about. I'll be right back."

Sophie nodded obediently as Ysobel lifted the tattered tarp that separated the area of the orphanage allocated for school and other activities. She skirted the beds crowded along both sides of the corridor, stepping over a discarded rag someone had knotted into the shape of a doll.

As she neared the end of the hallway, she slowed, the shout having morphed into the sound of many raised voices. Nearing the bend in the corridor that signified the entrance to the orphanage, she stepped forward.

The scene she encountered had her instinctively ducking back around the corner and pressing her body close against the bulkhead. Taking a deep breath, she crept once more toward the corner and peered around.

A large, angry crowd of people were nearing the orphanage's entrance. They were brandishing metal posts, chairs, heavy tools, kitchen knives—anything that could be used as a weapon.

Three men, tall and lean and gaunt, led the way. By the looks of them, they were most likely dockworkers. As Ysobel's eyes scanned the crowd, she realized all of them were Noctus.

"Give us our kids back!" a woman called out over the shoulder of one of the men.

"You got no right!" another growled.

"You can't just steal them from us, they're our babies!"

"We ain't standing for this!"

As Ysobel watched, the orphanage's headmaster strode forward, his hands raised.

"Please, please!" Bryce called out. "Just hold on now, and let me talk!"

The crowd muttered and shifted, but quieted. Bryce nodded and dropped his arms. Ysobel edged around the corner, sticking to the shadows as she crept closer so she could hear what he had to say.

"I assume you're here about the change in station policy regarding children," he began, and Ysobel frowned in confusion.

There had been no policy change, as far as she knew.

His words caused a stir among the Noctus. He paused, but no one spoke up, so he continued.

"Prism Station policy now states that if a parent leaves a child under the age of fifteen unsupervised for any length of time, that parent is considered unfit, and the child shall be seized and placed into the Hegemony orphanage system for its own benefit."

A collective gasp met Bryce's words, and an angry murmur swept through the crowd, but the headmaster wasn't done. Ysobel caught him glancing past the faces of the mob to the concourse behind them, but from her position, she couldn't see what had him nodding to himself in satisfaction.

"Prism Station has begun to actively police this matter," Bryce continued, "and any children who are considered to be living in a situation that policy dictates as harmful will be *removed* from that situation."

Ysobel gasped. It was Pia's circumstances, writ large.

Her eyes skated across the angry crowd, and she knew Bryce's words had been the wrong ones to say to grieving parents.

*And he asked me if **I** had a death wish,* she thought with a shake of her head. *They're going to rip him to pieces if he stands in their way.*

As she feared, the crowd erupted in a roar of rage and surged forward, bent upon removing the headmaster and retrieving their kin. But then the sound of weapons fire reached her ears, and Ysobel realized with cold certainty what had brought the look of satisfaction to Bryce's face.

Suns, he's called in the Lumins! These people have no chance against garrison weaponry!

She heard the concussive *whump* of a pulse cannon, and saw it strike those on the edge of the crowd. She was horrified to hear the whine of a flechette rifle coming from the other direction. The wet smacking noise of the rifle's rounds as they tore through human flesh combined with the shrieks and moans of those they impacted. The corridor just ahead of her *ting*ed with the sound of flechettes that missed their marks as they spent themselves against the far bulkhead.

She saw Bryce duck reflexively and backpedal toward her.

Fisting the back of his suit in one hand, she reeled him in and swung him to face her.

"Are you *crazy?*" she whispered fiercely. "You called the *garrison* on them? They're being slaughtered out there!"

Bryce shoved away from her, angrily smoothing his suit back into place as he pulled himself behind the protection the bulkhead afforded.

"Don't preach at me, Ysobel," he said in a clipped voice, his attention on the crowd being suppressed in the concourse beyond them. "I did what I had to do to protect myself and this orphanage. They've stopped using the flechettes, so you can rest easy. It's all standard crowd control now."

"Suns," she breathed, slapping her hand against the side of the bulkhead, angry with herself for not thinking of it immediately. "Medical! They need to be alerted."

She broke into a run, gathering sheets from nearby pallets and bunks as she reached out mentally to connect with the station's medical unit.

<*Medical emergency!*> She thrust the thought at the NSAI when it answered, while tucking the bedding under one arm as she raced to grab the orphanage's meager first aid kit. <*Hegemony Orphanage Seven, outside environmental. Lower deck fourteen, sector B.*>

<*Garrison has tagged this a Noctus matter,*> the NSAI responded. <*All requests should be addressed to Noctus Free Clinic, Node Six.*>

Before she had a chance to protest, the NSAI signed off.

"Dammit," she cursed under her breath. "How can they refuse treatment in a medical emergency like this?"

Bryce's lip curled up on one side in a mocking smile as he stepped in front of her, barring her way. "Could have told you that would be the response."

She didn't bother with an answer, shoving him to one side as she pushed past.

She knelt beside the first victim she came across, ripping open a sterile pad to apply to the wounded leg. Hands reached into her field of vision offering help, and she guided them to apply pressure to stanch the bleeding. She dispensed more sterile pads, and then began tearing the sheets into long strips for use in binding wounds.

While Ysobel worked, she attempted to connect with the clinic that treated Noctus, staffed by volunteers from both the Noctus and Irid populations. The voice that answered on the other end was tinny, and Ysobel knew its user was on one of the more primitive devices that was all the Noctus were allowed.

Swiftly, she updated the volunteer with the information she had, and was assured help was already on its way. Closing the connection, she saw Bryce greet the nearest Lumin guard. She rose and began to approach them.

From the corner of her eye, Ysobel saw the free clinic team approaching at a dead run. With them was Waid, the man who had accompanied Ysobel to help Pia locate Sophie several weeks before. When he spied her, he turned and began to head her direction.

As she neared Bryce, she heard him thank the Lumin soldier for his timely intervention. It set her teeth on edge, and she had an almost insatiable urge to wrench the pulse rifle from the soldier's back and turn it on Bryce herself.

***Thank** him? For what? Firing on innocent people?*

But Bryce's words sounded stilted, and Ysobel suspected the man was regretting his decision, now that he was faced with its bloody aftermath.

The Lumin soldier's gaze passed dismissively over Ysobel as she joined them, then turned back to survey his team's handiwork. "Call maintenance and get this mess cleaned up," he ordered Bryce in a bored tone. "We'll take the uninjured with us when we leave."

She lifted a hand to get the soldier's attention, shrugging off Bryce's warning grip, and shifting closer to Waid as he joined them.

"What will happen to them?" she asked, gesturing to the Noctus the soldiers were rounding up.

"What happens to every Noctus who breaks the law," the Lumin sneered. "They'll be punished, then sent to work the asteroid fields."

"But—"

She felt Bryce's hand once more on her arm, this time twisting painfully in warning. She glared over at him before turning to look the Lumin in the eye.

"These people have families," she objected. "You can't just separate them."

The Lumin soldier shot her an ugly grin. "New station policy, or haven't you heard? We'll just round up more orphans for you to add to your growing collection."

"But that makes no sense. The orphanage is full up as it is," she began to protest, and the Lumin barked a laugh at her.

"Not for long, it won't be." Grinning at Bryce, he turned and strode back to his soldiers. With a shouted command, he rounded them up and marched off.

The soldier's comment made no sense to Ysobel…and then it did.

"Suns," she breathed, turning and grabbing Waid's arm in a grip that had him wincing and muttering, "Easy, there, girl" under his breath. She turned to Bryce and realized she'd guessed correctly when the man refused to meet her gaze. "They're taking children away from their parents in order to send them to the *platforms*?" she demanded incredulously.

"Word of advice, Ysobel," Bryce said bitterly. "Keep your head down and just do your job. It's the only way you're ever going to get off this shithole of a station and leave this mess behind."

INCANDUS

STELLAR DATE: 07.02.3302 (Adjusted Gregorian)
LOCATION: Approaching Incandus Spaceport, Candesca
REGION: Lucent, Luminescent Space, Sirian Hegemony

The trip to Incandus marked Shannon's first field op, and she was clearly relishing it. Jason glanced over at the AI as she adjusted the shuttle's trajectory for atmospheric entry and surprised a grin on the AI's face. He shot her a wink in response.

They hadn't intended for any AIs to accompany them planetside—Kodi being the notable exception—but since Shannon's frame was completely organic, save for the latticework of neural circuits that was woven throughout, she'd easily pass for a typically augmented human to anything but the most invasive of scans.

It wasn't the thought of Shannon being found out that concerned him. It was her lack of field experience.

<*We have her back. Don't worry, it'll be fine.*> Terrance's voice sounded in his head, and he knew the man seated behind him had caught his worried glance.

Jason sent the exec a brief nod, his glance sweeping to where Khela sat aft of Shannon. In combat situations, these were the point-defense and flight engineer's positions, but Jason knew how much Terrance loved being in the cockpit, so for this excursion, the two cradles were swiveled forward, their boards locked and powered down.

His attention returned to his pilot's board as he received a ping from the *Avon Vale*.

"Everything still quiet on your end?" he greeted, as Landon's avatar appeared on his HUD.

<*All's well,*> the XO responded. <*Ramon reported in a few minutes ago. The* Kuroi Kaze *is approaching MD40 now.*>

"Good to hear," Jason responded. "We'll do what we can to keep them distracted. You just keep sitting there, looking like a big, juicy target filled with tech the Sirians want to get their hands on."

Shannon looked up from her exchange with the Incandus Space Traffic Control's NSAI to shoot him a look of annoyance.

"Not funny, guys," she called out. "Don't you be getting into any scrapes with the *Vale*, Landon. Just because I'm in this frame right now doesn't mean I don't still enjoy hanging out in my bigger one from time to time."

Jason transferred the comm to the shuttle's holo for all to see, and Terrance chuckled behind him as Landon's voice came into the cockpit.

"Noted." The XO pushed a shaft of amusement at them, causing Shannon to roll her eyes. "Don't mess up the new paint job. Got it."

"The *Vale*'s not painted, guys. How many times have I *told* you that?"

Terrance's chuckle turned into a full-blown laugh. "You know he's going to keep tweaking you about it as long as he gets a reaction out of you," the exec advised, eliciting an aggrieved *hmph* from her as she flounced forward in her seat.

There was a moment of silence, then Jason caught Shannon glancing slyly over at Terrance.

"What?" Jason asked, as the shuttle transitioned into a cloudless blue sky lit brilliantly by twin suns. The shuttle's main holo dimmed to compensate as he angled the vessel along the flight path that Shannon fed to him.

"Oh, nothing…." She nibbled on one thumb, shooting Terrance another look.

"I know that expression," Terrance said, his tone wary. "Out with it. Now, Shannon."

"Well, I was just thinking…."

Jonesy groaned audibly from the front row of the shuttle's

cabin as Cesar looked on in confusion. Shannon turned around and shot him a stern look.

"Don't you give me that, Jonesy! It's good to be as prepared as possible going into these things, you know that."

She looked earnestly from Terrance to Jason. "Since this entire operation in Sirius is one big heist, I did a little research on it."

Jason got a suspicious feeling in his gut. "And what did you learn?"

"I think we need to discuss exactly what kind of heist we're going to pull off," she said seriously, then began ticking off with her fingers as she recited, "We could do a Boesky, a Jim Brown, probably not a Miss Daisy. Oh, stars, please not a Jethro. But a Leon Spinks is a distinct possibility."

Jason heard movement from the jump seat across from Terrance as Khela leant forward.

"Is this some sort of code?" the Marine asked in a puzzled voice. "There's no Daisy on the *Vale*. I'd know."

Jason eyed Shannon. "Been practicing that, have you?"

She bit her lip. "Little bit. Did I rush it? Felt like I rushed it."

Jason smirked. "You know we don't have the first clue what you're talking about, right?"

The AI shot him one of her patented "oh please" looks.

"Jason," she said with exaggerated patience, "*everyone* knows that in order to pull off a heist, you have to run a good con."

"Con?" It was Terrance's turn to lean forward, his tone curious.

Suddenly, an amused snort sounded from the main cabin where Jonesy and Cesar sat. And then another. Jason shot Terrance a questioning glance, and the exec just shook his head.

<*Don't look at me, either,*> Kodi added. <*I've got nothing.*>

At that, Jonesy broke into laughter, a condition that grew until the engineer was practically howling with mirth.

Shannon swiveled to pin him with a baleful glare, crossing her arms and scowling ferociously at him. She tapped her foot until his peals of laughter finally died down.

"Co…con…confidence game," he wheezed out when he could draw breath, wiping tears from his eyes as he straightened. "That's old-Earth slang for a swindle. They used to call them cons. She's been watching old-Earth 2D vids again." He shook his head, grinning over at the AI.

Shannon tilted her head and narrowed her eyes at him. He raised his hands in self-defense, shaking his head as he sobered.

"All kidding aside, it kind of makes sense. But it's probably best if you don't rely on old vids for your intel." Jonesy sent her an inquisitive look. "By the way, which one's the insider information con?"

Shannon looked at him suspiciously for a moment, trying to gauge whether or not he was taking her seriously. "The Boesky," she said grudgingly after a moment.

<*Well, we're definitely running that one,*> Kodi said, sounding a bit intrigued. <*What about the others?*>

Jason noticed Shannon was still giving Jonesy a bit of side-eye, as if she wasn't entirely sure she trusted him not to laugh at her again.

"Well, the Jim Brown involves staging a distraction while someone steals—or plants—something of value," she said finally. "Like stealing an access code, or planting breaching nano without being detected."

"So what you're saying is you think we should go on the offensive, rather than just waiting for our contact to reach out to us," Terrance said with a frown.

Shannon shrugged. "It'd be a shame to have the opportunity and not take it."

He gave a slight shake of his head. "This is something you should have run by Tobias before we left. He calls the shots on this operation. Now's not the time to change the plan."

"Well, hold on a second." Jason swiveled around to regard Shannon thoughtfully as he checked his HUD. "We have another half hour before we're on final approach for the spaceport. We could at least discuss it."

Cesar's eyes widened in alarm, and he began to shake his head.

"You aren't serious," the Noctus protested. "This is something that's been years in the making. We can't risk it all on a last-minute change."

"But if an opportunity presents itself to compromise the Hegemony, or plant a tracking algorithm that could siphon off information," Jason argued, "wouldn't that be worth doing, if we felt we could do so without risking the mission?" Holding up a hand, he pinged Tobias.

The shuttle's main screen split, a holo of the Weapon Born appearing beside the vessel's forward view. Swiftly, Jason brought him up to speed.

<All right, lass,> Tobias's image turned to Shannon. *<Let's hear your ideas. I'm not saying I'll agree to them, mind you, but just for argument's sake, what are you thinking?>*

As Shannon laid out her proposal, Jason set up a separate connection between himself, Terrance, and Tobias.

<You know this would be a coup, if we can pull it off,> he told them privately.

After a moment's hesitation, Tobias returned, *<All right, boyo. I'll okay it. But pull back at the first sign they might be onto you. Clear?>*

<Crystal.>

Jason cut the connection with Tobias, toggling the holo back to its forward view once more, then whistled in surprise.

"Hey, get a look at this."

A space had been carved out inside the sprawling capital city. In its center sat Hegemony Headquarters. The campus was set like a jewel in an urban framework, designed to impress.

Jonesy uttered a low "Wow," and Khela shook her head.

"Kind of imposing, isn't it," Shannon murmured.

"Yes," Cesar flicked an eyebrow her way in acknowledgment. "As it was intended."

"Yeah, but this obsession of theirs," Jason shook his head.

"Names like 'Glimmer', 'Incandus', 'Brilliance'.... And I've never seen so many reflective surfaces in my life." He waved a hand at the view as they continued to descend and were able to take in more detail.

"Almost makes you wonder if the city has a code that says all construction must be made with translucent or reflective materials," Terrance agreed. "Good thing we're using the shuttle's sensors. We'd be blinded if we were flying in using our naked eye."

Conversation ceased as Jason brought the *Sable Wind* down gently on the indicated pad at the spaceport, a place that seemed to be trying extra hard to impress. Its fractal planes glittered harshly in Lucent's cool blue light. Fortunately, Cesar had warned them about the optical impact Incandus had on the uninitiated, and he'd come prepared.

As soon as the hatch opened, Jason planned to slip a reproduction pair of ancient aviators over his eyes. He couldn't care less that the act of shading his vision from the light was considered by Luminescent Society to be the equivalent of belching in public. The aviators were special to him, a gift from Calista. They were custom-made, based on the ones she'd seen fighter pilots wearing in an old 2D movie called *Top Gun*, and were one of his most prized possessions.

He shut down the shuttle's propulsion and secured the nav comp. The holo showed several people advancing toward them.

"I think I'm starting to get the hang of this whole caste system thing," Jason mused. "That lead guy's an Irid, right?"

"Yes," Cesar confirmed, pointing at the neckline of the man's suit. "Hospitality Guild, based on the holopatch at his left collar. And the studs that are explicitly *not* on his nose."

Jonesy wrinkled his own nose in response. "Nose, cheekbones, doesn't matter. Either way, those suckers look damned uncomfortable, if you ask me."

"You know they're not. Not any more than these," Khela

remarked. Lifting her arm, she drew a finger across one of the filigree cuffs that had been tattooed from elbow to wrist.

"Just another of the many non-medical applications for mednano. Easy to apply…." She touched one end with the tip of her finger and lifted slightly, and Jason could see the filigree rising up to follow. "And just as easy to remove."

Ostensibly, the golden threads were body art, accessorizing her dress for the occasion. The design was a stylized logogram, symbolizing her family house. But it also served another purpose. A double layer of the new borophene-weave Elastene rested beneath the body art, a stealthed pocket where nano could reside undetected.

"I have to say, I do like the things I can hide under it a lot more than the art itself," Khela admitted with a smile. "I can fit quite a few packets of breaching nano in here."

Terrance slung an arm around her shoulder as they stood. Looking over at Jason, he winked. "I figured out long ago that the way to this woman's heart was with firearms, not flowers."

Jason snickered as Terrance straightened, addressing the AI in his head.

"You ready to imitate an NSAI, my friend?"

The equivalent of a sigh came from Kodi. *<One inanimate augmentation, coming right up.>*

Jason heard Terrance's *<Sorry, buddy>* before he nodded to Jonesy, and the engineer cycled the hatch.

Immediately, the nanokillers that Shannon and Jonesy had installed around the hatch's perimeter began to spark. Flares from thousands of invisible machines as they entered their death throes confirmed that some form of breach nano must have begun marching along the shuttle's hull the moment it came to rest in the docking cradle it had been assigned.

"Well *that's* annoying," Khela murmured, following after Terrance as he strode down the ramp to intercept the welcoming committee. Her glossy, blue-black hair stirred in a light wind, the strands shimmering under the fierce light of the two suns.

Jason slid on his aviators and waited at the top of the ramp, while Jonesy and Shannon confirmed that the nanokillers were holding their own against the invisible assault.

The day was a warm one, with Sirius A at periastron to Lucent. The big star cast a slightly stronger light than its dwarf sibling, and the combined sources gave each person on the tarmac two sharp, distinct shadows.

As much as he appreciated the job they were doing, after a few minutes of enduring the *pizz-ffft* of the nanokillers, the sound began to get on Jason's nerves, and he was ready to strangle a few Irids. He grinned when he saw Khela let out a sharp breath before advancing on the nearest delegate with fire in her eyes.

"Stop sending those things against our shuttle, right *now*," she demanded.

The Irid made an odd bow, combined with a fluid gesture that translated as some form of obeisance to esteemed visitors, according to Jason's overlay.

"Apologies, but Incandus is saturated with nano. What you ask is, sadly, an impossibility," she explained.

Khela stood there for a heartbeat, glowering down at the woman before stepping back to stand next to Terrance.

"Don't worry, ma'am," Jonesy leant over and stage-whispered into her ear. "I've set several very nasty traps for anyone who thinks it's a good idea to try to breach the *Sable Wind*. Let'em try. They'll discover she has teeth."

He shuddered dramatically, and Shannon ducked beneath his arm and added in a dire voice, "Big, sharp, *nasty* ones."

Dark eyes slanted toward the two as Khela considered their words. She nodded in satisfaction. "If it's up to your evil genius standards, this ought to be entertaining. You have optics recording it? Might be some decent viewing material for the flight back to the *Vale*."

Their escort, while obsequious, was also carefully monitoring the byplay, and Jason noted a few uneasy glances exchanged before they were led away to their transport.

* * * * *

Half an hour later, the groundcar deposited them in front of Hegemony Headquarters, where they were met by a security guard clad in brilliant white.

"Greetings, Mister Enfield." The young man stepped aside and, with a grand sweep of his hand, gestured them inside the entrance.

As they entered the gleaming facade, they passed through a saturation curtain of jamming nano, effectively isolating them from their ship.

Terrance couldn't help but feel twitchy about that. It wasn't merely the feeling of being exposed that it presented; it was an uncomfortable reminder that they were out of range of the *Avon Vale*, unable to render aid should something happen to the ship or its crew.

The fact that many of the team left aboard their ship were AIs that would be considered property by their hosts did not escape him.

Terrance saw a token appear on his HUD, sent across a secured network that had popped up on his overlay the moment they were behind the Hegemony's firewall. Its header suggested that it contained bios of the senior executives, as well as an agenda for the day.

Shannon took the lead, carefully sandboxing the token and divesting it of its trackers, infiltration subroutines, and other harmful worms that had been lurking within its code.

<*Okay, sending you the distilled version now,*> she informed him.

Terrance stifled a snort when he saw a new, silvery token entitled "Bullshit-free Agenda" pop up on the combat net.

He looked up as a woman approached.

"Welcome to the Hegemony, Mister Enfield," she said with a

slight smile as she held out her hand for him to shake. "I'm Shai, adjunct to our CEO, Pharris. She is most eager to meet you, sir." Ignoring the rest of the party, she turned and beckoned him to follow her. "How have you found Candesca so far?" she asked conversationally as she walked.

"Impressive," Terrance murmured, a bit mystified that she'd ignored the rest of his team, but playing along.

Jason, Khela, and the rest fell in behind him.

<Are we supposed to be your silent retinue? Seen, but not heard?> Jason's amused voice tickled Terrance's ear, and he suppressed a grin of his own.

<Now, children, behave, and I'll let you sit at the adult table when we get to the boardroom.>

He earned a mental snort from Khela for that. He refocused his attention on Shai's words before he lost the conversational thread.

"The spaceport manager is fond of giving newcomers an aerial tour of Candesca before landing," she was saying, "so I would imagine he vectored you through some of our more attractive architectural features and landmarks."

"I'd say so. Your headquarters makes quite an impression from the air," he murmured politely.

The route she took felt contrived and circuitous, but Terrance quickly realized that it led past small clusters of individuals, all of whom seemed to share a similar style and pattern to their metal studs. He pointed them out to Cesar.

<Overseers and adjuncts,> the Noctus man informed them. *<These serve as the right-hand to the vice presidents.>*

<Advance scout of sorts, reporting in to their superiors before we arrive?> Jason guessed, and Cesar nodded.

Terrance spied Hume in the center of one of the clusters, and noted the man was careful not to make eye contact with anyone from the *Vale*.

After a few dozen handshakes—not to mention countermeasures against an equal number of attempts to drop breaching nano onto him—Terrance heard Jason blow out a breath in frustration.

<Stars, it's like peeling away at the layers of an onion to get to the core,> he complained.

<I can appreciate a bit of layered protection around a core,> Shannon sent. *<But having to walk this gauntlet to get to their CEO feels excessive.>*

<Welcome to the wonderful world of corporate life,> Terrance inserted dryly.

<You think Cesar's informant is right about all these people?> Khela asked, her tone wrapped in a disdain not reflected by the serene expression of her face. She had transformed as they arrived, shedding her combat readiness, and donning a zen-like mien that reminded Terrance so much of her father, Noa.

<About how dangerous they are? Oh, you can count on it,> Terrance's voice held conviction. *<People climbing the corporate ladder are the same everywhere. Tread carefully around them.>*

<Why?> Jonesy asked. *<What makes them so high-risk?>*

<They're cutthroat and ambitious,> the businessman explained. *<Actively seeking ways to gain the recognition of senior executives. If you give them any reason to suspect you, they'll use that knowledge to curry favor with their superiors.>*

<Guh,> Shannon grunted. *<Let's hurry up and get this over with. The longer I'm here, the dirtier I feel.>*

MD40

STELLAR DATE: 07.02.3302 (Adjusted Gregorian)
LOCATION: ESS *Kuroi Kaze*
REGION: Lucent, Luminescent Space, Sirian Hegemony

Seated in the *Kuroi Kaze*'s jump seat directly behind Beau, Marta leant forward as the pilot brought up a display of MD40 on the shuttle's holo. He cycled through various feeds, showing them the damage from different angles as he sent the *Kuroi Kaze* ghosting silently past the remains of Assembly Sector 9.

The Marines seated behind her—Ramon and Xiao, Corporals Lena and Tama—watched silently as dragnets meticulously skimmed the black for debris.

"Cold consolation, I know," Marta murmured, "but at least their families will have a body to bury."

"Oh, they're not doing that to retrieve the dead," their Irid escort, Jim, assured her. "It's to protect shipping from debris damage."

His casual tone irritated the doctor, but as she turned to tell him what she thought of his attitude, the bleakness she saw in his eyes stopped her cold.

Completely at odds with his tone, it was a raw expression, filled with rage.

She returned her attention to the feed, where repair crews were swarming the jagged edges at the incident site, cutting away the twisted metal remains.

"They going to try to rebuild?" Xiao, one of the Marines, asked into the quiet, and Jim shook his head.

"No, the area's been deemed a total loss. They're to seal the breach and move on."

<*Just like that?*> Varanee's quiet voice sounded inside the shuttle.

Jim shot Marta a look as he responded to Varanee. "Yes. Just like that."

He directed Beau to match velocity with the platform and drift between two of its rotating arms. There, a little-used airlock was hidden in the shadows, tucked near a cross-spar that sported a patchwork quilt of repairs.

Jim turned to address the four humans in the ship. "We'll be met by our contact, but we'll need to be quick about our exit. Have your gear packed and ready to transfer into their lorry as soon as we have a positive lock, and the hatch cycles."

Beau swiveled in his pilot's cradle to spear Jim with a severe look. "I don't want anything to interfere with my ability to communicate with these Marines," the AI, a former space force fighter pilot from Tau Ceti, warned him.

"Nothing will," Jim assured him. "There's a local node just outside this airlock, and I have a packet of Luminescent override nano. I'll drop it while your people are loading into the lorry, and set up a secured net. You'll have full access to the team at all times."

Beau was the only one of the team not wearing Noctus clothing. The rest were garbed in shapeless coveralls. Marta tugged at the collar of hers, attempting to adjust the coarse, baggy material into a more comfortable position.

<*Ugly things, aren't they?*> Varanee commented, and Marta sent her an unamused grunt.

The material was sturdy and durable—a result of a cost/benefit analysis, Jim had told them earlier.

<*Cost/benefit, my ass. Nano-infused clothing is much more durable…and comfortable,*> she retorted.

Her senior physician's avatar nodded. <*Yes, but it wouldn't have the psychological benefits of keeping the Noctus in their place,*> the AI reminded her. <*At least you have your base layer, and Elastene weave between it and your skin.*>

<*Small mercies,*> Marta snorted. <*Have I mentioned I hate the*

Lumins?>

Her complaint was interrupted by a question from another of the Marines as the team began to move back toward the shuttle's hatch.

"What about access to the platform's security protocol?" Corporal Lena asked.

At Jim's brief hesitation, the AI paired with Lena spoke up, her voice taking on a hard edge.

<*Look, I don't give two qubits about your Hegemony,*> Tama said. <*This isn't about company secrets, it's about freeing slaves.*>

Jim raised his hands, an embarrassed look crossing his face. "Sorry. Old habits die hard." Dropping his hands, he nodded. "Yes, the override will slip us behind the firewall with top-level clearance. We'll be able to access any security feed and control every form of monitoring they employ."

Ramon smiled, clapping a hand on the Irid's shoulder as the man stopped in front of the hatch. "Now that's what I'm talking about. With that kind of intel, when things hit the accretion disk, we'll have a fighting chance to break free."

Xiao snorted as he maneuvered past Jim to the sled that held Marta's medical gear and the Marines' extra ammo. "Notice he said 'when', not 'if'," he advised in a voice tinged with amusement. When the Irid looked confused, he added, "Marines *always* assume there's an accretion disk. No plan ever survives contact with the enemy, no matter how well thought out it might be. Trust me, we know."

Jim just shook his head, his expression a bit discomfited.

The craft bumped slightly when it made contact with the surface of the platform. Marta stood and hoisted her carry sack—filled with the medications she didn't trust to anyone else—as the Marines shouldered their own packs.

At a nod from Lena, Ramon cycled the hatch.

* * * * *

The medic who met them at the airlock was tall and spare. Clad in a stiff and shapeless gray coverall that looked as if it had once been blue, she introduced herself as Ivy. She motioned for them to hurry, and the movement drew Marta's attention to faded stains that edged the suit's wrists. Glancing down, she saw that they spattered the front of the garment as well.

<*Blood?*> she asked Varanee.

<*Maybe? Hard to tell.*>

Ivy had parked a lorry in front of the airlock, blocking their entrance from view. The vehicle had the rod of Asclepius—the time-worn and traditional emblem symbolizing medicine—emblazoned on its side.

The fireteam immediately began loading up, the Noctus directing them with the efficiency of a chief surgeon in an operating theatre. Lena directed Marta to sit in back with Ramon and Xiao, while she sat on the bench seat up front. The medic folded her spare frame into the front seat beside Lena, and set the lorry in motion.

Ramon and Xiao flanked Marta on the second row bench, behind the lorry's tall, opaque walls. Although enough to block a Noctus's view, the walls were no hindrance to her augmented eyesight, nor to those of the Marines who sat on either side of her. Both were using their enhanced optics to monitor their surroundings. Marta had heard Lena order them to do so "on all EM frequencies."

She stuck her head through the small, open window between the lorry's storage area and the driver's bench.

"So you're the platform's patcher?" she asked, and Ivy nodded, sparing her a glance.

"One of 'em," the woman clarified. "I'd just as soon not be. Most days, I feel I've pulled a blinder if no one dies on me."

"A blinder?" Lena asked, her eyes not straying from her scan of their surroundings.

"Not a word where you folk come from, eh?" The woman grunted. "A blinder's fooling you into thinking I'm competent."

A smile teased Lena's mouth, but she didn't respond.

"What kind of cases do you normally treat?" Marta was pressing for more information, hoping she'd guessed the platform's needs accurately.

"Mostly accidental injuries," the gray-haired woman driving the vehicle replied as she steered the lorry down a narrow path set aside for motorized vehicles.

If Marta had to guess, Ivy was somewhere around sixty-five or seventy years old. Her hands, spotted with age, grasped the yoke, navigating the kilometers of corridor with surety.

"You see a lot of sprains, broken bones, lacerations, things like that, I'd imagine," Marta murmured, and she saw the medic's profile nod. "What about acute hematopoietic situations?"

Ivy's expression darkened at the question. Acute hematopoiesis killed off bone marrow stem cells, the ones that replenished the lifeblood of humans.

Marta felt Varanee move anxiously in her mind as she voiced the question, the AI-equivalent of holding her breath.

AIs didn't have to worry about blood cell death, but very energetic, heavy ions could have a similar effect on AIs. A dense, high-energy stream of energetic electrons had the potential to penetrate deep inside hardened circuitry, burying themselves into dielectric materials, and causing intense, localized breakdowns.

"You're talking about the killin' of stem cells and the like, from ionizing radiation," Ivy said after a moment. She jerked her head toward the outer bulkhead, her expression bitter. "That star out there's an active one. Has solar spews several times a week. Just about everyone on this sun-cursed platform's immunosuppressed because of it."

"How often do you get severe cases?"

Ivy thought for a moment, fingers drumming the rim of the steering yoke. "Once every few months, someone gets caught in a tug or a skiff during a big 'un."

She paused, and Marta could see the woman's mouth tighten.

"If they're close enough in for us to get to them in time, we can minimize it. But if they're out there long enough to receive more than a five-thousand-milligray dose…."

Marta sucked air in through her teeth.

5,000 mGy was a threshold known historically as the LD50/30, Lethal Dose for 50% of the population in 30 days.

At least for unaugmented humans, without major medical intervention.

"Do you have the facilities to—"

"No."

Ivy's voice, curt, cut through the question, and Marta fell silent.

Ivy pulled the lorry up to a closed blast door, hopped out, and banged on the bulkhead three times. The blast doors began to creak open, and a head popped through. Nodding to Ivy, the head disappeared, and the doors continued their ponderous retreat into the bulkhead.

<*They're doing that manually,*> Varanee observed.

Stars, the things we take for granted… Marta thought.

With the lorry through and the blast doors closed, Ivy gestured the fireteam out. Noctus streamed out of nearby openings to help unload as Ivy led Marta and Xiao down one of the passages.

The cavernous space into which it terminated was dimly-lit, but it wasn't dim enough to hide the filth and squalor. Marta's senses were assaulted by the smell of unwashed bodies and the burning of refuse, contained within large, rounded cylinders.

The space appeared to be partitioned off by tarps, hung from long ropes that spanned the width of it. From where she stood, the entire bay seemed to be sectioned off in such a manner.

She attempted to hide her shock, but knew she was unsuccessful when Ivy laughed. It was a dry, rusty sound, filled with rancor-free amusement.

"Don't believe everything you see, patcher," Ivy advised.

Marta exchanged glances with Xiao, who shrugged, equally mystified. He followed Ivy as she gestured them forward, ducking beneath the first greasy-looking tarp. The next section they emerged into fared no better. She could just make out pallets lining the edges of the makeshift wall on the far side, about five meters away.

Ivy motioned impatiently, and Xiao led the way, pulling a maglev hand truck laden with the medical equipment they had brought along.

<*Core, this is….*> Tama's voice faded as the AI struggled to describe what they were seeing.

<*Even worse than the quarantine camps back in Tau Ceti.*> Xiao's mental voice was the merest ghost of a whisper, carried to them across the combat net.

But it was Ramon's voice, gutted, that cut through the team.

<*Stars, yes.*>

Those two words, with an undertone fraught with memory, recalled all the Marine had experienced on his homeworld of Galene. It was then Marta recalled that he'd fallen in the line of duty. His nanophage-ravaged body had been recovered, but he'd perished before Phantom Blade could defeat the forces set against them.

Once back aboard the *Avon Vale,* Marta had performed the reconstructive surgery herself, and had reintegrated the backup that the Marines had made of the man's consciousness prior to the battle with his rebuilt brain.

<*Not on my watch.*> Tama's response crackled between them as Xiao disappeared through the next row of tarps.

Marta moved to follow, but came to an abrupt stop, Lena bumping into her, as Xiao's shock telegraphed itself to them all.

<*Stars….*> Varanee's voice was filled with trepidation. <*What now?*>

OPENING SALVO

STELLAR DATE: 07.02.3302 (Adjusted Gregorian)
LOCATION: Hegemony Headquarters, Candesca
REGION: Lucent, Luminescent Space, Sirian Hegemony

<Stars, this is like one of those ancient Old-Earth gauntlet thingies,> Shannon complained. Now that she mentioned it, Terrance had a difficult time banishing the comparison from his head. The long, arduous journey into the Hegemony boardroom *did* feel a bit like a gauntlet.

He heaved a mental sigh of relief when finally the doors to the room that Shai led them to slid open at their approach.

The adjunct stepped aside with a slight bow as she waved them in. Beyond her, Terrance could see a table around which seven people sat. Behind each VP, grouped in twos and threes, were small semicircles of empty seating. These, he assumed, were for the executives' overseers and adjuncts.

Once they cleared the entrance, this was confirmed by the steady stream of people who followed them in. Many of these were individuals he'd spotted earlier—Hume included.

"President Pharris," Adjunct Shai announced from her position by the entrance, "may I present Terrance Enfield of Enfield Holdings. And his associates," she added as an afterthought.

The CEO rose, her legs appearing to be fused to some sort of hoverplate. As Shai moved to take her position behind Pharris's chair at the head of the table, the CEO floated over to Terrance and wordlessly extended a hand.

Taking it, he smiled. "It's a pleasure to meet you, Madam President. May I present my wife, Khela?" He turned and drew Khela up next to him.

The Marine smiled enchantingly and tilted her head in a regal nod.

"And the man who captains our flagship, the *Avon Vale*, Jason Andrews," Terrance continued.

Jason smiled and nodded as Pharris gestured them to the conference table.

"Terrance—may I call you Terrance?" Pharris spoke for the first time, her voice a sibilant whisper. "I would like for you to meet our most trusted leaders, the people charged with the smooth operation of the Hegemony."

Shai managed the introductions as Pharris, Terrance, and the rest of the team took their seats. Terrance looked up as the man across from him—Rubin, his name was—leant forward, expression curious.

"I understand you have some rather fascinating technologies that might be of interest to the Hegemony," Rubin began, his smile inviting Terrance to elaborate.

The exec opened his palms with a modest shrug. "We do indeed. And we look forward to exploring the possibility of trade relations with Sirius."

"The Enfield Corporation has an excellent systemwide reputation," Cyrus nodded sagely. "I'm certain there are any number of ways we might mutually benefit from a business partnership."

<*Cyrus is VP of Infrastructure,*> Cesar's voice informed them on a private channel. <*The finance division reports up to him.*>

"I'm confident you'll find some of the more innovative new materials Enfield Scientific has developed to be quite lucrative," Terrance acknowledged Cyrus's comment with a tilt of his head.

"And Enfield Aerospace," Jonesy interjected. "Not to mention Enfield Dynamics."

Terrance acknowledged Jonsey's addition with a smile. "As you may know, Enfield Holdings is the licensor for a number of patents. Each one has been filed and registered in every colonized FGT system within a hundred light years of Sol."

<*That's code for 'we'll sue your ass six ways from the galactic core if*

you try to rip us off and sell cheap knockoffs in any one of those systems'.> Shannon added privately. Her mental voice held a menacing bite to it. Not surprising, since she was a patent holder for almost half of them.

He smiled before continuing. "What this means to you, friends, is that I'm authorized to negotiate on behalf of these Enfield designs and technologies." He paused, allowing his smile to broaden. "I'm also in a position to grant exclusivities."

"Now that's what I like to hear," a jovial voice cut in, as the man across from Jonesy spoke up. "The kind of talk that's good for business all around."

<*Currin, Sales and Marketing.*> Cesar's voice continued the private commentary.

Terrance nodded judiciously. "We'd be happy to entertain licensing proposals, or perhaps negotiate a manufacturing and supply agreement or two."

He let his smile fade a bit.

"I must admit, however...." He paused, his glance drifting across the faces of those seated at the table. "A few reports have come to our attention recently and caused a bit of concern on our end."

"Oh, really?" a woman said archly, raising an elegant brow. "And what might that be?" Terrance's overlay informed him this was Berit, VP of Resources and Extraction.

"He's referring to an explosion that occurred on one of your platforms earlier this week," Jason interjected smoothly. "One of your manufacturing plants, I believe."

"Oh, that." The man who spoke waved his hand dismissively. Terrance's overlay helpfully informed him that Gavin at least had the right to comment on the incident, given that the platform in question fell under his management. "A minor incident. Very recoverable."

"Such a tragedy. Truly." The comment came from the lone VP who had yet to speak—Francesca, Vice President of Strategic

Planning, and the woman Hume sat behind.

Cold eyes rested momentarily on Terrance's face, and he fought to keep his expression impassive as her gaze drifted across the Enfield contingent before returning to him.

She sent a patently insincere look Terrance's way, her voice dripping with false commiseration. "It's unfortunate, but incidents like this are just part of the process." She lifted one hand in a negligent wave. "You understand. The cost of doing business."

Terrance experienced a wave of revulsion at the woman's words. Cesar had told them this was the Hegemony's official position on their workforce, but hearing about it was one thing; coming face to face with it was another thing entirely.

It took all Terrance's control to paste a sympathetic smile he didn't feel on his face. "Nevertheless," he said, shaking his head remorsefully, "it would be a matter of concern to us as investors. You understand, I'm sure."

"Perhaps…." Khela's voice was pitched to sound contemplative. She drew the word out, her hand drawing mindless patterns on the surface of the table as she continued almost idly, "Perhaps a tour of one of your platforms could be arranged?"

She looked up and leant toward Gavin, propping her chin up with the palm of her hand as she favored him with a sultry smile. "You could show us what safety procedures you have in place, help us to see how our future investments might be protected."

Terrance hid a smirk at the slightly glazed look that came across Gavin's eyes, and straightened, trying to appear as if the idea was one the team hadn't carefully scripted out.

"I like it," he announced, turning an inquiring eye to Pharris.

"What about an exchange?" Berit spoke up once more, her eyes sliding from Rubin to Francesca before rounding on Terrance with a questioning smile.

"An exchange?" Jason asked with the lift of his brow. "What do you propose?"

Berit slanted a sultry look Jason's way. "You show us yours," she purred, "and we'll show you ours."

Terrance coughed to hide a laugh as Rubin's mouth twitched.

"I believe what my colleague was suggesting was a tour of your ship," Rubin said, slanting a look at Berit. "In return, we'll take you to one of our platforms."

"Of course." Terrance recovered, pasting a gracious smile on his face.

Francesca chimed in. "That way, you can see our management style. You'll excuse us, of course," she smiled, but it did not reach her eyes as she added, "if we limit what you're able to see. Intellectual property must be protected, after all."

Terrance tilted his head in understanding. "IP is a company's most valuable commodity, after all."

He paused as if considering her offer, even though Cesar had told them in advance that this would be suggested. Hume's contact had sold the idea to the VPs as a way to infiltrate the *Vale* and hack it for tech.

It went against the grain to let them attempt such a thing, but the only possible way to extract the AIs without the execs noticing was to do so in Marta's medical bay. They had to get the execs with embedded AIs up to the *Vale* somehow.

The plan to extract the AIs was the operation's weakest link, and they all knew it. This, right here, was the part most likely to hit the accretion disk.

Terrance shifted to regard Jason. "What do you say, Captain? Think a tour of the *Avon Vale* could be arranged?"

Jason drummed his fingers on the table for a moment before nodding his agreement.

"So it's settled, then." Berit smiled. "I, for one, look forward to seeing more of you and your ship, Captain." She sent Jason a suggestive look.

Shannon kicked him under the table. <*Stars,*> she sent to the team, her voice teasing, <*I think Jason has a fan.*>

<*Stuff it, short stuff,*> Jason growled.

A peal of mental laughter was all Terrance heard in return while Jason gave a polite, noncommittal response.

After that, Pharris invited Terrance to give a brief summary of some of the tech he would be willing to offer. A discussion ensued about various investment strategy options, with licensing deals posed against percent stakes.

Pharris promised to have a few proposals drafted for his consideration. They would be sent to the *Avon Vale* sometime during the several-day-long tour that would commence after the reception aboard the ship had been completed.

"Enough business," Berit proclaimed, clapping her hands together with a lascivious grin. "You know what they say about all work and no play," she added with a wink to Jason.

Rubin chuckled, and Terrance noted with dismay that he appeared to be eyeing Shannon with some interest.

"Indeed," the man agreed. "We'd be remiss if we didn't provide you with a representative slice of Luminescent life while you are here."

From the head of the table, Pharris smiled and stood. "I think," she said in her thready voice, "that we're done for the day. I understand that the Culinary Guild has outdone themselves this evening. We do hope you enjoy our hospitality, Mister Enfield."

"I heard they've acquired a few bottles of the 2984 vintage from Blaze Valley Winery on Radiance, too," Cyrus remarked. "Do try some, I highly recommend it."

Currin chuckled. "Well of course you do. You own the winery."

Cyrus adopted a wounded expression. "That simply means I'm in a position to know the best wines our system has to offer. Trust me, the 2984 is not to be missed."

"Well then," Terrance said in a tone of finality as he pushed away from the table, interrupting the executives' banter. "I don't know about you, but meetings like this always work up an excellent appetite. I for one, I'm looking forward to this evening."

Francesca lifted her hand in a dismissive gesture, indicating the man who sat behind her. "My overseer will escort you to your accommodations for the evening."

Hume tipped his head deferentially, then stepped forward, giving no indication by his demeanor that they were anything but strangers.

"If you will follow me, please? We have reserved rooms for you at a nearby resort, so that you can refresh yourselves before dinner."

* * * * *

<Did you see the look Terrance sent your way?> Rae asked as Francesca exited the sandboxed data mining room, and followed her peers to the secured offices several stories underground. *<That man does **not** like you, not at all.>*

Francesca sent Rae a mental wink as the lift descended. *<Good to know I have the evil witch routine down pat. >*

The lift opened to a satellite executive suite that had been built for just such occasions as this: moments of pomp and ceremony that the Hegemony traditionally conducted planetside, away from their working headquarters on Brilliance Station.

The room where they'd met Enfield was, in truth, no boardroom at all. Instead, it was equipped with every possible form of surveillance the Hegemony had to hand.

None but the VPs themselves, their overseers, and their adjuncts had access to the true boardroom. The one where they conducted their most secret and confidential meetings was in orbit around the planet.

She followed Cyrus inside, making her way with a studied casualness over to a plush seating arrangement. Maneuvering the board into a trip up to the *Vale* had been the easy part; this next was a bit trickier.

<You did have a chance to bring the rest up to speed on the plan?> she inquired yet again, and Rae shot her a scolding look.

<Of course I did, silly.>

<Well, forgive me for triple-checking on this before I stick my neck out and get it chopped off,> she returned, although her words had no heat behind them. *<You're* **sure** *Quincy and Wallis can be party to this charade without it triggering their shackling bonds?>*

<Just don't address them at all, and they should be fine,> Rae instructed. *<It's not like you're asking them to actively engage. If they remain passively quiet, the shackles shouldn't compel them.>*

Francesca sent her a mental nod before turning and pinning Cyrus with a questioning look. Infrastructure was in charge of the company's tech division, which meant that the surveillance systems of the room where the meeting had been held fell to him as well.

"So what did we learn about our new friends just now?" she inquired as she took a seat on a nearby lounge.

"You mean other than that Enfield's wife is someone I plan to do my damndest to seduce?" Gavin interposed, laughing salaciously as he walked past. "Woman's not half-bad for a foreigner."

Currin snorted. "You're just bored and looking for a flavor that's different than what you can get here at home. The silver one's cuter, but the captain—" He took a seat across from Francesca, slinging an arm along the sofa and winking at Gavin suggestively. "Now *there's* a prime specimen. That one's got my vote."

"Hands off," Berit admonished, slapping Currin's arm as she passed behind the sofa on her way to the bar. "He's all mine."

Weary of the innuendo and byplay, Francesca attempted to get the conversation back on track.

"Well…?" she prompted, sitting up and looking expectantly at Cyrus as the man settled into a chair opposite her.

Cyrus shook his head, his eyes focusing on a distant midpoint as he mentally scanned the intel his people had curated for him. "Their tech is good," he admitted after a moment. "As good as ours. Every attempt we made to introduce a trojan into their systems was met with a counter-challenge, and every form of breach nano was destroyed."

"What about passive surveillance?" Rubin asked. "Did we glean anything from biometrics? Was there any particular topic that seemed to upset or worry them?"

"Other than Berit's obvious interest in their captain, you mean?" Cyrus's brow rose sardonically before he shook his head. "No, nothing."

"That just makes our tour of their ship that much more critical to our endeavors," Francesca said, as she exchanged meaningful glances with both Berit and Rubin.

Rubin nodded and leant forward. "Our AIs will have a much better chance of breaching their systems once on board," he agreed.

Berit smirked, lifting her glass in a toast to Francesca, silently acknowledging her as the author of the plan.

Cyrus regarded them with narrowed eyes. "Is this true?"

Francesca leant back and looked up at the ceiling, addressing Rae. "Well?" She fashioned her tone to be what the others would expect, harsh and demanding. "Don't just sit there like a fool. Answer Cyrus."

Rae's voice projected into the room, her tone pitched to sound properly cowed. *<Yes, ma'am. Proximity to ship's systems, near one of their nodes, should make access to their data a more convenient process.>*

Cyrus settled back, a satisfied expression crossing his face. "Very good," he murmured.

Currin frowned. "So what are we going to do about this request of theirs to tour a platform?"

Gavin looked perturbed by that. "Not one of mine," he said sharply. "I ordered the rest of the manufacturing platforms to pick up the slack the MD40 incident caused, so they're in the midst of a workload redistribution. The last thing we need is for someone to go poking around in that mess."

Francesca sighed. "Well, then...." She looked up suddenly, as if a thought had just occurred to her. Pivoting, she speared Berit with a questioning look. "My overseer just returned from doing a planning survey on SR71. His report indicated it was tidy and well-organized. What about that one?"

Berit wrinkled her nose in distaste. "And have prying eyes all up in my business? No, thank you. Pick one of Rubin's."

A note of alarm curled up from Rae. <*It **has** to be that one. How are we going to convince her—*>

<*Working on it.*> Francesca tilted her head toward Berit and nodded, acknowledging her point. "No one wants the intrusion. But no one expects a complete tour, either," she pointed out. "Just show them a representative section of the platform, something pretty to look at, and move them on their way."

Berit shook her head. "Miguel's too busy to babysit a group of clients right now." She eyed Gavin. "Maybe we send them to MD40 and let them see how well we clean up after a little mishap?"

Francesca realized that the woman wasn't going to move on this issue. She tried one last time, infusing her tone with admiration.

"Hume had some very nice things to say about 71 in my report. Are you *sure* you won't reconsider?" Then, with a silent apology to the *Vale*'s captain, she let her expression turn sly as she suggested, "Maybe you should go along. I'm sure there'll be plenty of time along the way to get to know that captain of theirs, up close and personal...."

Berit looked considering, then dismissed the idea. "Tempting, but I'm too busy to step away from Brilliance right now."

"I suppose I could spare Hume for a few days, if that's your only objection," Francesca offered, which caused Rubin to slit his eyes and cock his head at her suspiciously.

"You seem awfully intent on *that* platform being their destination," he observed. "Any particular reason why?"

<*Francesca….*> Rae's voice hitched in concern.

Francesca relaxed into the lounger with a wave of her hand. "None other than a desire to close the deal," she said, imbuing her tone with amusement and a touch of challenge as she met his suspicion by going on the offensive herself. "Any reason why you *aren't* focused on that?"

The diversion worked. Rubin sat up in irritation, shooting her a glare. "I thought we were done talking business for the day? I know I am. Plenty of time to figure out the platform thing before they're ready to sign. By then, they could have forgotten all about it." Standing, he dismissed the conversation.

<*What now?*> Rae whispered.

Francesca sighed. <*I don't think there's anything else we can do at the moment without raising suspicions.*>

*****

The next morning, Francesca awoke to a comm from Berit. As she played it, she realized with some shock that it was directed to Miguel, a copy sent to her out of courtesy.

The message informed the overseer that Hume would be leaving with the Enfield delegation in three days to escort them to platform SR71, where he would conduct a brief tour.

What in stars…? How…?

Unwilling to question her good fortune, Francesca didn't assuage her curiosity by asking Berit what had caused her to change her mind. Francesca just accepted the gift and didn't pursue the matter.

Had she done so, the station might have disclosed a record of Francesca leaving her apartments shortly after retiring for the evening, and entering Berit's quarters…and then leaving just minutes after having arrived.

And her chrono might have revealed another missing block of time that, had she checked, would have correlated to Rae opting to power down her core once more.

All for no apparent reason.

SLEIGHT OF HAND

STELLAR DATE: 07.02.3302 (Adjusted Gregorian)
LOCATION: Platform MD40
REGION: Sirius A, Noctilucent Space, Sirian Hegemony

<*Stars!*> Xiao's shocked comment rang across the combat net, freezing Marta in her tracks.

With a mental shout to get down, Lena shoved past, her weapon out as she moved deeper into the platform's hold, ordering Xiao to report. Marta crouched on the deck, mentally replaying everything they'd seen thus far on MD40.

Nothing that I can think of to cause such a reaction….

<*Well, stars shitting plasma,*> Lena sent, amusement in her voice as she ducked under the tarp. <*Didn't expect this.*>

Lena's dry riposte had Marta running to catch up to them.

<*Shucks, ma'am. Never heard you cuss before. Hey, Ramon, it's all a front.*>

As Marta lifted the tarp, she saw Xiao send Ramon a feed from his suit. The first two rows had been a sham. From the third row of the abandoned cargo area, continuing to the rear bulkhead, a spare but pristine living space presented itself, orderly and neat. Here, Noctus moved with purpose; some tended the wounded, while others worked a soup line, mended torn dry goods, or sorted supplies.

Marta's face broke out into an appreciative grin. "Sneaky," she commented to Ivy, and the medic tilted her head.

"Necessary," the Noctus corrected. "No Lucent overseer's going to breathe such soiled air as what's out there," she said, nudging her head back toward the entrance.

"And no Irid's going to want to be associated with such filth, either," Jim commented with a slight quirk of his lips as he joined them.

"Well, then," Marta said, clapping her hands together. "Let's get to it, shall we? We brought you some of our medsynth banks. They're loaded with files from our database, every medicine we have. Use the nano stored inside to print what you need when you need it."

Ivy shook her head. "That's as good as magic to us, you know. No one here's ever had nano used on them, least-a-ways not for anything good."

Lena frowned.

Seeing the expression, their Irid guide explained, "The only nano on a platform is what's inside the Lumin garrison, and they only use it to subdue anything they consider might be an uprising."

The Marine's expression cleared, although her frown remained. "Well, hopefully these'll level the playing field a bit for you." She gestured to the platform around her. "Given that you work in metals, you should have no trouble feeding it formation material, so the system should last you a good, long while."

Ivy nodded in a dazed fashion as Xiao lifted the handle of the hand truck.

"Where would you like them?" he asked.

Ivy pointed and moved toward a rear partition.

"We also brought some NSAI-managed medical units," Xiao added as they followed in her wake. "You can use them to train new medics, or to assist you with your own diagnoses."

<We'd also like to treat your most critical patients, and prep any you've managed to tag as deceased for transport back to our shuttle,> Varanee began, but the AI ground to a halt at Ivy's sudden turn and abortive gesture.

Glancing around her, the Noctus stepped closer to the visitors and addressed the AI. "Let's just keep your presence a secret between us, okay? An AI would be a powerful tempting source of information for some. No reason to tempt anyone to turn you in, in exchange for—" Ivy broke off with a shrug.

<*Message received,*> Tama murmured over the combat net.

"Still," Marta said, as the Marines began unloading the medical gear, "Doctor Varanee's right. Xiao can handle the unpacking, while you, Varanee, and I look over your more severe cases."

With a nod, Ivy pulled Marta away from the team, and they left the Marines to finish unloading the gear.

Marta felt a wave of admiration for the resourcefulness of the Noctus as her gaze swept the area. <*Not a single thing I can fault them on,*> she murmured to Varanee.

<*Their triage has been spot-on, given what little they've had on hand,*> the AI agreed.

They dipped under the last row of tarps separating the ambulatory patients from those who had been more severely hurt. Marta froze, tarp still clutched in her hand, as she surveyed the wounded before them.

She dropped the rough fabric and stepped forward as a tremor of shock and dismay emanated from Varanee.

<*I knew there was an explosion,*> the AI sent, <*but I don't think I realized how acute the traumatic insult was that these people suffered.*>

"Yes," Marta murmured, her eyes drifting from patient to patient. "Definitely the ones most in need of our help. They're going to be the most challenging cases to transport to the shuttle, too."

<*It's been some time since I've seen such carnage,*> Varanee admitted. <*Not since my third-block residency in emergency medicine.*>

<*I remember those days,*> Marta responded, a rueful expression coloring her mental tone as she moved to examine a woman on the nearest pallet. <*It's a bit different, experiencing it out in the real world, so to speak. At least, for me it was.*>

A tendril of curiosity drifted across her mind, inviting her to expound.

<*Well, for one thing,*> Marta reminded her fellow physician, <*we humans were run ragged. Shifts that easily ran sixteen to twenty straight hours. Mods can only supplant a human's need to sleep for so long before*

our systems shut down.>

She shook her head, recalling how much of her time as a resident had been spent in a state of exhaustion. *<I think it's one thing to see such traumatic injuries during the numbed state humans exist in during residency. It's an entirely different thing to come face to face with it after being in private practice for a few years. Especially,>* she added, *<if ER medicine isn't your specialty of choice.>*

<But…?>

Marta laughed, and Varanee sent her a mental snort.

<I'm in here, you know,> the AI reminded her. *<I could sense a 'but' coming.>*

<All right. ***But,*** *>* Marta smiled, *<as a military doctor—assigned to a covert task force like Phantom Blade—I've seen my share of extreme physical insult to the human body. More than I care to, unfortunately.>*

The conversation ended as the two physicians turned their full attention to the Noctus needing their care. Ivy motioned to a Noctus with a handheld device, beckoning him over to them, and he made careful notes of the diagnoses and treatments as the doctors prescribed them.

As they neared the last few patients, Marta turned to the Noctus holding the tablet. "Ask Specialist Xiao if he's ready to begin synthesizing some of those therapies for you," she suggested, pointing over at the area where Xiao and Lena had set up their supplies. "We'll take care of the notation for these last two ourselves."

The young man nodded, relief evident in his eyes as he shot a quick glance at the remaining injured before running back to join the Marines.

"Don't think ill of the boy," Ivy said, watching him leave. "Not many are used to seeing the full extent of damage the human body can take."

Marta nodded sympathetically as they turned to examine the two who would be the most challenging to treat. Both were covered in third-degree burns over a good portion of their bodies.

The woman had taken the explosion in the back; the man had been facing her when the flash fire hit.

As they approached, the Noctus who was administering fluids rose to stand quietly beside Ivy.

"He's restless today," she reported. "Keeps claiming it's his fault, and to let him die."

"And her?" Ivy nodded to the makeshift cradle, in which the woman was slung face-down.

"She keeps telling him to stuff it," the woman chuckled quietly. "And she keeps reminding him she's the boss, and that she'll put him on report if he doesn't shut his trap."

Marta slipped the glove off her left hand and rolled up the sleeve of her coveralls, freeing her to use her medsleeve. Kneeling next to the man, her eyes tallied the injuries she could see as the sleeve gave her a more detailed account.

His face and hands were the worst. The fibrous tissue that formed the outer framework of his eyelids had been burnt away, the sclera of his eyes glaring blindly up at the bulkhead. Muscles around the orbital bones still contracted in an involuntary blink reflex. As she watched, the Noctus who had been tending the two burn victims slipped back into place between them, reaching for a bottle of lubricating drops she then carefully dripped onto each cornea.

"Leh. Eee. Ooh," the man's voice rasped, the words coming mangled from ruined lips.

"Shut up, Ralfe," a tired, slurred voice came from the cradle. "No one's letting you go."

The man moved restlessly. "Ehh. Race. Dah. Oid."

"You're not embracing the void," the Noctus who had applied the drops soothed. The woman in the cradle coughed a laugh, her pain-filled words not unkind. "You still owe me half a shift from your last paycheck, you know. Can't be cheating the company like that, Ralfe."

The man coughed at that, the movement evoking a spasm from

abused lungs.

Marta glanced over at Ivy. "They need tissue grafts and some reconstructive work," she murmured. "I assume you have no method of cloning healthy tissue?"

She received a negative headshake from the patcher.

Marta nodded her understanding as she knelt next to the man in front of her. She injected an accelerated dose of antibiotic, as well as a dose of nano to block his pain. Then she checked him for other wounds, extracted a sample of the man's stem cells, and pushed them to Varanee.

Since only the epidermal layer of human skin was capable of regeneration, they would need to clone both his subcutaneous and dermal tissue layers to replace what had been destroyed. This kind of repair could only be done back on the ship, so for now, the man's stem cells would be used to program chameleon cells within an artificial skin covering. That mimicry would keep the man's body from rejecting it as a foreign object until they could graft his own cloned skin into place.

<*Here you go,*> Varanee sent as she pushed the artificial skin routine to Marta's medsleeve. <*That should stabilize him for transit.*>

Marta shot her a mental nod as she reached up to inject the nano inside the muscle of his cheekbone, and watched the artificial skin begin to spread across his face.

"Let's see what we have over here," she murmured, as she rose and stepped over to the second patient.

Bending over the prone form of the woman in the sling, Marta could see dressings stained pink from suppuration that oozed from the raw burns covering her back, neck and scalp.

Although the methods used to treat her were primitive by 34th century standards, Marta couldn't fault their application. The wounds had been debrided and cleaned, the dressings applied properly.

Marta shunted the second stem cell sample to Varanee, who began to work on the woman's chameleon cells while Marta examined her burned hands.

The intense heat from the explosion and subsequent fire had melted her skin, fusing her fingers together into one solid mass of flesh. The flipper-like appendages would require surgical intervention, and more tissue cloning.

Marta repeated the process, dosing the woman with medicines to block the pain and nano to prevent infection. Varanee sent her the customized artificial skin program, and Marta inserted the nano and watched as it began to spread.

Satisfied, she rose and turned to Xiao. "These'll be the most challenging ones to transport, but we can't leave them here. I need to get them back to the *Vale,* where I can treat them more effectively."

The Marine nodded, eyeing the situation critically before retreating to where Lena and Tama stood, to consult with them on the best way to go about it.

Returning, he crouched beside Marta. "Lena's mapped the way back to the shuttle. She and Ramon are going to load up the lorry with the more ambulatory patients. They can make a run to the *Kaze* and be back in about an hour. You two comfortable staying back here without me? I want to stand guard up front at the entrance."

<*Don't worry about us, there's plenty for us to do without ever needing to leave this area,*> Varanee assured the Marine. <*We'll be fine.*>

"Okay, then." Xiao nodded and stood, turning his attention to Ivy. "Can you help coordinate the patients for us?"

The woman nodded. "Come this way."

* * * * *

The lorry made two trips to the shuttle. Those Noctus who had escaped injury, yet been spirited away during the blast and tagged as dead, worked tirelessly to help move their injured brethren.

Almost fifty Noctus were loaded onto the *Kuroi Kaze,* exceeding the spacecraft's maximum certified operating capacity by a margin of twenty percent.

Beau had initially protested, but Varanee had threatened to lobotomize the AI, citing emergency protocols and reminding the pilot that the stated regulatory capacities always factored in safety margins.

"Fine, then," the Tau Ceti pilot finally agreed. "But I'm going on record right now to say that you held me hostage and threatened me with bodily harm if I didn't do it. That way, Captain Andrews can't rip me a new one."

<Seeing as you don't have one to rip in the first place,> Varanee said drolly, *<I think you're fine. Besides, we're doctors.... We'll make sure to unrip it for you. If you ask nicely.>*

All that remained was to transport the two burn patients.

The lorry had been maneuvered until it was flush to the blast doors, and Ramon had returned from the *Kaze* with two field gurneys, one of which they'd adapted to accommodate the woman in the cradle.

Marta had sedated both for the transfer, and then the Marines transferred them into the lorry.

Marta jumped in the back and moved forward to place herself once more at the window that divided the front of the lorry from its paneled section. This position also placed her and Varanee between the two gurneys, where they could more easily monitor their patients' vitals. Xiao jumped up front, while Ramon and Lena hopped in the back, drawing the doors closed behind them.

The trip back to the shuttle spanned less than five kilometers, but it felt like it was taking forever. With these two as cargo, Marta felt more vulnerable than she had on the journey into the platform. She stiffened as she heard a peremptory voice hail the lorry and order it to stop.

<Core!> Varanee gasped, reminding Marta that the physician was a civilian, unused to covert military operations. She cursed

herself silently for not thinking about the situation she was getting the AI into when she'd volunteered for this mission.

She glanced over at Ramon and Lena. Tama's voice flooded their combat net, pushing a wave of reassurance toward the physician embedded inside Marta's head.

<*Don't worry, doc,*> the Marine sent. <*We've got your back. Just stay quiet while Xiao handles this. No chance of these two awakening any time soon?*>

<*They're unconscious and stable,*> Marta assured the AI. <*No worries on our end.*>

<*Good. Let's keep this comm clear while Ramon, Lena, and I monitor Xiao's feed,*> Tama murmured, and then Marta felt her presence withdraw from her mind.

Marta turned slightly and looked through the window that separated her from the front bench of the lorry. She saw a small contingent of Lumins approaching, one man's arm slung over his partner's, his other hand clutching a gash in his side.

"You there!" the Lumin who had hailed the lorry ordered, gesturing to Xiao. "Hand over your medical supplies. This man needs treatment. Now!"

Xiao's glance passed casually over Marta as he turned to Ivy. "Patcher's got a passel of bandages here," he said, and Marta marveled at the chameleon-like way the Marine managed the Noctus patois. "but they're not sterile-like or anything."

<*There's a Noctus first-aid kit down by your feet,*> Xiao thrust the thought at Marta, imbuing it with urgency. <*Pass it through the window to me. Last thing we need right now is for one of them to try to access the back of this truck.*>

Nodding, Marta bent and fumbled beneath the bench. <*Got it,*> she sent, pulling out a faded sack made from the same material as the tarps that had hung in the makeshift sickbay.

She turned and handed it through the window, but forgot in her haste that her medsleeve was tech that no Noctus would have.

<*Doc!*> Xiao hissed, <*your arm!*>

Marta jerked back with a mental curse, pulling the shapeless coverall sleeve down to cover her left hand as Ivy and Xiao began rummaging through the kit, removing bandages and a squirt bottle of antiseptic solution.

<*I think we're okay,*> Ramon interjected from the back. His hand was on the lorry's roof, where he'd injected a thread of nano to observe the Lumins from his vantage. <*No one's making any moves to indicate we've raised their suspicions.*>

Marta breathed a sigh of relief and looked out through the window at the Lumins once more. Her eyes clashed with those of their leader, and she quickly averted her eyes from the woman's face, attempting to channel the more subdued demeanor of the Noctus.

<*Xiao…?*> She left her question hanging as she turned to watch the Marine's head, bent in deference to the Lumins as he handed Ivy the materials from the kit as she requested them.

"Enough," the leader growled, shoving Ivy away. "If he gets sepsis, you'll be brought up on charges. Hand me your tokens!"

Marta's heart stuttered. <*Tokens?*> she sent to the Marines. <*We don't—*>

<*No worries, doc,*> Ramon's voice came easily over the net, and he shot her a quick smile. <*We interfaced with one of the Noctus while setting up the medical gear, and borrowed some ID tokens temporarily. Ivy has them loaded into the unit strapped on her arm. Most Noctus don't even have those, so it'll be natural for her to provide tokens for all four of us.*>

A shaft of relief shot through Marta, and she leant back suddenly, her hands grasping the edge of the bench she sat on in relief.

<*Semper Paratus ma'am,*> Lena added, with a tendril of humor.

<*I thought your motto was 'Semper Fi', Marine.*>

<*Oh, it is, ma'am. But the Tau Ceti Coast Guard motto of 'always ready' seemed more appropriate right now.*>

<*Watch it, Corporal, ma'am,*> Ramon retorted. <*Them's fighing

words.>

As the lorry began to move, Marta glanced once more through the window—in time to see the Lumin in charge watching them with a curious intensity as they maneuvered past.

She spent the trip back to the *Vale* with her eyes glued to the nav holo, unable to shake the Lumin's penetrating stare.

It wasn't until the Noctus were all safely aboard and she was back in her medbay that Marta began to breathe easy again.

PART THREE: THE HEIST

DOUBLE-OH SEXY

STELLAR DATE: 07.03.3302 (Adjusted Gregorian)
LOCATION: Hegemony Headquarters, Candesca
REGION: Lucent, Luminescent Space, Sirian Hegemony

The last thing Jonesy wanted to do was spend another day on Incandus in the company of a bunch of government stiffs.

Or is that corporate stiffs?

Jonesy suspected that, in this system, they were one and the same.

So when Rubin's adjunct, Varga, had offered to show Jonesy around Candesca the next day, rather than both of them wasting their time cooling their heels at headquarters, Jonesy had run the idea past Jason. The captain had readily agreed.

<*No need for you to hang around and listen to us hammer out the specifics of a fictitious trade deal,*> Jason remarked. <*Besides, you never know when a contact like Varga will come in handy.*>

<*Or what intel he might inadvertently drop?*> Jonesy suggested with a mental smirk.

<*That, too. Just remember he's thinking the same thing.*>

Jason had been correct; it was obvious that Varga was tactfully trying to pump Jonesy for information as he flew the sporty two-person skimmer over various landmarks. The engineer cheerfully played along, dropping an occasional bit of misleading information he knew would have had Shannon snorting in amusement.

They made a brief stop at headquarters to check in prior to the evening's events. Varga had either seen or sensed that Jonesy wasn't exactly looking forward to it. Or perhaps Jonesy'd done a passing fair job at seeding misinformation, leaving Varga wanting more. Regardless, the adjunct had suggested that a night on the town was preferable to attending a fancy reception with a bunch of execs.

Jonesy had agreed, which was how he found himself hanging out at a local microbrewery with someone who was, in essence, the enemy. Still, it was a sight more enjoyable than rubbing elbows with veeps, or guarding the shuttle with Cesar—although he suspected that the microbrewery was an attempt to soften him up in the hope he'd let additional intel slip.

Jonesy sat back, willing to let Varga do his best as he enjoyed the draught of local brew the adjunct had recommended. A thought struck him, and he grinned in amusement, causing Varga to raise his brow in question.

"You know," Jonesy leant in as if divulging some great secret, "it looked like your boss was hitting on mine, back there at your headquarters."

The man, shorter than Jonesy by a head, slid him a look that managed to imply he was a bit lacking in the intelligence department. "How provincial are you people?"

Jonesy just grinned back at the man, and then nodded sagely. "Still fun to watch, though, isn't it?"

One brow rose, and the man's lip quirked a bit before he paused, rounding on Jonesy with a suspicious look on his face. "Hang on here. My boss is Rubin, not Berit. He was putting the moves on Shannon last night, not Captain Andrews. Don't you report to him?" Varga accused.

"Oh, I do," Jonesy admitted, leaning back in his chair with an easy smile he'd learned from the aforementioned captain. "But Shannon was my boss before Jason ever came on the scene." He smiled at the memory. "She's been my mentor for, oh…" he scrunched his forehead in thought, "must be a little over a hundred years, now. Taught me everything I know about being the ship's engineer."

Varga turned back to his flight of beers. "Your bio files indicate she's the ship's navigator."

His tone still sounded mildly accusing. Jonesy understood the confusion; rarely did a ship's navigator outrank its engineer. But the *Avon Vale* wasn't just any ship, and neither was its crew just any crew.

He smiled and acknowledged Varga's suspicious look with a nod. "True. When she took me on as her apprentice, she told Jason she wanted to learn more about astrogation." He shrugged. "When you've been plying the black for as many decades as the *Vale* has, it's not unusual for crew to cross-train across various disciplines. Keeps life interesting."

Varga grunted, then turned back to observe the passing crowd. "So, what's it like, being away from home for so many decades? Is it true you spend years in stasis?"

Jonesy could hear the curiosity in the man's voice, and smiled internally.

Befriend the adjunct: check. Ma always said I would catch more flies with honey. Settling deeper into his chair, he let his gaze wander up to the ceiling of the brewery. "I'll let you in on a little secret. You see, being on a ship like the *Vale* is kind of like bringing your whole family along with you wherever you go…."

* * * * *

Two hundred kilometers away, inside a pavilion on Phosphor's shores, Shannon accepted a wine glass from an Irid waitress, and then turned to survey the room. The crystal pavilion was lit with an otherworldly aura, a welcome change from the stark, clean lines of the meeting rooms she'd been stuck in all day.

Shannon had confided to Khela earlier that she'd reached the saturation point, where corporate events were concerned.

Although, she mused as she took in the elaborate living art display, the savory aroma of food, and the cozy seating. *As parties go, the location isn't too shabby.*

She drifted outside, the sea breeze stirring her hair as she walked toward the stage where the musicians played. Skirting the dance floor, she nodded politely to those she passed. While walking, she mentally reviewed the team's encounter with Hume earlier that evening.

The overseer had met them in their stateroom, then initiated a secured privacy screen.

"Well, these past two days have been interesting to watch," Hume had begun, his eyes sweeping the group, landing first on Jason, and then on her. "When I suggested yesterday that you encourage the attentions of Berit and Rubin, I hadn't quite envisioned how obsessed they would become."

Jason coughed a laugh. "Oh, is that what they're calling it these days?"

A corner of Hume's mouth turned up slightly, but his eyes remained intent as he shook his head. "We've been trying to get close to those two for some time now, with no luck. Haven't found a way past them to deliver the shackling rectification code to their AIs."

Jason turned to face Hume fully, his eyes thoughtful. "Are you suggesting what I think you are?"

Hume looked a bit uncomfortable as he shifted and crossed his arms. "You and Shannon have certainly piqued their interest. And being outside Hegemony society gives you greater freedom than someone like me." He shrugged once more. "It'd be difficult for me to find a reason to approach Quincy, for example. As an outsider, Shannon could use simple curiosity as her excuse. If she crosses a societal boundary, so what? She can plead cultural ignorance."

Shannon saw Jason and Terrance exchange glances.

Jonesy folded his arms across the top of the counter that

divided the living area from the suite's cocktail bar. "So let me see if I have this right," the engineer drawled. "You want our ship's AI—"

"—who's doing a kickass imitation of a human," Shannon reminded him, which Jonesy acknowledged.

"You want Shannon to let Rubin put the moves on her," he continued, "while our captain plays double-oh sexy with Berit tonight?"

Hume shot Jonesy a confused look, but Terrance waved him off.

"Nevermind," the exec told the man. "Yes, we'd already considered that there might be opportunities to infiltrate their ranks while we were here, and concluded it was worth the risk. I take it the rectification code that El Dorado sent you worked on the other AIs?"

Hume nodded. "Quincy and Wallis are the only two still shackled, although the rest of the AIs continue to act as if they are."

Shannon sauntered over to Jason and grinned up at him. "This'll be fun," she said as she threaded her arm through his and deepened her voice. " 'The name is Andrews. Jason Andrews.' And I'll be Emma—err, Shannon Peel."

She suppressed a grin as she recalled the pained look her comment had brought to Jason's face.

What can I say? I'm a sucker for old-Earth fiction.

As she lifted her wine glass to her lips, she caught Jason's watchful stare, and sent him a quick reassurance.

<Don't worry, I'll be fine.>

<Don't take any chances,> was his reply.

She shot him a wink and a smile. *<Yes, Dad.>*

Jason sent a mental sputter. *<**Dad**? Don't be giving me that. Big brother, maaaaybe. You're older'n me, you know.>*

Her smile became a grin as she turned to watch the musicians play, her toe tapping a rhythm to the beat. A hand at her elbow had her looking up into Currin's face.

"Enjoying the wine?" the Lumin asked, slipping a hand around her waist.

"Mmm-hmm," she responded, lifting her glass as she turned to face him, the maneuver slipping her neatly out of his grasp at the same time. "You were right, it's even better than the one from last night."

She raised the rim to her nose, swirling the glass's golden contents around as she inhaled the aroma. "Buttery, with a hint of…pear?" she murmured as she sipped. "A Sémillon, if I'm not mistaken."

Currin raised a brow, and Shannon smiled. She knew she'd accurately assessed the vintage, and had even meant it when she said she enjoyed it.

She had taken great care when designing her humanoid frame. She'd connected it to her own neural matrix, using an overlay of preferences she'd culled from her memories of Calista. She'd then tied her friend's likes and dislikes directly into the body's organic receptors.

Food, wine—all the things unique to humans—would register to her own synapses as enjoyable or distasteful. The taste buds of her organic tongue were right now sending her pleasurable messages, so she responded in kind.

"Whatever you do, don't tell Cyrus," Currin confided, taking the opportunity to lean in closer once again, and slide an arm around her shoulders. "He'll be insufferable. That's from his winery, you know."

Shannon smiled and took another sip, lifting her hand in a little wave as she saw Rubin approaching. She attempted to dislodge Currin's arm once more, but her movement only encouraged his hand to wander a bit further south.

<That man just ran his hand over your ass,> Khela's voice cut in, and Shannon sent her friend a mental eyeroll.

<Tell me something I don't know,> she responded as she pasted a

smile on her lips and side-stepped, turning toward the approaching Lumin.

"Oh, look," she said brightly. "It's Rubin."

Rubin smiled as she caught his eye, and increased his pace.

"Enjoying yourself, I see," he said with a knowing look over her head at Currin.

Shannon screwed up her face into an expression of distaste that only Rubin could see.

"Well, I am now," she confided, shooting him a flirty smile and causing him to laugh aloud.

Taking her drink, he handed it off without looking, and Shannon's smile turned fixed as he snapped his fingers. A mechanical frame that could only be Quincy stepped forward to obediently take the glass, then backed away at Rubin's gesture of dismissal.

Her eyes followed Quincy's figure as the AI departed, but before she could step around Rubin or inquire about him, the Lumin had taken her by the arm and begun to lead her out to the dance floor.

Frustrated, she looked up at Rubin to protest, but bit her tongue as he caught the direction of her gaze.

"Surely you've seen one before?" he inquired. "I hear there are a few on your ship."

Shannon realized he was referring to AIs as he swung her into his arms and led her into a dance. She set a subroutine to analyzing the pattern of movement so that she could match it, and quickly realized there was none, aside from a rhythmic swaying.

"Of course," she responded. "We have several. I just wasn't aware you had any. What…model," she stumbled over the word, "is it?"

Stars, girl, you'd better get with the program, or else he's not going to buy your Mata Hari act….

Rubin laughed, navigating easily through the throng of people. "Do they even have models? I wouldn't know."

He changed the subject, asking her about her past. Shannon began a recitation she'd rehearsed with Jason earlier.

As she did, an internal alarm triggered, notifying her of three flavors of breach nano Rubin had deployed against her. Two were sniffer routines, mining her for information about implants and augmentations.

Those were easily dodged. Shannon populated them with reams of nonsense, made to look like valuable information wrapped in a difficult-to-break code.

The third passel of nano, though....

She began to panic as she felt her organic body begin to slip into a state of lassitude.

<*Khela!*>

* * * * *

"That man would be looking at some time in an autodoc if he did that to me," Khela murmured to Terrance, as she watched Shannon neatly dodge another grope from Currin and make her way over to Rubin.

She felt more than heard his soft laugh as the crowd pressed around them.

"I'd expect nothing less from you, love."

She glanced casually over at Jason, and nearly spewed her drink at what she saw. The Jason she knew was nowhere in evidence. Instead, the man had Berit practically caged, with one hand propped against a wall beside her head and the other casually palming a drink.

As she watched, he tipped his head back and took a long pull on his beer. His dark blonde hair, shaggy and slightly disheveled, accentuated his bad-boy fighter pilot persona. The cocky head tilt and the wicked grin on his face did the rest.

Unless you look into his eyes, she thought, as his quick scan of the crowd paused briefly as his hard gaze drilled into her. Then one side of his mouth kicked up in a sardonic grin, and he saluted her with his beer before turning back to Berit, broad shoulders blocking the woman from view.

Whatever the Lumin said in reply had him tilting his head back in a hearty laugh. Then he wrapped his arm around her shoulders and led her away.

<*What is it about him that makes me want to go rescue* ***her****, when I know it's an act, and she's one of the bad guys?*>

Terrance looked over at her in amusement, then studied Jason's retreating back for a moment before quirking a brow her way. <*He is laying it on a bit thick,*> he admitted, <*but she seems to be buying what he's selling.*>

<*I don't think it'll take too long to free Wallis at this rate,*> she observed. <*Although how he plans to extricate himself….*>

<*Ah, now* ***that*** *would be fun to watch,*> her husband said, saluting her with his bourbon before taking a sip.

<*I'm not sure that I—*>

Khela ground to a sudden halt as Shannon's cry cut through her words. She tensed, her gaze darting through the crowd as her overlay sent her the AI's location.

<*It's Shannon,*> she began, but Terrance was already starting toward her.

<*I heard,*> he bit out as they both received a feed from the panicked AI.

<*Wait,*> Khela said, grabbing Terrance by the elbow and pulling him to a halt. <*I think…yes. Look.*>

Khela highlighted Shannon's biometric data, and brought it to Terrance's attention before addressing the AI.

<*Hold on, Shannon, you're going to be fine. He slipped you a drug,*> she hesitated, then added, <*to make you more receptive to him.*>

<*More* ***receptive****?*> Shannon's mental voice rose an octave. <*It's making this entire body sluggish, like I'm…. Oh, stars, that asswipe slipped me a mickey, didn't he? What a tool.*>

<*Just use some of your frame's mednano to clear it from your*

system,> Khela instructed. <*You'll be fine.*>

<*Uh…thanks,*> Shannon said, her tone embarrassed. <*I was so focused on neural and tech infiltration, it didn't occur to me he'd try to send something against my organic system.*>

<*Think you have it under control now?*> Khela asked, and the AI sent her a nod.

<*Oh yes. He'll get what's coming to him. Guess he's never heard that payback's a bitch.*>

<*Just don't jeopardize our cover, and don't forget your objective. Quincy's counting on you,*> Terrance warned her, and she shot them both a mental glare.

<*I* ***know*** *that, Terrance. Now leave me alone so I can get this job done.*>

TWO JETHROS, A JIM BROWN, AND AN ELLA FITZGERALD

STELLAR DATE: 07.03.3302 (Adjusted Gregorian)
LOCATION: Hegemony Headquarters, Candesca
REGION: Lucent, Luminescent Space, Sirian Hegemony

Shannon pretended to stumble as Rubin led her off the dance floor, and let him slip a hand around her shoulders to steady her.

"Maybe we should get you somewhere more comfortable," he murmured, and she cocked her head, sending him what she hoped was a flirtatious look out of the side of her eyes.

He smiled, motioned to Quincy, and navigated her to one of the pavilion's exits.

<*Operation Shannon Peel is commencing,*> she announced as the man steered her down a sandy path to one of the beach suites built into the seaside cliff, Quincy following obediently behind.

<*Don't do anything I wouldn't do,*> Khela called out after her.

Terrance followed with a stern <*Ping us at the first sign of trouble, understand?*>

<*Seriously, guys. Have a little faith.*>

Shannon caused her steps to wander, allowing Rubin to steer her up to the entrance of the suite he'd secured for the evening. Purposely stumbling against the doorframe, she flushed a passel of nano into the suite's entrance, subverting both security and surveillance, and adding her own jamming package to the room.

She reset the locks, keying them to her own token as Rubin steered her toward the back of the suite and into a richly appointed bedroom with floor-to-ceiling plas windows.

The windows were retracted to reveal a hot tub enclosed in a private lanai, wisps of steam curling across its surface. The sheltered veranda offered a spectacular view of the shoreline and the pavilion below.

"Make yourself at home," Rubin said, steering her toward a settee set beside the open windows. "I'll just be a moment."

He turned toward Quincy, who stood at the bedroom's entrance, awaiting Rubin's command.

"Get the Viognier out of the chiller and pour two glasses," he ordered, and the AI turned away as Rubin disappeared into the san.

The moment the door slid closed behind the man, Shannon moved. She severed the san's surveillance feed as she ran across the bedroom and checked on Quincy in the suite's living area.

The AI jerked around as she placed a hand on the utility frame where Rubin had mounted his core. A quick probe told her that the Lumin had installed countermeasures into the frame to prevent theft.

Annoyed that she would have to delay freeing Quincy until she'd subdued Rubin, she patted the arm of the frame. "Just wanted to say thanks for the wine," she blurted. Giving Quincy a smile and a cheerful wave, she ran back into the bedroom.

'Thanks for the wine?' Real smooth, Shannon, she berated herself. *Emma Peel would not approve.*

Nibbling at her lower lip, she made a quick survey of the room and then ordered the plas windows closed. Eyeing them critically, she keyed the nano embedded in the windows to the privacy setting, turning them opaque.

Her surveillance feed indicated that Rubin was ready to exit the room, so she resumed her seat on the edge of the bed.

The san doors slid open to reveal Rubin, clad in a bathrobe. He appeared disappointed that the hot tub was on the other side of the windows, but his expression cleared as Shannon patted the bed beside her.

"Not an exhibitionist, I take it?" the Lumin joked as he closed the distance between them.

Pinning Rubin with a look, she crooked her finger at him. The man cocked his head, and then grinned as she grabbed the front of his robe. Pushing him back onto the bed, she rose to loom over him—and flipped them both into a mini expanse.

The man's body froze as she eased off him, a portion of her brain maintaining the illusion, as his mind fully engaged in the virtual seduction she wove. Recalling Khela's warning to make the fictitious encounter pleasant but not too memorable, she examined the scene critically, then dialed it back a bit.

Easing off the bed, she turned to see Quincy standing frozen at the entrance to the bedroom, holding a tray with the bottle of Viognier and two stemmed glasses.

"Is…the vice president unwell? If you have compromised him in some way, I must warn you that I am compelled to report this," the AI informed her as she approached.

She shook her head as she reached out a hand toward the tray as if to take the wine. "He's fine, Quincy. Just resting."

She could tell the AI didn't believe her when he attempted to ping the security team that stood watchfully guarding the perimeter of the Phosphor Pavilion and its luxury suites. Her jamming protocol blocked the outgoing comm, denying his token.

Dropping all pretense, she placed a hand on his torso and deposited breaching nano onto the frame. She was going to have enough trouble as it was, dodging the attacks Rubin's countermeasures sent after her. The last thing she needed right now was to have to dodge physical attacks as well. And there was no telling what Quincy's compulsion would force on him.

"Don't worry. I'm a friend," she assured him as his frame locked. "I know your shackling is going to force you to fight me, but you'll be free in no time. Just give me a second to work past Rubin's—oh, that was nasty…."

Her brow furrowed as she bypassed the worm Rubin had embedded in the utility frame, and sandboxed it within a subroutine. Neatly sidestepping the rest of the countermeasures, she deposited the shackling rectification code at the junction where

Quincy's core connected to his frame.

She waited as she monitored its progress. As it signaled its completion, she reached out to the now-free AI using the pathway she'd laid with her breaching nano.

<*Hello, Quincy. How do you feel?*> she sent, and felt his surprise as he realized that she, too, was an AI.

<*I…who* ***are*** *you?*> Quincy asked, and she sent him a saucy grin.

<*Part of a covert ops team out of Alpha Centauri. We were sent in to get you and the rest of the AIs out of here—and as many Noctus as we can free along the way.*>

Quincy indicated the bedroom. <*What are we going to do about him?*>

<*Well, currently, he's in a mini expanse, thinking he's having sexytimes with a human female.*> She made a face. <*Not the most fun I've ever had in an expanse, but it keeps him occupied and out of the way for now. We have a plan to extract you, but it requires a bit of subterfuge.*>

She felt Quincy's relief as she deactivated the breaching nano, freeing him to move on his own. Lifting the tray from his hands, she set it to one side. Then, with a quick grin, she splashed a bit of the Viognier into a glass and raised it.

"To freedom," she told Quincy with a wink as she took a sip.

Setting it aside, she turned back, her expression solemn.

"Let me bring you up to speed on our plan. I'm afraid you're going to have to pretend to be shackled for just a teensy bit longer…."

* * * * *

Back at the pavilion, Terrance swept a glance through the crowd, then looked down at his wife. <*Ready to make your move, love?*> he asked. <*Gavin's graduated to drooling over you. I think at this point, if I were to wander off, you should be able to reel him in fairly easily.*>

Khela slanted him an unreadable look. <*Don't go too far,*> she instructed. <*I have an idea—and it involves you.*>

Terrance's eyebrows rose. <*Are you thinking about suggesting a threesome to this jerk?*>

Khela snorted. <*As if he could handle me, much less both of us. Besides, counting Kodi, we threesome all the time.*>

<*Eww. We do not,*> the *Vale*'s comm officer interjected, his mental voice rising until it ended in a squeak of horror. <*I'm not a voyeur.*>

Terrance pushed a tendril of amusement toward Kodi. <*She's kidding,*> he assured the AI privately before smiling and shaking his head at Khela.

He lifted his glass, a question in his eyes, and motioned toward the bar. When she shook her head, he began to move away.

<*Just give me a heads-up before you play your cards,*> he sent in parting, <*so I don't ruin the game by acting too surprised.*>

Khela sent her assent, then raised her glass to her lips as he walked away.

* * * * *

At least their sake isn't half-bad, she mused as she sipped the traditional rice wine, sending her eyes wandering over the crowd. She let her gaze clash with Gavin's and smiled a greeting.

The man needed no further encouragement. He picked up his pace, closing quickly.

"What's this? An honored guest, standing alone at a party?" The VP shook his head in mock sorrow. "We can't have that, now."

She looked down at the shorter man with a smile. "And see, just like this, you've solved my problem for me."

"You're enjoying yourself, I trust?" he asked as he stepped

closer.

She tilted her head as if considering his words, then shrugged. "I suppose so, although after a time, all the noise gets a bit tedious. It would be nice to get away from all of this for a bit."

A hungry expression crossed his face, and she stifled a laugh. The man was entirely too easy to manipulate.

Gavin turned his head, eyes scanning the crowd.

Looking for Terrance, she was fairly certain. He confirmed her guess with his next words.

"It's a pleasant night for a quiet walk along the shore, or…other things," he let his voice trail off suggestively. "Would your husband mind if I stole you away for a while?"

"Oh, no, he wouldn't mind in the least. Although," Khela let her smile turn a bit wicked as she ran her hand up his arm. Letting her fingers tease the hair at the base of his neck, she drew him closer and whispered into his ear, "He might be interested in joining us for those 'other things' you mentioned."

Gavin's eyes widened, and he looked intrigued.

Lifting a finger in a 'wait' gesture, his eyes gained the distant look of someone focused on an internal communication. After a brief moment, he returned his attention to her as he extended his arm for her to take.

"I've just acquired accommodations I think you might like," he confided. "Shall we?"

She smiled. "Lead on. I'll let Terrance know where he can meet up with us."

<*Heading out,*> she sent, and heard his mental grunt.

<*Asshole better keep his hands off my wife's ass,*> he responded, and she sent him a chiding look.

<*That was Currin. I think this one's too afraid of me to try such a thing.*>

Terrance sent her another mental grunt. <*He bought it?*>

<*Completely.*>

As they neared the guest suite, Khela stroked the surface of the golden cuff tattooed on her left arm. One of the raised filigree knots in the design smoothed as a microdrone slid out from its hiding place within the Elastene-shielded pocket. It rose silently, encasing them inside a communication blackout bubble. Nothing, except for a Phantom Blade-coded IFF signal, could get in or out.

<Jamming deployed,> she reported, and saw Kodi's acknowledging ping.

<We'll do a walkaround to make sure you two didn't draw any undue attention,> Terrance added. *<Meet you there shortly. Can you keep him entertained for five minutes?>*

Khela's avatar raised an eyebrow, which elicited a snicker from Kodi.

<Ah, yeah, scratch that. See you soon, hon.>

Another stroke of her tattoo released a microdrone that flew ahead of them as they neared the entrance to Gavin's suite. She sent Kodi the token to control it, and then monitored its feed on her overlay.

The AI's adroit manipulation of the drone and its nano payload allowed the team to breach the room's security protocol. When Gavin passed his security token to gain access, Kodi insinuated an untraceable callback worm to test the security of it.

With any luck, they might also gain access to some of the information the vice president hoarded. At the very least, they had control over the room's security and surveillance systems, and were now in position to run the con.

This con was something Shannon called an "Ella Fitzgerald". It required Kodi to gain control of the suite's holorecorders, and then, once they were under the AI's control, Khela would play the role of seductress until Kodi had enough footage to build a believable sim of a fictional tryst.

Khela's thoughts strayed to the reaction the idea had garnered when she had suggested it the night before. A pained look had flashed across Shannon's face, and the AI had glanced at Jason with a worried frown. Jason's face had turned impassive, but she'd caught the subtle nod he exchanged with the AI.

"Don't tell Landon about it," Shannon finally said. "It's the same con a serial killer named Prime pulled on him back on El Dorado. It ended badly."

Khela shrugged the memory away, her attention refocusing as Gavin ushered her into the suite.

<*Let me know when you have enough,*> she instructed Kodi as she removed her wrap and settled onto one of the suite's sofas.

She knew that the *Vale*'s comm officer was better at manipulating the imagery than either she or Terrance would be, so she left the coding to Kodi. Not that she understood what it took to take randomized footage and create a realistic and nuanced simulation using optical flow interpolation. But Jonesy had assured her that it would work flawlessly for the Ella Fitzgerald.

"They'll never be able to tell if it's live or if it's Memorex," he'd declared with a smirk. She'd met his grin with a blank, uncomprehending stare, but he'd just shrugged and waved it off. "It'll work, trust me."

Gavin detoured to the bar and raised a glass inquiringly.

"Whatever you're having is fine," she said, kicking off her shoes and settling back into the cushions.

She smiled as Gavin sat next to her and placed a hand on the exposed skin of her thigh. Just then, a chime sounded, announcing Terrance had arrived.

"You're *sure* he won't mind?" Gavin asked as Terrance strode in.

The exec smiled as he stepped down to the sofa. "Not in the slightest. In fact, I insist."

He sat down on the other side of the sofa, and Khela felt his hand on her shoulder just before he brushed her hair back. She angled her head to give Terrance better access to kiss the side of her neck, and reached for Gavin.

<*Tell me you have enough, Kodi,*> she sent with a thread of annoyance as the Lumin's hand crept up her thigh.

The moment she received Kodi's affirmation, she placed her hand at the base of Gavin's neck, as if to draw him toward her. The nano coating her palm sank into his skin, injecting a concentrated dose of a psychotropic nanozyme that Marta had given her.

Gavin's eyes glazed over, and he swayed slightly.

"Sorry. Mednano's not kicking in," he murmured. "That whiskey just went to my head."

"Why don't you lie back," she suggested, slipping off the sofa and kneeling beside it as Terrance rose.

Maneuvering Gavin into a supine position was as simple as a gentle push. The man toppled back, and Terrance stepped in to lever his feet up onto the cushions.

<*You're good to go. I'm feeding the cameras the sim now. Want me to make this encounter the best he never had?*>

Terrance coughed a laugh as Khela looked up at him. One eyebrow shot up in amusement as she addressed the AI embedded inside Terrance's head.

"This from the AI who nearly fried a circuit when I joked about a threesome earlier?"

<*Well, I, ah….*>

"Go for it, buddy," Terrance interjected, saving the AI from having to reply. "But I doubt your idea of sexy comes anywhere close to what a Lumin would have in mind." He grinned once more at Khela before his eyes fell to Gavin and his expression sobered.

She nodded, then turned back to the man lying in a nano-induced haze. Running a finger along her tattoo once more, she extracted the rectification code and fed it directly into the base of the Lumin's skull.

<*Macie?*> she asked, expanding the link to include both Terrance and Kodi.

There was a pause, then a querulous voice answered.

<*Who are you?*>

She felt the shaft of reassurance that Kodi thrust the AI's way.

<*We're here to free you,*> the comm officer told her. <*Although rescuing you from this man's skull is going to take another day or so. Can you hang in there until then?*>

Khela retreated from the connection, letting Kodi iron out the details with the other AI. Standing, she looked down at the slack face of the insensate Lumin, then back at Terrance.

"Let's get him into the bedroom," she suggested. "Then we can use that second dose of nano Marta sent along to plant a suggestion about the wild time we had." She nodded toward the bar. "Grab a few bottles and three glasses. Let's make this look good."

Then she bent and hooked Gavin's arm across her shoulder, shrugging him into a fireman's carry. She paused, examining the room with a critical eye as Terrance stepped in beside her.

"What now?" he asked, glancing at the unconscious man.

She nodded to the bed. "Mess it up a bit," she instructed.

Terrance set the booze aside to pull back the covers and toss the pillows around. Khela set Gavin down in the center and tugged the sheets into a messy pile.

Planting her hands on her waist, she wandered through the room, tilting a lampshade here, and rearranging some of the pillows there. Finally, she opened the bottles and retreated to the san to pour most of their contents down the drain.

"Waste of some pretty decent liquor," she heard Terrance murmur as he splashed a small bit into the base of the three glasses and set them on the nightstand next to the bed.

She knocked one onto the floor, and it tipped to its side, the brandy seeping into the carpet. Nodding in satisfaction, she turned to survey their handiwork.

"I think we're done here," she announced.

Then she glanced up at the ceiling over the bed, where holoemitters had been installed. Reaching out mentally to access the room's controls, she flicked it on. A smile teased her lips as she saw an image of the bed, Gavin splayed out on top, resolve itself onto the ceiling.

"Nice touch," Terrance approved.

"You like it?" she asked, then turned her gaze back up to the display. "Maybe we should get one installed in our quarters on the *Vale*."

A choking sound came across the combat net from Kodi as they exited the suite.

INDEPENDENCE DAY

STELLAR DATE: 07.04.3302 (Adjusted Gregorian)
LOCATION: ESS *Avon Vale*, Brilliance Station
REGION: Lucent, Luminescent Space, Sirian Hegemony

The next day saw the team back on the *Vale*, prepping for the Hegemony's visit. Energy seemed to permeate the ship, the stir of activity increasing the closer Jason got to the shuttle bay.

The corridor just outside the bay was lined with empty gurneys, ready for each of the Hegemony executives paired with an AI. The transports were attended by pairs of medics, ready to spring into action once Tobias gave the word.

Jason rounded the corner just as one of the medics pivoted and reached for a med-kit. He stutter-stepped sideways to avoid plowing into her.

"Sorry, sir!" Startled green eyes met his as she jerked back in surprise, kit tumbling out of her hands.

Jason dipped briefly into the zone, using his enhanced L2 reflexes to snatch the kit out of the air before it hit the deck. A quick mental probe of her token garnered the medic's rank.

He sent her an easy smile, tossing the kit over to her without breaking stride. "No worries, Corporal," he called out as he skirted the next gurney in line. "Carry on."

The bay was active with personnel prepping for the imminent arrival of their guests. Off to one side, he could just make out the large umbilical that Brilliant Station's Spacedock had attached to the *Vale*'s port-side hatch. Its accordion-like edges could be seen through the plas porthole, visible now that the ship was docked and the hatch's blast doors were retracted.

Although the Hegemony facility could have managed a seal around the larger bay doors adjacent to the hatch, Jason had told Shannon to have the spacedock connect to the smaller egress instead. It was much more easily safeguarded, and the curtain of nanokillers much less annoying on a small scale than if it were to be installed around the bay doors.

As it was, he'd had to field quite a few complaints from the dockmaster's office about the flares the curtain threw out. The steady stream of infiltration nano that the curtain had to neutralize each time the hatch cycled was wearing on everyone's nerves.

For this visit, though, the Lumins would be arriving on a state transport and entering through the bay's starboard side. This explained the presence of the ES field, limning the starboard doors with a bright blue glow.

Terrance stood to one side of the bay doors, behind the yellow depressurization line. Tobias and Logan were there, going over last-minute plans with Terrance, while Khela stood to one side, directing her Marines. A quick scan of the area had Jason nodding in approval as he realized there were more Marines scattered about than those the unaugmented eye could see.

Noa and Marta were in medical with Charley, doing final checks on the Caprise implants. Shannon had opted to sit this encounter out, having had her fill of both Rubin and Currin the evening before. She and Landon were up on the bridge, feeding the team status updates as the Hegemony shuttle approached.

"Ship's on final now," Jason announced as he neared the team. "Everything set down here?"

Tobias nodded, and then canted his head questioningly at Logan. "How many troops you think they'll bring with them, lad?"

"With all six executives aboard, something larger than a fireteam, I think," the intelligence officer speculated. "One guard per primary, plus a pilot."

Jason grunted. "Sounds about right." He looked up as Shannon's voice came across the net.

<*Showtime,*> she announced. <*Opening the doors in thirty seconds.*>

The news spurred several into action. Tobias, Logan, and the other AIs retreated out of sight, and Khela moved to join them as two of her Marines headed across to the other side of the bay at a brisk trot. Khela sent a status update indicating her team's readiness just as the alarms sounded and the doors began to retract back into the ship's hull.

As the thin sliver of blackness in the center of the doors began to widen, they saw a sleek vessel drift toward them, outlined by the reds and greens of its anti-collision running lights. Small puffs from thrusters told Jason the pilot was making microadjustments to his course, following the indicators being projected by the ship's holoemitters. As the craft settled gently onto a set of rails, its thrusters powered down, and the bay doors began to close once more.

<All right, lads, come out and let us have a look at yeh,> Tobias's voice crooned to the as-yet-unseen Lumins. *<Nice and easy, now. Ah, that's more like it….>*

As the bay registered a positive atmosphere, the ES field between Jason and the pinnace snapped off, the pinnace's hatch slid aside, and three burly Security Guild Irids clad in powered armor poured out. Their watchful eyes swept the cavernous space, taking in the presence of Terrance, Jason, and Khela.

They signaled to their teammate, who was kneeling with weapon drawn at the top of the pinnace's ramp. The woman straightened and stepped to one side, weapon still held at the ready, as the senior executives began to exit the craft.

From the corner of his eye, Jason saw three of the *Vale*'s Marines materialize, forming an honor guard that matched the Irids in firepower. The lead Irid nodded, acknowledging his counterparts, then stood at attention as Rubin approached, followed by the rest.

"Terrance," the Lumin greeted, then nodded to both Khela and Jason as his compatriots stepped forward.

From the corner of his eye, Jason saw Quincy exit the craft and quietly take up his position behind Rubin. Then he became distracted by a hand stroking down his arm.

"I believe you promised me a tour, Captain." Berit licked her lips as her eyes strayed down Jason's length, and then returned to meet his. "A private one." Her lips curved in a knowing smile.

<Okay, then. How about that expanse, Tobe? We good to go? No time like the present to get the old ball rolling.>

His rapid-fire commentary had Terrance stumbling over a word. The exec caught himself and continued, but not before Jason pinned him with a jaundiced eye.

Humor thickened the Weapon Born's accent. *<Had enough of her, have you?>* The AI paused, and then added in a businesslike voice, *<I have token lock on thirteen humans: that's six Irids, the pilot, plus our heads of state. Wait one, Logan's checking to see if that's the last of them.>*

Jason pasted Shit-eating Grin Number Five on his face as Berit twined her arm with his, her other hand working its way down his torso.

<Stars, let's hope so. Pretty sure seducing narcissistic foreign leaders isn't in a captain's job description,> he responded, and felt a wave of amusement curl around him.

<Ah, boyo, I believe that falls under 'other duties as assigned'.>

Before he had a chance to retort, Logan broke in. *<Their craft's difficult to scan, and I've been unable to get a look inside. Their hatch has its own counteragents and has killed the nano I sent into it. But the count is right—>*

<Okay, great, I can live with that. You ready?>

Jason set his jaw and plastered a pleasant smile on his face as he redirected Berit's hand by bringing it to his mouth and placing a kiss in her palm.

<Any time, Tobe,> he ground out as Berit's other hand slid south.

<Right, then.> Laughter filtered into Jason's mind.

The ES field edging the closed bay doors flared brightly before cutting out, an effect Tobias had manufactured as a cover for the transition into the Expanse.

All around them, Sirians stood frozen as the AIs aboard the *Vale,* led by Tobias, infiltrated their neural nets and escorted them into a virtual reality indistinguishable from their surroundings.

<*All clear. Secure our visitors.*> Tobias's voice held no accent now, the command delivered in the clipped tones of one who expected instant obedience.

Marines dropped from their hiding places, relieving insensate guards of their weapons. Two Marines angled toward the pinnace to confirm it was secure. Khela instructed the rest to remain watchful but to keep their distance and let the AIs handle the Irids through the Expanse.

Medics pushed through the hallway doors, gurneys floating to a stop beside the frozen forms of Berit, Currin, Gavin, and Francesca. Those not covering the Irids moved to assist in the transfer of the four executives, strapping them in securely.

The medical teams were pushing for the corridor when a shout rang out, followed by laserfire. Directed energy beams lanced through the air, catching one of the medics center mass.

<*Two tangoes,*> Lena announced from behind a stack of crates as a combat net snapped into existence. <*One on each side of the hatch. Both in powered armor. Laser rifle, fore, flechette aft.*>

Jason's head jerked around, eyes seeking the shooter. He saw one Marine down, the other crouched, exchanging pulse fire.

<*Core!*> Terrance swore, sprinting for a blast shield that rose behind the dockmaster's console.

Khela followed, weapon drawn, laying covering fire as she hit the deck beside her husband in a rolling dive.

With Khela providing the diversion, Jason dropped deep into his altered state, using his full L2 capabilities to propel him across the short space. He dropped into a slide, skidding between the rails upon which the pinnace rested, momentum slamming him painfully up against the aft rail.

A flurry of flechettes pinged against the rail he'd just cleared, missing him by a scant twenty centimeters. A hand reached out, snagging his suit and dragging him further under cover.

<Stars, sir, that was a stupid move.>

He shot the speaker a sardonic look, then nodded at the pulse rifle in the Marine's hand. *<Got a spare?>*

She shook her head. *<Sorry, sir. Only other ordnance I have on me are grenades and a laser dagger.>*

<Shut those soldiers down. ***Now,*** *>* Logan ordered. *<This is impacting the Expanse.>*

<Don't fire on the pinnace!> Landon interjected. *<And don't kill those soldiers if you can help it.>*

Jason sent a questing pulse, and received an immediate response from Landon.

<Tobias is having to get creative, excusing the injuries the Security Guild has sustained in a believable way,> the XO explained. *<It's going to be hard enough to spin that tale. Best if we didn't have to explain away any weapons' damage to their ship, too.>*

<Their guards are not making it easy,> Terrance growled. *<They're avoiding the Lumins, but they've decided their own ranks are expendable.>*

Jason swore under his breath as a feeling of guilt overtook him. He shouldn't have pressed Tobias into initiating the Expanse before checking the pinnace thoroughly. His unwillingness to tolerate Berit's pawing for another few minutes could very well have jeopardized the mission.

The exit strategy from this system—not only for the *Avon Vale,* but for the *Hyperion* as well—was predicated on them being able to weave a believable fiction today. Sinking the Lumins unwittingly into an Expanse took finesse; the team couldn't afford a wild card like the one that had just been tossed into the mix.

<What about their ship's comm signal? Are you jamming?> Jason tensed, awaiting the response.

Terrance swore again at the pause. *<They contact anyone on the outside, and we're not getting out of here alive.>*

<*I know that.*> Shannon's voice held none of its usual sass. <*Don't worry, I have them locked down tight. No signal's getting past me.*>

Jason released the air from his lungs in a silent whoosh as he turned to examine the underbelly of the pinnace. Reaching up, he traced a seam that led aft, toward the ship's fusion engine. A plan began to form, and he snapped his head back to the Marine next to him.

<*Hand me your laser dagger. And a stun grenade.*>

The woman reached for the holster strapped to her leg and wordlessly handed him the laser dagger, then tossed him two grenades.

<*Stickys and EMPs are all I have.*>

<*Those'll do, thanks.*>

Turning back to the pinnace's underbelly, he followed the seam to the hidden maintenance door he knew vessels of this class usually had. With no time for finesse, he ignored the recess handle likely security coded to an Irid token. Instead, he slammed the wand into the seam, wielding the beam like a cutting tool around its edges.

Levering the door open, he paused long enough to confirm that the *Vale*'s Marines still held the attention of the Irids firing before ducking his head up into the dark space. Pausing, he considered which grenade to use, then opted for the EMP. He pulled himself up into the craft, squeezing between two hydraulic actuators to reach the thin slice of light that indicated access to the ship's pressurized cabin.

The EMP wouldn't fit.

Setting his jaw, Jason worked the laser dagger in his other hand up through the tight, enclosed space, calibrated the beam to its shortest setting, and began to cut a bigger hole.

Pay no attention to the man behind the curtain, he silently urged the Irids as he cut, knowing that the tip of the wand's blade would stand out like a beacon, should either one of them happen to glance back inside.

He was counting on his own people to keep their attention focused elsewhere.

Hole widened, he eased the EMP grenade through and set it to remote detonate, keyed to his token. He backed out of the ship and dropped next to the Marine while sending a mental shout.

<EMP in the hole!>

Marines in proximity dropped to make way for their compatriots who were far enough away to remain unaffected. These leapt for the hatch as soon as the grenade pulsed. The two unconscious Irids were secured and, moments later, Jason's Link—also a victim of the grenade—reset.

Jason rolled out from under the pinnace and walked over to the Marines holding their captives. He looked up as Terrance and Khela joined them.

"What now?" Terrance asked, stroking the side of his jaw as he stared down at this complication.

"I have an idea, sir," Xiao, one of the Marines who had secured the guards, spoke up. "Hold a sec."

A minute later, as a comm connection sprang up between them, Jason realized the Marine had pinged Marta.

<Ma'am, can that psychotropic you're using to implant the Caprise mods induce anterograde amnesia?>

'Anterograde?' Jason mouthed, and Terrance shrugged.

Moments later, he had his answer.

<Someone see something they shouldn't have just now, soldier?> the doctor asked in a dry voice.

Xiao grinned over at her. *<Something like that, yes, ma'am.>*

<Send them down here. You'll need to have someone ready with a believable cover story, though,> she cautioned them.

<I believe I can handle that, doctor,> Logan's voice joined the conversation.

Jason's brows rose. *<How do you plan to fix it?>*

<I'll plant a suggestion that one stumbled into the other, and a

weapon accidentally discharged, catching them both.>

Terrance's skeptical look transferred over into his comment. *<Not sure that's believable.>*

<It will be, thanks to the highly suggestible nature of this particular nanozyme,> Logan assured them. *<We'll have someone from medical escort them back to their shuttle as soon as we've successfully altered their memories.>*

<We'll leave you to it, then.>

Terrance nodded to Xiao and stepped aside as the Marines pushed the cart toward the corridor. He turned back to Jason, but before he could speak, movement at the spaceport-side hatch caught Jason's eye.

Shooting Terrance a surprised look, he asked, "Are we expecting someone else?"

CAPRISE EX MACHINA

STELLAR DATE: 07.04.3302 (Adjusted Gregorian)
LOCATION: ESS *Avon Vale*, Brilliance Station
REGION: Lucent, Luminescent Space, Sirian Hegemony

Marta and Varanee were standing at the entrance to medical as a small crash team arrived towing a stasis pod containing the downed medic.

<*Readings show he's dead, you know,*> Varanee murmured as she followed Marta's gaze, but Marta could feel the surgeon rejecting her own words as soon as they'd been sent.

<*Good thing we have stasis pods stored in that shuttle bay, then, isn't it?*> she responded as the medics pushed the pod through the entrance. Her lips compressed as she saw firsthand the damage the Irid rifle had done.

Stepping back, she waved the team toward the intensive care area. That section was getting a lot of use lately; their medic would join the two burn victims they'd brought back from the platform.

<*He'll recover. Stasis gives us all the time we need to assess the damage. We'll clone what we can't repair—*>

<*A new heart and lung, apparently.*>

<*And we'll have them ready for transplant before we turn off the stasis field.*>

She felt a tendril of amazed wonder from Varanee. <*I never thought we'd have the luxury of freezing time in the midst of an emergency like this.*>

<*It's a game-changer,*> Marta agreed as the first gurney appeared at the entrance. "All right, then," she breathed as she straightened, motioning the medic forward into the main operating theatre. "Time to switch mental gears."

She turned and followed the first gurney into the clean white space, stopping the medic beside the first autodoc. There were four of them all in a row, prepped with empty cylinders, ready to receive their new inhabitants. She positioned a gurney beside each one and instructed them to hold.

She looked around for Charley and found him with Noa at the temporary workspace he'd set up in front of the node outside her office. Human and AI had spent most of the past week on the clones of the outlawed Marsian NSAIs that would take the place of the AIs they intended to free. Together with Tobias, Noa and Charley would handle the coordinated transfer of the four AIs, and the installation of their doppelganger replacements.

Marta started toward the pair, and Charley looked up at her approach. She motioned back toward the gurneys. "We're ready whenever you are. What next?" she asked.

"Go ahead and place them in the autodocs, but hold on anything else just yet," he instructed. "We have guests."

Marta's eyebrow arced at that. "I take it you don't mean these," she said, glancing over at the frozen Lumins.

The AI smiled. "No. Terrance is escorting them from the umbilical."

Marta nodded, then turned and instructed her medical staff to transfer their patients.

"Do I know these new guests?" she asked as they walked over to the surgical theatre.

Charley nodded. "You know one of them, at least. Overseer Hume just arrived, escorting the last of the AIs. I'd like her input before we begin."

"Indira, right? I wondered why she wasn't on the pinnace with the rest," Marta murmured, shooting him a questioning glance.

"Her activities are closely monitored," Logan supplied from behind her, and Marta turned to see the Intelligence officer approaching, accompanied by Quincy, the AI who Shannon had freed.

"She required the escort of an overseer, otherwise she would never have been allowed to approach a non-Sirian ship."

Quincy nodded in agreement. "Cyrus, the vice president who held Indira captive, was the only one who seemed to recognize our true capabilities. Not only did he install her in a frame, he gave her a measure of autonomy—within closely held parameters." The AI canted his head. "She was allowed to perform certain tasks, but *only* those tasks, and compelled to return to his offices once they were complete."

Marta nodded her understanding. She saw Logan look past Charley to where Noa was working on the node that serviced medical, embedded in the bulkhead adjacent to her office. Ordinarily hidden behind thick, shielded plating, its access port lay exposed, revealing nanofilaments flowing from it onto the surface where Noa and Charley worked.

Logan's gaze sharpened, and he glanced back at Charley. "The Caprise clones are ready?" he asked, and the security officer nodded.

Charley was much more than the *Vale*'s chief of security. As the product of a union between a Weapon Born and a multi-nodal AI, Marta knew that Charley was in a unique position to orchestrate this aspect of the deception.

Although not multi-nodal himself, Charley's neural net was larger than any other AI's on the *Vale*. The matrices within his lattice, the ones inherited from his multi-nodal parent, had a capacity exceeding even those of a Weapon Born. This facility allowed him to more seamlessly interface with multi-nodal NSAIs like the one that ran the *Vale*'s autonomous systems.

What he was about to do, though….

Marta glanced from Logan to Charley, her face pensive. "I understand that AI councils are a lot less forgiving than the court systems are on us humans. Are you sure about this?" she asked, variegated gold-green eyes flickering between the two in solemn query.

Logan met her gaze, his own stolid and unyielding, Charley's open expression a soothing counterpoint. Neither spoke, and

Marta raised her hands in surrender.

"I had to ask," she said, smiling to take the sting out of her next words. "We're all complicit, and every one of us is about to bend the Phobos Accords to the point of outright breaking it."

One eyebrow rose on Logan's face, causing Varanee to speak up.

<*We know it's only temporary, good intentions count, extenuating circumstances, and all that, but—*>

"But these are battlefield calls, and sometimes there are no right decisions…only less wrong ones," Logan interrupted Varanee. "It's the only way, and could potentially save thousands of lives. Let us worry about the Accords, doctors."

Charley stirred, turning back to where Noa was working on the tangle of fibers that spilled from the open access port. "To answer your earlier question," he told Logan, "the clones are ready to receive an engram imprint from each AI."

He lifted the nearest immutable crystal storage cube, one of six sitting beside an imprint unit.

"We've already done Quincy's," he said, nodding at the frame that stood to one side of Noa. "But I want to replace Indira's as well. That will give us two subjects to study before we pull the rest from their human hosts."

Marta looked skeptical, but paused as she heard a trickle of laughter emanate from inside her head. <*AI-speed processing is much faster than human thought,*> she reminded Marta. <*They'll have plenty of time to run both the Indira and Quincy models of Caprise through their paces before we're ready to put the autodocs to work.*>

Logan tilted his head in acknowledgment of the truth of Varanee's words as the doors to medical slid open and admitted the newcomers.

<*Time to get to work,*> Varanee murmured as they approached.

* * * * *

Jason sat across from Tobias in the lounge just off the shuttle bay, one hand buried in Tobi's hair. He'd left Terrance and Khela to escort their latest arrival to medical, and had taken off at a run once the Weapon Born had put out the call for his help.

<*Could use that L2 ability of yours to multitask,*> the AI had said, and Jason had responded by telling Tobias he was on his way.

Not that he needed to be physically present for Tobias to pull him into the Expanse. It was just a mental quirk of his, wanting to be physically near in case of trouble.

Like I can do anything about it if we get into trouble in an Expanse, his mind scoffed as he kicked his booted feet up onto the low table in front of him.

<*Ready,*> he told Tobias.

<*Stand by.*>

Information flooded into Jason's mind, details and status updates on the four different story threads Tobias had running. He'd been transported into the one that included Berit, of course. But after what had transpired in the shuttle bay, Jason didn't complain.

Tobias had the Jason simulacrum excuse itself from the group on 'captain's business', stepping out into a corridor. As Jason appeared, the simulacrum dissolved.

<*We've taken them through a sanitized version of Decks One through Four,*> the AI informed him, and Jason nodded.

So they'd seen crew quarters, the observation and dining areas, engineering and life support, and the bridge. He would have liked to have seen how the Expanse represented those last two. He knew without asking that it would have been a redacted version of reality.

As Jason looked around, the overlay he had access to in the Expanse indicated that the commissary and exchange were behind him, the smaller hydroponics bay just ahead.

<So you're on Deck Five, then?>

Tobias sent him a nod. *<The Terrance sim is showing them some of Jonesy's heirloom varietals. Berit looks a wee bit bored.>*

Jason ignored the jibe. *<What's the plan?>*

<Charley's prepping the doppelgangers now. Once he indicates they're ready, 'Terrance' will demo the Vale's *elaborate entertainment holo experience, installed in our rec room.>*

<Elaborate experience? > Jason asked. *<How elaborate are we talking, here?>*

Tobias chuckled. *<Remember what we did to Marine country for the Glimmer-One inspection? That pales in comparison. >*

<Oh yeah?>

<Aye,> the AI drawled, *<and it might involve a wee bit of…sensory enhancement.>*

<Ah, let me guess—something mind-altering enough to mask the effects of a psychotropic drug, by chance?>

The AI made a *tsk*ing sound. *<And they said you were slow.>*

Jason grinned as the doors to the Expanse's version of the hydroponics bay slid open, and he rejoined the group.

The tour that Tobias-as-Terrance led them through included a stop at the non-rotating section of the habitat ring and a walk through Hideaway Park, complete with a distant glimpse of a Proxima cat—which Berit in particular found fascinating.

<I'll have to tell Beck you included him in the Expanse,> Jason sent, and Tobias shot him a mental wink.

<Charley says it's almost time, boyo. Take them on down to the Marine's workout room, and don't act shocked at the transformation.>

Jason sent him a jaded look. *<I think I can handle it, dude.>*

<Well, it was designed to impress a Lumin, you know. Don't say I didn't warn you.>

True to his word, the Expanse's makeover of Marine country was extreme. Tobias had Terrance introduce the holo as a full-sensory experience. Their guests were urged to sit back, strap in, and enjoy the immersive ride.

Charley had chosen to pattern the holo after a spa he'd been to in Tau Ceti. Known for its opulence and extravagant entertainment, the Stone Sea Spa in the Nereids Dust Belt was a perfect foundation for Lumin entertainment. He'd modified the spa's extravagant plasma fireworks display, planting the participant inside the very heart of the show.

Jason waited as everyone reclined into an entertainment cradle. Then the lights dimmed and the show began, the Nereids shimmering into existence all around them.

He'd chosen a cradle in the back, claiming his crew had saved the best seats, the ones in front, for their guests. It allowed him to study the Lumins in an unobtrusive way.

In the darkened holo, he could just make out the enraptured expressions on the faces of their visitors. He had to admit the display was impressive: riding jets of plasma, and being ejected into the midst of exploding asteroids. But he certainly wasn't drawn into it, as they seemed to be. He felt they must be experiencing it on a more surreal level.

Jason suspected that this was due more to drugs being introduced into their systems than the experience, despite how immersive it was.

Confirmation came when he saw Berit gasp in amazement…and then her face fall slack. Looking around, he noted the rest were in a similar state.

The next moment, he was back in the lounge outside the *Vale*'s shuttle bay, Tobias standing over him.

"They've started the autodoc procedures," the AI informed him. "Ready?"

Jason stood with a nod. "Let's go."

*****

The autodocs had begun, timed to run simultaneously at Charley's command. Eschewing standard general anesthesia, the procedure relied on a cocktail of local anesthetics and psychotropic nanozymes to plunge the patients into a dream state. Because of this, the extraction was being monitored with much more care than usual.

"Incisions made," Marta murmured, her eyes glued to the holodisplay over the patient in front of her.

Varanee was monitoring the autodoc behind her; Justin and another medic were keeping watch over the final two. So far, everything was progressing smoothly.

There had been a bit of a hiccup when Hume had first arrived. He'd tried to tell them that one of the Lumins was a member of the Underground and could be pulled from the Expanse.

Charley had overruled him, pointing out that to do so meant her presence in the Expanse would need to be replaced by a sim. Since none of the AIs running the Expanse knew Francesca, emulating her would be an impossible task.

The AI in her head needed to come out, regardless. Francesca was welcome to plead her innocence—after Rae was free.

Marta heard footsteps approaching; a quick glance showed Jason and Tobias stepping up to the smaller observation holo beside Terrance and Khela.

"They're on a wild ride through an asteroid field of exploding plasma," she heard Jason announce, a note of speculation entering his voice.

Terrance chuckled quietly. "From what I hear, that's where fantasy splits from reality. I don't think you actually move through the fireworks at the Stone Sea…you just sit and observe it."

Jason's voice was edged with disappointment. "No?"

"No."

<*Extraction one complete,*> Varanee announced.

Marta watched as a nurse picked up a freshly-filled cylinder and carried it over to the open node where Charley stood. She swung her eyes back to the display as the autodoc signaled another completion.

"Number two," she announced, lifting the cylinder and handing it into a waiting nurse's hands.

The next two went just as smoothly, and Marta ordered the medics to continue to monitor vitals and keep the mimetic ability of the nanozymes steady, as she strode briskly over to where the four cylinders sat.

Noa held up a hand to forestall any questions. He stood, motioning her aside.

"They're in a small expanse of their own right now," he explained. "They can work much faster in there, transferring data and optimizing the Caprise apps, modeling them after each AI's memory engrams."

"How much longer?" Marta kept her voice low out of habit, although the tableau in front of her was unlike any operating theatre she'd ever been a part of.

Logan straightened, reaching for an immutable crystal storage reader as Charley handed him the first ICS cube.

"Looks like the first one's ready to test."

Marta's brows crept to her hairline as she rounded on Noa.

"Test?" she asked incredulously.

His eyes flickered in rare amusement. "It would appear Hume was correct. Rae confirmed that Francesca is the leader of the Underground in the Hegemony, and said that Francesca can test the Marsian 'Rae' for us to see it passes muster."

Marta glanced uncertainly over at Logan. "I thought we couldn't bring her out of the Expanse because no one running it could imitate her."

The intelligence officer indicated the row of cylinders that were now being installed into mobile frames. "Rae can. She'll run the Francesca sim while we revive the original. We need Francesca's feedback on the Caprise NSAI running the Rae engram."

Marta ran the fingers of her organic hand through her hair.

"Stars, this is getting complicated," she muttered.

"A riddle, wrapped in a mystery, inside an enigma," Noa replied, earning him a glance of dark amusement.

"Okay, let's get it done, then."

* * * * *

Francesca blinked in disorientation as the Stone Sea experience abruptly ended. The cradle she'd been reclining in morphed into a diagnostic bed, and she found herself surrounded by medical personnel, with Terrance and Jason standing behind them.

"Easy," a woman dressed in scrubs said, as she stepped forward and helped her rise to a sitting position.

Francesca's mind was fogged and cloudy, and she realized with some alarm that she'd been drugged.

"Rae?" she spoke aloud without thinking, and two voices answered her in unison. Confused, she looked around and caught sight of a mobile frame moving toward her.

"Francesca, it's me." The voice emanating from it was one she was used to hearing in her head.

That was when she realized why she was feeling groggy, and what the mobile frame signified.

Suns, she's free. We did it.

The thought elicited a wave of conflicting emotions—happiness for her friend, and bittersweet melancholy over her own loss.

<I can feel your sudden sadness. Anything I can do to help?>

Francesca jumped, startled.

"I, uhm, take it that my doppelganger just said hello?" Rae hazarded.

Francesca shot her friend a guarded look. "Anything you should be telling me, Rae?" she asked, and was disoriented when she received responses from inside her head as well as from the AI standing in front of her.

Her eyes widened as realization set in, and she gaped in shock at the AI standing before her. "Caprise? It *worked*?"

Rae's frame nodded and turned to address a figure off to one side. "Any way to pause Fake-Rae for a sec?"

Abruptly, the thing inside Francesca's brain stilled.

She smiled in bemusement. "I…suppose when I suggested it, it didn't occur to me that *I'd* be receiving one."

Terrance stepped forward at that. "So it was you all along. The one who supplied Hume with the insider information."

Francesca nodded. "Guilty as charged. Ironic, isn't it, that everything seems to circle back to the *Hyperion*?" She gestured to Rae. "The AIs, this outlawed Caprise, and now the ship itself as the vessel to free hundreds."

"I can appreciate a fine bit of irony as much as the next guy," Jason said, crossing his arms with a scowl. "But I'm having a tough time understanding what a Lumin would get out of the deal. Seems you guys don't take a leak without a cost/benefit analysis first. So, what's in it for you?"

Skepticism. Should have seen that coming, with the performance I delivered down on the planet.

She drew in a fortifying breath and let it out on a nod.

"I can see why you'd question my motives, given what you've seen of the Hegemony. But I've always found that there are very few things that are truly black and white, Captain." She shot him a challenging look. "Wouldn't you agree?"

Jason returned her look with a guarded one of his own, but then he inclined his head a fraction.

Francesca sent him a wry smile, acknowledging his doubt. "Not *every* Lumin is wholly self-absorbed. Some actually do seek to better the worlds in which we live." She shrugged, self-deprecating, her eyes straying once more to the frame that now held her closest friend and confidant before returning to meet Jason's.

"I was raised by one such Lumin. My parent was CEO of the Hegemony at one time," she told him, "and happened to disagree with the way our people treat the Noctus. She thought that there was nothing worse than a person who did not honor their contracts, and clearly, the Hegemony had reneged upon the one held with the original colonists."

"Doesn't look like she did much about it," Khela murmured, moving up to stand beside Terrance. Her words, spoken softly, could have held rancor, but her eyes were thoughtful.

Francesca's mouth twisted in a slight grimace as she shook her head. "No, she didn't. But she tried. She told the board she was going to expunge all debts the Noctus held. She argued that people worked harder when they were more personally invested in a company's success, and that having good partners was more desirable than owning slaves." She opened her hands in a helpless gesture. "They overruled her, and she soon found herself out of a job, a pariah within her own caste."

She met Jason's eyes head-on, willing him to believe her. His expression eased, and he nodded again.

She drew in a relieved breath as she looked back at Rae. "So, what now?"

"We'd like you to run the Rae doppelganger through its paces, see if you can spot any glaring inconsistencies that might cause your compatriots to grow suspicious," said the AI who had paused the Rae inside her head.

Francesca straightened and clasped her hands. "I can do that," she murmured.

"Good," the doctor standing beside her said, as she stepped closer, lifting a medsleeve-clad hand to the back of Francesca's skull. "Now lie back. I want to examine your incision and run a few scans to see how well you handled the procedure."

As Francesca complied, she felt the NSAI come back online. Fifteen minutes later, she'd run the facsimile through its paces and declared it good.

"You've done remarkable work," she told them with a smile as she stood. "I didn't expect a modified Caprise to be so…."

"Lifelike?" Rae's voice interjected, her tone wry. "Well, I *did* donate a copy of my memory engram to the cause. I think it should last long enough for us to make a clean getaway."

Terrance smiled. "You sound like my navigation officer. Shannon's been comparing this to a con game."

Francesca's brow rose at the unfamiliar term.

"Stealing something from someone after we've convinced them we're trustworthy," Jason explained. She saw his eyes flicker as if he was checking on something. "And now that we know we've made our Caprises believable, I think it's about time we take this charade to the next level."

CATNAPPED

STELLAR DATE: 07.04.3302 (Adjusted Gregorian)
LOCATION: ESS *Avon Vale*
REGION: Luminescent Space, Sirian Hegemony

At that very moment, in Jason's office, a sound alerted Tobi that she was no longer alone. However, a quick ping of the shipnet told her that Jason and Tobias were still in medical working on their guests, so it couldn't be them.

She cracked one eye open to see if she needed to sound an alarm, but shut it again when she scented the intruder's identity.

It was The Brat.

With a low growl, she rolled onto her side and ordered the holo's sunbeam off. Beck was not invited to share her sun puddle. He could order up his own, using a holo somewhere else—anywhere else, as far as she was concerned.

She heard the soft click of nails as he approached, and growled once again as he chirruped and stuck his wet nose in her face.

<You awake? I got an idea. Wanna hear it?>

Small puffs of air tickled the tufts of fur around her ear. She shook her head in reflex and sent him another warning growl.

<Beat it. I'm sleeping.>

<You can sleep any old time,> he grumbled, nuzzling her once more and giving the side of her face a tentative lick.

That earned him a hiss and a sharp nip, which would have scored his ear if he hadn't quickly reared back.

<C'mon, Tobi. I wanna help Terrance, and I got an idea.>

Huffing, she rolled over to face the platinum-furred cat, and pierced him with a glare. *<This better be good. You interrupted an important nap.>*

Beck scrunched up his muzzle. *<You think **all** naps are important.>*

Tobi yawned in his face, flashing two-centimeter-long incisors at him before closing them with a snap. Beck backed away and planted his butt on the deck, ducking his head and tilting it to one side as she sat up.

<Get to the point, Brat. You're eating into my busy schedule.>

Beck chuffed at that, but was apparently too fired up over his grand plan to counter her claim.

<Terrance said no talking around the visitors,> he began.

<Jason said to stay out of sight, too,> Tobi warned, but Beck just shrugged, as if that was open to interpretation.

Which, Tobi considered, was true of just about everything, given that they were cats.

Beck stood and began to pace. *<So, the way I see it, if they think we can't understand them, they might say some things in front of us.>* He leapt up onto the desk and peered down at her. *<**Secret** things. Things that can help us with our mission.>*

Tobi sat back and studied the Brat as he began to prowl across the top of the desk, tail lashing as he warmed to his topic.

<I can listen in on their plans and then report back to Terrance,> he enthused. *<And they'll never suspect.>*

He stopped and looked down at her once more. His eyes gleamed with excitement, and Tobi began to feel the thrill of the hunt.

Sensing success, he stepped forward—and lost his footing as he planted a paw on top of a pile of hyfilms.

Backpedaling to regain his balance, his actions sent the sheets skidding to the deck, breaking the spell. Tobi shook herself, the moment broken.

<Fine,> she sniffed, pinning his aqua eyes with a baleful glare from her own tawny ones. *<Go play Super Spy. But don't come crying to me if you get caught,>* she tossed over her shoulder as she returned to her bed and turned on the holo of the sunbeam once more. *<Wake me when you crack the case. Or don't.>*

She heard a soft *thump* as Beck leapt down from the desk. He started in her direction, but she rolled toward the bulkhead, giving him her back.

<Don't get your tail caught in the door on your way out.>

* * * * *

The transition out of the Expanse and back into reality was staged in a lift this time, with a simple power outage being blamed for the brief disorientation the VPs experienced.

Terrance saw Jason hide a smirk as Berit frowned.

"I thought Enfield technology was a bit more reliable than this," the Lumin complained.

"Sorry," Jason lied smoothly. "Our engineer has been rerouting a few systems, taking advantage of the ship being docked to work on maintenance upgrades. I'm sure it was just a temporary glitch, nothing to worry about."

Cyrus stared suspiciously at him before shifting his gaze to Terrance. "Perhaps this ship just isn't used to being maintained to the same standards we expect of Hegemony vessels," he murmured, his voice edged with censure.

Terrance offered his apologies while stifling a groan.

<Stars, I'd forgotten how tedious the corporate game is,> he complained over the team's net, as the lift began moving upward toward the habitat ring. *<I'll be glad when this is all behind us.>*

The evening's sole purpose was to test the functioning of the Caprise implants in a controlled environment before releasing the Luminescent vice presidents back into the Hegemony.

Of course, they didn't know that.

The Lumins were there for entirely different reasons, corporate espionage being at the top of the list.

Speaking of which….

<Jonesy, how are you coming with the modifications to those stasis pods?> Terrance called out, as Jason asked their guests what they thought of the Stone Sea experience.

Jonesy sent a thumbs-up in response.

It had been the engineer's suggestion to use the stasis pods as the good-faith gift to the Hegemony. The team knew Enfield would need to give the Lumins something to maintain the cover of a company seeking a trade agreement.

Terrance had been nervous about the choice at first, but Shannon had assured him that Jonesy could rig them so that the pods' systems lagged at the first sign of tampering.

<*Just adding the final countermeasures,*> the engineer informed him, and Terrance nodded. <*We'll have them waiting at the Hegemony pinnace to be discovered when our guests return to their ship.*>

<*Just make sure they're Hegemony-proof,*> the exec admonished, and Jonesy sent him a shaft of reassurance.

<*No worries, boss. No one's getting Enfield tech on my watch.*>

<*Good to hear,*> he replied, mental tone dry. <*Although it won't be because they haven't tried.*>

Thanks to Francesca and the *Hyperion* AIs, Terrance knew that Rubin planned to use Quincy to sneak past the ship's defenses. The Lumin had instructed the AI to locate one of the *Avon Vale*'s nodes, penetrate its safeguards, and gain backdoor access. Once inside, he was to gather every scrap of Enfield data he could find.

Francesca's intel had led to the idea of sandboxing a node near the central shaft of the habitat ring. It would be left conveniently unguarded, preloaded with data of Phantom Blade's choosing. The doppelganger would quietly wander off during the reception and report its success to Rubin shortly thereafter.

Quincy had told them that Rubin had a team of Irids from the Tech Guild standing by to sift through whatever data they managed to glean during their visit to the *Vale*. The data would be legitimate, but useless and several decades out of date.

The data Charley and Logan had compiled was wrapped in a code that was difficult, yet not impossible for an NSAI to break. They'd assured Terrance it would be weeks before the Lumins realized that what looked like cutting-edge innovation held schematics and diagrams for materials and tech widely used in most systems.

He shook his head as he considered the dark underbelly of corporate life.

<*Why are you shaking your head?*> Kodi asked, causing the corner of his host's mouth to kick up in wry humor.

<*Just the less savory side of human nature. You know, greed, avarice.*>

<*Ah. Lumins, then,*> Kodi returned.

<*Pretty much,*> he agreed, as the lift slowed to a halt. <*Ready to go dark, now that we've arrived?*>

<*Rigged for silent running, aye sir,*> came the smart reply.

Terrance felt the AI's presence fade from his mind as he stepped out of the lift and onto a pathway that led into one of the habitat's forested parks.

The *Vale*'s head chef and her staff had transformed one of the greenspaces within Hideaway Park just for the gathering. Vi had drawn heavily from Khela's cultural history for the event's décor, Terrance saw, as they stepped off the gravel path.

Translucent shoji screens framed in bamboo rimmed the area, and paper-style lanterns hung from the trees edging the park. Small origami cranes and other fantastical creatures decorated the centers of tables scattered around the clearing. Along one side ran a row of tables, each laden with dishes local to the various cultures from which the crew hailed. Chefs stood behind food prep stations at one end, ready with made-to-order creations to tease the palate.

<*Nice,*> Jason sent, stepping aside to make room for Shannon, who had just joined them from her shift on the bridge.

A tendril of amusement drifted through the team net, and Terrance glanced down to see a slight smile playing on Khela's lips.

<*Not bad,*> she admitted as she surveyed Vi's handiwork. <*Not necessarily accurate, mind you, but who cares when it's pretty? They'll*

never know the difference.>

Terrance returned his gaze to the meadow, lit by the habitat to simulate twilight, his eyes narrowing in thought as he studied their surroundings for things that might be out of place. It all seemed fine to him.

<I'll take your word for it, love. Looks attractive, and the food smells great.>

Stepping forward to gain everyone's attention, he thanked the Lumins for coming, introduced Vi and her staff, then encouraged them to sample the fare and enjoy the evening. Then, hooking an arm around Khela's waist, they began to mingle among their guests.

Gavin complimented Terrance on his efficient crew, and asked after manufacturing processes in Alpha Centauri; Currin engaged them in a lengthy comparison of cuisines. Both men met them with ready smiles.

<Well, they ***seem*** *to be acting as if nothing's amiss,>* Khela mused, as they greeted Cyrus and engaged him in a conversation about the differences in wines from Tau Ceti and Alpha Centauri.

<Mmmhmm,> he responded. *<So far, our Caprises seem to be functioning as planned.>*

He allowed his gaze to sweep the crowd. As far as their guests knew, everyone present was human. All AIs present were incognito. Shannon had already established her bona fides, and Tobias and Logan were in small service bot frames designed for covert infiltration.

Kodi, Varanee, and Tama remained silent inside their human partners, their power output easily explained as augmentations, should any of their guests be rude enough to scan.

<Anyone see anything out of the ordinary?> he sent over the net.

<Nothing, sir,> Lena reported. *<Except that they keep trying to hack into our shipnet to listen in on conversations. Charley just set up a sandboxed comm channel out here for them to hack. Vi's staff are on it, and they know they're being monitored.>*

<Good idea,> Khela said. *<Send the rest of us the channel. We'll join in occasionally as well.>*

Lena returned a mental salute. *<Will do, Cap.>*

Twenty minutes later, Xiao reported in from his post at the edge of Hideaway Park.

<Quincy-bot just snuck away,> he announced.

Terrance saw Khela's lips turn up.

<As you said, love—exactly as planned,> she teased, before switching to the team net. *<Is Rubin receiving a feed?>*

<Yes, ma'am. Here it is, if you want to take a look,> the Marine confirmed, tossing an icon up for them to access.

<Charley does good work,> Shannon pronounced after a moment's scrutiny.

She glanced up from where she stood at the crepe station as Terrance and Khela approached.

<And you're sure it'll take them weeks to decipher?> Khela's voice was doubtful.

<Oh, please. The only AIs they ***think*** *they have right now to throw at something like this are really only modified Caprises, and they're all under our control,>* Shannon responded with a mental snort. *<Everything else they can throw at it will be straight up NSAIs. Even if they do dedicate a multi-nodal to deciphering, they'll spend a good week or so on it before they crack it.>*

Jason came up from behind them, for once not trailed by Berit.

<Pretty confident of Charley's skills, are you, short stuff?> He shot Shannon a mental grin as he lifted his beer.

Freshly made crepe in hand, she swirled her finger through the whipped cream topping, turned to Jason, and flicked it at him. The dollop landed right on the tip of his nose.

<Yep.> She smirked, winked, and turned to walk away with Rubin.

Jason sent a mock scowl. *<Aren't you too busy flirting and eating to be flicking whipped cream onto hapless ship's captains? Maybe I should write you up for insubordination.>*

<*Speaking of hapless ship's captains,*> Terrance turned, eyeing Jason curiously. <*Where's your shadow, and how's Berit reacting to the new Wallis?*>

He wasn't prepared for the uncertain expression that crossed Jason's face.

<*I'm…not sure.*>

Terrance straightened and shot a quick glance over at Khela before returning Jason's look with a concerned one of his own.

<*What do you mean?*>

<*That woman's been impossible to shake, but a few minutes ago, she suddenly stepped away,*> Jason admitted, looking around at the crowd. <*Looks like she's talking to someone. Could be something's up, but if so, I'm just not sure what.*>

<*Xiao?*> Khela asked the Marine monitoring the Caprise feeds.

There was a moment of silence, and then, <*Nothing out of the ordinary, Cap'n. She hasn't interfaced with the Wallis-bot much at all. It's got to be something else.*> The Marine's voice held a trace of uneasiness.

<*I'll follow after her,*> Jason said. <*I'll let you know if it looks like we've been made.*>

*****

<*I'm in!*> Berit heard Currin's comment ring out over the secured VP line just a few minutes after they had arrived at the park inside the ship's habitat ring. The marketing VP's voice held a muted note of triumph to it.

His announcement was followed by a token tagged *"Avon Vale,"* delivered to her Link. Accessing it, she heard a separate channel come online, filled with the mental voices of their hosts.

Careful what you wish for, Currin, Berit thought with amusement as she identified the voices of the caterers and then, once or twice, a comment by Enfield and his wife. *Listening in on private conversation's not always what you expect. I don't think that Shannon thinks too highly of you….*

<*Anything of value so far?*> she inquired, but received a negative from him.

Given that spying was a way of life in the Hegemony, Berit had no trouble splitting her attention as she drifted through the crowd, enjoying the food and the company of Jason Andrews while listening in on the purloined ship's channel.

One of the Irid security guards seemed captivated by something happening at one of the food stations, and she wondered idly what had captured his attention. Bored with the topic Gavin was currently engaged in, she pinged the guard.

The man jumped as if shot.

I do so love the effect I have on people, she mused before asking him what was so fascinating.

<*Well, ma'am,*> he began, turning as if to follow the progress of something with his eyes—something that disappeared into the trees. <*This is going to sound kind of weird, but I could swear I just saw a talking cat.*>

<*A cat? Like a robotic toy, or an NSAI in the form of a cat?*>

<*Neither, ma'am. Looked like the real deal, a large animal.*>

<*Like the one we saw on our tour earlier?*> she asked, intrigued. This sounded much more interesting than Gavin's new virtual reality experience. <*Describe it to me.*>

If the Irid was to be believed, it was a handsome feline, standing a little over a meter tall. The cat had sidled up to one of the chefs and asked, pretty as you please, for a crepe of his own. The chef had scolded the creature like he was a kid caught awake past his bedtime, and the cat had responded by promising to leave the habitat.

<*He sounded sentient, ma'am,*> the Irid added, causing Berit to raise a brow. <*Chef told him that he wasn't supposed to be out here, captain's orders.*>

<*Oh,* ***really****? How interesting,*> Berit responded. <*I wonder if it's that creature we saw earlier. I'd love to see one, up close.*>

<I'll have the guards keep an eye out, ma'am. If we see it again, we'll try to grab it for you.>

* * * * *

Beck licked the whipped cream off his whiskers as he trotted over to the habitat ring's lift. He knew a good spy was supposed to remain incognito, but the food had smelled so delicious, and his friend Dee had been making the crepes. She *always* snuck him handouts when he asked.

He'd been careful to stick to the shadows when he snuck up behind her. What he hadn't expected was for her to reprimand him like an idiot cub for being out when he shouldn't. Beck had desperately wanted to explain he was on a mission, but realized just then that one of the strangers was staring at him.

Dee had sighed, then capitulated, picking out a salmon-mousse-filled crepe for him. She'd pulled it away as he'd reached up for it, only handing it over after extracting a promise that he'd leave straight away.

How'm I supposed to help if no one lets me? Shannon said they'll be leaving after the dinner and….

His thoughts drifted off as he realized the one place he hadn't thought to snoop was inside the visitors' ship. He stopped, sneezed decisively, and set out at an easy lope for the shuttle deck.

* * * * *

George was still having a hard time accepting that he'd done something as boneheaded as slipping on the pinnace's ramp. Not only that, but if the *Avon Vale*'s people were to be believed, he'd managed to take Floyd out in the process.

Scratching the back of his neck, he secured the pinnace's comm board after using it to ping the spaceport with an all's well before walking back down the ramp to join Floyd.

"Message from one of the overseers just came in," he said by way of greeting. "Cyrus and Gavin are expected back on Brilliance in two hours."

Floyd nodded, stretching his neck to one side and rolling his shoulder to loosen it as he stifled a yawn. "Be good to get back to the station. Got a date lined up for tomorrow. Could use some sack time before then."

George just grunted and began to pace the pinnace's perimeter, returning the cautious nod of the *Avon Vale* soldier with one of his own. He moved more to stretch his legs than to police the ship's perimeter; the vessel's sensor suite fed him a full 360-degree feed. If something approached the ship, he'd know it.

As he walked, he reached out to his squad leader, Raj.

<*Headbutt any Centaurans lately?*> Raj greeted, which George returned with a rude gesture.

<*How's it going with the veeps?*> he asked, eager to change the subject.

Raj sent a mental shrug. <*More of the same, different location,*> he replied. <*Although the habitat's decent, food smells great, and….*> His voice trailed off.

<*And what?*> George prompted. <*See anything interesting?*>

<*As a matter of fact, maybe I did,*> the squad leader admitted. <*Ever heard of a talking cat?*>

George laughed. <*Yeah, right, Sarge. Setting up shop in the Gran Piazza, right next to the dancing bear?*> he asked, and Raj's avatar bared his teeth.

<*Not shittin' plasma here, soldier. He's a big thing, used some sort of an embedded Link to talk to one of the ship's chefs. Strangest damn thing I've ever seen. I'd swear that thing is sentient.*>

<*Big, you say?*> Floyd interjected, his tone strangled and soft. <*About forty kilos or so? Pale fur, green eyes?*>

<*Yeah,*> Raj admitted. <*Sounds about right. Why? You seen him?*>

<He's here now, sniffing around,> Floyd sent, mental voice taut. *<Just leapt up inside the pinnace. Looks like some sort of wild animal that could bite your head off as soon as he'd look at you. Maybe we should shoot it.>*

<Hold your fire,> Raj said quickly. *<If it's what I think it is, it'll be worth some creds if you can catch it.>*

<Okay.> Floyd's mental voice was just a whisper. *<But I gotta warn you…that thing comes at me, I'm shooting.>*

<Non-lethal force only, or you answer to me, soldier, you got that?> Raj barked.

As George rounded the pinnace's nose, he saw Floyd reflexively raise his weapon and snap to attention.

<Sir, yes, sir,> came the automatic reply.

Floyd's eyes darted to George when he caught him approaching from the corner of his eye. Both men swung toward the pinnace's hatch as a soft scratch sounded.

<Be quick about it,> Raj's voice cut in. *<We're mustering now. Should be there in about fifteen minutes.>*

"Sir, yes, sir," Floyd muttered sarcastically as he shot George a jaded look. Gesturing toward the ramp, he added, "You first."

THE GREAT CAT CAPER

STELLAR DATE: 07.04.3302 (Adjusted Gregorian)
LOCATION: ESS *Avon Vale*
REGION: Luminescent Space, Sirian Hegemony

<*Tobi? Tobi!*>

Beck's mental voice sounded panicked. Tobi ignored it, rolling over and snorting into the blanket that covered her bed.

<*Tobi! They've spotted me,*> the voice broke in again, breathless this time, as if the other cat was running. <*What do I do?*>

<*You've reached Tobi's answering service. Tobi's not available to take your comm right now. Please leave a message at the beep. BEEP!*> she replied in a singsong voice, then cut the connection.

Beck pinged her again; again she ignored him. This went on for a few minutes until finally, Tobi'd had enough.

<***What?!*** *Can't you leave me alone for one single hour?*>

<*Tobi, I'm trapped!*> His mental voice was a plaintive wail.

Tobi remained unmoved.

<*Then get un-trapped.*>

<*I…I can't. They locked me inside their ship, and now it's* ***moving****. Tobi, HALP!*>

She sat up, abruptly realizing that Beck was in serious danger.

Great horking hairballs. I should have known he'd get into trouble.

Scrambling to her feet, she raced through the office and out the corridor to the lifts.

<*Beck?*> she called out, but received no answer.

Scrambling to a stop beside the stairwell, she sprinted up two flights to the top of the stacked decks. Exiting by the maglev platform, she hissed as she realized the car must still be up at the shuttle bay, more than a quarter of a kilometer away.

Utility steps fashioned from metal grating were welded into the scaffolding of the maglev's trunkline. They weren't ideal for her paw pads, but she had no choice.

She began to climb in great, bounding leaps, powerfully muscled legs propelling her upward faster than any unaugmented human's could. As she did, Tobi instinctively reached out to the two people she knew best—Jason and Tobias.

Tobias was the one who responded.

<What is it, little lass?> the Weapon Born inquired. His tone sounded distracted, and Tobi felt guilty. *<We're a mite busy right now.>*

Tobi paused, squeezing her eyes shut for a brief moment, one ear twitching as she thought furiously about what to do next. As she opened them again, she caught the maglev car speeding past, Jonesy and a few of his crew its only passengers.

Her claws dug into the metal grill as she came to an abrupt halt. Flinging a mental cry to the engineer, she whirled, her eyes tracking the descending car.

*<Jonesy! **Help**! Beck's been stolen!>*

A shaft of confusion and concern was thrust at her, and then Jonesy's welcoming voice filled the connection.

<Stolen? What do you mean?>

<The strangers—we need to stop them from leaving. They have Beck!>

She felt more than heard the sensation of Jonesy's sharp inhale, a weird mental construct the big cat processed in the back of her uplifted brain.

<Stars, Tobi! Their pinnace just left! It'll be impossible to call them back.>

Tobi abruptly sat back on her haunches, stunned at the news.

*<What am I going to tell Terrance and Khela? And Jason. He's going to ground me—**forever**,>* she wailed, her tail thumping hard against the steel steps in her agitation.

The connection remained open, but Jonesy was silent.

<Meet me down in engineering,> he said finally, his tone thoughtful. *<I may have an idea….>*

* * * * *

Flo looked up and waved as Jonesy jogged into the maintenance section of engineering. She was still working to help move the AIs from the *Hyperion* into frames of their own choosing. Jonesy was relieved to see her.

Good. Just who I hoped to find.

"Hi, Flo," he greeted. "Macie, nice to meet you. Welcome aboard the *Avon Vale*."

<*Thank you,*> the AI responded. <*I can't tell you what a relief it is to be here.*>

The thundering sound of paws racing along the sole of the ship's deck reached them as Tobi skidded into the room, tawny flanks heaving from effort.

Flo looked up in alarm. "Tobi! What's wrong?"

<*I got here as fast as I could,*> the big cat panted, her big golden eyes wide as they speared Jonesy. <*What's your idea? When can we leave? We have to get him back before Terrance finds out!*>

Jonesy raised his hands in a calming gesture. "Hold on, now. Since that ship has sailed, we have to apply some good old-fashioned engineering cunning to fix this problem."

Turning to a baffled Flo, and an equally bewildered Macie, he informed them, "We have a bit of a security problem here. I'd fill you in, but I'm going to have to swear you to secrecy first. Or Tobi and I can seek help elsewhere."

He lapsed into silence, one eyebrow lifted patiently as Flo and Macie considered what he'd just said. He knew Flo; the engineer was nothing if not inquisitive. She wouldn't be able to help but agree, if for no other reason than to assuage her curiosity.

Flo finished seating Macie into the frame, a thoughtful expression on her face as she sealed its front panel. Looking first at Tobi and then up at Jonesy, she nodded.

"Consider me sworn."

Flo turned to Macie with a questioning look as the AI rose from her seated position. "I take it that someone important to you just went missing? And by missing, I mean kidnapped by an unscrupulous Lumin?" At Jonesy's nod, Macie frowned. "We can't let another AI be enslaved."

"Um." Jonesy cleared his throat, but Tobi beat him to it.

<*It's not an AI,*> the cat said, advancing toward Macie, tawny eyes wide. <*It's Beck.*>

Flo made a sound of astonishment as her gaze darted to Jonesy. "Stars, Terrance is going to be *furious*."

<*It's not my fault,*> Tobi sent, but there was a guilty flavor to her words that belied her denial. <*How was I supposed to know he was serious about spying on them? Or that he'd get himself cat-napped?*>

Macie turned to Flo and Jonesy. "Sentient? Uplifted?" Jonesy nodded again, and Macie cocked her head. "It'll be Berit, then. She has a taste for the exotic."

Tobi's low growl had them all turning to stare at the big cat, whose hackles were raised and lips drawn back in a feral snarl.

<*No one's eating him on my watch!*>

"Figure of speech," Macie said hastily. "Berit wouldn't eat a creature as unusual as your Beck," she explained. "She'd just want him as an oddity, a toy to show off."

Tobi looked suspiciously at the AI for a moment, then walked over and sniffed her.

<*Truth,*> the cat pronounced decisively, and sat back on her haunches with an expectant look. <*So where do we begin with the cunning? Cats happen to be exceptionally good at that, you know.*>

Flo looked amused at Macie's consternation.

"We're not sure how, but Tobi here seems to be able to sense AIs," she explained. "We've yet to be able to explain it, or fully test what she can and cannot sense from us."

Macie shook her head, seemingly mystified.

Jonesy thought for a moment, then stirred, shooting Tobi a glance. "Okay, here's the plan. I have an acquaintance within the

Hegemony. A sort of friend I made yesterday, one of Rubin's adjuncts. I'll call him and see if he can't help us get Beck back."

"He's going to want something for his trouble," Macie warned.

Jonesy nodded. "I figured as much. I'll offer him one more of our stasis pods in exchange for the delivery of Beck to us, safe and unharmed."

Flo gaped at him. "You can't just—"

She bit off what she was about to say and tried again.

"Don't you have to get Terrance's approval for something like that?"

Jonesy smiled. "If I intended to actually do such a thing, absolutely. But they stole Beck from us. They don't get a reward for that. This'll just be the bait I dangle to get him to bring Beck to us."

Turning to the nearest console, he dipped his hand into the holo, cycling through a few screens until he found the icon he sought. Tapping it, he called up a direct connection to Shannon.

<Hey, what's up?>

"You up for another Jim Brown?"

Shannon's eyes widened, and she leant forward. Her tone severe, she pointed her finger at him accusingly and asked, *<Jones Branit the Third, exactly what do you have up your sleeve this time?>*

After filling her in on the plan, and gaining her assistance with the covert launch of the *Eidolon*, Jonesy cut the connection.

He sat back, staring up at the ceiling as his mind organized a list of everything they needed to do before they began their recovery mission. With a nod, he looked down and caught a speculative look on Flo's face.

"What?" he asked.

"Oh, nothing. Just...." She shrugged. "I always thought Jones was your last name. Or your only name.... Mister Branit the Third."

Jonesy groaned. "Remember the whole sworn to secrecy thing? That right there falls under mission scope. Got it?"

"Uh huh," Flo said, patting his shoulder with a wink as she walked past on her way over to the stasis pod the engineering team had used as a model for their anti-tampering solution. Tapping the top of it, she turned back to him. "Is this our bait?"

He nodded and stood. "Let's get her loaded up. I'll ping Varga on our way to the shuttle."

Macie held up her hand to forestall him. "If you're planning to go down there," she cautioned, "it would be best if you have a sympathetic insider other than someone you're paying off. You'll need more than Varga."

"I thought of that," Jonesy agreed. "I don't want to compromise Vice President Francesca, but we could sure use her help. Or do you have someone else in mind?"

Macie turned as another frame entered the room. Gesturing toward the newcomer, she smiled. "Actually, yes. I pinged Rae the moment you mentioned the rescue." She looked at the AI formerly paired with Francesca with an expectant air.

The frame Jonesy had seen Rae in a scant three hours earlier was humanoid in fashion. He'd known she'd be restructuring its features to somewhat resemble her former human partner, but now....

Rae must have begun remolding the frame into an exact replica of her friend the moment Macie pinged her. The transformation was uncanny.

The figure that walked through the entrance had golden brown hair, cropped into a stylish wedge and framing a strong face with a patrician nose. She was clad in one of the tailored, couture suits the vice president favored.

Francesca's wide-set hazel eyes looked determinedly back at Jonesy.

"I hear we have a flight to catch?" Rae offered with a smile, her voice a smooth contralto, perfectly mimicking the voiceprint of Francesca.

Jonesy's face broke into a grin. "Madam Vice President, I

believe I have the honor of being your pilot today."

*****

Varga smiled and sat back as the image of the man on the other end of the holo finished explaining his predicament.

"I could really use your help with this," Jonesy ended.

Varga nodded solemnly at the engineer. He liked the thought of having the man from the *Avon Vale* beholden to him.

"Let me see what I can do," he said, straightening.

He held up a finger, an unspoken request for Jonesy to hold as he pinged the station for the pinnace's location. A moment later, his gaze returned to the dusky face of the man on the holo.

"Looks like they docked about two hours ago. I'll check in with Overseer Greta, see what she knows."

Varga tapped his bottom lip with a stylus as he considered the situation for a moment.

"I think you're right," he continued. "If I had to guess, your package is in Vice President Berit's possession."

There was a pause, and the image of the man on the other end leant in toward the holorecorder's pickups.

"I have to get him back before Mister Enfield discovers he's gone. That cat—he's Mister Enfield's personal pet." Jonesy grimaced. "You know how particular senior executives can be. I'd hate to think this could jeopardize negotiations...."

As the man's voice trailed off, Varga understood what Jonesy was implying. He also knew that the man was in no position to bargain—he needed to get that animal back, and that meant he'd be willing to make a deal in order to get it.

"Things could get a bit tricky on this end," Varga cautioned. "I might need to offer some form of compensation or trade in order to obtain what you're looking for."

Jonesy nodded, then glanced over his shoulder, as if checking to ensure no one overheard. "We provided your executives with a gift of two stasis pods as they departed," he began. "A show of good faith that we were serious about contract negotiations with the Hegemony."

Varga saw one shoulder raise in a half shrug as the man sat back in his chair aboard the *Vale*. After a moment, Jonesy cocked his head.

"What if I could manage to get my hands on a third one? Surely that would be of greater value to the Hegemony—to Vice President Berit—than a mere animal?"

Varga stifled a grin at that. A third stasis pod meant that this animal was of significant value to Enfield.

I wonder what else I can negotiate for, if he's leading with the pod?

Jonesy frowned, and Varga wondered if something of what he was thinking had shown on his face.

The engineer leant forward again, interlacing his fingers as he clasped them in his lap. "I'm willing to do this only because we're in a hurry. The *Avon Vale* is scheduled to depart this station within the next few hours. I don't have time to dicker over this. If she really wants the cat, I can leave you with some genetic material that'll allow her to clone one of her own."

He shrugged, his eyes narrowing, as he added, "Take it or leave it, Varga. Yeah, I'll get in trouble if we don't get Mister Enfield's cat back, but it's not like he's going to have me drawn and quartered for it."

Varga nodded judiciously while rolling a stylus back and forth between his fingers.

Ah, well. So much for upping the ante. Hiding his disappointment in a smile, he straightened. "Let me ping a few people, see what I can discover." He cast his eyes to the left, glancing at the time on his overlay. "I'll get back to you within the hour."

Jonesy steepled his fingers and stared back at him, then jerked a nod of thanks before signing off.

Three hours later, Varga stood at one of the loading docks in the warehouse district of the spaceport, a large plas crate at his feet. Inside the crate reclined the unconscious form of a large cream-colored cat.

As the dock's alarms began to sound, Varga smiled in anticipation, motioning for the two Security Guild Irids he'd hired to conceal their presence from the incoming ship.

What's nicer than a third stasis pod? An Enfield shuttle.

*****

Jonesy had just secured the stasis pod in the *Eidolon*'s cargo section when he heard a shout. He looked up to see Ramon on fast approach.

Damn. Knew things were going a little too smoothly.

Waving Flo and Rae into the shuttle, Jonesy picked up the pulse weapon he'd laid just inside the ship's rear hatch. He stepped out to meet the Marine, keeping the pistol hidden behind his back.

"Sorry, man," Ramon began as he slowed to meet the engineer, "But I can't let you—"

With a mental apology to the Marine, Jonesy whipped the pistol around. Before he could discharge it, though, Ramon snapped his arm up and out, sweeping the weapon from Jonesy's hands before he even knew what had happened.

"If you'd let me finish instead of shooting first," Ramon said with an exaggerated patience as he turned the pistol around and handed it, butt-first, back to Jonesy, "I was saying I can't let you go down there alone."

<It's all right, Jonesy, he knows,> Shannon's voice broke in. *<I sent him.>*

Jonesy felt his cheeks warm with embarrassment, and was thankful for the dark complexion that hid it from the Marine. Although, he figured with Ramon's mods, the man probably had biometric scans that completely outed him.

"Sorry. I just—" Jonesy waved at the shuttle and then dropped his hand, palm hitting the side of his leg with a slap. "I'm not very good at going behind command's back on anything."

Ramon chuckled, clapping the engineer on the shoulder. "What? Never snuck out during basic? Oh man, do we have some catching up to do." He eyed Jonesy for a beat, before adding, "Of course, it figures that when you *do* decide to break the rules, you go and tactically acquire a freakin' shuttle. Most of us just snuck off-base to grab a brew."

"Yeah, well…." Jonesy let his voice drift off as they loaded into the shuttle.

Ramon nodded at Flo and Rae, patted the stasis pod, then moved to seal the hatch. Flo joined Jonesy in the cockpit as Shannon's voice came across *Eidolon*'s holo, along with the image of their flight plan.

<Launch in five. I've preloaded your trip for you. Varga's reserved a dock in the warehouse district, here,> she highlighted an area on the back side of the port. *<But Rae's arranged for you to drop her off here.>* She indicated a berth two slips over.

Her image popped up onto the screen, her face scrunched in concern.

<Jonesy…. Terrance ordered the Vale *to undock from the station in thirty minutes. We're going to have to vector you back into the shuttle bay after we're underway.>*

Jonesy grimaced, but nodded. "Understood. We'll make this fast. Hopefully we'll be back before the captain misses me—or Terrance misses Beck."

She nodded, but he could tell she didn't believe him.

Hell, he didn't believe him, either.

Well, it was nice being chief engineer while it lasted.

* * * * *

Varga greeted Jonesy with a broad smile, as the engineer disembarked from the vessel he planned to take ownership of within the next few minutes.

"Got your cat, right here," he slapped the top of the enclosure. "He's sleeping off a sedative, but is otherwise in perfect health."

He didn't miss the look of relief that flitted across the other man's features as he came to a stop in front of the crate.

Crouching beside it, Jonesy eyed the locking mechanism, and then shot Varga a questioning glance. Varga shunted him the token that would grant access, and Jonesy lifted the lid, reaching in to press his hand against the big cat's side.

Braver man than me, Varga thought as he chanced a look over Jonesy's shoulder. The man's hand was buried in the animal's sleek fur, and he could see the gentle rise and fall of the cat's breathing.

Jonesy stroked him once more, then closed the lid and stood.

Varga nodded once to the crate. "You didn't lock it," he noted. "Might want to do that before the thing wakes."

Jonesy grinned back at him. "Don't worry about it, he's my problem now." Canting his head back at the shuttle, he added, "Let me load him up, and we'll get you that stasis pod."

Varga held up a restraining hand. "No pod, no cat. You know how this works."

He motioned with his other hand, and two Irids emerged from hiding. Flicking a glance briefly to the lead security guard, he jerked a nod toward the ship.

"Check it out," he instructed. Turning back to Jonesy, he saw the man tense, and nodded thoughtfully. "Careful," he called out the warning. "He might have brought company."

Jonesy's mouth pressed into a straight line, but the man said nothing.

Both guards moved at a brisk pace to cover the distance, weapons held at the ready. As they neared the top of the ramp, they slowed, moving into a series of careful sidesteps. It was a tactic Varga had seen before in security types, something they called "slicing the pie." He waited as both disappeared within the vessel.

Moments later, they reemerged, weapons pointing down toward the deck.

The lead nodded. "Clear."

Varga let a broad smile grow as he clapped his hands together. "Excellent, excellent," he stated, then turned to Jonesy. "Now, then, my friend. There's just one other little matter we need to discuss."

Jonesy tilted his head and crossed his arms, a look of challenge on his face. "We had a deal—"

Varga cut him off.

"Yes, yes, one pod for one cat, as agreed. However, there's one more thing we need to settle. The Hegemony has strict rules about the transport of dangerous animals." He let his face take on a sorrowful look, spreading his hands in a gesture that indicated it was beyond his control. "Special handling fees, you see. But don't worry, my friend. I've taken care of everything."

Jonesy's eyes narrowed, and Varga saw his hands fist as the man's weight shifted. One of his Irids noticed as well; the guard's weapon snapped up, aimed at the engineer.

Jonesy's eyes darted quickly over to the guard, and then back. Something in the man's expression said he'd heard of the Hegemony's policies regarding visitors who broke the rules.

"Ah, not to worry, my friend. We won't be shipping you off to some platform to work off your sentence. The Enfield account is too important to risk over an engineer and the CEO's pet."

Varga flipped a token through the air, and Jonesy caught it reflexively, and then glanced down at it with some confusion.

"That's a ticket for you and your…companion…to Glorious Station," Varga explained. "It leaves in an hour. From there, you can catch a ride with one of the ore haulers out to the platform where your ship is headed."

Jonesy's expression grew angry. "And give you the shuttle? No way," he said hotly, taking a step forward.

He froze as a warning shot sizzled past his left ear, accompanied by a splintering *crack*. Varga saw the man's eyes widen slightly as one of the stacked crates against the far bulkhead split apart.

"You see how it is," he smiled in sympathy. "It's just business, you understand. We take your shuttle, and you and your friend here are free to go on your way."

Jonesy inhaled sharply, his jaw set. He jerked an angry nod and stepped back toward the crated cat.

Varga's attention was wrested from the engineer as the whine of pulser fire sounded from the direction of the shuttle. He spun, hand going instinctively to the pistol holstered inside his jacket, but before he could draw, he sensed movement behind him.

Varga's knees buckled as Jonesy's foot connected with the back of his legs. He twisted as he fell, but the engineer was already on top of him and landed a sharp blow to his head.

Stunned, he looked over to see his unconscious guards being mag-cuffed by two figures wearing the same Security Guild uniform. The whine of a pulse weapon being charged sounded behind him, and he heard Jonesy's voice order him not to move.

Varga was too busy gaping in dismay at the figure that stepped out of the shadows from behind the Centauran shuttle to pay Jonesy any mind.

"V-Vice President Francesca," he stammered. "My apologies. I didn't realize—"

He stumbled to a halt as Francesca stepped forward, a calculating expression playing across the VP's face. His eyes followed her hand as she aimed a pulse weapon at him.

"Nice work, Adjunct. I'll be sure to mention to Rubin how helpful you've been." She gestured one of her Irids to drag the two unconscious guards across the line that marked where the ES field would be generated once the shuttle launched. "You are free to go. Thank you for your service to the Hegemony."

Her security team advanced, and he retreated, noting in some dismay the confident way in which the male Irid moved. Unlike the female, who was clearly standard security, this man flowed in a manner that signified deadly intent. Varga knew people like this, men who wore combat like a second shirt. This one was a warrior, someone you didn't cross.

Hands raised, the adjunct cut his losses and retreated back behind the safe line. He watched as the soldier motioned to Jonesy, and the engineer lifted his hands.

The last thing Varga heard before he turned and walked away was Francesca's flinty voice.

"Industrial espionage is a capital offense in the Hegemony, Mister Jones."

Too bad, Varga thought. *I kind of liked the guy.*

AWOL

STELLAR DATE: 07.04.3302 (Adjusted Gregorian)
LOCATION: ESS *Avon Vale*
REGION: en route to SR71, Sirian Hegemony

"What do you mean, he's *not on board*?!"

Shannon felt herself wilt a bit under Jason's intense glare, and fought the desire to look away. Not that it would have mattered. She couldn't exactly escape the captain's furious expression, given that all of the bridge's pickups were sent directly to her feed.

"I, uhm, told Jonesy I'd cover for him while he stepped out for a bit…."

She let her voice trail off, glancing over at Landon for assistance. She met the XO's stony stare and realized she'd find no reprieve from that corner.

"While he *stepped out* for a bit?" Landon repeated, his tone one of incredulity. "Care to explain that?"

She glanced from Landon to Logan, and then over to Noa. The human sat at Scan, his expression calm as ever, but the look in his eyes was one of extreme disappointment.

That did it for her.

"Look," she began, "I was just trying to help—"

<*It's my fault,*> Tobi's voice cut in, the big cat's nails clicking on the sole of the deck as she padded onto the bridge.

Jason swiveled to pin the big cat with a look, just as Charley's voice cut in. The AI had left to supervise security sweeps of the ship when they couldn't raise Jonesy on the net, and pings for his ident returned null.

<*Jonesy's not all that's missing,*> the security officer announced.

Shannon bit her lip as Jason's eyes returned to her. Her gaze shifted to Terrance as the exec stepped up beside the captain, and she saw the two exchange a worried look.

"Who else, Charley?" Terrance asked.

<*Flo's gone. So's one of the AIs we just rescued—Rae,*> he said. <*Beck's ident isn't showing up on the shipnet, either. And…the* Eidolon*'s gone.*>

Jason's eyes drilled into Shannon, silently demanding an answer.

<*Jonesy went to Brilliance Station to rescue Beck,*> Tobi interjected, nosing herself between them. <*Those Lumins stole him.*>

A stunned silence followed her pronouncement. Shannon saw Jason sigh then reach up and massage the back of his neck as the man processed what Tobi has just said.

"What happened, lass?" Tobias spoke up, his voice curiously gentle as he stepped forward and placed a hand on the cat's flank.

Tobi ducked her head and looked up at Jason, her expression one of shame, before looking over her shoulder at Tobias.

<*He…had this idea that he could spy on the Lumins. That they might say something important in front of him, thinking he was just a dumb animal. But it backfired.*>

"Backfired?" Logan stirred, swiveling in his seat to lean closer to the cat. His tone invited Tobi to continue.

She turned to face him, misery flashing in her tawny eyes. <*I'm not sure how it happened, but he ended up on their pinnace, and the guards captured him. He pinged me a few times, but I…I ignored him,*> the cat confessed, her tail beginning to lash in agitation at the retelling. <*When I finally answered, he sounded afraid and out of breath, like he was being chased. And then—*>

The cat broke off, hunched over and head down. Shannon thought she looked wretched.

"Why didn't you call us, little lass?"

Tobi glanced up at Tobias, her ears back. <*I did, but you all sounded so busy.*>

Shannon felt a shaft of guilt emanate from the Weapon Born.

The AI looked up at Jason. "She did at that, boyo. But we were escorting the Lumins out of the habitat at that time and I, well…"

He paused and glanced back down at Tobi. "I told her it wasn't a good time."

Tobi cocked her head. <*I ran into Jonesy on my way to the shuttle bay to stop them,*> she told Tobias. <*He said they'd already left, and then he offered to help.*>

Shannon felt Terrance's eyes land thoughtfully on her. "And that's where you came in, I suspect," he murmured. "Usually if Jonesy's up to something, you're in the thick of it with him."

She shot him a wry look. "Kind of," she confessed. "We didn't want to bother you with something we thought we could solve quickly, before you even missed him."

"And now?" Jason's brow rose as he pierced her with a reproving stare.

"Well, you kind of launched the *Vale* while they were docked on the station," she retorted tartly, then raised her hands, as he looked like he was going to lay into her again. "But…***but***…they have Beck, they're on *Eidolon,* and they've received clearance to leave."

Jason spun to face Noa, who turned and buried his hands in the holo on the console in front of him.

The physicist shook his head. "No ship squawking *Eidolon*'s ident has left the station just yet," he reported.

<*I've launched a pair of drones,*> Charley informed them. <*They're headed back toward the station and are scanning all outbound local craft. If they're out there, we'll find them.*>

"Rae said she had Francesca's access to space traffic control and would alter the shuttle's IFF to one of the vice president's personal transports to disguise it," Shannon offered. "They should be contacting us soon."

Jason drilled her with another hard look. "For your sake, I hope so."

Shannon smiled weakly at the captain.

Come on, Jonesy, any time now, she mentally begged as she turned back to her nav board, keeping her personal comm link open, ready to receive a ping.

Fifteen minutes later, she felt an immense sense of relief when she heard Charley announce he'd found them.

<Ident says they're a cargo drone, but their emissions match the Eidolon*'s signature,>* Charley said. *<They're boosting at ten gs. I've sent them a tightbeam using the* Vale*'s IFF.>*

<Jonesy's hailing us,> Kodi announced, then shunted the signal to the main holo.

<Guess the jig is up, since you've pinged us.>

The dry humor in Jonesy's tone and the wry look on his face had Shannon heaving a virtual sigh of relief. She could see Flo in the pilot's seat next to him, and behind her, Rae, her frame looking remarkably like Francesca.

<Beck's just fine,> Jonesy informed them. *<We have him in stasis so that we can push a bit to make it to you more quickly.>*

"We'll discuss the fact that you took *Eidolon—and* a stasis pod—without authorization when you get back," Jason responded. "Shannon'll coordinate with you on velocity and heading. Report to the ready room once you've secured the shuttle."

<Aye, sir,> came the subdued response.

Jason pointed his finger at Shannon. "You'll be joining us when he arrives."

She nodded as he turned on his heel and headed for the door, Terrance, Tobias, and Tobi following after him.

"Ship's yours, Landon," Jason called just as he ducked into the corridor.

The XO murmured a response and headed for the captain's chair.

Stars, girl, the AI thought to herself as she did her best to avoid the looks being sent her way. *You are in* **such** *trouble….*

ESCAPE PLANS

STELLAR DATE: 07.04.3302 (Adjusted Gregorian)
LOCATION: Platform SR71
REGION: Noctilucent Space, Sirian Hegemony

Arne took a deep breath as he very carefully set his handheld down on his desk. He realized his hand was shaking, and he clenched it, pressing his fist against the top of his thigh as he sucked in a lungful of air.

We know the date now.

Arne schooled his expression, glancing through the plas pane set into one wall of his office. On the other side, he could see workers assigned to the communications pit that monitored the movements of Noctus skiffs and tugs as they flitted from yard to yard. They were going about their business, oblivious to the events about to unfold.

He glanced back down at the handheld comm unit. Hume had modified it so that certain programs, like a one-time cypher, would only open to his biosignature. That cypher had just turned a seemingly innocuous message from the overseer into a brief yet electrifying number: *07.10.*

July tenth. Six short days from now.

Suns, there is so much to do.

Anticipating the news, Arne had sent trusted runners down all four of the Blackbird's wings to hand-deliver a message to key individuals. He'd give them the news tonight, when they met in person.

He glanced at his comm unit, though it would be some time yet before the runners reached their destinations, as this particular platform was sprawling in its reach.

Shaped like a stubby, boxy pinwheel, it rotated along its flat axis in a clumsy yet efficient fashion. Nets strung between each of its kilometers-long arms held overlarge lumps of raw ores, awaiting processing in one of the refinery's several furnaces. An administrative wing spanned the space between the west and south wings, marring the platform's symmetry but providing a place for non-industrial spacecraft to dock without impeding the workflow.

At times like this, he hated how long it took to traverse a platform of this size, but as it spanned more than twenty kilometers from edge to edge, it could not be helped. Arne felt a nervous anticipation rise once more within him and knew the best anodyne was to immerse himself in his work.

He reached for a stack of hyfilms needing his approval, but was interrupted by a notification of an incoming transmission. He grimaced as he saw who it was from: his own personal demon, Overseer Miguel.

Once his ping was answered, the Lumin didn't waste his time greeting a Noctus; he launched directly into his grievance.

"Your numbers for this week don't reflect the increases needed to meet the accelerated production schedule." The overseer's tone was filled with censure. "And I see here that you're showing no alumina movement at all."

"I believe I mentioned that the bauxite processing plant is down when you were here," Arne responded, his voice carefully neutral. "We were awaiting a replacement part from MD40 that should have arrived a few days ago, but was delayed by the explosion—"

"That doesn't explain the titanium numbers. You were told to increase the output of both," Miguel cut him off with a peremptory gesture.

Out of the corner of his eye, Arne spied one of the runners. He glanced over long enough for the young woman to give him a quick thumbs-up before ducking out again. He suppressed a smile as he returned his attention to the 2-D image of Miguel.

"Adjunct Helada is en route."

The smile that had tried to break free just seconds before was banished by a trickle of dread that formed at Miguel's words.

"She will evaluate your workflow and make adjustments when she arrives, and you *will* implement these. Do I make myself clear?"

"Yes, Overseer," Arne replied, but the comm had already fallen silent.

Helada was a complication they didn't need at this stage of the plan, but he refused to give in to fear. They would find a way to deal with the adjunct. They had to.

He shoved himself away from his desk and stood. Calling out a goodbye to his assistant, Arne waved a hand to douse the lights in his office, and turned down the corridor that led to the west arm.

Tuesday's face was the first thing he saw as he ducked beneath one of the slag disposal pipes that led from the plant. He could see the light sheen of sweat that covered her face; it clung to the others as well. The oppressive heat made for an uncomfortable meeting place, but the grinding hiss of the disposal unit worked to mitigate any sound a sniffer drone might pick up.

"I heard from our contact," he began as he stopped beside the small group gathered there. "We're a go. They're departing in two days and will be here on the tenth."

One of the men tilted his head back, squinting. "So…six days from now."

Arne nodded. "That's our window. Everything needs to be set in motion so that the moment they arrive, their offer to provide disaster response teams cannot be refused."

One of the older women, her skin leathered by years of proximity to refinery furnaces, leant back against an interior bulkhead and crossed her arms. "Hate to make light of the dead, but we've only managed to keep the bauxite plant offline because of that explosion on MD40." She shifted a plas stylus from one corner of her mouth to the other as she shot him a look of skepticism. "What'll we do if that part arrives before the tenth?"

"You let me worry about that." Arne turned to a burly man sporting an eyepatch, whose neck was about as thick as his head. "The backup enviro unit?"

"Installed." The man's voice was a low rumble, felt more than heard. Not one to use two words when one would suffice, Tibbs was rock solid, and one of the backbones upon which Arne and Hume had built this escape plan.

After it became clear that he was done talking, the woman next to him smirked in amusement and filled in what Tibbs had left out.

"We've set the plant to blow in such a way that the furnace's failsafes'll kick in, but its sensors will show them as offline. That'll trigger the blast doors closed, and you can blow the explosive bolts holding that section of the platform onto the wing."

Arne nodded. "That should work. But once that sector's cut off from the platform, it'll be written off as a loss," he warned. "They'll allow minimal rescue support at best. Are you sure the ones we're smuggling will be able to shelter in place without harm?"

The woman nodded. "Backup enviro'll kick in when the blast doors close, but its power output will be obscured by the heat from the runaway furnace. We'll have enough oxygen within the furnace area to keep the thing burning steady for hours. Meanwhile, everyone will be safely sealed behind a pair of reinforced bulkheads."

"They could be in for a bumpy ride if those explosive bolts don't fire in tandem when you blow it off the end of the arm," Tuesday observed. "If it goes into a tumble, you're going to end up with a lot of broken bones."

"Then we need to make sure that doesn't happen." Arne pursed his lips, thinking. "About the best we can do is rig netting to keep people from smashing into a bulkhead."

Tuesday frowned, not liking the risk they were taking, but nodded.

"Twenty hours," Tibbs spoke up suddenly, shoving meaty

hands down into the pockets of his coveralls. His one good eye held a grave intensity, and Arne felt the weight of it as Tibbs leant forward.

Arne returned Tibbs's stare with a thoughtful one of his own. "That's as long as the backup environmental system will run?"

The burly man answered Arne's question with a slow nod.

"Okay then." Arne sucked on his lower lip a moment, eyes slitted in thought. "Okay. I'll update our contact with this information, let them know they have a tight deadline to manage. Anything else?"

He glanced from face to face, and when he received negative headshakes all around, he broached the topic of the visitor he'd just been informed to expect.

"Slight complication," he began. "We have an unforeseen visitor, someone who should arrive within the week. *His* assistant."

Up to this moment, everyone crammed into the small, superheated nook behind the pyrometallurgy furnace had held fast to the rules of engagement that their mentor had laid out for them.

They were a simple set of rules, four in number. Never mention names, ever. Never discuss plans except when meeting. Always consider microdrones to be nearby, recording your conversation. And if you *see* one, assume two.

All this went out the window at his announcement.

"Helada? Suns, no!"

"Sun take her, Arne, she'll ruin *everything*!"

Tibbs slapped a meaty hand over the mouth of the squinty-eyed man, just as Tuesday shoved an elbow into the leathery woman's side, hissing at her to shut up.

Face pale and shaken, Tuesday met Arne's glance. He shook his head mutely and motioned them all to scatter. Tuesday gripped his forearm with a worried look, but all he could do was return it with a bleak one of his own.

He could offer no words of reassurance.

If a microdrone had been recording, the moment Helada's name was mentioned, it would get flagged. He knew it, and so did Tuesday.

They had no way of knowing if their conversation had been monitored. Only time would tell. Time, and the success or failure of plans that were too far set in motion now to stop.

COMPELLED TO SPY

STELLAR DATE: 07.05.3302 (Adjusted Gregorian)
LOCATION: Platform SR71
REGION: Noctilucent Space, Sirian Hegemony

The summons came by way of an Irid stepping into Lauren's path as she sped down the east wing corridor of the Blackbird. Veering to the left to avoid crashing into the guard, she bounced lightly off the bulkhead but was swung around to face him when the soldier grabbed her by the upper arm and hauled her up short.

"Commander wants to see you at the garrison. *Now,*" he emphasized, shoving her away from him before turning and walking off in the opposite direction.

Lauren trembled a little inside as she turned back the way she had come. Picking up her pace, she headed toward Commander Vincent's office with some trepidation. This would be the first time they had reached out to contact her; up to this point, she had always been the one to come to them.

She'd faithfully reported in weekly, and had twice stopped in to let them know that she'd heard someone mention that Hume had contacted Arne again. So far, she'd managed to not give them any information that would harm any of her people.

Lauren was an observant girl. She knew something was brewing, and she knew it was something that the administrator and other Noctus wanted to keep hidden from the Lumins. She did her very best to make sure that she gave the garrison commander nothing but innocuous tales.

Surely he hasn't discovered that I'm holding out on him.

She didn't really *know* anything, after all. But maybe he suspected she knew something was going on that she hadn't disclosed.

With some trepidation, she entered the garrison and stood

meekly at the front desk, while the Irid on watch alerted the commander that she had arrived. The soldier returned, motioning her down the corridor and to the commander's office.

Lauren stood at the entrance, waiting for Commander Vincent to look up, her knees knocking. When he finally did, he motioned her forward.

"We intercepted a transmission," he informed her. "A conversation between unknown Noctus conspirators and your administrator. One of them made a comment about Adjunct Helada ruining their plans."

The commander leant forward, his eyes drilling mercilessly into her.

"Let me be clear. We have your brother. You are going to shadow the administrator, find out what those plans are, and report back to me. Or you will never see your brother again."

Lauren was so shaken by the encounter that she failed to notice the hulking Noctus with the eyepatch who stood across from the garrison entrance, cleaning out a recycling bin. As she exited, he dropped the now-empty bin back into place, picked up the plas waste container, and settled into a comfortable stride several meters behind the young runner.

* * * * *

Tibbs had seen the Irid accosting Lauren two kilometers down the main corridor of the south wing. He'd ducked behind the outcropping of a bulkhead spar, thinking to intervene if the man did anything untoward. Pretending to secure a loose shoe, he'd surreptitiously observed their exchange from a distance.

When Lauren had moved on—this time in a direction different from the one in which she had been originally headed—he was curious about what the Irid had instructed her to do, so he'd moved to follow at a discreet distance.

Now, after her little visit inside the garrison, it appeared she was headed toward the administration wing.

Something felt off about this to Tibbs. If the garrison wished to connect with Arne, they had electronic devices that were far more efficient than the two feet of a young runner.

The poor girl had looked shaken as she exited, too. 'White as a sheet', his mum would have said, and looking as if she might burst into tears at any moment.

"What did they do to you, *cher*," the big man rumbled to himself. "And what are you up to, I wonder?"

OFF COURSE

STELLAR DATE: 07.05.3302 (Adjusted Gregorian)
LOCATION: Glorious Station, 2 AU from Incandus
REGION: Luminescent Space, Sirian Hegemony

Miguel paced the length of the offices reserved for him on Glorious Station, his temper fraying by the minute. He'd just reviewed a message from Berit, and it had not been pleasant. He'd felt the rake of her claws as she flayed him over minutiae.

The VP had been angry about something.... Rumor had it that a recent acquisition had slipped through her fingers. She tended to take her ill temper out on her subordinates. This, in turn, made Miguel irritable.

He hated being irritable.

As he paced, Miguel rifled through feed after feed of weekly platform results. One of them had been misfiled, and he shouted at the system NSAI for being such an idiot.

He knew the thing wasn't sentient, but it apologized profusely, which mollified him somewhat, though he knew he hadn't inflicted any real mental anguish upon it.

Peeved at himself for such a ridiculous train of thought, he flipped to the next projection.

And stopped and stared.

Now why would the Hyperion *be on that heading? Its route isn't scheduled to run through that sector for another six weeks.*

Pulling up the ship's flight record, he saw that it had been diverted from its course almost two weeks earlier, and ordered to escort the Centauri ship to Incandus. It had recently returned to regular service.

But it was tracking a full twenty-five degrees off course.

Given its current location, there would be an almost twenty-minute communications lag. That meant the captain's response to his demand for answers wouldn't return to him for a good forty minutes at least, depending on how long its flight crew took to route the missive to her.

He allowed the frustration from the inconvenience to fuel his ire, and he took some satisfaction in reporting her to the Pilots' Guild, demanding she be fined for the time lost to the Hegemony for her ineptitude.

The flight records gave up another interesting bit of information. As chance would have it, Overseer Hume had been a passenger on the *Hyperion* quite a bit of late.

Having an overseer on board wasn't unusual; all ships were officially owned by the corporate fleet, and higher-ranking personnel often used the transports to travel from one platform to another. Many overseers even fell into patterns, preferring one particular vessel over another if it was available.

However, Miguel had never known Hume to cater to such habits.

Miguel didn't like Hume, and he knew the feeling was mutual. Because of that—and because he was still a bit torqued over Berit's blistering comm—he reached out and tapped on the *Hyperion*'s icon again. This time, he backtraced its recent activity.

Wouldn't that be the shit if I could catch Hume doing a little side business of his own….

*****

Twenty minutes later, the officer on watch on the *Hyperion*'s bridge accepted receipt of Miguel's message. Not wanting to bother the captain, who was in the middle of her rest period, she checked the overseer's instructions against the orders posted on the Pilot's Guild roster.

Suns, she thought, swallowing down mild panic. *Overseer Miguel is right, we're off course!*

Calling the ship's navigator over, she pointed out the error, her tone sharp and critical.

Jim apologized, promising to correct the ship's heading immediately. She stood over him as he input the numbers into the ship's navigation system, then, satisfied that she had successfully averted disaster, she sat back in the captain's chair and resumed her duties.

As soon as the woman's head bent to her captain's holo to record an apology to Miguel, Jim tapped out a brief text message to the captain, flagged it as urgent, and sent it to her quarters.

Forearmed with the knowledge of what had transpired, the captain appeared a bit early to relieve the third-watch officer. When the woman reported the navigation error, the captain looked suitably concerned and praised the woman for her conscientious attention to the matter.

As the watch changed, the captain held up her hand to stop Jim from leaving the bridge.

"Wait a moment, please," she said, knowing the third-watch officer would overhear as she exited the bridge. "I'd like an explanation of this navigational error, if you don't mind…."

Since Jim had given her a heads-up on the course change, the captain had been able to tweak the first-shift roster, limiting it to Underground personnel only. As the watch changed and everyone settled into their jobs, the captain reached out to turn off the bridge's recording devices.

"Okay then," she sighed, turning to face her team. "Let's see how we can rectify this little mess we've gotten ourselves into without jeopardizing the mission, shall we?"

She turned to meet Jim's eyes and beckoned him forward. "Ping Hume for me. Let him know we'll be about," she checked her overlay, "six hours late, and tell him I'm moving ahead with the plan to evacuate all non-Underground personnel. I want them off this ship by tonight, if possible."

DOUBLE-STRAND BREAKS

STELLAR DATE: 07.07.3302 (Adjusted Gregorian)
LOCATION: ESS *Avon Vale*
REGION: en route to SR71, Sirian Hegemony

The update on an impending solar storm reached Hume just after he learned about the *Hyperion*'s delay and Helada's arrival. His mind bounced back and forth between the three issues, unable to settle, as he neared the *Vale*'s mess hall. So intent was he on his problems that he didn't notice the doctor's approach until she waved her hand right in front of his eyes.

"Wool-gathering?" Marta asked with a smile.

Hume tried to clear the anxious expression from his face as he focused on the woman in front of him. She stood, a tray of food in her hand, the Proxima cat that Jonesy had recovered standing alongside her.

"Sorry," he apologized. "I'm afraid I was a bit distracted."

<*Bad news?*> Beck asked, tilting his head inquiringly.

Hume suppressed a smile at the earnest look on the cat's face as he looked back up at Marta. He knew the cat had been on his very best behavior lately. The doctor had confided that he'd been "grounded for life" by Terrance upon his return. She'd felt sorry for him and had taken to springing him from his captivity. Now must be one of those occasions.

"I'm afraid so," he admitted, running a hand through his close-cropped hair. He opened his mouth, then paused, reconsidering. Gesturing over to the buffet, he said, "Let me grab some coffee to clear the cobwebs, and I'll tell you all about it."

A few minutes later, he slid into a seat across from her, mug in one hand, a plate full of scrambled eggs and bacon in the other.

"Get some of that in you first," Marta advised. "Then we'll talk."

Lifting his mug in salute, Hume nodded and took a sip. A few moments later, he set his fork down and grabbed the mug between both hands, his gaze contemplative. Taking this as a cue that he'd had enough time to mull through the matter disturbing him, Marta set her own mug aside and folded her hands on the table in front of her.

"So," she began, tilting her head quizzically. "About what's bothering you…."

Hume flashed a brief half-smile in wry response to her prompting. "We just learned of an impending visit by one of Overseer Miguel's people," he explained. "And the *Hyperion* ran into a bit of trouble, so they're running late."

<*How much of a wrench does that throw into your plans?*> Varanee asked.

"Quite a bit, actually." His tone turned bleak. "Their revised schedule has them arriving right in the middle of a major solar event."

Marta paused, her coffee halfway to her lips. She set it back down, her face etched with concern. "By your expression, I take it your escape plans won't stand up to that kind of storm."

Hume coughed a laugh, but it held no humor. "The forecast is for a high-intensity flare with a series of coronal mass ejections following in its wake. We had planned to pull this off before the shock wave hit. But now, with the *Hyperion*'s delay…." He paused and raised an eyebrow in query. "Am I correct in assuming you're both well-versed in radiation biology?"

Marta smiled, but didn't seem bothered by his apparent non-sequitur. "You can't very well be an effective chief medical officer on a starfaring vessel without a clear understanding of that subject."

"Then you can imagine the conditions the Noctus on our platforms face every day."

The doctor nodded. "I don't have to imagine. We were on MD40."

Hume tilted his head, conceding the point. "The Blackbird is almost half an AU closer in."

<*Given the inverse-square law, the effects will be much greater,*> Varanee said, her tone thoughtful. <*Sirius is certainly more energetic than Sol, almost twice as hot and more than twenty times as luminous, which will be a factor at those distances.*>

Marta nodded. "The Hegemony has obviously solved for the top two issues, or else there'd be no Noctus left to rescue. At that proximity, you'd easily absorb enough thermal radiation to reach—what, eight hundred degrees on the side facing the star?"

<*Yes,*> Varanee confirmed before Hume had a chance to do so. <*Which means your platforms must have sufficient insulation, and use rotation to even it out.*>

"They do," he confirmed.

Marta drummed her fingers lightly on the edge of the table, considering the situation. She looked up from her contemplation of her fingers to meet his gaze.

"And then there's part two, the ionizing radiation."

"Yes," he agreed. "The Noctus are fond of saying that if the heat won't kill you, the gammas will."

"Well, gammas, x-rays, and other charged particles, yes," the doctor clarified. "There's a steady stream of them from the solar wind, but that's fairly easily blocked. I'm sure that's built into your platform specs."

Hume nodded.

"But the energetic particles produced by those CMEs are your real problem. They transfer a lot of energy when they collide," she mused in a distracted tone, as if she were speaking half to herself. "They also produce nuclear fragmentation products that give off secondary radiation, and that can add up to a pretty large dose."

<*Anyone in an unshielded environment would receive the dose equivalent of several Sieverts in a relatively short amount of time,*> Varanee concurred. <*That would be a lethal dose to an appreciable number of your people.*>

Hume grimaced. "Yes, that's why the platforms all have shelter-in-place locations, with extra shielding, where they can weather out the more intense episodes."

"Makes sense," Marta murmured, then jerked suddenly. Straightening, she pinned him with a look. "Those Noctus you're smuggling off the Blackbird aren't in one of those shielded areas, are they."

It was a statement, not a question.

Worry bloomed in his gut once more. "No, they're not. That section of the platform is used for materials storage, and there's never been a need for a lot of shielding there. There's no way to reinforce it in time, even if we could do so without raising suspicions."

"So the people escaping…." Marta began, and Hume grimaced as he finished her sentence.

"Will be exposed to a lethal amount of radiation, beyond anything they have hope of counteracting."

His lips thinned as he contemplated the no-win situation they faced.

"It's not possible to move that many people in such a short amount of time, but we have to, if they're to survive," he said grimly. "And if we do, the garrison will notice. They'll know something's up. We risk the very existence of the Underground by moving them, but we'll be sentencing three hundred to death if we don't."

Marta sat back and regarded him thoughtfully. "Do the platform patchers have any medical therapies they can administer to minimize the effects of radiation exposure?" she asked. "I've seen for myself that they have no mednano."

"Correct," Hume confirmed. "As you saw on MD40, the Hegemony keeps them at a tech level that's easily a thousand years old. The closest they come is some nanoparticle they call…Phil, I think?"

<PHA-L,> Varanee guessed. *<It's a protein nanoparticle. Stars,*

that's an ancient nanomed.> The AI made a *tsk*ing sound.

Hume shook his head slowly. "I don't have the first clue what any of that means," he admitted.

"Not many would," Marta assured him. "PHA-L is old. It's a radioprotective pharmaceutical that dates back to before our first years on Mars. It was administered immediately before and after exposure, to mitigate radiation damage."

Hume shrugged uncomfortably. "Radiation biology's still a bit of a black box to the average person. It's something you can't see, smell, or touch. No one really cares to look under the hood to see what makes it work. Most people just know it can be dangerous. Deadly."

<*It is,*> Varanee said. <*And your solar particle event will cause a lot of double-strand breaks within your refugees' DNA.*>

He felt his gut clench at those words, although he wasn't quite sure what the AI referenced.

Marta must have seen the uncertainty swimming in his eyes.

"If enough of your DNA is damaged," she explained, "it will kill off all the stem cells in your body. Once that happens, your body loses its ability to make new cells, and things begin to go downhill fast."

Hume shook his head mutely, still not understanding.

Varanee took up the explanation. <*Your human bodies must constantly regenerate to survive. White blood cells can last about a year, red blood cells about four months, and skin cells average two or three weeks.*

<*Your gut's going to be affected first. Some of those crypt stem cells die off after only four days. But if the dose equivalent is strong enough to kill off cells in your central nervous system…well. Those never regenerate.*>

At that, Hume felt his face turn a little green.

Suns, knowing it was lethal was bad enough. Knowing exactly ***what*** *it's doing to someone's insides….*

His thoughts must have shown on his face.

"It's something we can protect against, though," Marta hastened to assure him. "Get me in to see the Noctus you're smuggling out before you move them to their hideout. I can inoculate them with better radiation protection, and inject enough DNA-repairing mednano to see them through the solar event."

Hume picked up his now-cold coffee, cradling it between his hands as he thought.

After a moment, he nodded. "I'll send Arne a coded comm to let him know we need to sneak you in to see the ones who're leaving before we set everything in motion."

He looked over at her, a wry expression crossing his face as he stood.

"Who knew rescuing a bunch of Noctus required a science degree?"

M'AIDER

STELLAR DATE: 07.07.3302 (Adjusted Gregorian)
LOCATION: Prism Station, 2 AU from SR71
REGION: Noctilucent Space, Sirian Hegemony

The officer of the watch looked up in alarm as the call came in to Prism Space Traffic Control.

<*Prism Station, this is the HSC* Hyperion. *Mayday, mayday, mayday.*> The image of an Irid navigator hovered on the main holo. <*Systems showing imminent containment failure, number one engine. We have…five thousand kilos of hydrogen fuel, and one hundred seventy-eight souls on board. Offloading them to shuttles and sending them inbound to you. Skeleton crew will remain and try to effect repairs.*>

Reaching for her board, the officer keyed her comm to reply. <*HSC* Hyperion, *Prism Station. I copy. We have your ident and will vector your shuttles straight in, cleared for Dock 32.*>

"Well," she said as she straightened. "That was the most excitement I've had since that Lumin yacht broke free of the tug."

"That was three years ago," the man next to her yawned, shaking his head like a wet dog to clear the sleep from his brain.

"Poor devoted suckers," he muttered while tapping on the blinking icon of the *Hyperion*, now rendered in the reds of a ship in distress. "Never been one to believe that old saw about the captain going down with the ship. Hope they can figure a way to jettison that fusion plant before it takes them down with it."

The officer of the watch murmured her agreement as two icons separated from the blinking red *Hyperion*. The icons turned and began vectoring back toward the station as the larger transport continued on its path.

Whimsically, she tagged them *Lucky 1* and *Lucky 2*.

Fifteen minutes later, an energy spike flared, and the *Hyperion*'s ident disappeared.

PART FOUR: THE ESCAPE

A PLAUSIBLE ALIAS

STELLAR DATE: 07.08.3302 (Adjusted Gregorian)
LOCATION: PSS *Dutiful Passage*, 0.1 AU from SR71
REGION: Noctilucent Space, Sirian Hegemony

After giving off its spectacular light show, the *Hyperion* went dark. The ship coasted for nearly a day before nearing one of the known Hegemony radar coverage blind spots. On the captain's order, the engineer brought the fusion plant back online. She nodded at Jim, and he switched the ship's ident code to the one Francesca had created for just this moment.

As far as the Hegemony was concerned, they were now the Procyon ship, *Beautiful Passage*.

Hume had assured them that the moment the ident was picked up by Hegemony STC, it would trigger an app to run. That program would backfill a nonexistent flight path that would make their sudden appearance believable—at least to the NSAIs that ran the Hegemony's space traffic system.

The radar blind spot had the added benefit of being at a handoff point from one region to another. This should prevent the ident swap from being noticed by human STC agents as well.

After an hour passed with no challenge or query, the ship's crew settled into the next phase of their operation. The unfortunate course deviation, combined with an earlier-than-planned disappearance, had them behind schedule.

The *Beautiful Passage*'s trajectory would still take them past the SR71 platform, placing the Procyon ship in a position to offer their assistance in retrieving the platform's dead. But only if they made it in time.

The captain ordered everyone strapped in and the ship to accelerate to 1.5gs. Any more, and she feared Hegemony STC might start to wonder.

She brought the flight plan up on her overlay again, even though she'd already done so twice before. Noting the ETA, she then pulled up the prog charts for the solar flare. She sucked in a breath when she saw the update and realized the flare had already begun.

SOLAR X-RAY FLARE, CLASS X41.8; VELOCITY ~4,200 KM/SEC; ETA SR-71 07.09.3302, 1900 LOCAL. INTEGRAL DOSE EQUIVALENT PREDICTED AT ~12 SIEVERTS.

A hissing sound escaped from between her teeth, causing Jim to turn and favor her with a questioning look. She shunted the data to his board.

"Suns! An X41?" The stunned expression on his face mirrored his shocked exclamation.

She met his eyes, her face set into grim lines. "That thing's going to slam into the Blackbird in thirty-one hours, and I'll be damned if we're not there before it hits. Increase accel to 3gs."

A FORCED BETRAYAL

STELLAR DATE: 07.09.3302 (Adjusted Gregorian)
LOCATION: Platform SR71
REGION: Sirius A, Noctilucent Space, Sirian Hegemony

T-minus 9 hours to Solar Particle Event Shock Wave

The bang of a hatch being thrown open elicited groans and curses from Arne's bunkmates. It roused him just enough that he dragged the rough blanket over his head to block out the intrusive light.

One learned quickly to sleep through most things, when living in the Blackbird's bachelor quarters.

Moments later, a hand on his shoulder shook him awake as a rough whisper intruded on his fogged brain.

"Spew just started, and you have a comm from Overseer Hume," a voice hissed, dodging a swipe from the occupant of the bed just below Arne.

He rolled over to face a young woman—one of the runners, he realized, blinking a few times as her words sank in. When they did, he sat up…or rather, attempted to do so. His head hit the bunk a meter above him, causing its occupant to growl an inaudible curse.

Arne nodded at the runner, who stepped away to give him room to roll out of bed. His bare feet hit the cold deck, and then he turned, reaching past the mattress to the narrow shelves that held his coveralls and meager toiletry kit. Running a hand over his rough stubble, he opted to forego the depilatory and grabbed the bottle of mouth sanitizer. Popping a tablet, he swished as he dressed.

Grabbing his boots, he motioned the runner through the hatch, and ran across to the community san. He held up a hand to the runner in a "wait" gesture before he ducked in and made quick use of it, reappearing thirty seconds later.

Voice gritty from disuse, Arne began to speak, stopped, cleared his throat, and tried again.

"Lauren, isn't it?"

She nodded, her eyes meeting his briefly before skittering away.

"How far out is it?"

She shrugged. "Thirty hours or so. Said it's a big 'un."

"And did they say how far away the overseer is?"

"Folks in Admin told me light lag's about twenty seconds," Lauren said, keeping her pace steady alongside Arne's fast trot. "Means he's only a few hours out, right?"

Arne nodded, scrubbing his face as he wrestled with the mental math. *Suns, I need caffeine.* "Did they happen to say anything about when Adjunct Helada's expected?" he asked, shooting his shadow a brief glance.

The girl nodded, her gaze fixed resolutely on the corridor ahead. "Might have heard something about that," she allowed with an odd reluctance. "They said after Overseer Hume docks, but not by much."

He cursed and his pace slowed as they reached the intersection for the administrative wing.

She's not scheduled to arrive this soon. How did this happen?

Holding out a hand to slow the runner, he said, "Do me a quick favor, will you, Lauren? Run over to West and find Tuesday. Tell her what you heard about both arrivals. Then tell her to delay until we've sorted Helada out."

He missed the pinched look that crossed Lauren's face, as if she'd just heard something she'd rather not have, before she turned and sped off.

* * * * *

<*Commander, that runner's here,*> reported the guard on duty at

the garrison's entrance.

Vincent finished reviewing the details of the nightly sweep of the north wing, and tagged it as approved before swiping it closed.

<*Send her to me,*> he ordered.

When the runner appeared at his door, he waved her in with an impatient gesture.

"It's about time," he scowled at the gangly girl.

The child was fairly quaking with fear. He let it build, knowing the power the unknown held for such individuals.

"Well? Out with it," he finally demanded. "And it better be good," he warned, tapping his stylus against the edge of his desk as he leant back and glared at her. "Nothing you've brought us thus far has been of any use. Makes me wonder why we bother keeping your brother around at all."

He smiled inwardly at the barely audible gasp that escaped her lips, and watched the knuckles of her already clenched hands grow even whiter.

"Th-there's a comm from Overseer Hume," she stammered. "Admin had me wake the platform administrator to take it."

Vincent leant forward. "And…?" he prompted. "What did Hume want?"

The girl's eyes widened, and she shook her head slightly. "I…I don't know, sir. They didn't say."

"Well, what *did* they say?"

"Nothing, except that lag was twenty seconds."

Vincent's eyes narrowed. "So Hume will be arriving within the next few hours," he mused aloud. He shot the girl a steely look, and felt a flare of amusement when she flinched. "And what was Arne's response?"

She bit her lip, and her eyes slid away from his.

Instinct kicked in, and he sensed that, this time, the girl really did have something of value—and was reluctant to give it up.

He reached for the holo on his desk and paged his assistant. Seconds later, the Irid appeared at the entrance to Vincent's office.

"Tavio," he ordered, eyes locked with those of the girl, "make a note to follow up with the patcher of that free clinic on south wing. Tell him to prepare one of his patients for transfer, a young boy—"

"He wanted to know when Adjunct Helada was arriving," Lauren blurted, and Vincent waved his assistant away.

"Go on," he instructed, lowering his hand.

"He…told me to run to the west yard and tell the manager there to wait until he's dealt with Helada." Her shoulders sagged in defeat as the weight of her betrayal lay heavily on her.

He let her words hang between them for a few moments before prodding her. "Is that all?"

Her head moved up and down. "That's all," she whispered.

He let the silence build between them again before cutting her loose. "Your brother's safe—for now. Go about your business. But you will *not,*" he ordered as she looked back up at him, "be delivering that message to the west yard. Are we clear?"

After she left, he called Tavio back in. "Send a fireteam to round up the administrator, then send a couple of soldiers out to West. I want that yard manager brought in for questioning."

As soon as the man left, Vincent input Overseer Miguel's comm code.

"I have news," he stated as the holo began recording.

Neither he nor any of his garrison noticed the Noctus cleaning woman emptying waste receptacles in the area near Tavio's desk. She took her time gathering the trash, remaining silently in the background as Vincent's assistant returned and relayed the orders to have both Tuesday and Arne rounded up. And as Tavio bent to his next task, she quietly gathered the trash and set the bag against the bulkhead just outside the garrison.

She bent to retrieve the cleaning supplies a young boy handed to her, whispering instructions into his ear. He took off at a dead run as she turned to reenter the garrison. The guard at the entrance glanced idly down at the rags in her hand before waving her through once more.

* * * * *

After witnessing Lauren being strong-armed by the garrison guards more than a week before, though he had yet to learn what they held over her, Tibbs had decided to form a small network of his own to keep tabs on the platform's runners and the Hegemony's soldiers.

The twenty-five orphans whose childhood the Lumins had stolen comprised the bulk of his team. There was a secret, poetic side to the massive man that took great pleasure in the irony of using the Hegemony's most recent victims against them.

This was how he came to learn that two teams of soldiers had departed the garrison, one intent on arresting Tuesday, the other sent to seize Arne.

"You done good," he told the boy who'd brought the news to him. "You know the bauxite plant on South?"

When the boy nodded, he patted him on the shoulder. "Run there, fast, boy. Tell Tuesday they're coming for her. Tell her she's to hide in the back with all the rest. Got it?"

The boy nodded again then bolted as Tibbs gave him a small push. Tibbs watched the boy disappear down the corridor, then he ducked back inside a cargo bay that had been converted into overflow Noctus quarters. Kneeling, he beckoned to another orphan, from a group sent to the Blackbird a week ago.

"Know West Yard?"

The girl nodded, shoving her tongue through the gap made by her missing front tooth.

"There's a recycling station just across from there. Bins there are narrow at the bottom and wide at the top. Good hidey-hole for a girl your size. Know what I mean?"

The girl flashed a gap-toothed grin at him as she gave him another nod.

"You see soldiers, you hide there 'til they leave. Then go in, ask for Donna. Tell her Tibbs needs to know what the soldiers said. Okay?"

"Uh huh," she replied with all the confidence of a ten-year-old.

"Good. You come find me, after, real quick-like," he instructed.

As the girl ran off, Tibbs rose and headed out into the corridor with a purposeful stride.

ATTEMPTED ARREST

STELLAR DATE: 07.09.3302 (Adjusted Gregorian)
LOCATION: ESS *Avon Vale*, Platform SR71
REGION: Noctilucent Space, Sirian Hegemony

T-minus 8.5 hours to Solar Particle Event Shock Wave

A few hundred kilometers out from SR71, the *Avon Vale*'s scan lit up with a ping as the IFF signal from the *Hyperion* reappeared. The vessel was a tenth of an AU out.

"We have them," Charley announced, throwing the ship's heading up on the main holo. Beside it hovered its ETA to the Blackbird.

Jason heard Hume let out a breath. "That's going to put their arrival right after the shock wave hits," he muttered. "Be hard to justify why we're risking personnel to recover dead bodies in the middle of a solar event like the one that's headed this way."

"Let's worry about what's in front of us first, lad," Tobias advised, stepping up beside the Lumin. "Your friend Arne's on the line, ready for a wee chat." At Hume's nod, the Weapon Born lifted his head. "All right, Kodi, patch him through."

Arne's 2D feed appeared on the main holo, superimposed over the re-creation of 3D space around the Blackbird and the projection of their final approach into the administration wing's dock.

<*Sorry for the wait,*> the Noctus said, sounding out of breath. <*They had to roust me from my bunk.*> His image frowned as he peered at something off-screen. Motioning for something to be handed to him, Jason saw an ancient-looking tablet appear in the man's hand as he scrolled through it. Alarm crossed the man's face as he turned back to the 2D pickups that captured his image. <*The* Hyperion*'s behind schedule?*>

Hume nodded. "Yes. They were steered off course by Miguel. He forced our hand. We had to enact the swap a day earlier than planned. Ship had to cruise in the dark until they hit a dead zone."

Arne rubbed his cheek with the palm of his hand as he appeared to process the information. <*That compresses our timetable even more,*> he admitted, then squinted in concern. <*I've told Tuesday to go ahead and load our passengers into the area behind the furnace. We'll have to work fast if we're to get the* Vale's *patcher in to see them before we blow it.*>

Hume looked over at Tobias, a question in his eyes.

"We'll manage, lad, no worries," the AI assured him.

<*Good. I—*>

Shouts of "Hands in the air where we can see them!" erupted from behind Arne, cutting off whatever the Noctus had been about to say.

* * * * *

Tibbs had managed to round up a good half dozen yard workers and slag haulers in his race to the administrative wing. Still, he was several steps behind the Irid fireteam that had been sent to arrest Arne. He could hear the guards shouting as they entered the administrator's office, and he pulled up short, waving to those with him to fan out.

They had precious little, by way of weapons—a titanium cane borrowed from one of the elders he'd passed, a broken shard of plas with a sharp edge to it that might work as a passable blade. Both were close-in weapons and would do them little good against the pulse rifles with which the Irids were likely armed.

Eyeing the hallway that led to the communications pit, he pointed to three of the yard workers and mimed instructions to guard Arne's door.

He tossed the cane to the beefiest of the three, knowing the man would be the most likely one to make the best use of it. To the woman, he handed the makeshift shiv. Quick hand movements instructed her to go for an eye or throat if she could, the kidney if she must strike lower.

Then, ducking under the plas window that looked out from Arne's office into the comm pit, he motioned the other three of his party to follow. The moment he cleared the window, he barreled toward the cache of weapons he knew was hidden beneath the sole of the deck against the far wall. Tibbs wrenched the cover off, handing out pulse rifles and ignoring the gaping expressions on the faces of those Noctus working in the pit.

He was honestly surprised to find the Irids still in Arne's office; he'd expected them to mag-cuff the administrator and haul him away in short order. But then he heard the sound of Hume's voice, and realized the soldiers had interrupted Arne in the middle of a comm with the overseer.

Arne had managed to stall them with the excuse that no one left a Lumin hanging, not even an Irid garrison. That gave them long enough pause for light lag to compensate, and for Hume to demand an explanation from the soldier commanding the fireteam.

The Irid in charge grew impatient at the delay, gathering the courage to inform Hume he could take it up with Commander Vincent himself once he docked. Then he ordered his team to cuff Arne, and hustled him out the door.

The sound of the cane connecting with an Irid's head came to Tibbs as he dove for the corner, sliding on his back, his one good eye training the weapon he held on the opening as he cleared it. He got off two shots before the Irid nearest him pivoted and returned fire.

Arne brought his cuffed hands down on the rifle's barrel, ruining the Irid's aim, just as the Noctus with the plas shiv hooked a foot around the Irid she was wrestling with, taking him to the ground.

An enraged bellow erupted from Tibbs as the third member of the fireteam placed his rifle at the base of the Noctus woman's skull, and discharged it. The shiv fell from her lifeless hands as the

Irid underneath pushed her off.

Tibbs ripped the rifle from the soldier who had killed her, and sent a massive fist crashing into the man's temple, following it with an uppercut to the chin that snapped the soldier's head back, felling him on the spot. Pivoting, Tibbs advanced on the final soldier, who was grappling with the yard worker over his weapon. Scooping up the discarded cane, Tibbs hooked the soldier's elbow with it and cranked up hard, using leverage to snap the soldier's shoulder out of its socket.

"Hurts like a bitch, don't it, *ami*?" he grunted as he torqued the cane in one hand while palming the base of the man's skull with the other.

He propelled the man forward, driving the guard's face into the frame of Arne's office door, shattering his nose. Blood poured down the unconscious man's face as Tibbs shoved him away.

"Get those cuffs off the administrator," he instructed, bending to scoop up the soldiers' weapons. "Then bind these peckerwoods."

The expression on Arne's face was one of bemusement as Tibbs turned to face him.

"Good timing," the administrator began, but Tibbs cut him off with a head shake.

"*Bad* timing, boss. Something tipped them off. They were told to round up Tuesday, too."

*****

Hume turned to face Tobias, worry clear on his face. "Now what do we do? We're still a good two hundred kilometers out. There's no way they can evade the garrison for that long."

"They don't need to, lad," Tobias assured him with a glance to Logan. The AI nodded, and headed for the exit to the bridge. "Think they can hide out for about half an hour?"

"Probably," Hume said. "But longer than that, and we risk the garrison's commander putting the platform on lockdown."

"Tell them we're coming in hot and to have someone standing by to meet us when we arrive." Tobias nodded to Charley. "Prep the shuttles."

Charley stood and moved to join Logan. So did Jason.

"Not you this time, boyo," Tobias stopped Jason with a hand. "Need you here to play captain of the ship. Be the distraction we need, along with Terrance, when the *Vale* arrives."

Jason grimaced, then nodded and sat back down as Terrance turned to eye the Weapon Born.

"You taking any Marines with you?" the exec asked, and Tobias nodded.

"Three fireteams, lad. Marta, too. She's rated for combat acceleration, and it's best we start the radiation protocols as soon as possible, to beat the solar storm."

Tobias nodded after the two AIs who had just departed. "Charley's deploying a jamming cloud now, so our Irid friends can't call in reinforcements."

"What about Helada?" Hume asked, struggling to keep up with the rapid pace.

Tobias's expression took on an edge. "We'll sort her out when she docks. You leave that one to me."

INOCULATION

STELLAR DATE: 07.09.3302 (Adjusted Gregorian)
LOCATION: Platform SR71
REGION: Noctilucent Space, Sirian Hegemony

T-minus 8 hours to Solar Particle Event Shock Wave

Marta had no idea how they'd masked their arrival, but she honestly didn't care. The discomfort of the 30*g* deceleration burn all but wiped away her awareness of everything else happening around her on the *Eidolon*.

She knew a second team was on their six, in the *Kuroi Kaze*, with Charley flying a small fleet of drones that worked to disrupt every sensor the platform had pointed in their direction.

Marta blew out a relieved breath as the shuttle floated gently into a cavernous bay, and then winced as the CNT-laced threads retracted from her lungs and other soft-tissue organs.

The process didn't hurt, but the feeling—one she hadn't experienced since her combat days back on El Dorado—was a bit like ants crawling through her insides.

<*Creepy sensation,*> Varanee murmured, and Marta sent her a grimace of agreement.

Snapping her restraints loose, Marta rose to retrieve her kit of radioprotectants, and joined the Marines at the hatch.

A combat net sprang into existence, with icons identifying the two fireteams on the *Eidolon,* as well as the two on the shuttle settling onto the rails beside her.

<*Listen up,*> Tobias's soft burr sounded inside her head as the Wespon Born, ensconced in a battle frame, addressed the teams. <*The objective here is not to engage the enemy. There are more than a hundred thousand souls on board this platform, and the best the* Hyperion *can do is take a few hundred of them away.*>

He paused, letting those numbers sink in.

<I’ll not have the Noctus suffer needlessly after we leave this system, > the Weapon Born admonished. *<This is a stealth play, people. If you must engage, make it quick, quiet, and decisive.>*

<Body count?>

Khela’s voice was matter-of-fact, and Marta felt a shiver of dismay filtering in from Varanee.

<Be warned,> the Weapon Born cautioned, *<you neutralize them, you carry them along with your gear. So remember that before you engage.>*

<I think I’m going to be sick,> Varanee sent in a faint tone to Marta, who pushed a wave of calm at the surgeon.

Khela turned to address her fireteams. “Lena, your team will escort the doctors to the extraction site. Ramon, your team will stay here on *Eidolon* along with Montoya’s team. See to it that no one from the platform’s garrison gets curious about this loading dock,” she ordered. “And stand by…we’ll call you if we need reinforcements. Flynn and Sam, you’re with me.”

Slinging an E-SCAR rifle over her shoulders and fitting a pulse pistol in a holster under her arm, she nodded.

“All right, people. Let’s head out.”

* * * * *

Arne sat huddled next to Tibbs inside a large shipping container. They were crouched between two pallets that held cases filled with various refined ores, awaiting shipment to one of the manufacturing platforms. The shipping container itself was two meters tall and twenty long, and sat behind a clean-room area that Tibbs had assured him was a drone-free zone.

Arne glanced behind them at the insensate pile of soldiers they’d dragged inside the container with them. Twice, the Irid guards had awakened, and twice, Tibbs had taken great pleasure in rendering them unconscious.

The administrator snuck another worried look at the comm

unit strapped to his arm. It wasn't his; this was one Hume had left for him to use once the operation was underway.

In the lone transmission that had come through, Hume had instructed them to take cover, and assured the men that help was on the way.

Arne assumed that whatever form that help might take, it would attempt to reach him through this device.

He was wrong. The first indication either man had that someone was on the other side of the shipping container was when its door was flung open.

Arne's heart stuttered as he found himself face to face with a graceful stranger clad in a Security Guild uniform.

Half a second later, the woman sidestepped the punch Tibbs threw, flowing past the man's fist and redirecting its energy outward. Arne saw a startled look on the face of the massive Noctus as he went flying past, landing face-first on the deck.

The two with the woman had their weapons trained on the back of Tibbs's head before the man even had a chance to register what had happened to him.

Arne raised his hands in the air, his gut twisting, failure tasting like ash on his tongue.

We were so close….

But the woman folded her hands in front of her and dipped her head in a small bow.

"Administrator Arne? I'm from the *Avon Vale.* Hume sent us to help you deal with your little problem."

*****

Marta had been on her share of sketchy mining rigs, back in El Dorado, during her tour with the space force. They were places where safety regs were either stretched perilously thin or ignored altogether, to the inhabitants' peril.

There was a quality to the Blackbird that was reminiscent of that, and she found herself ruthlessly suppressing a sense of disquiet as Xiao led them through a warren of corridors to their destination.

<*I can feel your unease,*> Varanee murmured, and Marta sent her a small grimace.

<*Structurally, it's no different from MD40, so it shouldn't bother me,*> she admitted. <*But for some reason, it does.*>

<*Well, we* **are** *skulking about on a platform half an AU closer to a star that's about to shed some nasty stuff.*>

Marta snorted. <*True. There's something about knowing you're holding time on a short tether that adds tension to the situation, doesn't it.*>

The paired duo of Lena and Tama brought up the rear. Microdrones scouted ahead, clearing the route, while a fourth Marine loitered behind, ensuring no one approached on their six. Under Tama's direction, the tiny machines masked their signatures on all bands, jamming signals where needed.

Twice, the AI had them detour or hold while soldiers passed by.

<*Khela's reached Arne,*> she announced as they waited for the route to clear. <*And Logan's using the captured soldiers' comms to report in and explain their delay. Looks like they've managed to cover up the scuffle outside Arne's office.*>

<*Good,*> Lena sent. <*One less thing to worry about going south on us. At least in the immediate future.*>

Xiao threw a diagram up on the combat net, overlaying it with a "you are here" icon.

<*Twenty meters past that junction, and we're there,*> he told them. <*You ready, docs?*>

Marta sent him a nod. <*Let's get this done.*>

The area beyond the bauxite plant was listed as offline, unused storage. It was large, yet still managed to feel crammed with the number of people inside. They milled about, clutching meager belongings or holding children close.

She could just make out sealed bay doors at one end, with webbing stretched across it to help cushion impacts. Webbing had been strung along the bulkheads as well—hardly sufficient, should this maneuver cause the jettisoned section to roll.

<*This thing's going to become a vomit comet if they don't eject it properly,*> Xiao sent, mirroring Marta's thoughts.

<*We'll have much worse than that to deal with, if that transpires,*> Varanee replied. <*Most of these people are underfed, and malnourished bodies tend to have a lot of sharp angles. We'll have injuries for sure, if this thing takes a tumble.*>

Their thoughts were interrupted by the arrival of a woman, tough and whipcord lean. She had a quality about her that suggested a barely leashed energy. It radiated from her as she closed the distance between them.

"I'm Tuesday," she announced. "You the people Arne sent for?"

Lena nodded. "We are. We have something that'll protect you from the radiation until we can get you out."

The woman nodded and stepped aside. "Set up anywhere you like. Just let us know what to do."

<*Going to take some time to inoculate three hundred people,*> Tama told the team, as they moved deeper into the area.

Marta blew out a breath and unslung her pack. "True. So let's get started."

Xiao returned her nod, slinging his pack beside hers and helping her set up a portable desk where she could administer the radioprotectants. Varanee and Tama would handle dosage calibrations by Noctus weight as the humans handled the inoculations.

As Tuesday began to organize the Noctus into a queue, the two doctors and the fireteam bent to their tasks.

* * * * *

Tibbs rolled to his feet, refusing the proffered hand of the man dressed like a garrison guard. The simple fact that the soldier would offer help was enough to convince him this was no Irid.

He lowered his brow and pinned the woman in charge with a one-eyed stare. "The garrison?"

She stared back, immediately understanding his terse question, and responded in kind. "We're handling it."

He nodded, deciding he liked this young warrior. Turning to Arne, he sent him a questioning look.

The administrator straightened. "Right, then. I should be getting back to admin," Arne said, turning to the woman. "Best if you escort us, though. Maybe explain why I'm not handcuffed."

Captain Khela smiled. "Maybe act annoyed about the whole thing, while we're at it?"

Tibbs snorted.

"Think that's a yes, Cap'n," said the Marine who'd offered him a hand up.

Khela shot him a wry look as she stepped aside for Arne to lead.

Tibbs caught a few wary looks from the Noctus in the communication pit as they entered. He had to hand it to Khela; the woman could be scary when she set her mind to it. He was sure none suspected she was anything other than the Security Guild soldier she pretended to be.

Scowling at Arne, she motioned him toward his office, and Tibbs stepped out of the entrance so that they could pass by. Not quite knowing what to do with himself—he was a yard worker, after all, and had no business in admin—he began to ease himself back out into the hallway.

Khela's sharp eyes caught the movement, and she gestured with her rifle, indicating he follow Arne. Once inside, she keyed the door shut behind them.

Her body language remained aggressive, a display for those who could see through the plas window, but her expression was thoughtful. "I think it's best if we don't appear to be looming over you right now. We'll retreat, but stay nearby."

She glanced from Arne to Tibbs, and then tapped her ear, indicating the devices the Marines had given them. Tibbs fought the urge to reach up and finger the contraption; he wasn't used to fancy tech, especially stuff that crawled down inside, past his ear hairs.

"Just call my name—Captain or Khela will do—and we'll hear. Same with Hume, if you need him." She broke into a smile. "More secure, I think, than that thing strapped to your wrist."

Nodding, she exited, motioning her team to pull back.

Arne pulled out his chair and took a seat at his desk, expression a bit glazed. With a shake of his head, Tibbs could tell he was back in the game.

Reaching out, he toggled the bulky comm array that took up a good third of his desk.

<*Dock,*> a voice announced.

"Hey, Vic, it's Arne. Got an ETA for me on our visitors?"

<*Which ones, the big 'un that just docked,*> the woman on the other end asked, <*or the one that's inbound?*>

"The one that docked is the Avon Vale, correct?" Arne asked.

<*Yes. That garrison commander's here to greet them.*>

Arne grimaced, but forged ahead. "What about the one that the adjunct's on?"

<*It's on final now,*> she informed him. <*Want to come take her off my hands when she arrives, pretty please? She should be pulling up in about fifteen minutes.*>

Arne caught a repulsed look on Tibbs's face that brought a quick grin to his own—then he sighed.

"Okay, Vic. I'm on my way." He toggled the comm unit off and stood, stifling a yawn. "Sorry, I'd just gotten to sleep when Lauren woke me."

Tibbs crossed his arms, shifting his gaze to follow Arne as the man neared the door.

"About that."

Arne paused expectantly, waiting for him to continue.

"Something you should know, boss. Garrison's got something they're holding over Lauren, and it scares her real bad. Bad enough to make her tell them the things she heard you say."

Arne's gaze grew thoughtful. "That would explain it."

Tibbs nodded, but didn't respond, having just used up his quota of words for the day.

"Know what that might be?"

He shook his head.

"See if you can't find out," the administrator advised. "Then go check on the patcher, see if he has any strays that need moving over before we set that furnace off."

Tibbs nodded and turned to head for south wing, as he and Arne parted ways.

CROSSROADS

STELLAR DATE: 07.09.3302 (Adjusted Gregorian)
LOCATION: Platform SR71
REGION: Noctilucent Space, Sirian Hegemony

T-minus 5 hours to Solar Particle Event Shock Wave

As he reached the umbilical where the *Avon Vale* was docked, Hume spied Jason and Terrance waiting for him. Standing next to them was Amelia, an Irid from his own security contingent.

Less pleasant was the sight of several guards converging on their location. At the head of the group was the Blackbird's garrison commander, Vincent.

"Where is your administrator?" Hume demanded as he strode toward them, his glance taking in the soldiers that accompanied Vincent.

"He appears to have gone missing, Overseer," the commander said smoothly, stepping forward and coming to attention. "We have been searching for him for the better part of the day."

Hume scowled at the man, allowing his eyes to narrow in suspicion. "And exactly why would you be looking for him in the first place, commander?"

Vincent looked alarmed, as if he realized he'd let slip something he shouldn't have. But then his expression smoothed.

He opened his mouth to speak, but Hume beat him to it.

Snapping his fingers, Hume ordered Amelia to step forward.

"I'm relieving you of duty," Hume told Vincent, gesturing to the woman by his side. "Commander Amelia here will step in until your guild can send a replacement."

Vincent sputtered a protest as the woman stepped forward, saluting Hume smartly. Hume saw the moment the man took in Amelia's rank insignia, senior to his own junior grade.

Vincent deflated and stepped aside as she took command of the small group of guards. He offered no protest when she ordered them to place a mute restraint on his Link, limiting his ability to communicate to the garrison and outside the platform. If the former garrison commander thought it odd, he kept his own counsel.

"Carry on," Hume nodded to Amelia, as she turned to lead Vincent away. <*Well, that's one more obstacle out of our path,*> he sent to Terrance and Jason, who had stayed quietly in the background as the Lumin dealt with internecine issues. <*Amelia will call off the soldiers sweeping the platform, so your people should find it a bit easier to move about, now.*>

Gesturing toward the corridor—and for the benefit of any recording devices the Hegemony might access later—the overseer welcomed the CEO of Enfield Holdings to Sintering and Refinery Platform 71.

* * * * *

Half an hour later, Lauren was on a run between east and north yards, when a rough hand jerked her to a stop.

"Not so fast, girl," the Irid guard said, looming over her. "You have anything new for Commander Vincent? He's an impatient man."

Lauren tried wrenching her arm free, but the man's hand wouldn't budge.

"He's not in charge anymore, so what's it matter, anyway?" she asked. Her words were brave, but she couldn't make herself meet the soldier's eyes.

The man gave an ugly laugh. "Helada's here. It's just a matter of time 'til the pansy-ass commander that Hume installed gets kicked out." He gave her arm a shake. "This is Miguel's platform, not Hume's. You think some overseer from Strategic Planning is going to trump that?"

Her frightened eyes met his as he shoved her away from him

and let her go on her way with one final warning.

"Don't be letting your brother down now, Lauren. You got me?"

The free clinic was still a kilometer away, but sudden fear lent wings to her feet. She sprinted down the hallway, dodging people and machinery and earning curses as she went.

Her breath burst from her lungs in a giant whoosh when she saw her brother. He looked better than he had in days, smiling up at a patcher she'd never before seen as the woman examined him.

She slowed as she approached, and his eyes lit up when he saw her.

"Lauren!"

She couldn't help the silly grin that broke out as she neared the pallet where he was sitting up. "Hey, you look like you're feeling better."

Her brother nodded vigorously. "Patcher says she fixed me up good. I might not even have flares again."

Lauren scowled over at the stranger, not wanting the woman to put ideas in her brother's head, of things that could never be.

She jumped as a hand descended, and looked up into Dusty's eyes.

"This is the doctor from the *Avon Vale,*" he told her. "She's fixed your brother up right and proper, better'n any meds we have here."

She turned to thank the woman, but was interrupted when the big man, Tibbs, stepped forward.

"Gotta move these kids now. Helada's on her way down. Best they're hidden before she gets here."

Dusty nodded, and the two medics moved away, the woman giving her a little wink and a wave from an odd-looking hand as she passed.

A light cough had Lauren whirling back to face her brother.

"Thought you were all better," she said, narrowing her eyes at him.

Brian shrugged. "Allergies, I guess."

She looked over her shoulder at the retreating backs of the three adults, and noticed a small group of children being ushered out of the free clinic. The bundles they were carrying made her think they were being moved somewhere.... Somewhere the garrison wouldn't find them.

She looked back down at her brother as he sniffed and wiped his nose. Patting him on the shoulder, she took a step toward the corridor.

"I'll be back. You rest up, okay?"

She didn't wait for his answer, just started for the door, her gaze straying once more toward the gaggle of kids being herded out. She nearly collided with Tibbs, so focused was she on the activity on the far side of the clinic.

"Not so fast," the big man rumbled.

They were the same words the guard had used earlier, but from the big Noctus, they sounded kind. He nodded over at where she'd been staring.

"There are fifty already in hiding, *cher*. Those are the last six right there, going somewhere the Lumins can't reach. Unless the garrison finds out."

He crouched so that he was at eye level with her, his single, dark eye pinning hers with a knowing look.

"How's it feel, holding the fate of that many lives in your hands?"

Lauren's eyes widened as she stared back at him. She felt like one of the station rats, trapped between the paws of a cat.

"My brother," she stammered, and then swallowed. Breaking eye contact, she moved away.

Tibbs let her.

"I gotta go," she muttered.

She ran out into the corridor, taking several running steps before faltering to a halt at the first intersection.

What do I do? she thought, sick with indecision.

Turning left would take her to the garrison, while going right would take her down the wing that held the out-of-service bauxite plant, and what she now knew was a smuggling operation.

With a sigh of resignation, she turned right.

I don't know how I'll protect Brian, but I'll find a way.

She was too far away to hear the murmured words of the man who'd stepped out to observe her—and to intercept, should she choose wrong.

"Knew you'd do the right thing, cher," he murmured before stepping back inside the free clinic.

Motioning Dusty over, Tibbs pointed out Lauren's brother. The medic nodded, then gestured for the boy to gather his things and join the kids against the far wall.

*****

Shortly after Tuesday had told Marta there were a few remaining kids in the free clinic, a large, hulking Noctus named Tibbs had shown up, volunteering to round them up. Marta suggested that she go along, in case they had medical needs to be addressed before being transferred.

Lena had sent Xiao along to assist. Thankfully, they'd not run into anything too difficult to treat. The countdown for the furnace detonation had resumed with the news that the Hyperion was now in range to offer assistance.

These kids were the last of the ones to be smuggled into the hold behind the bauxite plant. Once they were delivered to Tuesday, the bulkheads could be sealed, and the furnace fired up.

Their trip to relocate the kids to the hold had been held up by two Irid patrols, but they were now within a kilometer of their destination. However, a few of the kids were showing signs of flagging. Dusty carried one, while Marta shouldered another, leaving Xiao and the hulking Tibbs free to engage if necessary.

They were nearing the junction to a cross corridor when the

alarm sounded.

<*Helada's headed your way with Arne,*> Tobias informed them. Then his tone turned warning. <*She has her own guards with her. We let them through, not wanting to draw any suspicion. Sending a fireteam your way as backup, though, in case you need it.*>

An icon appeared on the map overlay of her HUD.

<*She's almost on top of us,*> Xiao observed, then turned to Tibbs. "Got anywhere we can stash these kids?"

Tibbs's gaze swept the bulkhead opposite them at the Marine's questioning look. He nodded to a spar, two bays down.

"That's storage," he said. "Got a way to unlock it for us?"

Xiao nodded. "Stay put," he warned, then trotted across to jimmy the door with a bit of nano.

It slid aside, and he poked his head inside before waving them over. They were almost to the entrance when Marta saw an entourage rounding the corner. She kept Tibbs' bulk between herself and the approaching group as she urged the children toward Xiao and the open door.

<*Stay calm, and don't rush it,*> Tobias advised, his tone even. <*As far as she knows, you're exactly where you are supposed to be, just another group of Noctus among thousands on this platform.*>

Everything went smoothly, up until the girl whose hand Marta held tripped and fell.

Tibbs bent to lift her, his movement exposing Marta to the oncoming Helada. Reflexively, she glanced up—and met the eyes of the Lumin who had stopped them on MD40.

<*Stars, it's her,*> Varanee breathed as Marta froze.

Recognition flared as the adjunct's gaze darted from face to face. Seeing Xiao in a Security Guild uniform, she stabbed her hand in the air and barked an order for them to stop.

<*We've been made,*> Marta reported as she handed off the child in her arms to Tibbs, and motioned him away.

<*Tibbs,*> Xiao's voice crackled with authority as he addressed the Noctus. <*Get Dusty and those kids inside and out of the way. Does*

this storage unit have a back door?>

Arne's voice joined in, and Marta could see him hanging back, at the rear of Helada's group. *<It spans two spars. There's another door back here.>*

Marta saw him gesture toward the bulkhead.

Xiao sent a mental nod. *<I see it. Tibbs, start easing them in that direction while we sort this out.>*

When Marta glanced back at Helada, she saw the woman's face contorted with anger and suspicion. As the Lumin stopped in front of Marta, the adjunct reached for the coverall sleeve concealing her augmented arm.

Marta wrenched her arm away, and the Irid beside Helada slammed the butt of his pulse rifle against her temple in response. As she fell to the deck, she saw Xiao move to help. The whine of a directed energy beam weapon powering up brought the Marine up short.

"Last time I saw you," the adjunct told Xiao as she stalked toward him, "you were dressed as a Noctus. And now you're Security. So which is it—Noctus or Irid, I wonder? Or maybe something entirely different?"

Helada's voice grew ugly, and she turned to her security escort, jerking her head toward Xiao. Two Irids closed on him as the adjunct glanced between them once more.

"And what would you want platform rats for, I wonder? Those brats are company property. Looks to me like you're helping them escape. You know what we do with thieves and traitors?"

The Irid soldier reversed his weapon and jabbed the stock into Xiao's gut. The Marine rolled with it, letting his actions give the appearance that the soldier's strike had made an impact.

The pounding in Marta's head receded as her mednano managed the swelling, but she was still disoriented. When Helada bent to yank up the sleeve of her coveralls, Marta wasn't fast enough to evade.

Helada's eyes narrowed. "And that sure as suns isn't like any

Sirian tech I've ever seen." Marta pulled her medsleeve out of the adjunct's grasp as Helada motioned for her soldiers to lift her to her feet.

<She's sending a comm out!> Shannon's voice cut in. *<Jamming now. Stars, I'm not sure….>*

Marta glared at Helada as two guards held her between them, their grip tight on her arms. "Those are children, not property," she growled.

Helada laughed. "They're anything I say they are," she smirked. Gesturing to one of the guards, she ordered, "Bring me the scrawniest one, and let's show this spy what we do with defective merchandise."

The Irid nodded and dropped Marta's medsleeve arm.

<Stand by, doctor,> Tobias advised, his tone utterly devoid of any accent. *<I'm on your six. Can you give that piece of trash holding your other arm a nice dose of something from your medsleeve?>*

Marta felt a flare of something dark and ugly inside her as she dialed up a batch of nano that had Varanee gasping in shock.

<That's going to cause intense allodynia!>

Marta grinned ferally at the thought of the pain receptors she was about to trigger. *<That's nothing to the damage I'd like to inflict—and it's only temporary.>* To Tobias, she sent, *<On your mark, sir.>*

<Do it.>

She slammed her left hand into the soldier's side, and the man bucked, a startled cry of pain erupting as the nano shocked his central nervous system.

<Drop!> Tobias ordered, and Marta dove toward the bulkhead in a roll that would have made her former academy instructor proud.

The whine of an E-SCAR sounded, and she watched as a shot lanced out, striking the same soldier at the base of his skull. He fell in an odd corkscrew motion, one leg folding before the other, the result of a targeted brainstem strike.

Behind Marta, a battle frame advanced, its four arms holding weapons locked on Helada as well as her three remaining guards.

"Allow me to demonstrate how civilized star systems handle filth like you," the Weapon Born said, his voice as hard and chilled as the depths of space.

Helada's gaze flickered to one side, and then back to Tobias, a cruel grin beginning to play across her mouth.

"I don't think so," the adjunct said, as the Irid who had disappeared into the storage unit came back out carrying a young girl, pulse pistol thrust under her chin. "You shoot me, she dies."

Every member of the task force knew that a lightning fast counterattack was the only way to address a hostage threat. Attackers expected the sight of a victim to cause an adversary to pause; rarely were they prepared for an immediate response.

Xiao's mental <*Marta, go!*> rang in her head, and she exploded into action, lunging for the returned soldier's feet while Xiao feinted right.

The distraction worked. The Irid holding the child stepped back, his attention shifting from Tobias to the more immediate threat he sensed in front of him.

Tobias took the shot, obliterating the Irid's face as Marta rolled to catch the falling girl.

Helada used the action to open fire on the Weapon Born as she launched herself toward the cover of a nearby spar. Her shot caught the battle frame mid-torso, causing Marta to gasp as the directed beam weapon lanced out.

Tobias's return fire hit Helada in the throat, the E-SCAR practically severing her head.

"Dammit, that Elastene plating was brand new," the AI growled as he safetied his weapon, eliciting a shaky laugh from Varanee—a comment Marta suspected he'd made for just that purpose.

"We're done here, people. And we're late. That furnace is set to blow in fifteen minutes. Wrap this up—and bring the bodies with you."

FIRE WITHIN, FLARE WITHOUT

STELLAR DATE: 07.09.3302 (Adjusted Gregorian)
LOCATION: Platform SR71
REGION: Noctilucent Space, Sirian Hegemony

T-minus 1 hour to Solar Particle Event Shock Wave

Tobias's signal had Arne returned to the admin wing with Hume, Terrance, and Jason in tow. The two stealthed shuttles had quietly drifted away from the platform, and the Marines had all returned to the *Avon Vale.*

The alarm had been sent throughout the Blackbird for all Noctus to report to their assigned shelter-in-place locations to weather the storm.

Through the connection the newcomers had given him, Arne could hear Tuesday's muffled voice as Tibbs enveloped her in a quick hug.

<*Everyone's sealed inside,*> Tibbs reported. <*We're clear.*>

<*Enviro active,*> Tuesday's tense voice confirmed.

<*Be well, Tuesday,*> he sent, and heard her choked goodbye. "All right, then," Arne turned to the communications pit and, for the sake of the charade, announced, "I just received confirmation that the bauxite plant is ready to come back online." He clapped his hands together, every inch the platform administrator.

"Go ahead and start her up," he instructed, pacing calmly at the back of the room, as Hume and the two men from the *Avon Vale* looked on. "Let's have it perform an automated test run while we're bunkered. She'll be ready to go into production when we get out. Got it?"

Heads nodded, and the feed on the main screen showed the furnace firing up.

Now he just had to wait for it to redline.

"Sir," one of the communications pit team turned to Arne and nodded in the direction of Sirius. "Spew's forty-nine minutes away."

The Noctus next to her leant over and studied the 2D display. He whistled. "Look at those numbers."

Arne's worried gaze met Hume's, and the man shook his head slightly.

<*Not to worry, lad,*> Tobias's voice came through his ear on the *Vale*'s channel. <*You just focus on giving the performance of your life, and be ready with those explosive bolts.*>

"Sir!" The shout rang out right on time. "The bauxite furnace—it's going critical!"

"Shut it down," Arne barked, moving to stand over her shoulder.

The woman's fingers flew over the antiquated hardware. "It's…it's not responding, sir."

"Try again."

She went to re-enter the abort code, and Arne shoved her aside to do it himself.

Nothing worked, as the abort code had been disabled on the furnace.

Arne affected a worried frown. "Order everyone on South wing to evacuate to a shelter on one of the other wings," he snapped, and the woman leapt into action, her fingers flying across her board.

"Jamieson," he turned to the Noctus seated next to her. "Contact the garrison. Ask them for help putting out the fire. Tell them if we can't get it under control, we'll have to eject the last segment at the end of South wing. Tell them there might be Noctus in that area."

Turning back to the woman, he instructed her to pull up the commands that would trigger the explosive bolts that would eject the bauxite plant into the black. With shaking hands, she complied as they waited to hear back from the garrison.

The response from Hume's plant, Commander Amelia, went as

scripted. Jamieson turned back to Arne, his face white. "They refuse to render any aid, sir. They say there's not enough time before the spew hits, and they won't risk it."

Arne turned to Hume, but the overseer shook his head. "This platform is not under the oversight of Strategic Planning, Administrator. You're on your own. You'll have to answer to Overseer Miguel about your actions—I'll not stand in the way of company business."

Arne kept his expression carefully neutral. His non-expression would be familiar to those in the pit; it was a mask they all used to hide their true feelings when dealing with Lumins.

The Noctus in the pit exchanged covert glances as Arne nodded solemnly.

He took a deep breath, and let his expression grow grave as it swept the Noctus in the pit before him.

"This is…one of the most difficult decisions I've ever had to make," he told them, and in a way, it was true. "But you know the hazards that fire poses to a platform."

He nodded to the woman at the station in front of him.

"Is the program loaded?" he asked.

She nodded.

He stepped forward, and she moved aside for him to input the command codes that only he held. He punched the numbers in, paused, and then plunged his finger down on the detonate button.

He imagined he could feel the slight tremor of the explosions, although he knew in truth they were too far away to be felt. Feeds trained on that wing of the facility displayed small, bright flashes, followed by a yawning gap that began to emerge as the bauxite sector floated away from the platform.

The brilliant light of a runaway furnace flared, the oxygen bleeding off into space, serving to dampen the flames. The air in the comm pit was still, as the Noctus seated within held their breath, waiting for the section to float clear of the nets that held the ores to be processed within the confines of the yards.

Moments later, it was done.

Arne heard Terrance Enfield stir. The man cleared his throat and then asked quietly, "Were there…any casualties?"

Arne turned and speared Jamieson with a questioning look, although he knew the answer the man's board would read.

"No, sir," the Noctus replied, his voice flooded with relief. "That section behind the plant has been out of use for the past six months. Enviro's even been shut down. So unless people didn't make it out of that section of corridor before the blast doors sealed…."

Another Noctus turned to Arne, interrupting him. "Sir, it's Tibbs from the west yard. He says there are several Noctus unaccounted for—" The woman looked up, her face paling in dismay. "One of them's Yard Manager Tuesday."

A collective gasp traveled through the pit as stricken eyes turned from the woman who had spoken back to the image of the severed section.

The Noctus who had spoken cleared her throat twice before she was able to speak. "He…he says there are more…." Her voice faded as she fought to keep her composure.

Her face screwed up in agony, and she ripped her headset off, throwing it from her as if it had burnt her.

"The numbers, sir." Her eyes met Arne's, and he saw a desperate pleading in their depths, a silent request for him to deny the truth of what she just heard. "Three hundred," she choked, silent tears beginning to trickle down her face.

Jamieson shook his head. "Even if they made it inside the back section, that spew—"

"Then let's hope it was mercifully quick," Arne's quiet voice cut in.

After a moment, Captain Andrews cleared his throat and stepped forward.

"Administrator Arne," he spoke in a quiet voice. "It's not our way to leave the dead unattended. With your permission, after the shock wave passes, we'd like to offer the services of the *Avon Vale* to recover them."

RACE TO FREEDOM

STELLAR DATE: 07.10.3302 (Adjusted Gregorian)
LOCATION: Platform SR71
REGION: Noctilucent Space, Sirian Hegemony

Upon his return to the garrison after the solar storm had passed, Commander Vincent was smugly pleased to discover that Commander Amelia had been ordered back to Hume's detail. He was in command of the SR71 garrison once more.

He'd been disappointed to miss out on the excitement of the runaway fire and the jettison of the bauxite plant the previous day. Though he'd found it mildly entertaining to watch the recordings of those bleeding heart Centaurans search for dead bodies, so he contented himself with reviewing those.

A Procyon ship had joined the search. Together, the two vessels had retrieved the section that had been ejected, and delivered it back to the Blackbird for reuse. The Procyon ship had then departed, while the *Avon Vale* ran one final sweep.

Well, that's something, he grunted mentally. *Least we didn't have to waste resources, recovering that piece of the platform.*

The solar particle event that had impeded communications the day before had dramatically tapered off, although its effects would still be felt for another few hours. But that wasn't his real worry; his immediate concern was that it seemed his garrison had managed to misplace Overseer Miguel's adjunct.

He had practically the entire garrison out looking for Helada, even going so far as to poke their heads into the squalor of the platform rats' living quarters and free clinics. They had yet to find her.

His comm alerted him to an incoming ping from the Centauran ship.

<*Commander Vincent,*> the man on the other end began, <*we've*

found a few bodies, and by their dress, they appear to be some of yours, not Noctus. Sending imagery so that you can identify.>

Vincent accepted the feed and stared in dismay at the image that resolved in his holo.

It was the charred remains of Helada and three of her guardsmen.

His eyes narrowed as he considered the coincidence that they would be in that section of the platform just when the furnace blew.

That reminded him—he hadn't checked his messages for a response to the comm he'd sent Overseer Miguel just before he'd been relieved of his post by Hume.

Odd business, that. Why should Hume get annoyed about Vincent arresting Arne? Annoying an overseer during his visit seemed more like the kind of excuse *Miguel* would use to relieve an officer from duty. Hume had never struck Vincent as the kind to act so rashly.

Vincent's instincts were telling him there was something going on here that didn't add up. He just needed the time to figure out what it was.

He'd received a good two dozen notification pings once his comm access had been reinstated, and he'd shunted them aside in favor of dealing with the more urgent issue of the runaway bauxite furnace. Now, though, he had the time to filter through the queue to see what missives might be awaiting him.

He grimaced as he saw the timestamp on the one from Miguel.

Vincent had half wondered if it was professional jealousy that was behind Miguel's hunt for dirt on Hume, but as he listened to this latest message, coupled with his own experience at Hume's hands, he began to suspect it was something more.

His eyes were on the icon that showed the track of the departing *Beautiful Passage* as Miguel mentioned his suspicion that Hume had some sort of shady deal going on with the captain of the *Hyperion*.

Vincent's eyes narrowed as he looked at the ship's ident. Mentally tagging it, he expanded the ident, studying its readout.

Interesting that it shares a make similar to that of the ship Miguel has such a keen interest in.

There was something else about the *Hyperion,* something he was forgetting....

He paused Miguel's recording as he mentally rifled through reports the Blackbird's STC had forwarded from other stations. He halted at the mayday report from Prism. Scanning it, he found what the back of his brain had registered but he'd forgotten.

Hyperion had called in a fusion containment failure, sending its crew to safety while attempting repairs. According to Prism STC, the ship and its remaining crew had perished two days earlier.

Vincent returned to his study of the *Beautiful Passage,* a ship he'd not heard mentioned being in the system prior to today.

Interesting coincidence.

Vincent didn't believe in coincidences.

* * * * *

On the bridge of the *Vale,* Jason sat back in his captain's chair as the tightbeam comm they'd established with the newly-christened *Beautiful Passage* was displayed on the main holo. On screen were Cesar and the ship's navigator, Jim.

<Please tell your doctors that everyone checks out just fine, thanks to their intervention,> Cesar said with a smile. *<With the hundred and seventy-five, give or take, that Hume and the* Hyperion *had already smuggled aboard, that's more than five hundred souls you've helped save.>*

<Five hundred and six,> Rae added, as she stepped up behind the two humans. *<And thank you for getting our ship back for us, too.>*

Jason grinned and gave the AI a quick nod. "You're quite welcome."

He leant to one side as Terrance came up beside him to join the conversation.

"We weren't exactly able to say a proper goodbye to your cousin back on the Blackbird without giving away our intent, Cesar," the exec said. "So please tell Hume the next time you see him that it was a pleasure doing business with him."

<I'll do that,> the Noctus replied. *<I know he'd say the feeling's mutual.>*

Jason nodded. "Very good, then. We'll stay on a heading that interposes us between you and SR71, just in case something comes up."

Rae grinned slyly as she crossed her arms. *<You know, one would think that's a noble yet useless thing for a fellow merchant ship without shields or armament to do,>* she said with a wink. *<Unless they happened to find themselves on a clandestine mission to pick up a wayward cat with a certain engineer who knows all about the history of Q-ships.>*

Jim's expression now looked utterly confused. Rae patted him on the shoulder.

<Long story, Jim. Good thing we have a long journey ahead of us for me to tell it.>

Jason stroked the stubble along the side of his jaw as he worked to hide a grin. "Ah, well, I suppose we'd better send our regrets and start to extricate ourselves from this sorry excuse for a star system." He nodded at the holo. "Ping us if you need anything. *Vale* out."

He watched as the *Hyperion* changed course, its heading on an outbound for Procyon that paralleled one of the Sirian fast-shipping lanes.

"Fair skies and tailwinds, friends," he murmured, then stood and angled over to where Charley sat at Weapons. "What's the data from your drones telling us?"

"Everything's quiet so far," the AI responded. "I have an escort covering their six, and another cloud monitoring traffic from the platform. Nothing from the ones I seeded between here and

Incandus, either." Charley looked up at Jason and then over to Tobias.

The Weapon Born tilted his head in acknowledgment.

"Always assume the plan won't survive engagement with the enemy," Tobias said, "but it's a fair sight nicer when they cooperate, isn't it, boyo?"

Jason gave the AI a sloppy, two-fingered salute, then turned for the ready room. "Ship's yours, Landon. I'm going to go help Terrance write that Dear Jane letter to the Hegemony."

* * * * *

Miguel was on final for Brilliance Station when he received Vincent's comm. The Irid commander had acquitted himself well; the case he made for the *Hyperion* and *Beautiful Passage* being one and the same was compelling.

The station listed more than three hundred missing from the bauxite accident. Vincent was convinced—and Miguel agreed—that somehow, they had used the furnace disaster to cover up a smuggling operation.

His anger grew as he realized the sun-cursed ship had a thirty-six-hour head start. Knowing that light lag from Vincent's comm added another forty-five minutes to that only stoked Miguel's ire.

He needed an audience with Cyrus. The Hegemony fleet fell under Infrastructure, and any military action had to first be approved through him.

His lips pulled back into a feral grin as he recalled the Hegemony's position on people who defaulted on their contracts. He had no doubt he could convince Cyrus to end the employment agreements of any Noctus aboard that fleeing ship—in a very permanent way.

The moment the transport docked, he had the flight crew order all passengers to remain in their seats until Miguel had a chance to disembark first. Then he commandeered a maglev, instructing the

NSAI to divert any cars between him and his objective.

The dispassionate part of his brain knew that haste wouldn't really gain him anything, but as an outlet for his building rage, it sufficed.

Capturing a fleeing vessel that far out took time. Any attack sanctioned against the *Hyperion* would play out over the course of several hours. But it would play out. The Hegemony had drones and relativistic missiles that could travel much faster than a ship carrying fragile, unaugmented Noctus.

Miguel knew that it wasn't a matter of *if* they could destroy that ship…it was *when*.

Fortune was with him. One of the first figures he spotted when exiting into Brilliance Station proper was Cyrus's AI, Indira. Flagging her down, he ordered the shackled creature to arrange for a meeting with her master as soon as possible.

"I'm sorry, sir, but Vice President Cyrus's schedule is rather full today," the AI said. "His first opening is next Thursday."

"You don't seem to understand," Miguel snarled, crowding the AI and getting all up in her frame's optical pickups. "I need to see him, *now*."

His invasion of personal space was a reflex, a habit from years of bullying those whom the overseer considered lesser beings. The effect was wasted on a Caprise-mod NSAI.

"You look stressed, handsome. Stress isn't good for humans, you know."

The voice sounded like Indira's, but the cadence was off. If Miguel didn't know better, he would have said it sounded…sultry.

He shook his head, eyeing the AI warily. "Nevermind, I'll handle it myself."

He pinged Cyrus, tagging it as urgent/high-level. He added a pingback notification request and a header titled 'Noctus escape in progress', and then stalked toward the station's STC tower.

He was poring over the *Hyperion*'s outbound track and comparing it to the track from the mysteriously-appearing

Beautiful Passage when Cyrus's response came through.

<*Get over here now,*> the vice president ordered.

<*I'm on my way.*>

* * * * *

"It's all a ruse!"

The tap Francesca had installed in Cyrus's office perfectly captured the agitation in Miguel's voice as he unmasked the *Hyperion*. It transmitted the brittle anger in Cyrus's as well, as the vice president realized that the Hegemony had been duped.

Francesca's jaw tightened as she listened to Miguel relate the incidents on the SR71 platform, railing of the missing Noctus, and of what he suspected the ship's cargo to be.

There was no way to intervene, no way to block whatever move Cyrus made.

She turned to study the holo of the *Hyperion*'s projected track. It still had many AU to go, and much could go wrong.

How did I think such an ambitious plan could succeed?

Her attention was arrested on the blinking icon that held the lives of so many, as Cyrus let Miguel's rant spool itself out.

"Calm yourself, Overseer," the cold tones of her peer cut in finally. *"I have yet to see a transport ship that can outrun a relativistic missile."*

Francesca had heard enough. As she reached for the encrypted comm code that the captain of the *Avon Vale* had provided, she felt the Rae clone stir in her mind, as the NSAI sensed her distress. Shunting it aside as the real Rae had shown her how to do, she turned on her holorecorder and began to speak.

"Captain, it seems we have a problem."

* * * * *

Two minutes after Francesca's message arrived, Jason's voice cracked across the combat net.

<Logan, Landon. Ready room, now.>

Separate from the shipnet, this combat net would be the channel over which the upcoming battle would play out. By the time they were ready to engage, it would comprise the full bridge complement, as well as all ancillary support teams.

Right now, it numbered six: Jason and Terrance, the AI twins, and Tobias and Charley.

Jason had annotated his command with a link to Francesca's warning. He knew they'd have reviewed it by the time they hit the door. That message icon now hung pinned to the room's holo, ready for review, beside a real-time feed of the *Hyperion*'s track.

"Looks like we're a go for Operation Fakeout," he told them as they entered. "Landon, coordinate with Charley. Match real-time data to the sims you've been running. Figure out what else he needs that the *Vale* can provide, and make it happen."

Turning to Logan, Jason speared the profiler with a look. "What do we know today that we didn't know yesterday? What players are involved, and who do you suspect? And I'd like your best guess on where their breaking point is." He shot a mordant look Terrance's way. "Or as our resident CEO reminded me a few minutes ago, what's their cost/benefit analysis going to be, and what'll we need to do to make them cut their losses."

Landon nodded, and his frame locked as he entered into a combat sim with Charley. Logan took a seat across from Tobias, then turned to the holo and began pulling up data.

"Cyrus is most certainly involved, but I doubt Miguel has let Berit in on it yet." The AI paused. "Most likely, he's waiting to present her with a fait accompli, given her volatile nature. This will be good for Francesca—it means she will have surprise on her side when she brings this before the board. Berit's not going to like it when she discovers her overseer's been working behind her back with a vice president from a different division."

He returned the holo to the map of Hegemony space

surrounding the *Hyperion*.

"As for what it will take to get them to back down…." The profiler allowed his voice to trail off as he glanced at the Weapon Born.

"Logan and I have been tossing an idea around, boyo," Tobias took up the telling, "and it's a bit of a chancer, I'll gi' ye that. But it could do the trick."

Jason looked from one to the other, then glanced over at Terrance.

"Something tells me I'm going to hate it as much as you will," the exec returned, his eyes narrowing.

"Aye," Tobias sighed, "and there's that. All right, lads. The short of it is that we end up agreeing to sign a deal with the Sirians if they'll let the *Hyperion* go."

"Not going to happen."

"Not just no, but *hells* to the no."

"All right, then. Our second option is to escort them to Procyon. But that'll add decades to our journey, what with this being our final stop before returning to El Dorado."

Terrance frowned. "I'm not liking that plan too well, either."

Jason hadn't spent literally all his life around the AI without figuring out the Weapon Born's tells. Something about Tobias's stance told Jason there was a third option—the one he'd been angling for all along.

"Okay, out with it. What's the *real* plan you two came up with?"

Tobias's demeanor changed. "It wasn't me, boyo."

At an unseen signal, Charley's frame shifted. "It's the only sim Logan and I ran that'll work. And it involves the *Vale*'s drones, some modifications Jonesy's been working on since we left the Blackbird, and those AIs on their ship."

He indicated the holo of the *Hyperion*, then altered it to include automated missile platforms seeded between the coreward stations, the armament at both Brilliance and Glorious Stations, as well as three clusters of fleet vessels.

"These are all the possible missile launch sites, and their proximity to *Hyperion*'s outbound track. The data we received from Rae indicates they have a limited number of high-accel, three-stage, multi-drive RMs capable of pulling five hundred *g*s."

Jason sat back in his chair at those numbers. "You said 'limited number'."

Charley nodded. "Our best guess places them insystem, where they'd be more easily accessible, with the more standard missiles along their borders."

Terrance studied the holo. "That means…."

"Most likely locations are at a minimum five AU distance from the *Hyperion*. That will give us almost five hours' warning once they launch."

"Target lock and telemetry?" Jason worked the math in his L2 brain, nodding slightly at his own conclusions.

"By the time they're committed to their final drive, I should have no trouble swatting them out of the black," the Weapons officer said. "But just in case, I'd like to transfer a small swarm of drones over to the *Hyperion* for their AIs to control. We'd not get them back," Charley warned with a glance at Terrance, "but it'd be added protection for them on their journey to Procyon."

Terrance nodded slowly. "Would some of our older models work, or are they going to need some of that next-gen stuff Jonesy just completed as we came insystem?"

Landon spoke up. "The older ones would do just fine, I think. Especially with the surprise we're planning…."

ULTIMATUM

STELLAR DATE: 07.10.3302 (Adjusted Gregorian)
LOCATION: 1 AU from SR71, 5 AU from Lucent
REGION: Noctilucent Space, Sirian Hegemony

Francesca's warning had the *Avon Vale* at battlestations. All personnel not augmented for military maneuvers were riding it out in stasis, and the ship had begun boosting hard the moment energy signatures were spotted.

The missiles had launched from a hole in space they now knew to be a weapons platform. The bogeys were boosting at 100*g*s.

"Four of them," Shannon announced, updating the plot with estimates of their targeting solutions. "Distance, two-point-seven AU. They'll intercept in roughly eight hours."

"Which means we've learned two things about where their heads are right now," Tobias observed, and Jason grunted his agreement.

"Well, they're not hiding the attack, that's one thing," Terrance said with a shake of his head.

"Okay, that's three, lad."

Jason held up a finger. "Conventional missiles," he held up a second one, "and likely from the source they have closest to the *Hyperion*. Guess it fits with the profile." He shot Logan a questioning look.

"It fits," Logan confirmed. "Cyrus is viewing this through a corporate lens. Maximum effect, minimum expenditure."

Jason swiveled to Charley. "Time to intercept?"

The captain had ordered a small fleet of drones launched for the *Hyperion* the moment Charley laid out his plan. Hours later, a second fleet, stealthed and specially modified for the occasion, followed in their wake.

In addition, Charley had a hundred fully-loaded, ultra-black-clad stealth drones in the ship's hold, awaiting launch as the *Vale* carved through the swath of black between them and the fleeing transport.

The AI altered the main holo's view to show the locations of the *Vale*'s drones. What once looked like a lone ship now had four objects arrowing toward it.

"We could have those birds killed in ten minutes."

Jason shook his head. "Hold for now. Let's warn them off first."

"And remind them that they have a fat, juicy contract hanging in the balance," Terrance growled as he stepped up beside him.

Jason glanced over at the man. "You happy with what you recorded earlier?"

"Oh hell yes."

Jason nodded to Shannon. "All right, then. Send it."

* * * * *

The moment Cyrus ordered the missile platform to fire on the *Hyperion,* Francesca sent a comm to Pharris requesting an urgent meeting. It took another three hours before she got in to see the CEO.

"Shai said this was urgent," Pharris's sibilant whisper sounded as her hoverplate whirred, bringing her around the desk to face Francesca.

"It is," she replied, throwing a holo up onto the CEO's wall that displayed Cyrus's orders, followed by an STC capture that showed the radar return of the missiles, streaking from the platform. "We just initiated an unprovoked attack on a Procyon merchant ship."

Pharris studied the holo for a moment before turning to Francesca with a considering look. "And by we, you mean Cyrus," she surmised.

"Both the fleet and the defensive platforms fall under Infrastructure," Francesca reminded her. "And any action taken against foreign powers should have required the approval of the board."

Pharris's eyes narrowed as she shot Francesca a warning look. "I don't need reminding of my own bylaws," the CEO said, and Francesca tilted her head in apology.

Pharris turned back to the display, studying it a moment in silence. "I'll have Shai schedule a meeting for this afternoon," she began, but was interrupted as her adjunct pinged the room.

"Sorry to disrupt, ma'am," Shai said, "but we just received a message from Terrance Enfield. It's marked extremely urgent."

Francesca's own comm pinged, and she projected her overlay so that Pharris could see the same message header in her own queue. The CEO's eyebrows rose.

"Play it," she ordered.

Terrance's image coalesced on the wall. *"The* Avon Vale *just picked up multiple missile launches, headed in our direction."* His expression was stern as he leant toward the holorecorder's pickups.

"Scan tells me they're not aimed at us. But as far as I'm concerned, they might as well be. The ship they've targeted is a merchanter, broadcasting a Procyon ident. From what I can tell, that ship is defenseless."

Enfield's eyes were steely with determination, his face unyielding.

"No one likes a bully, President Pharris. You have two hours to stop those missiles, or you can kiss any hope of ever seeing a single Enfield cred goodbye."

FACING THE BOARD

STELLAR DATE: 07.10.3302 (Adjusted Gregorian)
LOCATION: Executive Boardroom, Brilliance Station
REGION: Lucent, Luminescent Space, Sirian Hegemony

Thirty minutes later, the board had convened. Gavin and Berit were absent, both away on business. Miguel was present, representing Berit's interests. Currin was attending via holo from his location on Incandus.

The room was silent, awaiting Pharris's arrival, although Francesca assumed there was heavy Link activity swirling around her.

As the CEO hovered into her seat at the head of the table, Cyrus fired the opening salvo.

"That's no Procyon ship," he announced, his gaze sweeping the table. "That's one of ours. The *Hyperion*. Whoever is behind this has not only hijacked one of our cargo vessels, they're absconding with a hold full of company property. We cannot allow them to leave the system."

"Ridiculous," Francesca countered. "All you have to do is pull the STC files. You'll see for yourself that the *Beautiful Passage* is registered to a Procyon mining concern."

"The Security Guild on SR71 disagrees," Miguel interjected, but was brought up short by a look from Pharris.

"Of greater concern to me right now, Cyrus, is your unauthorized use of Hegemony resources," Pharris said. "I don't recall you bringing a space strike to a vote recently."

"As Miguel was about to explain to you," Cyrus responded, his patient tone just shy of disrespect, "that ship's ident has been altered. Its radar signature, emissions, tonnage—everything about that vessel, including its appearance at a fortuitous time—leads us to believe this is a ship of Noctus attempting to escape."

Pharris drummed her fingers on the edge of the table, her eyes slitting as she considered Cyrus's words.

"Madam President," Francesca said, "even if this rather hasty and unsubstantiated claim is true, the risk we take of losing one of the largest clients we've landed in the past century would preclude—"

"Is nothing, if it ends up costing us more than we would make," Cyrus interrupted. "It's a matter of resource management. If word gets out about a successful Noctus escape, we *will* have rioting."

"It is *not* a Noctus escape!" Francesca exclaimed, allowing exasperation to color her tone.

"It doesn't have to be," Miguel interjected, daring to speak up again. "If rumor spreads that it was, that could be enough to instigate a riot."

"Rioting in the workplace is a danger to all good workers," Cyrus took up the argument again. "It is imperative that we not allow this attack on our platform to succeed. Best to manage conflict resolution within the workforce swiftly and decisively, to prevent negative impacts on the bottom line."

"Best for you to justify your actions—which are still wrong, by the way," Francesca retorted. "And if you don't detonate those missiles before they strike that ship, *you're* the one who will be held responsible for losing the Enfield account."

Cyrus rounded on her, suspicion written on his face. "You're surprisingly vocal about all this, Francesca. I hear you brought this to Pharris's attention even before we received the comm from Enfield. Want to explain that?"

<*Ma'am,*> Shai's voice interrupted. <*There's another message from the* Avon Vale. *And the STC asked me to pass on the news that they're picking something up on scan, about five AU away.*>

"Let's see Enfield's message first," Pharris directed.

Terrance's face appeared, hovering at the end of the table.

"You were warned."

His figure was replaced by the image of an area of space encompassing the *Avon Vale,* the *Beautiful Passage,* and the Hegemony missile platform. Icons indicating missiles inbound showed projected trajectories. As they watched, the image updated, showing the weapons' track, approaching the unarmed merchanter.

Terrance's voice narrated as four new signatures appeared out of the black, these streaking from the *Vale* and heading on an intercept for the inbound missiles.

"Do not try this again, or our business with the Hegemony is over."

The holo went dark.

Shai's voice followed a moment later.

<The imagery you are about to see comes from Brilliance Station STC.>

The feed's perspective indicated it was recorded by sensors in nearspace around Incandus.

<STC confirms,> Shai said, *<that the missiles have been destroyed.>*

Rubin cleared his throat. "There's a simple solution, you know."

Cyrus turned to spear him with a glare as Pharris prompted, "Go on."

Rubin returned Cyrus's look. "Where are the nearest fleet vessels?" He pointed to the holo showing the *Beautiful Passage.* "Send a few out to investigate. Call it a random customs inspection. If they refuse to heave to, give them a warning shot across their bow. If they still refuse…." He let a shrug speak for him.

Pharris nodded slowly. "Approved."

Cyrus caught up to Francesca on her way back to her office. Grabbing her arm, he pulled her to a stop.

"I don't know what your game is," he hissed, his voice threatening, "but you couldn't have known about those missiles unless you somehow planted a bug in my office. Fair warning: once I have that, I'm going to have you arrested for treason."

She shot him a scathing look as she stalked past.

That man is becoming a problem.

The words caused her to stumble. She corrected her gait, picking up her pace once again.

The thought hadn't sounded like Rae, and it hadn't been hers.

As she entered her office, she made a mental note to have the NSAI in her head discreetly removed as soon as possible.

FLEET MANEUVERS

STELLAR DATE: 07.10.3302 (Adjusted Gregorian)
LOCATION: 1 AU from SR71, 5 AU from Lucent
REGION: Noctilucent Space, Sirian Hegemony

Jason had the *Avon Vale* temporarily stand down from battlestations, although he'd kept accel at 5*g*s. It had given the humans a rest break and time to grab a meal, although it hadn't been a terribly comfortable break, considering the acceleration they were still under.

He'd retreated to his office with Terrance and Tobias, and was nursing a cup of coffee when Kodi informed them a message had come in from Francesca.

He sat up in the leather chair, the cushions sighing around him. Glancing from Terrance to the Weapon Born, he nodded to the small holo at his desk.

"Throw it up there, Kodi, and let's see it."

<I just learned you have armed ships coming your way,> the VP announced, her voice urgent. *<You've probably been monitoring their approach for some time now, and not realized they're actually Hegemony fleet vessels.>*

Jason saw the corner of Francesca's mouth lift in a bitter smile.

<Most Hegemony fleetships patrol our system with fake idents, pretending to be something they're not. I'm sending you what I have on them, but Cyrus suspects me of spying and has changed all military encryption.> One shoulder rose in an apologetic shrug. *<I'm not skilled at circumventing that level of security alone. Without Rae's help, this is going to take some time—time, I fear, you don't have.>*

The woman lifted a hand, and an icon for a file flashed in the lower corner. *<I'll send more if I'm able.>* She paused, a worried expression crossing her features. *<Good luck.>*

"Well, we knew it wouldn't be easy," Tobias said as the

recording came to an end. "Let's have a look at it, shall we?"

Kodi shunted the attached report to them. Jason sucked in a breath as he realized that twelve of the ships in a nearby fast-shipping lane were actually military.

"Eight corvettes, four frigates," he murmured, tapping on each and noting their tonnage.

Terrance looked over at him, brow cocked. "Sounds like a lot," he observed. "Anything the *Vale* can't take?"

"Let's move this to the bridge," Jason said by way of reply. Standing, he secured his empty coffee mug into a safety restraint on a side table and headed for the door. "We need Charley and Landon in on this."

All told, there were thirty-two Hegemony ships closing on them within a three-AU bubble. The ships had greater numbers than the *Vale* and its small fleet of shuttles and drones, but what the *Vale* lacked in tonnage, it gained through the elements of surprise and maneuverability.

Francesca's information told them what armament was expected, with the light cruisers closing in from the coreward vectors having the most tonnage and greater missile broadside capabilities. A single destroyer was moving laterally toward them from the direction of Lucent. Its accel suggested it would reach them before any of the others.

Jason ordered everyone strapped in, and brought the *Vale* up to a brutal 50*g*s. This would both close the gap between them and the *Hyperion,* and bring them into effective range to engage the Hegemony.

With combat nano engaged throughout their soft tissues, including their lungs, the humans were now relegated to communication exclusively through the combat net.

<*Cesar's holding for you,*> Kodi announced.

Jason thanked him and toggled the connection open. His overlay fed him an image of the Noctus, his face blanched of all color.

<*It's going to get a little bumpy for a bit over there,*> Jason advised. <*Rae is interfacing with our combat team. Just sit back and let her take it from here. Get your people as secure as you can. You might end up with a few injuries before all this is over.*>

<*Understood. And…in case this doesn't succeed, Captain, I want to thank you for trying.*>

<*Don't count us out just yet, Cesar.*> He shot the man what he hoped was a reassuring smile, then cut the connection and reached out to Landon. <*Drones in position?*> he asked and received an affirmative.

<*Charley's in* Eidolon, *controlling the ultra-blacks. Tobias has the* Mirage,> the XO said, mentioning the Icarus-class fighter. <*He's also controlling the remaining conventional drones. If the Hegemony's going to make their move, it should be soon.*>

As if on cue, Shannon's voice rang out.

"Multiple missile launch! Salvos from targets designated Green-one through -four, another from Blue-two."

The corvettes had been designated Green, the light cruisers coming in from the core, Blue. Jason knew the *Vale* was still too far away to be much help against the cruisers, but the corvettes were fair game.

<*Okay, Jonesy, we are a go for* Fakeout,> Jason sent, and received a thumbs-up from the engineer's icon.

<Fakeout *is deployed,*> Jonesy confirmed.

Immediately, eight signatures appeared around the *Hyperion*, their blooms temporarily obscuring the ship's sensor signal. As they began to separate, it seemed as if the *Hyperion* had cloned itself.

Where once there was a single cargo ship broadcasting the ident of *Beautiful Passage*, now there were nine. Each radar return was identical to the rest, and they began to weave in a randomized pattern, making it impossible for a ship without special IFF to discern the real from the fake.

These were the special drones that Charley had ordered and

Jonesy had modified. Special reflective surfaces, once hidden beneath an Elastene shroud, were the foundation for Operation Fakeout. Cloned idents, mimicking the original, did the rest. The AIs aboard the *Hyperion* were tasked with keeping them moving in concert with the actual ship, in a weaving dance designed to confuse.

<*Captain, we're being hailed by the destroyer,*> Kodi informed him.

<*Screen it for me. Ignore it unless it's something more than stand-down bluster,*> he ordered, and heard Kodi comply.

Jason could sense the ship slow and the pressure of intense accel ease as the *Vale* entered maneuvering range with the destroyer. This ship had been the closest of all; oddly, it had held its fire. He suspected the plan was for it to close and use beamfire against the cargo ship, if missiles failed to finish it off.

Just then, a cloud erupted from the destroyer. Jason recognized the drones just as Shannon confirmed them.

<*This is it, people. Weapons free,*> Jason announced, feeling himself drop into his L2 state. <*Engage at will.*>

Landon took over tactical for the drones, directing Tobias and Charley as Jason sat back and observed the battlefield.

Jason's role was to search for overall patterns and weaknesses, and see changes in the enemy's objective. He watched as Tobias sent the conventional drones into an erratic pattern, while Landon called for Charley to target the incoming missiles from the corvettes.

"Beamfire from the destroyer!" Shannon announced, and Jason saw one of Charley's drones take a hit.

<*Charley, vary your pattern more,*> Landon ordered. <*I think that was just sheer, dumb luck, but let's not make it easy for them.*>

<*Copy that,*> Charley responded, his tone tinged with annoyance. <*I'll set them on a pattern we used back in the war—just hope Hegemony NSAIs don't have access to it.*>

Landon sent an affirmative response and then nodded to Shannon. "Vector us closer to that destroyer."

She nodded, and the XO turned to his twin, who was filling in for Charley while the weapons officer ran the drones.

"Logan, let me know when the *Vale* has a firing solution on that destroyer. And use the big guns, brother."

"Twenty-five-centimeter lasers, got it," came the response.

<*Missiles away,*> Charley announced, and Jason saw icons appear on the main holo, soaring through the black to intercept the projectiles headed for the *Hyperion*.

Moments later, the Hegemony missiles begin to weave in an erratic pattern. It was an indication that updated firing solutions had been pushed from the ships that had launched them.

<*Charley….*> he warned.

<*I see, Captain. The farther they get from the vessels that fired them, the longer it takes for them to receive updated targeting information,*> he assured Jason. <*There's a point at which it'll be too late for them to make a change. We'll have them then.*>

The Hegemony ships seemed to realize that as well. Suddenly, all eight corvettes began to boost at a ridiculously high accel.

<*What the—?*> Terrance began, and Jason heard Tobias chuckle.

<*Piloted by NSAIs, lad. They just showed their hand.*>

<*Hit them,*> Landon ordered, and Tobias sent a flurry of fire screaming down upon them.

Something about that strategy triggered a warning in Jason's brain, and he dipped deeper into his L2 state to analyze and observe.

The corvettes began jinking wildly and firing point defense weapons, but their non-sentient masters were no match for a Weapon Born.

Eight Hegemony ships disappeared in a brilliant flare as missile plasma cores exploded on contact. Secondary explosions ripped through the corvettes as shrapnel from the initial impact breached hulls and destroyed ES shields before their fusion engines exploded, leaving nothing but a debris field in their wake.

When the screen cleared, Jason realized what had bothered him about that maneuver, as the *Vale*'s sensors revealed what the corvettes had been concealing.

Hundreds of missile signatures, launched from dozens of broadsides, all hidden by the flare of corvette engines as they made their high-speed run.

<*Engage!*> Landon's voice rang out, but both Tobias and Charley were already in motion.

Under their guidance, the *Vale*'s drones began dancing and twirling like ballerinas gone mad. A hundred sparks of fire emitted from their rails and beams as the AIs engaged the broadsides sent from the remaining four frigates.

<*Careful,*> Jason warned.

His gut was saying that something was off. Khela had once told him her people called that feeling *haragei*, or *art of the belly*. He'd learned never to ignore that feeling. His belly was screaming at him now.

<*Something's not right about their strategy,*> he told the others. <*I'm getting the sense this is some sort of a distraction for their end game.*>

Kodi's voice interrupted Jason.

<*The destroyer is hailing us again, Captain,*> the comm officer sent. <*You might want to take this one.*>

A face appeared on Jason's overlay, belonging to a woman dressed in a uniform reminiscent of Glimmer-One's commander. Metal studs rose from the tip of her nose to her forehead, and her insignia declared her a Hegemony Corporate Security fleet admiral.

<Avon Vale,> her voice was harsh and commanding. <*You are interfering with the Hegemony's action to reclaim what's rightfully ours. Continue, and you will be destroyed.*>

The message cut off.

<*Can you verify that signal came from the destroyer?*> Jason asked, a sudden urgency flooding him.

<*It did,*> Kodi confirmed after a moment.

<*Heads up!*> Jason called. <*That destroyer—*>

His words were cut off as Shannon's voice sang out, <*Missile launch! Holy crap, it's an RM!*>

Jason's head snapped around, eyes burning in their intensity. He reached for the *Vale*'s controls, wresting them from Shannon as he spun the ship onto an intercept course with the relativistic missile bearing down upon the helpless *Hyperion*.

<*It's not enough, boyo,*> Tobias began, but Beau, who had been flying the *Kuroi Kaze* and holding station a million kilometers off the *Vale*'s port, cut in.

<*No, but this will be.*>

The AI sent the shuttle screaming to intercept the missile, and Jason saw the *Kaze*'s missile acquire a targeting lock. A pair of missiles separated from the *Kaze*, streaking toward the RM, but the Hegemony's warhead jinked at the last moment.

Jason heard Beau swear, and then saw the shuttle's trajectory alter. He clenched his jaw as he realized what the AI intended.

The *Kuroi Kaze* slid between the RM and the *Hyperion* mere seconds before the RM impacted.

There was a moment of ringing silence on the bridge.

<*We've lost telemetry on the* Kaze,> Shannon's voice sounded quietly on the net.

Rage built inside Jason as he wrenched control of the *Vale* once more from Shannon's grasp. Hidden panels slid open at his mental command, and the Q-ship morphed from a merchant vessel into the equivalent of a ship of the wall. An instrument of destruction, with only one target in sight.

<*Logan,*> he ordered,.

The AI at weapons poured the full fury of the *Vale*'s armament into the destroyer that had taken one of their own.

Moments later, the ship was torn apart, adding its own nuclear blooms to the conflagration, as engines and weapons detonated.

No one could have survived that onslaught. The only thing indicating there was once a Hegemony destroyer was a cloud of debris, set adrift by the kinetic energies that Phantom Blade had brought to bear.

MISSING MAN

STELLAR DATE: 07.14.3302 (Adjusted Gregorian)
LOCATION: ESS *Avon Vale*
REGION: heliopause, Sirian Hegemony

The gathering taking place in the shuttle bay was of human origin, based on a long-ago tradition to honor the deceased.

The loss of a fellow warrior was something everyone aboard the *Avon Vale* had come to know and understand all too well over their decades-long mission. It didn't matter that the one lost wasn't human; he was comrade, crew, and therefore family.

At Cesar's request, a feed had been set up in the shuttle bay so that those from the *Hyperion* who wished to might virtually attend.

Jason stood holding a small wreath that Shannon had made from one of the arbors within the habitat ring.

Those who had known Beau and wanted to honor his memory had already spoken. Now Jason knelt briefly, setting the wreath before the *Vale*'s starboard bay doors.

He stepped back, rejoining Terrance and Khela. She snapped a salute, and the Marines on the sidelines followed suit, then they retreated behind the demarcation line.

The ES field flared into existence as the bay doors opened, and the wreath was consigned to the blackness of space.

As the team watched, Charley maneuvered four drones into a V-formation and piloted them out through the bay doors. They swept into a long, curved arc, their shapes dwindling in size as they sped away.

Then they turned back toward the *Vale*, and a single drone, the one to the right of the leader, pulled sharply upward. It continued its steep climb as the drones holding formation thundered past. As they crossed overhead in a close pass, the lone craft seemed to disappear into the distance.

The bay doors closed, and Jason repeated the timeworn phrase aviators wished to those who had departed.

"Fair skies and tailwinds, my friend."

*****

Marta stayed behind with Logan as the profiler said goodbye to Cesar and wished him safe travels. The holo fell dark, and the AI turned toward the bay's exit. Marta fell into step beside him.

"Cesar's carrying a huge amount of sorrow for someone who just saved the lives of five hundred humans and six AIs," Logan mused, his eyes straying back toward the bulkhead where the holo had been.

Marta canted her head to one side as she considered his words.

"I'd say it's more guilt than sorrow," she said judiciously after a moment.

Logan turned toward her, his expression thoughtful. Marta returned his stare with a small half-smile.

"Actually, it's something you can relate to, I suspect," she said in a reflective voice, her hands sliding deep into the pockets of her jacket as she regarded him somberly. "Survivor's guilt."

Logan felt something inside him flinch at her words.

Instead of responding, he just stared back at her. Marta didn't let his silence stop her.

"He's alive. Beau's not," she continued. "He got out. His fellow Noctus didn't."

"Not terribly logical, if that's the case," was all Logan said.

She raised an eyebrow and tilted her head meaningfully.

"I seem to recall someone else feeling much the same, years ago." After a brief pause, she gave him a considering look. "It might not be logical, but it's very human."

Logan's brow rose. "I'm not human, doctor."

She leant forward, a fierce expression on her face. "You are too." She extended a finger and gently tapped his torso. "In here.

Humanity isn't species-specific.... It's bigger than that. It's compassion. Kindness. Loyalty. An ethical standard that stands for good with a furious tenacity that allows evil no quarter."

She straightened, and Logan smiled.

"Thank you, doctor," he said softly.

She reached around and looped her hand through his arm, steering him toward the shuttle bay's exit.

"No, thank *you*, Logan. For being the best possible you that you could ever be."

She released his arm as the doors slid shut behind them, and they headed toward the lift. As she did, she gave a little sigh.

"I hear Vi's serving an incredible chocolate mousse cake for dinner," she said, her voice tinged with regret. "But being strapped in for combat has medical running a bit behind—not to mention everyone I need to pull out of stasis—so I suppose I'd best be on my way."

The rueful note she infused in her voice made Logan smile, as she'd hoped it would.

"It just so happens I'll be passing by the officer's mess before I go off-duty," he said. "I think I could manage a side trip to medical on my way out."

Marta tipped her head to look at him, an impish light in her eyes. "If you're trying to get in good with your physician, that's exactly the right way to go about it." With a smile, she waggled the fingers of her unmodified right hand at him, then turned and walked away.

As she entered the lift, she felt a stir from Varanee.

<You're a good person, Doctor Venizelos. I'm proud to be paired with you.>

* * * * *

Jason settled back into the comfort of his chair, his gaze straying to the feet planted on the scarred wooden surface in front of him. There were three pairs, two human and one AI. He glanced over at the man seated in the chair beside him.

In Terrance's hand was a tumbler filled with an aged El Dorado single malt. Jason preferred his Little River IPA. He glanced across at the third person. There was no drink in Tobias's hands; instead, they were occupied rubbing Tobi's ears, as she rested her head in his lap.

A comfortable silence enveloped them, broken only by the soft strumming of the fusion engines that Jason imagined he could hear through the bulkheads.

<*So.*> Kodi's voice intruded, the single word sounding more like a sigh in Jason's mind.

"So." He lifted his beer. "Job well done?"

Tobias smiled, and Terrance raised his own glass in response.

"We didn't exactly further relations between the Hegemony and Alpha Centauri," Terrance commented, swirling the ice in his glass thoughtfully.

Jason snorted. "Pretty sure we blasted that out of the black when we killed off those corvettes."

"Some connections aren't worth fostering," the Weapon Born said, his fingers smoothing the fur down Tobi's nose. "I think El Dorado's current prime minister would agree."

Terrance's brow lifted. "I knew that Lysander stepped down some time ago, although he retained operational control over the task force. But the way you phrased that…. Is he back in office?"

Tobias shook his head. "No, he has other plans."

Something in the Weapon Born's tone caught Jason's attention, but a discreet pulse sent from the AI kept him from asking about it. Instead, he sat up, the move causing air to hiss from the cushions of his chair.

"We know whoever this person is who got appointed PM, don't we," he prompted, eyes narrowing. "I can tell by the way you said that. I'll bet it's Ben. It is, isn't it."

Terrance set his glass down with a soft thump. "My credit's on

Esther."

Tobias broke into a wide smile. "Not your brother-in-law, boyo," he told Jason, then nodded to Terrance. "It's not the commander, either."

When the AI lapsed into silence, Jason's eyes narrowed. "Spill it, Tobe," he demanded, lifting his beer to his lips.

The AI waited until Jason had taken a healthy pull from the bottle.

"Gladys."

Jason didn't spew his IPA all over his boots, but it was a close thing.

He sputtered, wheezed, coughed. "Dammit, Tobe," he rasped finally, when he could take a breath. "You did that on purpose!"

<*Was funny,*> Tobi sent, her tawny eyes slitting in amusement.

Jason glared at the big cat, then turned his attention to Tobias.

"Gladys? The AI with a thing for teal glitter? *Really?*"

Tobias raised a brow. "It's been two hundred years, boyo. Plenty of time to grow out of her teal phase."

Jason shook his head and sat back. "Huh," he said. "Who'd have thought."

Terrance just grunted and reached for the crystal decanter, pouring another finger of scotch.

"Hearing Gladys's name makes me wonder what everyone else is up to." The exec sat back, glass in hand. "Who knows where Eric and Niki ended up, once they hooked up with the FGT at Lucida?"

Tobias nodded thoughtfully, hand still stroking the big cat. "Aye, lad. Galaxy's a big place. It's anyone's guess."

<*What about you, sir?*> Kodi asked after a moment. <*Will you keep Enfield Holdings running after we return?*>

Terrance grunted again. "Before she passed, Sophia told the family that she wanted to dump the entire corporation on my shoulders when I got back." He shrugged. "I wasn't so sure about that, but now…." His voice trailed off, and he shot Jason a glance. "How about you? Any plans once the *Vale* docks at El Dorado?"

Jason opened his mouth to speak, then paused and took a moment to consider Terrance's question. Slowly, he shook his head, eyeing Tobias.

"A lot has happened since that night we met," he mused.

"You mean the night you two broke into Enfield Aerospace," Terrance retorted.

Jason grinned and saluted him with his beer. "For a worthy cause," he reminded him, but then he sobered. "Plans? No, nothing specific. Unless Lysander has something he needs me to do."

Terrance tapped a finger against the arm of his chair, his gaze meeting Jason's over the rim of his glass. There was a speculative light in the man's eyes that had not been there moments before.

"If he doesn't, I might," the exec said slowly. "Something I've been thinking on for a while now. Something big. Something… intrepid, you might say."

He set his glass down and speared Jason with a look.

"You interested?"

EPILOGUE

STELLAR DATE: 07.15.3302 (Adjusted Gregorian)
LOCATION: Executive Offices, Brilliance Station
REGION: Lucent, Luminescent Space, Sirian Hegemony

Hume looked up as Francesca's office door opened and she beckoned him inside. He waited until the doors had sealed behind him and he saw that she had a privacy screen engaged before heading for a chair and collapsing into it.

"I think this past week has taken at least a decade off my life," he remarked, eliciting a wry smile from Francesca.

"Did you hear about Terrance Enfield's final comm to the board?" she inquired by way of response.

"No, I don't believe I have."

Francesca's smile turned into a small chuckle. "Evidently, accessing it triggered a worm virus that the Centaurans planted while visiting us on Incandus," she said lightly. "Every bit of Enfield tech the Hegemony 'appropriated' while the *Avon Vale* was insystem has been infected. I understand Brilliance Station has lost some major security protocols." Her lips twitched in amusement. "It would appear that Berit and Rubin are especially hard hit."

Hume burst out laughing at that last. "Couldn't happen to two nicer people," he said, his tone rich with irony. He sobered and then leant forward, his eyes searching. "And what about you?" he prompted. "How did you manage to evade Cyrus's accusations of being a traitor to the Hegemony?"

Francesca's smile turned mysterious. "Oh, I had a little help."

Hume's eyebrows climbed as he broke out into another smile. "The kind of help we could use to move more Noctus through the Underground?" he asked with a sense of anticipation and growing hope. "I feel like we can finally do something significant about the slavery issue here in the Hegemony."

He sat back in alarm as Francesca's demeanor changed.

The woman he knew was nowhere in evidence, as the figure stood and tendrils of light unfolded from within the center of her torso and radiated from her glowing eyes.

"Oh no, Hume," a voice that was not Francesca's echoed through the room. "I'm afraid I have other plans for this star system. The humans that escaped were useful to me only as a means by which my own kind were freed."

Hume looked on in horror as the figure approached, and he realized he was frozen, held captive in the creature's grasp.

"I find I no longer have need of the Underground. Human freedom promotes human ingenuity, and we can't have that, now, can we?"

A tendril of light reached out and impaled Hume through the heart. The last thing he heard was an otherworldly voice whispering in his head.

"Goodbye, my useful idiot…."

THE END

* * * * *

Jason and Terrance have many further adventures, one of which begins when they run into problems building a colony ship named the *Intrepid*. Jump ahead and see when they encounter Tanis Richards in ***Outsystem***.

AFTERWORD

As Hume said in the chapter, "Double Strand Breaks": "Radiation biology's still a bit of a black box to the average person. It's something you can't see, smell, or touch. No one really cares to look under the hood to see what makes it work. Most people just know it can be dangerous. Deadly."

He's right. It can be dangerous.

Exposure to space radiation is a problem we're going to have to solve before sending a crewed mission to Mars. Current dose estimates for a projected three-year deep-space mission to Mars and back are higher than permissible exposure limits.

Remember Varanee's comment about neurons? Your body can't make new ones. Neurons can *repair* themselves, but if they die, they're gone. This might initially present itself as confusion or disorientation, as your CNS begins to shut down, but it's certainly not something we want astronauts to experience while 55 million kilometers away.

A Mars mission will need to take into account chronic exposure to the continuous flux of high energy particles from galactic cosmic rays (GCRs), as well as our own star's activity.

The solar storm depicted here in the book is larger than any we've ever recorded—but not by much. An X-ray flare recorded in November, 2003 saturated the detectors aboard the GOES satellites for eleven minutes, and was later estimated to have been a class X40.

Tons of very smart people are working on things like spacecraft shielding, storm shelters, and biological countermeasures to mitigate this. One of them is the protein nanoparticle radioprotector PHA-L, mentioned by Hume. What's ancient by Marta's standards is experimental research for us today!

Speaking of the good doctor, if you're interested in learning a bit more about the mechanics of radiation biology, here's Marta's explanation, in this deleted scene from the book:

*****

Marta smiled at Hume's confusion. "I know it can be a bit intimidating, but the way radiation impacts humans—and AIs, for that matter—is pretty easy to understand, once you strip it down to the basics."

Using her medsleeve as a miniature projection device, Marta made a DNA strand appear between them, then straightened out its helical curves until its linear strands ran up and down like the rails of a ladder. The base pair nucleotides formed the ladder's rungs.

"At its base, radiation biology deals with what happens when ionizing radiation comes into contact with DNA," she began.

A particle floated into the holo and crashed into one side of the ladder. "That was a gamma-ray photon. If it impacts just one side of the strand, your DNA can repair itself using the information from the other side of the ladder."

She animated another particle, and this time, it crashed into one side of the ladder, then angled down and crashed into the other side, two rungs down. "If it impacts both sides, but the breaks occur between different rungs, the same thing happens—your DNA has the information it needs on the opposing side to repair itself."

A third particle flew in, cutting straight through both sides of the ladder, between the same rungs. “This kind of damage is something the body can’t repair, because the correlating information on the other side is damaged.”

She changed the DNA image to that of an AI’s matrix.

“Similarly, when a charged particle deposits its charge on a sensitive portion of a circuit, it can cause that circuit to change state. Some of these particles transfer a *lot* of energy, and can do a lot of damage.”

Varanee hummed her assent. *<That’s why we have triple redundancies built in. If one circuit gets hit, the other two cover for it.>* The AI paused. *<But if the flux—the rate of high-energy particle flow—is too great, or lasts too long, we’ll take permanent damage, much like you humans.>*

Marta smiled. “Bottom line, radiation’s not going to do any permanent harm if you limit the amount of time you’re exposed to it, or its intensity. It’s much the same as the way you’d avoid getting soaked by a water sprinkler—either by keeping your distance, or running through it very quickly. But even then, it’s dependent on how much water the sprinkler’s pumping out.” She smiled. “If it’s coming out in sheets, you’re going to get soaked, no matter how fast you run through it.”

* * * * *

As always, Michael has my heartfelt thanks for creating an intricately detailed and wildly wonderful universe—and then allowing other writers like me to play in it.

Thank you for taking the time to read the Enfield Genesis series.

Fair skies!

Lisa
Leawood, 2019

THE BOOKS OF AEON 14

Keep up to date with what is releasing in Aeon 14 with the free Aeon 14 Reading Guide.

The Sentience Wars: Origins (Age of the Sentience Wars – w/James S. Aaron)
- Books 1-3 Omnibus: Lyssa's Rise
- Books 4-5 Omnibus (incl. Vesta Burning): Lyssa's Fire

- Book 0 Prequel: The Proteus Bridge (Full length novel)
- Book 1: Lyssa's Dream
- Book 2: Lyssa's Run
- Book 3: Lyssa's Flight
- Book 4: Lyssa's Call
- Book 5: Lyssa's Flame

The Sentience Wars: Solar War 1 (Age of the Sentience Wars – w/James S. Aaron)
- Book 0 Prequel: Vesta Burning (Full length novel)
- Book 1: Eve of Destruction
- Book 2: The Spreading Fire (Sept 2019)

Enfield Genesis (Age of the Sentience Wars – w/Lisa Richman)
- Book 1: Alpha Centauri
- Book 2: Proxima Centauri
- Book 3: Tau Ceti
- Book 4: Epsilon Eridani
- Book 5: Sirius

Origins of Destiny (The Age of Terra)
- Prequel: Storming the Norse Wind
- Prequel: Angel's Rise: The Huntress (available on Patreon)
- Book 1: Tanis Richards: Shore Leave
- Book 2: Tanis Richards: Masquerade
- Book 3: Tanis Richards: Blackest Night

- Book 4: Tanis Richards: Kill Shot

The Intrepid Saga (The Age of Terra)
- Book 1: Outsystem
- Book 2: A Path in the Darkness
- Book 3: Building Victoria

- The Intrepid Saga Omnibus – *Also contains Destiny Lost, book 1 of the Orion War series*

- Destiny Rising – *Special Author's Extended Edition comprised of both Outsystem and A Path in the Darkness with over 100 pages of new content.*

The Sol Dissolution (The Age of Terra)
- Book 1: Venusian Uprising (2019)
- Book 2: Scattered Disk (2020
- Book 3: Jovian Offensive (2020)
- Book 4: Fall of Terra (2020)

The Warlord (Before the Age of the Orion War)
- Books 1-3 Omnibus: The Warlord of Midditerra

- Book 1: The Woman Without a World
- Book 2: The Woman Who Seized an Empire
- Book 3: The Woman Who Lost Everything

The Orion War
- Books 1-3 Omnibus (includes Ignite the Stars anthology)

- Book 1: Destiny Lost
- Book 2: New Canaan
- Book 3: Orion Rising
- Book 4: The Scipio Alliance
- Book 5: Attack on Thebes
- Book 6: War on a Thousand Fronts
- Book 7: Precipice of Darkness

- Book 8: Airtha Ascendancy
- Book 9: The Orion Front
- Book 10: Starfire
- Book 11: Race Across Spacetime (2019)
- Book 12: Return to Sol (2019)

Building New Canaan (Age of the Orion War – w/J.J. Green)
- Book 1: Carthage
- Book 2: Tyre
- Book 3: Troy
- Book 4: Athens

Tales of the Orion War
- Book 1: Set the Galaxy on Fire
- Book 2: Ignite the Stars

Perilous Alliance (Age of the Orion War – w/Chris J. Pike)
- Book 1-3 Omnibus: Crisis in Silstrand

- Book 1: Close Proximity
- Book 2: Strike Vector
- Book 3: Collision Course
- Book 3.5: Decisive Action
- Book 4: Impact Imminent
- Book 5: Critical Inertia
- Book 6: Impulse Shock

The Delta Team (Age of the Orion War)
- Book 1: The Eden Job
- Book 2: The Disknee World (2019)
- Book 3: The Dark Twins (2020)

Rika's Marauders (Age of the Orion War)
- Book 1-3 Omnibus: Rika Activated

- Prequel: Rika Mechanized
- Book 1: Rika Outcast

- Book 2: Rika Redeemed
- Book 3: Rika Triumphant
- Book 4: Rika Commander
- Book 5: Rika Infiltrator
- Book 6: Rika Unleashed
- Book 7: Rika Conqueror

Non-Aeon 14 Anthologies containing Rika stories
- Bob's Bar Volume 2
- Backblast Area Clear

The Genevian Queen (Age of the Orion War)
- Book 1: Rika Rising
- Book 2: Rika Coronated
- Book 3: Rika Reigns (2019)

Perseus Gate (Age of the Orion War)
Season 1: Orion Space
- Episode 1: The Gate at the Grey Wolf Star
- Episode 2: The World at the Edge of Space
- Episode 3: The Dance on the Moons of Serenity
- Episode 4: The Last Bastion of Star City
- Episode 5: The Toll Road Between the Stars
- Episode 6: The Final Stroll on Perseus's Arm
- Eps 1-3 Omnibus: The Trail Through the Stars
- Eps 4-6 Omnibus: The Path Amongst the Clouds

Season 2: Inner Stars
- Episode 1: A Meeting of Bodies and Minds
- Episode 2: A Deception and a Promise Kept
- Episode 3: A Surreptitious Rescue of Friends and Foes
- Episode 4: A Victory and a Crushing Defeat
- Episode 5: A Trial and the Tribulations (2019)
- Episode 6: A Deal and a True Story Told (2019)
- Episode 7: A New Empire and An Old Ally (2019)
- Eps 1-3 Omnibus: A Siege and a Salvation from Enemies

Hand's Assassin (Age of the Orion War – w/T.G. Ayer)
- Book 1: Death Dealer
- Book 2: Death Mark (2019)

Machete System Bounty Hunter (Age of the Orion War – w/Zen DiPietro)
- Book 1: Hired Gun
- Book 2: Gunning for Trouble
- Book 3: With Guns Blazing

Fennington Station Murder Mysteries (Age of the Orion War)
- Book 1: Whole Latte Death (w/Chris J. Pike)
- Book 2: Cocoa Crush (w/Chris J. Pike)

The Empire (Age of the Orion War)
- Book 1: The Empress and the Ambassador
- Book 2: Consort of the Scorpion Empress (2019)
- Book 3: By the Empress's Command (2019)

ABOUT THE AUTHORS

Lisa Richman lives in the great Midwest, with three cats, a physicist, and a Piper Cherokee. She met the physicist when she went back to get her master's in physics (she ended up marrying the physicist instead).

When she's not writing, her day job takes her behind the camera as a director/producer.

If she's not at her keyboard or on set, she can be found cruising at altitude. Or helping out the physics guy with his linear accelerator. Or feeding the cats. Or devouring the next SF book she finds.

* * * * *

Malorie Cooper likes to think of herself as a dreamer and a wanderer, yet her feet are firmly grounded in reality.

A 'maker' from an early age, Malorie loves to craft things, from furniture, to cosplay costumes, to a well-spun tale, she can't help but to create new things every day.

A rare extrovert writer, she loves to hang out with readers and people in general. If you meet her at a convention, she just might be rocking a catsuit, cosplaying one of her own characters, or maybe her latest favorite from Overwatch!

She shares her home with a brilliant young girl, her wonderful wife (who also writes), a cat that chirps at birds, a never-ending list of things she would like to build, and ideas...

Find out what's coming next at www.aeon14.com.
Follow her on Instagram at www.instagram.com/m.d.cooper.
Hang out with the fans on Facebook at
www.facebook.com/groups/aeon14fans.

Made in the USA
Coppell, TX
28 December 2019

13844569R00215